THE GOD OF MIRRORS

THE GOD

)F MIRRORS

a novel by
ROBERT REILLY

The Atlantic Monthly Press
BOSTON / NEW YORK

FIRST EDITION

LIBRARY OF CONGRESS CATALOGING IN PUBLICATION DATA

Reilly, Robert.
  The God of mirrors.

  1. Wilde, Oscar, 1854–1900, in fiction, drama, poetry,
etc. 2. Douglas, Alfred Bruce, Lord, 1870–1945, in
fiction, drama, poetry, etc. I. Title.
PS3568.E4848G6 1986   813'.54   85-20145
ISBN 0-87113-029-7

MV

Published simultaneously in Canada

PRINTED IN THE UNITED STATES OF AMERICA

For H.P.

PART ONE

A Young Man
with All the Vices

SIFTING through a thin screen of fog, the afternoon light gilded the domes and steeples rising over Russell Square, making the city seem to tremble with some secret illumination from within.

"Can we draw the blinds, Frances?" said Oscar Wilde. "It threatens to be a particularly harrowing sunset."

She laughed, dipping a long, narrow brush in turpentine and rubbing it clean with a bit of muslin. "You don't expect me to paint in darkness, Oscar!"

Frances Richards was a handsome, olive-skinned woman with searching brown eyes, a long intellectual nose, and dark hair cut in bangs like a medieval page's. Her voluminous frock was protected by a billowing smock of sage green chintz, patterned over with leaves of a darker green and with tiny muted spring flowers, in the manner of an ancient tapestry. The amazing thing was that, encumbered by so much fabric, she was able to work at all. "And I *forbid* you to make Mr. Somerset laugh," she said, laughing herself. "I shall never capture the melancholy look about his eyes."

The house was rented from a brewer of uncompromising tastes, and Frances had tried to soften the stern effect by tinting the walls gray and violet, right up to the moldings, and adding a dado of dragonflies and butterflies in silver Japanesque. She had covered the Roman *scagliola* mosaic on the floor with mattings of rush, and scattered about quaint musical instruments and vases of peacock feathers and painted fans. Nevertheless, the room's original fixtures — the ceiling with its painted grim night sky, the four-square panelings of satinwood, the all-seeing mirrors of beveled glass — seemed ever to be bursting through. An awfully somber background for the likes of Oscar Wilde, she thought worriedly, glancing over at him on the wickerware settee.

He was slender and handsome in a coat of emerald velvet, trousers tighter than they should be, cheeks as bold a pink as the orchid languishing in his lapel. As he puffed at his gold-tipped cigarette, his great blue eyes were fixed on the modeling stand where young Somerset, in a morning costume that appeared almost lavender in the waning light, was trying not to sag. Wilde seemed to be searching for something in the younger man's petulant, handsome face.

"Do you really think I look melancholy, Miss Richards?" Somerset drawled, the blue embroidered silk of his waistcoat echoing the azure of his eyes, his tousled blond head gleaming like burnished copper.

"Very near forlorn!" she replied, motioning for him to sit still. Amidst etchings of Palladian villas and a large sepia photograph of a Titian Venus hung several of her own nudes, male and female forms looking oddly similar, in tints of listless gray-pink.

"Allow me to stay, Frances, and my behavior will be exemplary," said Oscar Wilde, fingering the pearl stickpins in his tie of peacock blue. "I am desperate for artistic inspiration. I have just spent a long — a *very* long weekend in Torquay, with my wife and our darling baby, who is training to be a coloratura. Cyril delighted us with arias from *La Favorita* all the while." He crossed his legs, as if to give a better view of the white spats gleaming over his rich brown Russian leather boots.

"How *was* the country?" said Somerset plaintively. On the table beside him, tasteful objects were carefully arranged to look spontaneous: a tiny magnifying glass with a handle of mother-of-pearl, a perfume flacon of Wedgwood jasperware, *The Earthly Paradise* lying open with a jeweled dagger marking the page.

Wilde gave him a pouting smile. "Full of strange, garish-colored things. Flowers, I believe they're called."

It must be four — no, five years since she and Oscar Wilde had met, Frances was thinking, as she toned down a harsh cobalt with a dab of earthy green. How different that younger Wilde had been: callow, brash, a bit crude. Yet full of endless promise. Full of a coarse hopefulness that seemed somehow to have dimmed.

"You must be about thirty now, Oscar," she said. "Or thirty-one?"

"I have scarce seen twenty-eight summers, Frances!" he cried, as if insulted. He snatched up a small oval hand mirror from her worktable and gazed fretfully at his reflection. "I look older because I am exhausted. I spent the entire morning removing a comma from a sentence."

"And how did you spend the afternoon?" said Somerset, with a fetching smile.

"Putting it back."

A pixie face hovered out of the shadows of the doorway, gaped at Wilde, and withdrew. Wilde, fortunately, was so interested in Somerset that he did not notice.

Quickly, Frances Richards said: "Marriage has improved you, Oscar."

"Do you really think so, Frances?"

"It has made you happier." She hoped the question in her tone was not too obvious.

"Heavier, you mean. What an exquisite red, Frances!" He was glancing over her shoulder at the palette, onto which she had just squeezed a spiral of alizarin crimson. "Lovely," he said. "Like one of the deadly sins."

"In *my* opinion, it is a mistake to marry young," said Somerset. "It is such a *serious* step . . ."

Wilde smiled at him ruefully. "There is a great deal of truth in what you say, Mr. Somerset. And you looked very picturesque as you said it, which is much more important." Just then a cloud passed from before the sun and lemon light danced down over them, lighting up a small plaster Venus de Milo next to a vase of jonquils. Somerset threw back his head, squinting at the light. "The moment!" whispered Wilde.

Frances Richards smiled. "The moment?"

"This one. Now. Are you *experiencing* it, Frances? Are you, Mr. Somerset? We must! It is our *duty* to grasp at life, to seek out startling experience, to ever be on the lookout for a new, a truly new sensation . . ."

His voice, to Frances Richards's ears at least, disclosed no trace of his native Ireland, except perhaps in its exceptional musicality. If anything, it was more essentially English than the voice of any

Englishman — but of a purer strain. It was thus that she liked to imagine Shelley had spoken, or Chatterton, or Byron.

After the brief drama of his dissertation, Wilde looked slightly ill at ease. From the table beside him he lifted a small ivory elephant toting on its back a crystal ball. In the crystal all the room curled round : the windows and the yellow-green trees beyond, the golden lantern suspended from the ceiling, Somerset on the modeling stand . . .

"Would either of you care for a cigarette?" Wilde said. "They are imported from Egypt. It is only when I am deeply in debt that I can afford them."

Somerset accepted one, and Wilde lit it, holding the match lingeringly before his face. "Isn't it odd," he said. "The blond physical perfection we seek among the Greeks — in vain — is actually quite common among our young Englishmen." Replacing his embossed silver matchbox in his coat, he sank back on the sofa with a sigh. "I suspect you must commit a great many sins, Mr. Somerset. It is the only way one ever keeps an air of innocence."

Somerset chortled. "I should be found out at once, I fear."

"Would there not be more to fear if you were found *in?*"

Frances Richards dropped the palette on her worktable with a clatter. "You are impossible, Oscar," she said, laughing helplessly. "No more painting today." Somerset let out a sigh of relief.

"Don't you agree, Frances?" said Wilde. "There is only one way to develop strength of character. That is to be constantly faced with temptation. And give in."

In the entranceway the varnished oak door suddenly rattled on its hinges. "Tell us — tell us more about our duty to sin," said Frances Richards.

But it was too late. "I believe, Frances, you are providing shelter for a ghost," said Wilde.

"Come out, Robert," she called, laughing. "You've been discovered." She wiped her hands clean with a length of spirit-soaked flannel. "I believe, Oscar, you have a secret admirer."

A slender adolescent inched into the studio, head hanging. He was wearing a black suit of excellent wool that seemed too large for him, as if he had not yet attained full growth. As Frances put an arm around his shoulders, chucking him under the chin, the boy squirmed, his features wrinkling up in an elfin grin.

"Mr. Robert Ross. A dear friend from Canada," she said, moving toward the screen and unbuttoning her smock. "He has read all your works, Oscar."

"That cannot have taken very long," said Wilde, appraising the youth, the top of whose tousled head reached barely to his shoulder.

"Even *Vera*," the boy volunteered, in a high, frightened voice. "I found a first edition at the Millman's . . ."

"With my works it is not first editions that are rare, but second ones. Robert seems altogether too straightforward a name for such a — surreptitious young man. I shall be forced to call you Robbie, I fear. But only if you will call me Oscar."

Frances stepped out from behind the screen. She was wearing a magnificent princess tea gown of a pale chutney color that harmonized with her warm skin. Its lace undersleeves swirled frothily about her arms as she tossed the smock onto a coatrack. "Robert and I were neighbors in Canada," she said. Hugging Ross close to her, she added : "Oscar is a great connoisseur of North America."

As if irritated at losing everyone's attention, Somerset began collecting his things. "Is that story true about the reporters in New York, Mr. Wilde?" he asked languidly. "Did you really tell them that the Atlantic was a disappointment?"

"If you knew how I regret that statement, Mr. Somerset! I never intended to ruin the poor ocean's reputation. It seems no one will receive it anymore. But the nearest I got to Canada was when I lectured in a city called, if I remember, Buffalo — in honor of the more intelligent inhabitants. There was some intolerably noisy body of water nearby . . ."

"You saw Niagara!" said Robert Ross.

"I was told that every American bride is brought there on her honeymoon. In American marriages, it appears, Niagara is the first, though certainly not the keenest, disappointment."

"Mr. Wilde," said Ross, with some indignation : "the falls are one of the world's great wonders."

"I would think it more wonderful if the water *didn't* fall, wouldn't you? And the name is Oscar." He turned back to Somerset, but the young man was drawing on his gray suede gloves. Wilde frowned.

"The same time tomorrow, Mr. Somerset?" said Frances Richards.

"I — I must go, too," said Robert Ross. "I must be home in

time for tea.'' He turned as if to say something further, but when he saw that Wilde's attention was concentrated on Somerset, now making some minor adjustment to his hair in the pier mirror over the great stone fireplace, Ross edged quietly out of the room.

When Frances returned from seeing them out, Wilde was sitting in the window, with the silhouette of the West End behind him warm as amber in the soft twilight. She paused to study him. He was excessive, and absurd — two pearl stickpins, indeed! — and there was something about him slightly wilted, even effeminate. Yet at the same time she could think of no man who exuded more of a sense of strength.

''At what are you staring so intently?'' she asked, opening a cabinet of polished hardwood, the twisting claws and finials of which dominated one whole corner of the room.

Wilde turned from the window. ''Shall I ever conquer it, Frances? That harsh, golden city?''

She selected a pair of bamboo-patterned Minton cups. ''If you can't, no one can.'' She was about to take out dishes of the same pattern, but changed her mind, and instead lifted down two of the precious blue-and-white plates from the narrow shelf between the windows.

''But I have produced nothing in over a year, Frances. Nothing to speak of. Except Cyril.''

''And what of that notorious comma, that you rejected and re-placed? You produced that, at least.'' She lit a spirit lamp and slipped it under the hanging kettle. ''I should think writing would come so easily to you, Oscar. You have so much to say!'' Now she peeled a Valencia orange and divided its sections on the plates: more for aesthetic satisfaction than nourishment.

''Shakespeare and Balzac — between them they have said every-thing worth saying. They have left me nothing.'' Then, as if in fear of being suspected of sincerity, he added: ''Nevertheless, I am a *little* closer to my lifelong ambition: to be the first well-dressed philosopher in the history of thought.''

Finishing the orange sections, he picked up his plate, holding it up to the window and nodding in approval at its transparency. Then he turned to the portrait, which in the darkening room re-tained its glow. ''I have done nothing since my marriage,'' he said, sighing. ''Perhaps I am too happy to work.''

The picture might have been painted by Manet himself, Wilde thought — if one could envision a Manet without genius. Against a background of solemn umber, the surfaces of the youthful face gleamed pink and ivory. There was bravura in the brush strokes, but little more. Dear Frances. In striving to plumb the boy's depths, she had come up with only surfaces. And yet how skillfully she had captured Somerset's wistfulness. More touchingly, perhaps, than a finer painter might have done. "Youth," Wilde said. "What a precious thing. I would do anything to retain my youth — other than eat properly, avoid strong drink, and get sufficient quantities of sleep. Is that tea ever going to be ready, Frances?"

She had poured the boiling water into a white teapot embossed with a stork and bamboo motif. "Another minute," she said. "You were right about Mr. Somerset, Oscar. He does have something Greek about him."

"So much more so when he is absent and only the aura of that golden blond perfection remains behind. The gods, being jealous of Somerset's beauty, bestowed on him that fatal combination: a tongue that works too readily and a mind that works not at all."

He glanced at the other paintings on the walls. A small flower piece caught his eye: peonies and lilacs. Slowly it dawned on him that there were several arrangements of the same flowers in vases about the room. He even became aware of their fragrance for the first time. It was as if, he thought, they were vying for attention with the little painting.

Frances laughed her low, embarrassed laugh. "Fortunately, Mr. Somerset's portrait will remain ever silent."

Wilde nodded dreamily. "Ever silent. Ever young."

He said nothing for a time, smoking thoughtfully as the shadows gathered in the corners of the room. Then: "What of the other fellow — Ross?" he asked.

"Isn't Robert a darling?" She poured the tea. "You don't mind his 'spying,' do you? He was *so* eager for a look at you — and too shy to be introduced."

Each moment told on her face, Wilde thought, bringing a higher or lower flush to the curves of her cheeks. But it was only when she stopped smiling that a different kind of smile revealed itself, forlorn and detached and a little cold.

"Is he a Londoner now? Or only here on holiday?"

She passed him the cream and sugar in Chantilly bowls painted with boughs of pine. "His mother is only here long enough to install him at Cambridge — if they will accept him. Bright as he is, Robbie seems uneducable!" She sipped at her tea meditatively, frowned, and heaped in another spoon of sugar. "He was a joyous, happy baby. A happy little boy. And then — something changed. I never knew what, nor why. Robert is still joyous, still delightful. But something in him is — broken."

Wilde downed his tea and held the cup forth for replenishment.

"The Rosses are one of Canada's best families," Frances went on. "Robert's grandfather was Prime Minister of Upper Canada. And his father had an important position back home — Attorney General or something. He died when Robert was two, poor little leprechaun."

But Wilde was hardly listening. He was staring at the unfinished portrait. "What a pity that such a face must change with time. For Somerset, every wrinkle will be a tragic poem."

She moved closer to the easel, and reached the hand mirror from her worktable. "Tragic? Somerset?" Now she turned her back to the picture, and studied its reflection in the glass.

"What are you doing, Frances?"

"Seeing my efforts fresh. You are painfully accurate, Oscar. Poor Somerset has beauty — and nothing else!"

"One *needs* nothing but beauty — while beauty lasts."

She replaced the mirror and rubbed her thumb into the crimson about the cheekbone, darkening it slightly. "Strange, though — now that he is gone, something seems to be gone from the picture as well."

The oil lamp had dulled the hues; aside from that Wilde saw no alteration. "Something is gone?"

At the far end of the studio she regarded her painting with arms folded. "It looks somehow *older* than it did," she said, with a little laugh. "Or is it my imagination?"

He carried an oil lamp over to the easel. "Perhaps at this very moment, Somerset is discovering that he is five years younger!" Confronting the guileless painted face with its quizzical smile, he grew solemn. "Ah, well," he sighed. "We shall all of us suffer for what the gods have given us. Suffer terribly. Of that I have no doubt."

"Oscar!" She took a seat on the wickerware sofa, giving him a reproachful look. "I never know when you're being serious."

"When I'm joking, of course," he said, joining her. "And now I am going to ask you a *very* serious question, Frances. Perhaps the most serious I shall ever ask you."

"Well?"

"How is it you have never asked to paint *my* portrait?"

) 2 (

On the steps of the brownstone, he paused to button his greatcoat of green-dyed suede and fur. Over four years old now, it was still ahead of the fashion.

The city beyond Russell Square was a medieval illumination in blue and gold. Even as he watched, though, the gilt evaporated from rooftops and towers. Like toast soaking up tea, the trees absorbed the last of the sunlight, and the buildings turned a soiled gray.

His eyes, attuned to Frances Richards's pictures, were still strained towards art, and he swaggered eagerly into the park, appraising every passerby with wonder, as some visitor might who had just arrived from the moon.

How strange Londoners would appear to that visitor, thought Wilde, the women puffed out with bustles or crinolines, those still old-fashioned enough to wear them, while the men, with their spindly long hats jutting chimneylike out of their heads, loped past like giants. Then there were the aesthetic young ladies simpering through the square in limp garments without stays, a magdalen in a purple dress with slashed sleeves, long train dragging over the cobblestones, a mater dolorosa in a flapping azure cloak. A stooped elderly woman stared after them, scowling, her ferocious eyes seeming to say: *I am not supposed to be old.*

He had left the studio rather abruptly; too abruptly, perhaps, just when Frances Richards seemed to be warming to his company, even opening up.

He adored companionship, craved it — yet was forever pulling subtly away from people, from the demands they unwittingly made, escaping into what all too often turned out to be even greater demands: for time, attention, money, love. He had none of these to spare.

Except love, perhaps. The scent of sweet young buds rose up, pleading, from the park. How could the poets have dedicated so many stanzas to the joys of spring, when it was in fact a time of deepest sorrow? Yes, he thought, of love he had much to spare.

He reflected on home, and an emptiness pulsed somewhere near his heart. (Where did Somerset live?) Was this all he wanted of life? Was this all life wanted of him? What was the purpose of it — or were wife, child, home purpose enough? (And was the dusk in some shadowy glade darkening at this very moment the blond tangles of Somerset's hair, were his clear blue eyes growing fretful over the coming night?)

Yes, Somerset, for all his shallowness, had indeed touched something deep. A function of the season, no doubt: one's emotions in April were always erratic. Still, this golden youth reminded Wilde of something, someone from long ago — someone he had lost all trace of. Someone whose absence made all life dreary and false. Only — who?

And then he was staring into a grinning visage, bloated and gray, the features bulging and uneven, the nose and cheeks scarlet with tiny veins. "Got your eye full, Guv'nor? 'Ow's about a few shillin's for a man what's truly 'ard up? A toff like you wouldn't miss it none."

So filthy was the man's face that his features seemed to be outlined with charcoal, like the face of an actor in some masque of horror. His shoulders were stooped, his chest narrow, his legs bowed; yet the soiled clothes he was wearing looked as if they once might have fit him well.

An absurd self-satisfaction emanated from the derelict, as if he were mocking both himself and Wilde. He was stout and healthy; if he would clean himself there should be no difficulty for him in finding work. He seemed to imagine himself above such considerations. He stared at Wilde with a half smile, as if to say: *I know you.*

Wilde pulled a coin from his pocket and dropped it into the filthy outstretched hand, quickly pulling back his own, afraid the fingers might touch. Not a word was uttered: the derelict merely kept regarding Wilde as if he were expecting something more.

Striding through the park, Wilde tried to annihilate all memory of that mocking face's lineaments. Footsteps came clattering up

behind him. He increased his speed. The footsteps came faster. Taut
with fear, Wilde turned.

"Isn't this a little — silly, Mr. Ross?" he gasped.

"I wanted — so badly to — I had to speak with you."

Wilde was frowning at the road behind them. "Is there no one
in back of us?"

"A bit of human flotsam? He is gone."

Wilde composed himself. "Detestable creature," he said.

"Detestable?"

"We must save our better energies for the joy, the beauty, the
color of life. The less we see of its sores, the better." He began to
stroll, and Robbie followed. A dry, faded smell rose up to greet
them from the pavement, and mingled with odors of shrubbery,
tobacco, sausages steaming on a grill in the park's refreshment
stand. "So," Wilde said. "Not only do you bribe poor Frances to
let you spy on me. I now apprehend you trailing me through the
streets of London like an avenging angel. You are relentless, Mr.
Ross. You are incorrigible. You are unscrupulous. I think we are
going to be great friends."

At the far end of the square, they turned into a side street where
girls in ragged dresses skipped rope in front of a public house; a
row of men sat at tables watching them, smoking pipes. Robbie
darted ahead, and peered up at Wilde guiltily. "She is a splendid
painter, Miss Richards, don't you think?"

Wilde said nothing for a moment. Then, "Frances feels too
deeply," he said. "It ruins her painting."

Robbie reflected on this for a moment. "She is developing an
excellent reputation."

Wilde nodded gravely. "And that is always so hard to live down."
At Robbie's shocked look, he smiled. "Before dear Frances can
become a true artist, Robbie, she is going to have to learn the subtle, torturous art of being shallow."

Below a swatch of unruly hair, frizzed by a hint of mist in the
atmosphere, Robbie Ross's forehead was too high, his nose too snub,
one almond eye tilted higher than the other. He had a zany look
that kept him from being truly attractive. But what charm. The
boy fairly pulsated with it. Gazing down at the hobgoblin face, so
alive though hardly beautiful, Wilde was reminded of Somerset,
so beautiful though hardly alive.

"Your poems have had a great influence on my life, Mr. Wilde. I read them over and over, as others do the Bible. Masterpieces — nearly every single one!"

"*Nearly* every one!"

"I thought of writing a letter of admiration to you — but didn't dare."

"Good, for I never answer letters. I know of men who came to London full of bright prospects and wound up wrecks in a month or two, simply from answering letters." Ross hadn't a profile, his face was fresh and winsome, no more — and yet, how much that was, at seventeen. "I quite like frank appraisals of my work, provided they're utterly complimentary," Wilde said, thoroughly enjoying himself. "What is your opinion of London?"

Robbie hesitated. "It seems a very — lonely place. I had expected it to be so much more — romantic."

"Ah," Wilde said, "but one has to make places romantic for oneself! Any city I find myself in always seems the most romantic place in the world! Well, I am on my way to Chelsea." The boy's face fell. Wilde signaled for a hansom, though in the heavy traffic there were no free ones in view. "May I drop you, Robbie?"

"Oh, I should like that very much! But there is an omnibus stand at the corner. Would that not be more economical? And every bit as fast?"

"Omnibuses should be reserved for the use of the rich," said Wilde, staring with distaste at the carts and wagons rolling past. "They are in a better position to endure discomfort. When one is not rich, one must console oneself — with extravagance."

As if by magic, a splendid new Gurney cab cut through the traffic and rumbled up to them, as from all sides cabmen, busmen, vanmen swore at the driver.

Robbie looked from the cab to Wilde, amazed. "Shall — shall we take this coach, then?"

The cab's body was painted a luxurious wine red, and the horse was clean and well tended. "I would prefer, Robbie, that the coach take us."

Not only was the cab brand-new, the driver appeared to be sober. He had flaming cheeks and a look of deep serenity, and made no argument as they discussed the fee to Chelsea, with a stop at Gros-

venor Square; indeed he made them feel he would be delighted to
take them without charge. Robbie gaped up at Wilde as if he were
a sorcerer. Wilde smiled, feeling no compunction to erase this
impression.

As they rolled through the crowded traffic in the direction of
Oxford Street, a heavy fog was closing over the city with the dusk.
"Ah," said Wilde. "We are going to create a romantic London
for you, after all!"

And indeed, as the boy craned for a look at the buildings on
either side of Oxford Street above the traffic, it was as if an enchanted veil fell slowly over London. The houses blurred; the slow-
moving faces in the crowd appeared for an instant beautiful. Even
the cries of the vendors, over the dull clatter of truck wheels and
wagon wheels and horses' hooves, became briefly harmonious.
"Muffins!" "Brooms and brushes!" "Chairs to mend!"

And the passing omnibuses, red and cinnamon and blue, took on
a magic of their own with their bold advertisements for Horlick's
and Pear's Soap and Sanitas Disinfectant. Oxford Street was a
faded etching: black-bonneted old women on the corners selling
matches, tinsmiths carrying backloads of gleaming pots and pans,
shoppers peering excitedly into the glittering shops. The clothing-
emporium windows, glaring from the magnified light of gas reflec-
tors, were filled with colored coats and dresses, watches, jewels,
shining silverware.

"A pity this part of London is so flagrantly commercial. I have
spoken to Her Majesty about it. She only says, 'What can I do,
Mr. Wilde? My hands are tied.'"

"You are not on speaking terms with Queen Victoria!"

"Poor dear Queen. She never makes a move without consulting
me. Ever since Albert's death . . ."

The fog had deepened. Now they could barely make out the figures sitting on top of the passing omnibuses, and the streetlights
and lantern lights blurred into dim stars and trembling, misshapen moons.

"Fog," Wilde said. "It transforms our shabby city into a composition by Monsieur Claude Monet. If the smoke were to be pur-
ified and the air made clear, we all would flee from London, horrified, having recognized it as the most dreadful spectacle ever seen
by man." The coach lurched at this as if in disagreement.

It was indeed a remarkable cab. The inside was as clean as the outside, and the window sashes were unbroken, so the windows opened and closed. No scent of dung or straw or unwashed driver reached their nostrils, and the seat was as welcoming as an easy chair.

"Every city, like life itself, is unspeakably ugly," Wilde said, lighting a cigarette, very nearly purring with pleasure. "When here and there one finds a saving grace or two, one must seize upon them."

Over Regent Street, angry soot-edged clouds obscured the moon, as if in homage to the galaxies of ladies of the night, gathering across from Liberty and Company, ready to start their evening promenade. Picture-hatted, overdressed, their eyes aglitter with belladonna, they sauntered down towards Leicester Square like pillars of the highest society, mocking the startled look of the passersby, regarding women with disdain and males with a knowing smile. In their midst was one who had fallen a few steps farther down, her looks gone, her clothes in tatters, offering flowers to anyone who deigned to glance her way. "Only a penny, sir, only a penny for a whole bouquet."

The coach turned into Bond Street, where a cool deep silence welcomed them. They passed chapels, churches, an almshouse, houses of so many styles it seemed as if all the architects of Italy and Greece and Alexandria had been hired to add some porch or pediment. There was less and less traffic, fewer people, fewer lights. The buildings on either side seemed to be leaning towards them for a better look.

"The whole art of living, Robbie, is to ignore ugliness, heighten beauty." The coach filled with the sweet smell of tobacco smoke. "One must create fogs of one's own."

The boy smiled. "You are teaching me to see."

"Or not to, which is equally important." The coach paused at a corner and a woman rushed up, waving a sheaf of crudely printed booklets. "The wages of sin," she cried, "is death!"

Wilde accepted a tract and handed her a coin. "Just as most Englishmen are unable to see anything that is beautiful," he said, as the coach started up again, "we must train ourselves to see nothing that is *not*." He tore the tract in little pieces.

"Might not she be right, Oscar?" Robbie asked, disturbed. "What *is* the wages of these 'exquisite sins' of yours?"

Wilde grinned at the way the words sounded in the boy's North American twang. "The only sin is boredom," he said.

In the gaslight and thickening fog, nothing looked real anymore. They seemed to have ridden into a city in the clouds.

"I am tempted to believe you," Robbie said.

"Good. For one must always be on the lookout for new temptations. There aren't nearly enough, you know." He chuckled. "I sometimes pass an entire day without coming across a single one. It makes me quite ill." Their bodies bounced against each other as the coach turned out of Audley Street. "Speaking of temptation," Wilde went on, "I was invited to Lady Kendall's for dinner. Lady Kendall always serves the very best caviar. But instead I am going home to dinner with my lovely wife. Is that not dutiful of me? Now — which house is it?"

For they were slowly rolling past the shoulder-high shrubbery of Grosvenor Square. Robbie pointed to a row of gloomy houses. "The one in the very center." As the coach drew to a halt, the shrubbery, full of murmurous cricket calls, formed a cloister of shadows.

Robbie stared up at Wilde. Suddenly the park grew silent as if waiting for something — a nightingale, perhaps.

"Oscar, come up," Robbie said. "For just a minute."

"I am already late."

"Do come. Please." Something about the insistence in the boy's eyes was not to be denied. Puzzled, Wilde told the driver to wait, and followed Robbie into the Millman family's elaborate Grecian temple.

"I am on the third floor," Robbie said, as they ascended a curving marble staircase. "Where no one need bother with me." The Millmans, he explained, were abroad. His mother was at Windsor for the day.

"Then why did you have to rush home?"

"Ah." The top floor was less impressive, room after darkened room of dust-sheet-covered furniture, with a hallway of anterooms lined with ancestral portraits.

Throwing open a door, Robbie led Wilde into darkness. The

lamppost in the street sent twisting blue reflections through the layers of sheer curtains. Robbie pressed the door shut and leaned against it. He made no move to turn up the light. Wilde made out the forms of a desk, a sofa, a case of books, a bed.

"Are we to have no light?"

But the boy did not reply. In the silvery gloom, he darted across the carpet without a sound and reached up his face to Wilde's — a half-seen form, warm and ghostly in the darkness.

"Robbie, what are you —"

The softness of the boy's lips was as the searing of a flame. In Wilde's abrupt recoil, something was knocked over. His knees seemed to be giving way, and stumbling across the room, he grasped for the door. A herd of demons chuckled in his brain. Worse, something, *someone* behind him seemed to be pulling him, trying to drag him back.

Then the room materialized as, in a corner, Robbie Ross turned up the oil lamp. Wilde crossed the floor as steadily as he could, and reaching the desk chair, collapsed into it, his overcoat bunching up about him.

Robbie Ross moved to the sofa. For a moment he sat in silence, his head bowed, expressionless as a sleeping cat. At last he said: "Isn't that what — you wanted?"

"How dare you think such a thing?"

Robbie threw his head back, staring up at the coffered ceiling. An unhappy smile flickered over his lips. "You were speaking of — temptations. And wonderful sins. I thought —"

"There are sins and there are — how *could* you have imagined such a thing?"

The boy met his gaze with a certain haughtiness. "You said that one must forever seek out new experiences. You are giving me one. I never felt hated before." He made a twisted effort at a smile. "Thank you for that."

"I cannot — you have startled me out of my wits, that is all. I don't hate you. But I am a married man. With a child."

"I am aware of that."

"Then how — I must go."

"Yes, Oscar. Mr. Wilde. Go."

Making for the door, Wilde caught a glimpse of the pile of books scattered at the bedside, prominent among them his own book of poems. He derided his vanity and yet could not but feel touched. As he reached for the door handle, an image filled his mind of Robbie's strange, childish features — a face designed for joy. The memory of his own youth loomed up before him, with all its hurts and contradictions, and pity squeezed his heart for Robbie's pain, for all pain. He traced his way back to the desk.

"You have found out my secret," he said, drawing his coat up, buttoning its top button. His lips seemed to taste of gall and wormwood. "I am not really very wicked at all. There are even those who accuse me of never having done a naughty thing in my life. They say it behind my back, naturally. We will forget this little incident, Robbie. We will pretend it never happened. We shall be friends. I want very much for us to be friends. You are a charming young man and a connoisseur of literature, as you prove by enjoying my work. There is lunch at the Café Royal any day you wish, and as often as you wish. But about this evening, Robbie, we must never speak."

Whatever the boy was feeling, sorrow, remorse, or shame, his face had taken on a dignity that aged him, made him seem in a curious way the older of the two. "I understand, Mr. Wilde."

" 'Oscar' is what you mean." He grasped the lad by the shoulders and regarded him sternly. "We shall speak of sorcery, and journeys to Cathay. Of cunning devices bordering the collar of a princess's dress, of politics and poems. We shall weep at witticisms and laugh at the philosophers' graver words. We shall eat of pomegranates and costly viands and soups made of monsters drawn from the seven seas. But of these past ten minutes, Robbie, we shall never, ever speak. Do you agree?"

"I agree," said Robbie. A sad smile played about his lips. "Do you grant me absolution? I am a Catholic, you know. And a very good one." The trace of hauteur had come back.

Wilde laughed, but his heart was nowhere in the laughter. "It is counsel I should be giving you — the wisdom of an older man. But it is always a silly thing to give advice, and to give *good* advice is absolutely fatal." He pried open the door. "I must leave. My wife will be furious with me for my lateness. No, she will be kind and understanding — and that is so much worse . . . ."

) 3 (

The cold air was like water after long thirst. Heaving himself into the waiting coach, Wilde could feel nothing in his legs, his hands, his heart. His voice was foreign to him, instructing the driver to move on to Chelsea — as quickly as possible. And as they turned into Bond Street a slow, rising influx of terror made him want to leap out of the jiggling cab and run into the night.

"Driver?" He tried to sound casual. "Make that Park Lane."

"Park Lane, sir? Did you not say Chelsea?"

"Never mind Chelsea!" Wilde snapped. "Park Lane. And *somehow* make that horse move faster."

The driver frowned at him, and continued at virtually the same cautious pace. Wilde sat back and closed his eyes, trying not to think, trying to concentrate on the sound of hooves on cobblestones.

The house, looming silent and forlorn in the wavering blue light of a single lamppost, had been a splendid edifice at one time, but now the stone had eroded, the carved flowers of the facade were blurred and featureless, the fence's metal fixtures were caked with rust. Wilde paid the driver with an apologetic air.

"Good evening, Delia," he said, his voice shaky. "Has there ever been a lovelier spring evening?"

"There has," snapped the maid.

As the front door closed behind him he had the sense, as always, of slipping away from the harsh and wounding real world into the sweetness of the warm, protected past.

"Tell my mother I am here," he said, sniffing to discover if there were any alcohol on Delia's breath.

"I'll ask if Lady Wilde will see you."

"Don't be absurd, Delia. Of course she will see me."

The maid raced to the stairway ahead of him and mounted it two steps at a time. He went up at his own slow pace, noting how the flowered wallpaper was peeling in ugly coils, how the banister was coated thick with soot.

When he got to the salon door, Delia was standing in it with her hands clasped beneath her apron. "Her Ladyship will receive you," she said in a sardonic tone. She admitted him and left, slamming the door.

The windows of the salon, like all the house's windows, were barred and shuttered, and the blinds were drawn. Stale perfume and cigarette smoke hung thickly over the credenzas and armoires and horsehair chairs. The house was barely half the size of the one in Dublin, yet every stick of furniture they had ever owned was crowded into it: desks and tables and lamps of questionable periods were crammed together in long narrow rows like pieces in an auctioneer's showroom. His mother had refused to surrender a single chest of drawers, a single dish, after his father's death. The huge, heavy sofas seemed to be writhing under a sense of their own ugliness, with a nymph smirking at every angle and a dragon mouthing on every claw. A single candle guttered in a corner where, on an enormous high chair gleaming in the shadows like a golden throne, his mother sat reading, tapping her fingers on the chair arm to some inner rhythm of her own.

"Mother."

Eyes glued to the page, she raised a hand. "I must finish this stanza," she boomed in her deep, musical voice.

Upon the mass of her dyed ebony hair rested a coronet of laurel leaves fashioned of a metal something like gold. The heavy creases of her throat were nearly concealed by the necklaces clattering down the front of her low-cut bodice, and there were bracelets of all descriptions jingling on her arms. The lace trim about her bosom was held in place by brooches hung like a general's medals, in each of which was affixed a painted miniature portrait of some ancestor.

At the far end of the room the "shrine" to his father was illuminated dimly by a candle glowing in a blue glass cup. A vase before it held a bursting bouquet of blossoms, all of fabric: silken roses and lilacs and irises, perfectly arranged and, despite their dustiness, more beautiful than real flowers could ever be.

Dabbing at her eyes with a lace handkerchief, Lady Wilde rose. For an instant, in the gloom, she looked the way he always saw her in his mind's eye: youthful, even beautiful, a dark-eyed goddess glowing with wisdom and disinterested love. "Sophocles affects me too deeply," she said, wafting a scent bottle before her nostrils. She reached her book towards a cabinet in the shadows, but missed. She took no notice as it crashed to the floor.

"I am glad of company," she said. "It will make the night — less lonely."

Natural-seeming she might appear, and even young, yet the presence that rose thus so strangely beside the tea table was in fact painted with makeup like an actress on the stage, her heavy face ghostly white except for streaks of scarlet rouge blurring across the cheeks and into the temples. She was nearly as tall as he, and as she brushed her cheek against his, Wilde felt as if he might be shrinking. Petals were scattered over her bosom: but the rose she was chewing only seemed to intensify the smell of alcohol emanating from her crimson-tinted lips.

"I am sorry, Mother, if you are lonely," he said, sinking into a seat beside her. A spring jutted out of the upholstery.

"Lonely? I am too busy to be lonely. Still,

> *'Who ne'er his bread in sorrow ate,*
> *Who ne'er the mournful midnight hours*
> *Weeping on his bed has sate,*
> *He knows you not, ye Heavenly Powers . . .'*

I would quote it in the original, but it is impossible for a woman to speak German without looking plain. What is on your mind, my boy? Trouble at home?"

"I was feeling — in need of a cup of tea. And Chelsea seemed such a very long way off. And then I —"

"Tell the truth and shame the devil, my boy. Is everything as it should be between yourself and Constance? Not that you would confide in *me* about it, of course. Delia!" she cried. The door flew open. "Bring up tea for my son."

"I will not bring it up, I will send it up," said Delia, and turned on her heel. Again the door slammed behind her. Lady Wilde grimaced.

"Everything between myself and Constance is heavenly, thank you, Mother," Wilde said coolly.

From beneath the golden chair she reached a tall glass filled with macerated fruits, and tilted it to her lips. "I have been feeling ill," she said with a heavy sigh. "I don't think you will long be troubled with me . . ."

"Mother, you are being silly."

"Sit up straight, Oscar. Even when a poet broods, he never slouches." She gave him a knowing smile. "And how *is* poor Constance?"

"Why 'poor,' Mother? She is not devoid of capital, and I do not beat her."

"There are females who enjoy nothing more than an occasional wallop. I, needless to say, was never one of them. Nor, I am sure, is your sweet wife. Constance is a dear little thing. It is a great pity . . ."

"Why is it a pity? *What* is a pity?"

"I said, 'Constance is very pretty.' You must not put words in my mouth, Oscar. I am capable of producing my own, as the volumes on those shelves will attest." She groaned voluptuously, and took another sip of the fruit-filled concoction. "I am exhausted after a visit to the Duchess of Warwick. She has become interested in Methodism and is quite unbearable."

"Mother, you *mustn't* speak of Constance as if she —"

"I never saw anyone so altered. Virtue is unflattering to anyone, but to a woman of a certain age, it is a catastrophe."

"Mother —"

"Never trust a woman over thirty-five who wears pink ribbons, Oscar. Nor a woman who wears mauve, no matter *what* her age. And now the duchess is speaking of baptism! Well, they say it is a form of new birth, and certainly to be born again would be a great advantage to the duchess."

Sulking, Wilde picked up a book and pretended to find it fascinating. She pulled it away from him. "Shall I read you the piece I am writing for the Irish press?" She was grasping at a handful of papers on the table beside her. "Even if my Irish song has been somewhat dulled by London's din, 'Speranza' has managed to put together an amusing paragraph or two."

"Please — not tonight, Mother."

"It may inspire you to write something of your own."

"Then I would rather you read me — a fairy story, Mother."

She made a scoffing sound. "You will find this far more interesting. It is about the flowers of Kensington — ostensibly. Naturally, I do not limit myself to so paltry a subject." She cleared her throat, balancing a magnifying glass before her face. " 'Tis the spring again, and London wakens from her winter sleep . . .' "

Her voice, dark and hypnotic. The warmth she seemed to cast. The aromas of the deep-shadowed room. He was seeing her, not as she was now, obscured by time and veiled by the tints and powders of her vanity, but as she once had been . . . and he was back in childhood, seated in troubled silence on the dusty carpet, listening to the strange, musical phrases of her compositions without understanding, yet glued to the magic of each new incomprehensible idea like a fly in honey, the lovely-falling syllables mingling in his imagination with her mysterious fragrances: ink, female scents of hair and cool flesh, a whisper of patchouli, as she had chanted on of ruined convents and castle walls, knights and bravery and witches.

He had secretly believed that she had intimate knowledge of all those things, that whilst he slept she rode abroad upon the winds, discovering all the mysteries of the hidden world and translating them into passionate sobbing phrases.

Alas, venturing forth outside the sanctuary of home, he had learned that there were other worlds than hers, ugly ones, and that he could be despised as well as loved — and so could she. His eyes were drawn to the white wall behind her golden chair, filled with cracks like a vase of ancient porcelain, covered with rows of photographs, pictures he had known for so long that he no longer knew them at all. Himself as an infant, looking vaguely like her and dressed in skirts (he would *never* allow Constance to follow that preposterous fashion in dressing Cyril!). Himself in boyhood, scholarly and well behaved in one after another idyllic setting. But where was the pain, the humiliation, the harsh, all-destroying laughter?

Most terrible, it had not been him only whom they had mocked, but her and his father as well. And in the echoes of that laughter the chivalry had died, the abbeys and the castles all had crumbled together into ruins, and all the dreams, desires, beliefs, convictions of his boyhood had passed away, never to return.

No, there could be no true picture of his childhood; it was a ruined mosaic full of missing parts that he seemed ever to be in search of. And invariably he found only sorrow in those unfixed memories that he seemed always to be trying to repair — as he came back always to this room, her room, her salon, remembering it as the place in all the world fullest of warmth and welcome — and yet whenever he found himself in it once again, he would sit impatiently, just as he was doing now, counting the moments till he could once again pull free.

"You were the most adorable child the sun has ever shone on," his mother said, abandoning her recital and replacing the manuscript on a pile of dusty pages.

He saw her for a moment as an old woman, ravaged by conspiracies of sorrow from without, and sorrow from within.

"Yes, Mother."

"If only you might have stayed that way. If only we all might have stayed the way we were . . ."

And he thought of Somerset's features, the room of blue light and cold shadows, a young boy's searing kiss.

The dumbwaiter bell tinkled. "Will you get the tea, Oscar? Delia has become quite impossible."

"Why do you put up with her, Mother?"

"She amuses me."

Yes, he thought with irritation, and makes a stalwart drinking companion as well. He opened the dumbwaiter door and carried the rattling tea things back to his chair.

"Now tell me, Oscar," she said, pouring into a cup that was none too clean, "why are you wandering about London at this hour? Why are you not at home, perfecting your craft?"

His voice was tired and old. "I have no more poetry in me, Mother."

She nearly dropped the teapot. "I, who never slapped you once, should slap you for that! Have you forgotten who you are? Have you forgotten who *I* am? And the powers at Trinity College — were they all mere fools to heap laurels on your adolescent brow? Or at Oxford? Was the Newdigate Prize bestowed upon a youth who had no poetry in him? For shame, Oscar Wilde! You are the sure, clear voice of the younger generation, the most sensational discovery since Byron."

"Yes, Mother."

She nodded towards the shrine where his father in a framed brown photograph, circled by SIR WILLIAM WILDE in cutout letters of gold, scowled out at them from behind his votive candle. "Even *he* was an accomplished writer."

Wilde nodded dismally, staring at the photograph and hearing her voice from long ago: *Your father is a sensualist, Oscar. You must ever be on guard against that tragic flaw* . . . And once again the scene came back: the darkened room in Grosvenor Square and the kiss of the trembling boy.

"Brilliant as your father was as a scientist, of course, he betrayed an ignorance of the artistic temperament that reminded one of the worst excesses of the Counter-Reformation. Nevertheless, he was a fine writer, even if he did limit himself " — she spat out the words in a spray of mist — "to folklore. Of the most pedestrian kind."

The tea, which tasted like pure tannin, might have been brewing for days. "I must start off for Chelsea," he said in a weary voice. "Constance is keeping supper for me."

His mother was looking at him sorrowfully, her eyes full of perishing dreams and the wrecks of forgotten aspirations. With a sigh she said: "It *is* unfortunate that, in spite of marrying into such a family as ours, Constance remains a wallflower."

"Mother!"

"The wife of a poet, Oscar, should be fascinating, strange, unpredictable. She owes it to him, and to society. People expect her to be astonishing. I have tried on many occasions to point out to Constance the necessity for spectacular behavior, but she remains, alas, an unwilling pupil."

"Constance is full of interesting schemes," he said, turning away from her, trying to find a mirror. He adjusted his clothing as best he could without one. "She is even thinking of taking up writing."

"Writing!" cried Lady Wilde with such a start that the golden coronet tilted sideways on her head. "What can Constance know of writing?"

"She is thinking of becoming an expert on costume and modern dress. She is very good with clothes."

"Constance? Modern dress?" His mother choked with laughter. "I have always thought it was extremely fortunate that you and she had such a short engagement. You had no opportunity to learn the truth about each other!" She reached a hand over to him, resting it on his arm. "Poor dear Constance is far too sensible to be a writer, Oscar. Artistic excellence can never be achieved by one who is entirely normal. It is the province of those who are larger than life. Now, have another cup of tea and let me finish reading my article," she said. "And this time, pay attention."

"I am late for supper."

"You have not yet heard the loveliest phrases!"

"Constance will be furious."

Still grasping his hand, she drew him down to the floor at her feet. ''Hush, my child. You will seem all the more precious to her for the wait . . .''

) 4 (

The coach creaked down the dark streets of Chelsea, and as the gas lamps grew fewer and the trees more plentiful, Wilde felt for once a sense of relief to be going home, even of something like happiness.

The air became clearer and sweeter, and deeply he inhaled the green wet smell of spring. The hansom's side windows were still coated with moisture, transformed by every passing light into trembling jewels. Across the river the sky flashed red from unseen industrial furnaces.

Except for the ringing of the horse's hooves, there was little sound — only an occasional squall of song or laughter from a public house. Though the mist had cleared, the pavements were still damp. They mirrored the candle lamps of passing bicycles, the lantern of an oilskin-wrapped police constable, the glowing drawn curtains of passing windows, orange from the fires within.

The Chelsea sky was a reservoir of powdered stars, and far to the north hung a cold white moon. Artemis, he thought, watching with serene indifference from her summit of self-glorifying light.

Why could he not enjoy these sights, he asked himself, without pondering on ways to describe them in a poem?

Were there for him no simple pleasures left?

Then he reflected that he might, perhaps in an essay, write of the poet being only able to see things as jeweled phrases or magical sounds, and thus saw them more beautifully than anyone else, and this mollified him, almost made him smile.

They drew past the graveyard of the Royal Hospital, traversed the brooding slum of Paradise Walk, and turned into Tite Street, to the neat brick house identical to the ones on either side. Wilde paid his fare, but on the steps he hesitated. He longed to be inside and safe in the loveliness and warmth — and yet, reaching for his key, he felt as always an urge to turn back, to flee, to disappear into the beckoning mysteries of the night.

She was in her sitting room, reading, surrounded by heavy pieces of tapestried furniture, her own small collection of books, sentimental pictures, keepsakes of Ireland. It was the only uninteresting room in the house. When she heard him, she slipped the pamphlet she was reading inside the pages of *Costumes of Greece and Rome*.

"Darling," he said. He went to kiss her, but his lips felt tainted. He pressed her to him instead.

Or could it be that he wanted, in some way unknown even to himself, to preserve the memory of that forbidden kiss intact? Surreptitiously he wiped his hand over his mouth. "Has it been a pleasant day?" he said. Casually he flipped open the costume book. *Christ the First Theosophist* dropped out.

She looked up at him expectantly. The peonies in her cheek were faded and sere. Yes, she was angry with him for being late and determined not to show a bit of it. She was wearing a new dress, a serviceable brownish thing with a pattern of field flowers — the kind of garment she knew he detested. And now he was expected to compliment her on it.

"Cyril has been awful, awful, awful."

In the dim light thrown by the flower-painted oil lamp, she looked winsome and sweet — but alas, no more than that. Her loveliness had been budding when first they met; what had kept it from blossoming forth? Time was edging her towards a kind of resigned handsomeness instead. "It's not much of a life I've given you," he said, drawing her to him impulsively. He had not lost hope of turning her into a great beauty.

"Whatever do you mean?" she said, dabbing at the overplain arrangement of her glistening, well-brushed hair, which went from dull red to a vivid chestnut brown, like the wood of a cello.

"Can't we go into the salon, Connie? You languish in this dreary room all the time when you could —"

"But it's *my* room. I like it here." She smiled in embarrassment.

He drew open the sliding doors. In the silvery light filtering through the window slats, everything in the salon gleamed white, clean, perfect, like a room preserved in crystal, or in ice. It seemed too beautiful to be real, a painting of a room, where nothing could ever alter or fade or grow dusty. Even the shadows seemed to be hung with lace.

"I neglect you," he said, lighting one of the lamps. "Shamefully. I pursue my interests and pay no mind at all to yours."

She watched the room come to warm life as he lit one lamp after another, beside the Japanese dado, beside the slender white mantelpiece, beside the piano that was a sonnet in ivory and the table that was a masterpiece in pearl. The room was a musical composition, he liked to say: his variations in the key of white.

"You are a man. It's only natural." She sat rather fearfully on one of the Grecian chairs. It was still difficult for her to accept that its slender turned legs could support a human's weight. The floor was carpeted in mellow cream rugs woven with threads of gold, and the white walls on one side of the room had an ocher tone, while on the other they were tinted with blue. The woodwork was a gleaming harsh white, shading to palest gray.

"We must spend more time in here, darling," he said. "These rooms grow fretful when there is no one here to appreciate their loveliness."

"Like you, they need an audience," she said.

"Connie!"

Giggling, she stretched up on her toes, primping his lapels. "I have become a tour guide, leading your admirers through the glittering exhibition galleries of your home." She said it as if in jest, but he knew her dislike for parties, company, excitement. For society she had no patience, for entertaining no gift.

"*Our* home, Connie."

But when he turned to kiss her cheek, she pulled away though he knew she had been waiting to be kissed, was always waiting only for that. Proof. That he loved her. And, of course, the more the proof was demanded, the more difficult it was to give.

He smiled at her helplessly, finding her fragile and somehow pathetic, pacing in her clumsy printed dress past the row of Whistler nocturnes of Venice, all shadowy palaces and somber moonlit lagoons, past the pearl-white vases filled with snow-white heather, past the white azaleas in their bone-white jars.

"You hate it, don't you," she said with a little smile.

"It's very pleasant as a dress. I just don't think —"

"*I* happen to like it very much." She sat at the piano, removed her rings one by one, rubbed her fingers.

Smoking on the cream satin divan, Wilde pretended to listen as she played. Just as his eyes began to grow heavy, she raised her voice in song:

> *"It may be that Death's bright angel*
> *Will speak in that chord again.*
> *It may be that only in Heaven*
> *I shall hear that grand 'Amen'!"*

She stared down at the keys, exhausted, gloomy.

"Bravo, darling," Wilde said, gently applauding. "I adore Wagner."

"Oscar — it was 'The Lost Chord'!"

"Wagner is nothing *but* lost chords. I wish you were wearing your white moiré dress as you sat there, darling. The one with the little pearls all over the —"

"Pearls. Satins. Peacock feathers." She spun around so her back was to him. "Oscar, *why* must we waste so much time on frivolities?"

"They are the only things of importance. Frivolity is to the rest of existence as —"

"Please!" she snapped. "No epigrams. I believe you are more interested in my clothing than in me! To pay so much attention to the look of a dress, or a room — don't you think it's a little — a little —" Her hands crashed down on the keys.

"Vulgar? Constance, I am *incapable* of being vulgar. That is why I am not a successful writer."

From the floor above came the shrieking of the baby — all too familiar a sound. Constance crumpled at the piano, clamping her hands to her ears, looking as if she might begin screaming, too. Hurriedly she composed herself, sat up straight, even forced a little smile.

If only, he thought, she had released that scream!

"I will see to Cyril," said Wilde. "Ask Bridie to put dinner on the table, will you, darling? I am starved."

"But you don't know what to *do* with an infant. At least that is what you keep telling me."

"Of course I know what to do with an infant," he said, starting up the stairs. "I was an infant for years. Some say I am still an infant!"

The nursery was bare: there was no telling yet what turn Cyril's personality would take, thus it seemed too soon to decide upon an appropriate decorating scheme. Wilde looked down into the crib and twisted his features into an exaggerated smile. The baby stopped crying and stared up at him.

"Why do you look surprised, Cyril? You recognize me by this time, surely. It's the least I would expect. And how *is* my little darling? Do you require changing? Is that what all this screaming is about?"

Looking down at the small squirming bundle of fresh, unspoiled existence, an ache of self-reproach coursed through him. He *must* become a better father, a better husband. He must set all his best efforts to improving himself, to affirming life, to nipping his slothfulness in the bud.

He must change his ways.

Unpinning the diaper, he stared down at the mess the wailing baby was writhing in. At the smell, a swirl of dizziness rushed over him. He turned away, head reeling. There must be a clean diaper somewhere — perhaps in the sideboard. He yanked open drawer after drawer. At last he found them, under the sheets.

As he tried with finger and thumb to detach the sticky soiled diaper from the tender skin, the baby began to shriek again, in that unbelievably loud, insistent way. A wave of nausea came over Wilde. "Constance!" he cried out. "Connie, please — please take care of this child."

She came flying up the stairs, but halted in the nursery doorway. He was leaning over the crib, reciting, in a stentorian voice:

> "Darkling I listen! And for many a time
> I have been half in love with easeful death!
> Wooed him in soft words! In many a mused rhyme . . ."

"Have you gone mad? Oscar, what are you *doing?*"

Wild-eyed, he moved away from the crib. "Trying to stun him into silence. If Keats cannot do it, whatever can?"

She poured water from the ewer on the sideboard, reaching for a towel and murmuring consolations to the screaming child, as Wilde stormed from the room.

"To my conversation you will barely lend an ear," he shouted petulantly, starting down the stairs. "Yet you will listen to that infant's dithering for hours on end . . ."

They had little to say over dinner. ''I thought you were hungry, Oscar.''

''Ravenous.'' He was leaning on an elbow, eyes traveling without interest over the cunning patterns of shadow on the jade-green lacquered walls.

''You haven't touched your meat.''

He was thinking of caviar, and of the way Lady Kendall served it, heaped up in glass bowls sunken into silver ones, cushioned in crushed ice. ''The meat is overcooked.''

''I didn't find it so. I thought you were fond of calf's liver.''

''I adore calf's liver. But not boiled.''

''Bridie wouldn't boil calf's liver!''

He stepped over to the sideboard and poured himself a generous serving of brandy in one of the wedding crystal glasses she was afraid to use. ''Bridie would boil her own liver, provided she could serve it with her hideous mint sauce.'' He broke off a piece of the dessert mince pie. ''Why do we never have gingerbread pudding anymore? It is the only thing the woman knows how to make properly.''

Constance sliced another piece of meat, making a great show of relishing it. ''There is a theory that ginger causes consumption.''

He collapsed into his chair again, exhaling a great sigh. After a few sips of the brandy, he said: ''It's my fault. If I were bringing in some money, we could afford a decent cook.''

''Bridie is an excellent cook. When she's asked to do regular English food.'' She seemed to regret the tone of reproach in her voice, and looked up from her plate apologetically, stretching a hand to him across the table. He would almost have preferred for her to throw her plate.

''We must do things together, Connie,'' he said, forcing himself to squeeze her hand tight.

''Yes. Yes, we must.'' There was a hint of desperation in her low, sweet voice. ''But not go out to a lot of dinners and parties. I don't want that, really I don't. Unless, perhaps, once in a while, to the Monmouths.''

''Anyplace but there, my darling. Their cook is worse than Bridie!''

''But they are such good people. They are active in *all* the charities.''

He gave her a pained smile. "Dearest, all the cardinal virtues put together cannot atone for a half-cold entrée."

He felt he could read her mind. Even though she was thought of as the sensible one, there were ways in which she was by far the more romantic of them, given to long sieges of dreaminess and fits of sorrow, seeing herself always in a kind of stage moonlight, while he by contrast could be very much a realist, even a cynic.

She wanted to make love. Or, rather, wanted to be reassured in endless subtle ways, and lovemaking had become the most important of those ways. He was hardly expected to take part as himself, only as the Reassuring Other.

And so it had become an obligation, and as with all obligations he put it off for as long as he possibly could.

"I'm quite content to be here in our own lovely house," she went on. "I wish — I wish you were as content. I wish we could have dinner here more often. In the salon, sometimes. Just the two of us."

"We shall, Connie. We'll do *your* things." He reflected a moment. "What *are* your things, nowadays?"

She lowered her eyes. "I haven't had much time . . . the baby . . ." Then abruptly she sat up erect in her seat and looked straight at him, her hands clenched. "I have been working with — the Missions."

"Ah."

"I've been afraid to tell you."

"The Missions."

"We've all been laboring with special diligence, ever since poor Bishop Harrington's tragedy." She reached for the brandy bottle, and to his surprise took down another of the crystal glasses.

"Refresh my memory, darling," he said. "Who was Bishop Harrington and what was his tragedy?"

She seemed astonished that anyone might not know. "Slaughtered. By savages." Suddenly she seemed younger, fresher. Perhaps the brandy. Perhaps the soft light of the guttering candles. "Surely you heard, Oscar! We must do our part, Lady Sandhurst is quite set upon it. Those same savages would like nothing better than to discourage us. We're only the more determined to reveal to them the *true* meaning of Christian charity! In return for their cruelty we are going to show them the way to God."

"That is very worthy," he said. He knew that if he had more brandy his mind would race faster and faster, and he would be up till all hours. And tomorrow he was determined to rise early and make a fresh start. He stared into his empty glass moodily, and pushed it away. "And your research on clothing?"

She drew her finger down the length of her dessert spoon, round the swirling edges, over the shining ridge. "I have so little time . . ."

"Do you not see how you are *cheating* yourself of a pleasure I know you would adore! There is a great need for someone to write about costume. So *little* has been said!"

"Yes, darling."

"You could begin by learning all about one century. Then branch out to all the others . . ."

She stole behind his chair and placed her arms around him. "If you're *really* interested in the Missions, Oscar, I am thinking of inviting Bishop Hall down, from Manchester, to address our group. He has done some remarkable work among the savages of East Africa. I am sure you would like to meet him . . ."

"East Africa?" Reaching over to the sideboard, Wilde poured himself a finger of brandy. "I shall keep it in mind, darling." He rose and took her in his arms, nuzzling her ear fondly. "Connie?"

"Yes, darling?" she whispered, breathless.

"Have you ever looked closely at the Gainsboroughs in the National Gallery? I mean, truly closely?"

She smiled up at him expectantly. "Why, no, darling. Why?"

"I can think of no finer way to learn about brocade . . ."

) 5 (

Decency, common sense, and the most rudimentary principles of self-respect warned Wilde to stay away from Robbie Ross; almost at once he sent a telegram inviting Robbie to luncheon at Tite Street.

In the first place, it would be unthinkable for a man like himself, who prided himself on openness and the liberal point of view, to begin casting stones, or to neglect to offer friendship, which in this case would amount to the same thing.

More important, there was all the good he might effect by way of reforming the unfortunate lad. Robbie was like a sheet of white foolscap, as ready to be scrawled over by vice's scented plume as by the careful quill of virtue. Clearly the boy needed guidance, and what better guide could he find than Oscar Wilde?

"How do you do, Mr. Ross," Constance said, giving him her loveliest smile.

"Robbie is from North America, and like all Americans believes we English are more cultured and intelligent than he is. We must do nothing to disabuse him of this illusion."

Wilde watched them carefully as they conversed. Good. It was clear that Robbie was well on his way to being infatuated with Constance — perhaps had been half infatuated before they met.

Though he was now enrolled at Cambridge, Robbie began to spend most of his weekends in London, nearly always in the company of Wilde. Together they admired Hawksmoor steeples, Sloane ceilings, Nash facades. They listened to Handel oratorios at the Albert Hall and Irish come-all-ye's in Trafalgar Square. In the Grosvenor Gallery they bickered over modern paintings, and in the National Gallery over old ones (if Robbie lingered over the portrait of an attractive male, Wilde would carefully steer him back to the Vermeers or Claude Lorrains).

"I have always been an incorrigible student," Robbie confessed.

"I am glad to hear it!" said Wilde. "It is always an advantage not to have received a good education."

Robbie listened intently to Wilde's advice on clothes. Together they haunted the Burlington Arcade, looking for just the shirt, or cravat, or pair of boots, to add some touch of distinction to Robbie's wardrobe.

"Those boots are too naive."

"Naive!" said Robbie.

"You need something at the same time in the best of taste and subtly unexpected . . ."

Wilde took Robbie to dine at his club, so that he might see the comforts of righteous living; his plan was to ease Robbie away from his leanings towards wickedness by convincing him of the superior gratifications of decency.

Sometimes when Constance begged to be excused from attending some dinner or ball, Wilde would take Robbie along instead, keeping a careful eye out for all the eligible young ladies in the vicinity, like a watchful dowager seeking mates for her offspring.

But along with showing Robbie the pleasures of wholesome living, Wilde was ever vigilant to stress the consequences of digressing from life's salutary paths.

"So this is the notorious Café Royal!" Robbie said. They were in the Domino Room, seated at a marble table under a gilded caryatid and sipping a tart young Château des Mille Secousses claret.

Over the talk and laughter could be heard the click of domino tiles from addicts who could not stop playing even as they dined. The amiable giant of a chucker-out was walking about, nodding to the regular customers. Wilde pointed out people at various tables who were known to be leading sordid lives. Unfortunately they all seemed to be enjoying themselves enormously.

"You must not be swayed by the charm of the decor, Robbie, nor by the splendid costumes of the women. In its own way the Royal is as dark a den of iniquity as anything to be found in the most sordid corners of the East End."

Robbie smiled dreamily, looking into the great long mirrors, placed at such angles that their images bounced back and forth in an endless corridor of reflections that seemed to pull one subtly inside. Through the door he had a view of the lobby, with its smart tobacco-shop kiosk selling newspapers from all over the world.

"How did you meet?" Robbie asked. "You and Mrs. Wilde?"

Wilde softened at the memory. "I courted her in Dublin all one short wintry week. We sat in a frozen garden and I asked her to be my bride. When she accepted, the air filled with the scent of roses . . ."

They went on night tours of Limehouse and the East End, to sections where the policemen walked in pairs, past workhouses and coffee stalls, German beer shops and Israelite cafés, down dank alleys where every third house was a tavern with a name like the Black Cat or the Red Rat, filled with drunken men and women dancing round and round.

They drank a concoction named blue ruin in an evil-smelling pub with eggshells lining the floor, their faces distorted into masks by flyblown mirrors lining the walls. "Delicious," Robbie said. "It tastes like raspberries and licorice mixed."

In a dim shop near the waterfront a brooding Chinese offered "Sloe leaves, China clay, yellow ocher, tragacanth, poison?"

"What, no opium?" said Robbie, and laughed so effusively that the Chinese began to laugh as well.

Once after the chimes of midnight they wandered through dark twisting streets, towards a great illumination that welled up in one of the alleys before them, and in the midst of it, as they slowly advanced, a palace of electric lights seemed to lift itself visibly up from the broken cobblestones, making the ugly old buildings on either side appear, for a moment or two at least, as lovely as country churches. Inside, a conductor was playing a piano with his left hand and manipulating a harmonium with his right, while a crowd of men and women stood watching impatiently, eating fried fish, or sucking oranges, or cracking nuts. The curtain jerked open and two women came out and began a row with each other. "Do you know," said the first, "that I have blue blood in my veins?"

"I know that you'll soon be havin' *red* blood on your nose," the other replied. And while the audience roared its approval, the two began tearing at each other's faces and hair.

"Isn't this dreadful," Wilde whispered, but it was obvious that Robbie was thoroughly enjoying it, and Wilde had to admit to himself that he was enjoying it, too. Ugliness of any kind could make him shudder with distaste, yet he was forced to admire its unrelenting vitality. The coarseness of the Irish peasants reeling drunkenly through the crowd, the pathetic efforts of the jugglers and magicians and dancers to entertain so demanding an audience, the very gaudiness and disorder were more vivid, in their way, than all the measured ecstasies of art.

At the same time as he was trying to rescue Robbie, Robbie was making a discreet effort to rescue him.

"My religion, Robbie? Why, I don't believe I have any. I am an Irish Protestant."

And repeatedly he would listen, with amusement, as Robbie endeavored to persuade him of the beauty and the depth of the Roman Catholic faith.

"I once had an audience with the Pope," Wilde said.

"Oh?" said Robbie. "Did you convert him to paganism?"

"I was a very, very young man, in Rome for the first time. A teacher took me to meet Leo the Eleventh. He was quite delightful. We had a wonderful chat."

Robbie grew serious. "What did the Holy Father have to say?"

Moved by the memory, Wilde was silent for a moment. "He told me I must seek the City of God."

"Well! That was good advice."

"My reply — though being so young I was far too cynical to make it — was that I much preferred a City of Gold. I very nearly became a Catholic at Oxford. And several times since. But I could never accept it as a *system*, Robbie. One must not try to take up residence in an inn meant for the sojourn of a single night!"

Nevertheless, when it transpired that the old Cardinal was making a special excursion from Birmingham to speak one Sunday at the Oratory, Wilde agreed to accompany Robbie to the service.

In the morning sunlight the blindingly white church looked, Wilde thought, like a cathedral the angels had wafted over from Rome, powdered with snow from the flight. Its interior splendidly reproduced all the gesticulations and excesses of the Italian Baroque.

The white marble saints in their alcoves appeared to be performing some hectic dance. An unseen orchestra struck up a rippling accompaniment, and the choir on their high platform soared into a lush Kyrie Eleison from France as incense rose over their heads in a slow-drifting cloud. Higher and higher rose the white smoke, up past the archivolts, blurring that continuous painted chain of language and of life so that all the bishops and seraphim and early fathers, the miracles and Bible scenes, seemed to be quivering with emotion.

Wilde was, at moments, moved to tears — though they were very nearly tears of laughter.

But Robbie — the incorrigible — seemed to be concentrating on a well-built young chorister in a gray cassock with lips as red and full as a harlot's.

The Cardinal sat hunched over on his wooden throne, and at one point two priests in green vestments, moving in a stately saraband, assisted him up the pulpit steps. Framed by cherubs in shining carved black wood, Newman peered down at his congregation, his face pinched and white and weary, and in a frail, unhappy voice spoke on the theme, What doth it profit a man if he gain the whole world and suffer the loss of his soul? He seemed to be reciting from memory and, for all the exquisite harmony of his phrases, to have very little faith that anything he said was true.

Wilde leaned back watching Robbie, who was gawking up at the steamy apotheoses crowded across the church's ceiling as if the painted saints might at any moment come spiraling down on top of them, or perhaps escort them up to their own dizzying heights. How absurdly romantic the boy was. How absurdly young.

"Well?" Robbie demanded outside, seeming to half expect Wilde to request baptism on the instant. "Was it not thrilling?"

"The best spectacle I have seen since *I Puritani* at Covent Garden," said Wilde. "I admit I am fascinated by your Roman Catholic Church. In all her seeming goodness the 'Scarlet Woman' is so utterly depraved." He sighed. "In any case, for myself, I believe salvation is required more by my senses than my soul." At Robbie's interested look, he blushed. "You realize, of course, I am talking nonsense," he said — and hailed a coach to take them to Kettner's and a sumptuous lunch.

For all their appearing to have so little in common, Wilde and Robbie began, in those dreamy months together, to set up a curious harmony. Robbie was the perfect audience, bright, untutored, throwing back a clear reflection of all the best in Wilde, of all Wilde hoped to be. Looking back to the time before Robbie, in fact, he began to feel he had not been entirely alive.

He dismissed the boy's praise as the rantings of an overimpressionistic youth ("I am keeping a scrapbook of your sayings," Robbie told him one day, as they strolled through Trafalgar Square. "One day I shall publish them and become rich.") Yet something about it encouraged him, and deeply. He would get home from one of their outings and find himself unable to sleep, filled with ideas inspired by their conversation. And then he would sit up in his bed and by the light of a candle begin to write.

At first they were only sketches. But the sketches began to expand. Soon he had a long essay on the theme of art, and the way nature forever copies it — little more than a reverie woven around several of their conversations, and yet he felt it was in many ways the best thing he had ever done.

"Wonderful!" Robbie said, when Wilde gave him the essay to read.

"But it is almost a collaboration, Robbie! I could never have written it if I were not imagining you listening to every line!"

There was something else robbing his sleep. The books he read, the plays he saw, the pictures he admired in the galleries seemed suddenly to be filled with strange, inexpressible emotions he had never been troubled by before. He could not bring himself to examine them too closely; at the same time he was unable to free himself of their fascination.

"You are always talking about your sins, Oscar," Robbie said one afternoon, walking under clouds of pigeons wheeling over Piccadilly. "But you are absolutely secretive about your lapses into goodness."

Wilde roared with laughter, causing the passersby to turn and stare. "Did you invent that, Robbie? Or did you hear me say it?"

"I spent all morning working it up. I wanted to be certain it appeared *impromptu.*"

Still laughing, Wilde gave his arm a squeeze. "What a delightful distorting mirror I have found! Do you know you quite inspire me? I will tell you a great secret — provided you solemnly promise to tell everybody. I have never in my life worked so well, nor been so happy, as in these past few months."

But between his hunger to write and the strange sensations swarming through his thoughts, he found it more and more difficult to adapt to Constance's regular hours of sleep. At last he decided that, for a month or two, he must set up a bedroom on the top floor, next to the nursery. There he could write or brood all night long, if write or brood he must.

"If that is what you think you need," said Constance, looking hurt.

He was always impatient for the weekends. Improbable-looking scamp though Robbie might be, Wilde's thoughts were full of him, and he was forever catching himself reflecting on the changing humors of that sly little face, trying out plays on words that might make the irregular features tighten with laughter, thinking of little gifts to make the clear hazel eyes shine. Robbie was almost too easy to delight.

But easy to hurt as well. "I am cross with you, Robbie," Wilde said one Saturday noon when they met at a shabby little Chinese café in Soho. "You have been neglecting me shamefully. I haven't seen you in almost twenty-four hours."

And he went on with an anecdote about Cyril's adventures learning to walk. Robbie said nothing, only looked down at his hands.

Without Robbie's enthusiasm, the story was stillborn, and Wilde too lapsed into silence.

"You are not yourself, Robbie. Something is wrong."

"Nothing. Nothing is wrong."

But when their meal arrived, the boy was unable to touch it. Finishing his tea, Wilde pushed his own plate aside and motioned for the check. As they turned out of the alley leading to the main road, he was about to reproach Robbie for his secretiveness when the boy burst into tears. "Don't — don't waste your time with me, Oscar."

"Dear boy, whatever are you — ?"

"If you knew me you wouldn't have anything — anything to do with me," Robbie sobbed.

Wilde stopped and made Robbie stop as well. "We are not moving another step until you tell me what has happened."

"A crowd of — of men from one of the colleges. They — they waited for me outside my room."

Wilde felt a surge of nausea rise in him. "And then what, Robbie?"

The boy had turned away, and when Wilde tried to tilt up his chin, Robbie covered his face with his hands. "They tore off all my clothes," he sobbed. "They tied — tied me with ropes. They called me terrible names. And beat me. And then they — and then they made me commit — the unpardonable sin."

"Robbie —"

"Then they dragged me to the fountain. And threw me in. For everyone — everyone to laugh at."

"Schoolboy tomfoolery," said Wilde in a strangled voice. "There is only one unpardonable sin, Robbie, and that is to wear silver accessories with a yellow waistcoat."

"I shall never go back to Cambridge. Never."

"We are going to have a beautiful lunch, an unforgettable lunch. At the Royal. No, at Frascati's. No, at Kettner's."

"I cannot. I shall never eat again."

But by the time the menus were placed in front of them, Robbie had to admit he had an appetite. His face was washed clean of tears, and he looked like a kitten fresh wakened from sleep.

"You are to order anything — absolutely anything on the menu that pleases you," said Wilde. "Some Cancale oysters, perhaps. They are extraordinarily large here. A salad made with one of those enormous Piedmont truffles, sliced into dark, transparent disks . . .''

"Can I order *escargots?* I have never tasted a snail."

"So young, and so eager for disappointment?" Wilde took a long sip of champagne. Through the sparkling liquid and the crystal, Robbie looked very nearly beautiful. "Snails, dear boy, only taste like *escargots* in Paris."

"I have never *been* to Paris. So I should like to try them here."

Wilde gaped in disbelief. "Dear boy," he said, as if Robbie had confessed to having some grave illness. Then suddenly Wilde's face lit up. "You shall be my guest. We will go to Paris together. Soon. Next week. Tomorrow."

Where the money would come from, he had no idea. He was already in debt, hadn't enough for coach fare or new shirts. But it was imperative that Robbie be distracted from this humiliation — Robbie, and himself as well.

They would go to Paris. So long as one took care of the luxuries, he told himself, the necessities would take care of themselves.

) 6 (

It was raining when they arrived at the Gare du Nord, and looked as if it had been raining for weeks. Wilde was perplexed. Paris was so different from what he had expected, so unlike the Paris he knew — or thought he knew — from his youth, from his honeymoon, from his many delightful visits.

The city was ugly. He had never dreamed it could be so ugly. The grimy water-splotched monuments were surrounded by English tourists uttering in hideous accents exclamations of innocent delight. The Parisians were surly, badly dressed, unhappy. A miasma of evil stenches oozed through the narrow streets : sulfur and horse dung and sizzling animal flesh.

The city was beautiful. He had never dreamed it could be so beautiful. Everywhere they turned they saw lovely things : noble youths and worldly, kind-eyed women; shops filled with wonderfully crafted furniture and jewels; an apotheosis of oranges glowing in a roadside cart; the Seine a ribbon of gray silk unfurling under a cloud-packed sky. Under an umbrella they promenaded through the deserted Luxembourg Garden, past pink nasturtiums and purple-hued petunias spiraling over the terrace of the queens of France, past mossy wet statues of forgotten poets, past the ivy-garlanded Medicis Fountain, with needles of rain chipping its green water into shimmering squares.

The city was dismal. It was iridescent. It was glossy, somber, gay. It was lachrymose, effervescent, haunted, hateful, funny, stately, sad. It seemed willing to be anything, so long as it could always be a surprise.

Robbie, too, kept changing. At moments he seemed almost too homely to look at; at others his quirky bemused features had a charm and dignity that moved Wilde more than any handsome face had ever done. Robbie had smiles that filled Wilde with pity, and others that made his heart thicken with affection. Like the city, Robbie refused to limit himself to expectations; refused to stand still.

They ate too much, drank too much, talked too much, laughed too much. In a café overlooking Saint-Sulpice they gulped down Calvados, smiling out at the glittering cobblestones of the square with its fountain of white stone bishops seeming to flinch miserably under the raindrops; and then they had a coffee in an artists' restaurant on the gloomy rue des Beaux-Arts; and then it was time for another liqueur, this time in a cozy warm workers' tavern pressed up against the crumbling house where Balzac wrote *César Birroteau*.

After dinner at Foyot's with far more Château Mouton-Rothschild than was good for them, they took a coach for Montmartre, stopping off at Château Rouge, where an impromptu spectacle was thrown together at a long odoriferous bar, with mendicants and blind men and cripples of every sort dragging their bodies along the sawdust floor, groping at each other or tapping canes.

"How dreadful!" said Robbie.

Then, as if at a signal, all the beggars leaped up and began dancing a quadrille, shouting and laughing and kicking their legs up higher and higher, pulling Wilde and Robbie into the fray.

"I am dizzy, Oscar! I am drunk!" cried Robbie, weaving along the dark street outside.

"Good!" said Wilde. "For I have something very, very interesting to show you next."

The waiting coach drove them on to a mansion in a dismal side street, where a woman in a gown of black and silver, her aristocratic face framed by a high collar of stiff white lace, led them to an upper floor.

She opened the door to a large bathroom, fragrant with pine and powder, painted with copies of lascivious murals from Pompeii. On a tiled dais, a great red copper tub rose like an ancient sailing vessel, its figurehead the body of a woman with the wings of a swan. From there they passed into a monk's cell, with rows of wooden pews, a *prie-dieu,* and a set of paintings of the temptations of Saint Anthony.

"If messieurs wish, we can perform a *messe noire* in this very room," said their hostess.

"We are not feeling particularly devout this evening," said Wilde.

In the next room, people seemed to be coming forth from all sides to greet them: but no, it was a chamber lined with mirrors from ceiling to floor. Next she showed them a Russian room, with a large sleigh for a bed; an Arab room with tented ceiling and passages of the Koran inscribed on large gold disks; a Chinese room; an Egyptian room. The *Chambre des horreurs,* as it happened, was occupied and could not be seen.

When at the end of the tour the ladies of the establishment were brought out for inspection, Robbie whispered timidly that he would like very much to leave. Almost relieved, Wilde tipped their hostess excessively, and led Robbie out into the lilac-scented night.

He was lighthearted as they walked the misty streets along the quai Voltaire en route to their hotel. He had another surprise in store, he announced. The following afternoon Robbie was going to meet Sarah Bernhardt. "She is a very dear old friend."

Robbie laughed. "Like the Queen?"

"You wound me, Robbie," Wilde said, stopping to gaze at the steaming waters of the Seine. The lanterns of the bridges shone like melting jewels in the racing coal-black waves. "You must *always* believe me, Robbie. Except when I tell you the truth. I met Sarah at the Folkestone boat when she made her first English tour, years ago. She floated down the gangplank onto English soil, and I tossed lilies in her path. Compared to her lovely feet, of course, they looked like vipers twisting in the dust." He sighed. "In my bachelor days, Sarah and Her Majesty were the only two women whom I thought of marrying. Victoria would in many ways have been a more suitable match. But Sarah was a goddess, and she was merely a queen . . .''

As he lay in his room that night, with the rain tapping at the long windows and all of Paris outside hiding in the dark, Wilde thought: *Today was a happy day. A truly happy day.* He remembered the eager face of the boy in the next room, and an ache throbbed through him that was very like pleasure, and very like pain. Only a wall between us, he thought. And an idea came that he quickly pushed away.

His eyes grew heavy, and he listened all the harder to the rain, reluctant to let go of the day's last moments.

A delightful day, he told himself. *The happiest day I have ever spent.* And a tremor like fear went through him as he cast off into the warm, dark lake of sleep.

The next afternoon they stopped at a flower market on the quai. A group of art students had set up easels and were painting the long stalls, with their rows of zinnias and daisies, acacias and pampas grass. A small hunchbacked woman weaved in and out among them, staining sheafs of wild oats a cool scarlet, her dye flowing over the cobblestones like fresh blood. In the distance rose the solemn stone mass of Notre-Dame, a dark mirage in the hazy afternoon.

''Now what,'' Wilde demanded, ''does one take as an offering to a goddess?''

Robbie investigated the banks of green-painted pots. They held plumes and papyrus, roses, funeral chrysanthemums with brown and orange buttons. There were tiny yellow flowers that looked as if they'd just awakened, red flowers as assertive as thistles, white ones with petals bunched together like glockenspiels. ''For Sarah Bernhardt — orchids, I should think,'' said Robbie, stooping to inhale the lilacs.

''You cannot be serious! Sarah walks on carpets of orchids every day.'' The stooped old woman was watching him suspiciously. He asked what she could recommend for a friend more beautiful than any flower.

The woman shrugged, gesturing without interest at a vase of long-stemmed roses.

"Have you no spikenard? Or nenuphar? Some sprigs of bougainvillea?" She stared at him with disgust. "Alas, then," said Wilde, pointing to a canister of tiny marguerites, "I believe I shall settle for these."

"Daisies!" cried Robbie. "For Sarah Bernhardt?"

"I'm certain Sarah hasn't seen one in decades." When the old woman complained that she could not change the large note he presented her with, Wilde airily said she was to keep the change.

Over the shrieking horns of traffic on the avenue Villiers, the slate-blue house, all towers and turrets and machicolated walls, seemed to float like an enchanted castle in a book of fairy tales. The massive black gate clanged shut behind them, and they passed through a curved avenue of topiary foliage to the Renaissance palazzo front door.

The dull ring of the knocker — a serpent caught in a lion's mouth — echoed through empty corridors. At last the door creaked open an inch or two. "Madame is having her nap," said the maid, a whey-faced child with raisin eyes.

"I know that. You are to tell her Oscar Wilde is here."

She drew the door open all the way and waved them in. "Right this way, messieurs. Madame Sarah is expecting you."

They ventured inside, and suddenly there sprang forth before them potted trees and hanging plants and flowers, with their vases and their trellises, and labyrinths of sweet mimosa and rose, and alcoves of lilacs, and an old cloister thick with entanglements of impenetrable English ivy. The scents of the flowers blended in an aroma powerful as incense in a church, but there was another odor hanging heavily over it: the sharp, bitter stench of cat urine.

Wilde led Robbie into the vast salon, and they threaded their way amidst sculptures of Brahmas, Sivas, Buddhas and saints in porphyry and alabaster. The walls were draped with lengths of red silk and Oriental rugs, and round about were set pillars of variegated stones, their capitals encrusted with acanthus leaves and vines. Wonderful and terrible paintings covered the walls, along with fans, swords, pistols, crosses, a samurai's cloak in shimmering satin, a priest's chasuble in crumbling lace.

Robbie turned to Wilde, as if for protection. "You seem right at home!" he whispered.

"I am at home anywhere, Robbie. Except, of course, at home."

Suddenly from a clump of bamboo trees a black figure slithered forth to greet them — a full-sized panther with sullen yellow eyes. The animal loped towards Wilde, without much interest sniffed the cuff of Robbie's coat, then stalked away, its tail slowly swishing from side to side.

"The thing appears to be tame," said Wilde uncertainly. Just then a parrot swooped down from a palm tree and landed on his shoulder. "*L'amour triomphe! L'amour triomphe!*" the parrot squawked, and began to nibble at the pearl in Wilde's cravat.

"Messieurs! Messieurs!" cried the maid, halfway up the winding staircase. "One must not be late for Madame Sarah."

They hung back, scrutinizing the portraits lining the stairwell: Sarah as painted by Bastien-Lepage, by Alfred Stevens, by Toulouse-Lautrec, by Sarah herself; paintings and photographs, drawings and prints of Sarah as concubine, socialite, princess, slave, Sarah in furs and laces or banked in blossoms or veiled in rags, Sarah pouting, preening, wanton, wan, as Cleopatra and Teresa of Ávila, as Ophelia and Lady Macbeth. Waif with flowing russet tresses, smirking woman of the world, melancholy Pierrot, she was in each portrait a new person, and in each she seemed unhappy in a different way.

"Which is the real Sarah Bernhardt?" Robbie said.

"There is none," Wilde replied, and hurried up the steps.

"Madame said you were to wake her from her nap." The maid opened a velvet-covered door and tiptoed away.

Gathered curtains of dark quilted silk shaded the room from daylight. Blossoms in muted pinks and browns and lavenders were painted over the walls, their stems and tendrils looping and knotting into tortured patterns like bars of an exquisite cage, and somewhere far beyond them, unseen fingers brushed softly across an organ's most solemn keys. Thick draperies of a faded pink, drawn back in curves as elaborate as the curtains at the Opéra, lined one end of the room, and in front rested a spacious coffin of polished rosewood, illuminated by a long, flickering church candle. In the coffin, hands folded across her chest, Sarah Bernhardt lay, ghostly pale and still. Nosegays of dried field flowers bordered her unmoving form.

Robbie gasped.

"This is how Sarah always sleeps," Wilde whispered. "They say she even receives her lovers here."

There was a white marble bust of Sarah on a pedestal beside the coffin, so that she seemed to be staring down at herself, one exquisite statue admiring another. They tiptoed over the entwined leaves and lilies of the thick-piled Aubusson carpet for a closer look. She wore a dress of cream brocade with a high ermine collar. A spray of lilacs was affixed to her breast with snow white ribbons.

"Awake!" whispered Wilde,

> 'Awake! For Morning in the Bowl of Night
> Has flung the stone that puts the stars to flight . . .' "

Her eyes flickered, opened wide — great blue flowers bursting suddenly to life. Her mouth, touched with carmine, was a trembling, new-blown rose. Still half asleep, she frowned, puzzled, trying to place herself. She seemed to feel no joy at the world she was waking into; rather, to greet it with fear, horror, revulsion.

"Oscar," she whispered, slowly rising to a seated position. He gave her his hand and reluctantly she pulled herself up, leaping out of the coffin with a graceful little jig step and falling into his arms. She wore white satin slippers covered with blossoms in mother-of-pearl; the heels were of silver. "You must not look at me too closely," she murmured into his shoulder. "I am the worse for wear."

She had a small head over her long, lovely neck, like the heads of saints in medieval manuscripts. Her nose was fine and curved just enough to give her a look of haughtiness, and her eyes, a deep liquid blue, expressed a hungry fascination for all they lit upon. But even more wonderful than her face was the glowing red hair that streamed down her back and that, as Wilde smiled adoringly at her, she began to wrap into an impromptu crown atop her head.

"You are even lovelier than I remembered," he said, and handed her the bouquet.

Moodily she stared at the flowers, then whispered: "Marguerites?"

Then her voice rose from a low groan to something like a shriek. "Marguerites! The flower I love best!"

And then she began to babble about Brittany and her childhood and her mother abandoning her in a cottage banked with lonely little marguerites, drinking in the sun — all in a melodic, heavily rhythmed monologue that sounded like a speech from Racine. How, she demanded, had Oscar known? Was he a sorcerer? No gift, she insisted (drying a tear), could have pleased her more.

"I should like you, Sarah, to meet a dear, dear friend," Wilde said now. Robbie fell to his knees. A peal of laughter rang forth, and Sarah Bernhardt presented a hand for him to kiss.

That hand seemed to glow, Wilde thought, smiling at Robbie's look of awe: in fact, rays seemed to issue from the woman, turning everything around her to shadow, so that it was impossible to estimate what she really looked like, her age, whether she was indeed beautiful. Perhaps his words on the staircase had, after all, been true, and she did not exist at all. Perhaps she was the only one who did exist.

She led them into an adjoining room, this one a jungle of painted foliage and real trees, with stuffed birds tied upon their limbs. The walls were hung with moose heads and Japanese masks and Mexican sombreros, with yataghans and Turkish sabers, with coral-studded spears; and tinted light glowed down from windows diamonded with Gothic glass.

The maid was placing shell-like cups on the table, where one of the chairs was already occupied — by a skeleton, staring at himself in a large round makeup mirror.

"I want you to meet the great love of my life," said Sarah. She bent to kiss the top of the polished cranium. "His name is Lazare — in English you call it Lazarus, no?" Then to Wilde she whispered: "I am so cold!"

"Cold?" He had been wondering how she could bear to live in a house so warm.

She placed a hand on his cheek. "See?"

The cheek seemed to undergo a kind of paralysis. For a moment he thought he would never have feeling in that cheek again.

The room was filled with chairs and settees, each covered in deep-tinted silks or laces or priests' stoles. But there were few places to sit, for most of the seats were occupied by gilded Buddhas. Far from Lazare, Robbie found an empty chair and sat at attention, hands in his lap. Wilde sat next to the skeleton and engaged in a conversation with him, commenting that he bore a startling resemblance to a drama critic on *Punch*.

When she had poured each of them tea, Sarah splashed a few drops into a cup for herself, and carried it across the room where onto a divan covered with animal skins she sank with a low moan. "Oscar, I asked you here because I want you to tell me something truthfully. And you are the only one I know who will."

"What is it, goddess?" said Wilde.

She pouted for a moment. "Is it true I resemble an antelope?"

He smiled, but before he could reply, she had turned to Robbie, eyes blazing — a more fiery version of the panther downstairs. "You must not sit like that!" she said. "In my home, everyone reclines."

Obediently Robbie slid down in his chair. How wonderful he was, Wilde was thinking: his very clumsiness was a kind of grace. What a joy to be presenting him to Sarah Bernhardt, and her to him.

Her ferocious look had melted into a smile. She spoke of the play she was rehearsing and how difficult it was for a European to play an Arab woman. Her fragrance was a smoky orange scent, and it mingled with the tanning odor of the animal skins and the sweetness of lilacs and roses withering in urns all over the room. Why did not Wilde write a play for her, she demanded. They spoke of music, of interior decoration, of ballet. They commiserated over the relative stupidities of French and English audiences, of critics in general, of people in general.

"Your home, Sarah, is superb," said Wilde.

"Trinkets. Toys. What good are they when I have lost the person most important to me in all the world?" She wrapped a chinchilla blanket about her, peering out from it with her great blue eyes.

"Whom have you lost, dear goddess?"

"Myself. I am dead, Oscar. It is only proper that I sleep in my casket, for I long ago succumbed." Now her eyes seemed to have turned into topazes, and she dabbed at them with a handkerchief of white cambric, trimmed with lace.

For one small corner of that handkerchief, Wilde thought, half the men in France would have given their souls.

A slim white borzoi padded across the floor and rested his head on her lap. "Not now, Boris. I am speaking with my guests. Is he not handsome? I adore Russians." She pushed the dog away from her and resumed her despairing mood. "Can you advise me what to do, Oscar? I feel my life has lost all meaning."

"What you need, dear Sarah, is to find a new mask to wear. Then you will discover yourself all over again." He glanced at Robbie thoughtfully. "May I suggest you fall in love? That always provides the most interesting masks."

"I am never *out* of love, Oscar. To be without love would for me mean death. Yet no one — not a single person, ever — has loved me in return."

"We are all in love with you!"

"You adore me. That is not the same."

There was a tap at the door and the maid peered in. "The model from Julien's, madame."

Sarah nodded, and a husky youth in a silk wrapper was shown in. "Your back, monsieur," said Sarah from the divan.

The man let fall the robe and waited, nude, in the center of the room. His skin in the soft light was the color of copper. Robbie slid down farther in the chair, and Wilde frowned at him.

"Very good," said Sarah Bernhardt. "Now the front. Hmmm. Very good, indeed. Be here in the morning at eight."

The model's body rippled as he reached for the robe.

"Everyone praises my sculpting," she said, when he was gone. "Which delights me, because I know how terrible it is. I have no talent for sculpting. Nor for painting. Nor for acting, either. Truly! I do something — I don't know what. And everyone is fascinated. It has nothing to do with me. Nothing at all."

"Goddess!" said Wilde.

For once the word seemed to irritate her. "I am *tired* of being adored as a goddess. I want to be loved as any peasant woman is loved. Ah, would that not be magnificent! Love that touches the soul, and not the vanity. And such a love — it is denied me. In all my romances, there is always the sense of a curtain rising and falling. Of an audience. It is the same with you, Oscar, is it not?"

Wilde was tittering behind his hand. "Sarah, whatever do you mean?" Robbie quickly turned to study the photographs on the wall.

"Would you like one of those?" Sarah said to him kindly. She rifled through an armoire packed with silken and feathery things, and reached out a silver box of photographs. They were of herself as Phèdre, as Fedora, as Delilah, as Adrienne Lecouvreur. She reached for a quill pen.

"Do you see my inkstand? It is the only true portrait of me. I sculptured it myself."

The thing was of bronze and indeed had Sarah's face, but with the wings of a bat and a lion's claws, grasping the well of ink. Wilde looked away, shuddering. It was in the worst possible taste.

Giggling, Sarah dropped a blot of ink on a sheet of translucent lavender paper. "And now we are going to learn all about Oscar and love." She handed Wilde the paper. "Fold this and press the blot until it makes a picture."

Wilde did as he was ordered. The page, opened, revealed a form-less black shape.

"A heart!" she cried. "No — a broken heart."

The configuration on the paper did not, to Wilde's intent scrutiny, look anything like a heart, broken or otherwise. Now Sarah, bored with reading fortunes, snatched up one of the photographs and smiled at Robbie sorrowfully. "What did you say your name was, young man?"

As she signed the photograph, Wilde served himself more tea. "I should like to know, dear Sarah, why you are so *convinced* that I shall be unhappy in love."

"Because I feel it in my bones. They say I am a witch, you know. And it is true! Let me see your palm. Ha! Exactly like mine! The moon's cruel influence. Poor Oscar. You have never wished to live as ordinary mortals live. How then can you love as ordinary mortals love?"

Robbie kept Sarah's photograph clutched to his chest, not even glancing at it, as if the sight might turn him to stone. Outside, with dusk tinting the avenue Villiers a milky lavender, he stepped under a lamppost, and in the flickering light read the inscription. In a bold hand she had written:

> *"Beloved Robbie — closest of friends,*
> *to whom I owe everything.*
> *Your — Sarah."*

) 7 (

"So that was Paris," said Wilde moodily, as their ferry coursed through the murky green waters of the Channel. "Thank you, dear boy, for showing it to me."

Robbie was holding on tight to the railing as the wind fluttered their coats and whipped their hair. "You have been to Paris a thousand times before!"

"Never before."

To keep his hands warm, Robbie was holding them about the sides of his teacup. After a moment he said: "About my wounds, you were right, Oscar. They are healed."

Wilde smiled at him, and gave his shoulder a squeeze.

"*All* my wounds. For there were worse ones than at Cambridge."

Wilde nodded, not wishing to hear any more.

But Robbie, suffering the pleasures of a rebirth, seemed determined to divest himself of all memories of sorrow. He told the story with utter calm. It had happened in Toronto, when he was eleven years old. He had befriended an older boy at school. A good, generous fellow, he had seemed, and very kind to Robbie. "I was so fond of him — so very fond. He seemed so sure of himself, so wise, whilst I —"

"Robbie, there is no need for all this! Please, let us stop investigating our hidden depths. The true mystery of life is in the visible, not the invisible. Forget the past."

But there was no longer any need to forget, Robbie went on, his face aglow — and plunged into the sickening details of that early humiliation, the betrayal, the leering face, the pain, the shame.

"Robbie, please —"

"But the thing itself was not the terrible part, Oscar. The terrible part was after. Because this wondrous idol of mine, this paragon — made everyone in the school believe that it was I! I! Who seduced *him!*" For a moment it seemed he would begin to sob. "I was the laughingstock of the school. And there was no one I could go to. No one I could tell. And for all the rest of my time there — years! Years! I had to walk in shame. For what *he* had done."

Wilde was looking at the water whipped into tiny whitecaps by the gale, thinking and trying not to think. He was remembering

his own undergraduate days, the gibes and mockery, his rooms pil-
laged, his photographs of Botticellis and Titians torn in bits, his
pitiful collection of inexpensive wines poured over the Magdalen
lawns. Had he not earned the right to be insolent with all of them
now? But the brutalities of adolescence had brought to him a
strength that he feared Robbie would never find in them. Wilde
had never wavered, never bent, had accepted persecution as part
of his destiny. How could he ever have toured the wilds of North
America, dressed in suits of velveteen, preaching the gospel of
Aestheticism to midwesterners and miners, if he had not gone
through that earlier baptism of scorn? He remembered an afternoon when stones and insults had rained down on him from the
quadrangle windows of Trinity College, and how he had stared up,
defiant, at the handsome, chortling imbeciles, and for the first time
had felt a strange participation in the passion of Jesus Christ.

"Now all of that is healed," Robbie was saying. "I am going to
become an upright member of the community. Find a wife. Anything you say. I'll even go back to one of those dreadful houses. If
you think it is necessary."

Wilde studied the boy's face. When you love someone, he realized, you no longer see him, you see a portrait of your love for
him, and it grows more beautiful every day.

"Well, Oscar?" Robbie said.

For once, Wilde could think of not one word to say.

) 8 (

The driver heaved the valise up the front steps, and Wilde hesitated in front of the door. The coach window was patched with a
bit of cardboard, so Robbie was barely visible, waving good-bye.

"Mrs. Wilde has guests in the salon," Arthur said, reaching the
valise up onto a broad shoulder.

"Guests? Mrs. Wilde?"

"A number of ladies, sir."

"I see." Wilde turned to watch the coach disappearing past the
Royal Hospital. It seemed he still could hear it, long after it was
gone.

The chatter of the women carried down to him as he trudged up
the stairs. "Oscar, you have missed the most stimulating discus-

sion," said Constance, hurrying across the room. "I am most eager for you to — how was Paris?"

He nodded in answer, and nodded again at various ladies pointing to him, tittering and whispering to each other. "By choosing solitude of spirit," said a pink-faced clergyman, perched on the edge of one of the exquisite white chairs, "we come into possession of the most delightful social organization in the universe. I am referring to the Kingdom of Heaven."

"I know you have been anxious to meet Bishop Hall, Oscar," said Constance. Wilde appraised the wispy little man as she made the introductions. "And you know Lady Sandhurst, of course. At least you know *of* her."

"Ah, Lady Sandhurst," Wilde said. "I am *so* impressed with your good works."

The way Lady Sandhurst's hair was arranged in careful curls about her face, like the stylized locks in a statue of Antinoüs, only served to emphasize her beady eyes and the steely squareness of her chin. "There is nothing particularly *'good'* about my works, Mr. Wilde. It is our *Christian duty* to help the savages in *any way we can*. It is what *Jesus wishes* us to do."

"Ah, yes, Jesus," said Wilde, scrutinizing the others in the room. "Such a delightful personality."

Lady Sandhurst's nose jutted forth like a pointing finger. "Jesus is *more* than a *delightful personality*, Mr. Wilde."

"Of course, Lady Sandhurst, of course . . ." He had turned to join a circle in which the ladies were diligently sewing, among them Miss Pattle and the Misses Orr. "Whatever are you working on, Miss Pattle? An enormous tea cozy, is it?"

"Gowns for the heathen ladies," Miss Pattle snickered, standing to model her work. In prim flowered muslin, the formless dress billowed about her like a collapsed tent. "It completely conceals their — their nakedness," she said, with a triad of rising giggles.

"Gwendolyn!" whispered Miss Spencer, who was so refined as to be barely visible at all.

Wilde sighed inaudibly, determined to make the best of it. "Would the heathen ladies not prefer something a bit more fashionable?" he said. He reached the dress up over Miss Pattle's knotted braids. "May I demonstrate?"

"Oscar!" warned Constance.

Miss Pattle hushed her. "I should be delighted to have Mr. Wilde's expert advice, Constance. Truly."

"Loose, flowing robes of the Grecian kind would be most comfortable — and becoming — in Africa's warm climate." Wilde held the unfinished dress up over his chest. "By letting the fabric drape from beneath the shoulders, the ladies would get an exquisite play of line and light. How smart they would look if only you —"

"Enough of fashion, Oscar!" said Constance quickly, smiling at her friends. "What a pity my husband missed the bishop's lecture on his African adventures. We shall all be having nightmares for weeks."

"Poor Bishop Hall was very nearly caught by cannibals," Miss Pattle volunteered enthusiastically.

"I *was* caught, Miss Pattle," the bishop said, his mustache quivering as if he were trying not to sneeze. "I escaped."

How very far away was Paris, Wilde was thinking. "That is one thing about cannibals I have never understood," he said — "their fondness for human flesh." Without thinking, he offered a cigarette to Bishop Hall, who with a horrified look rejected it. "They tell me the taste is very like chicken," Wilde went on. "Depending, of course, on the age. Myself, I don't think I could bear to dine on it. Not, at least, without a *very* high seasoning . . ."

She confronted him in the kitchen, where he had sneaked down for a quiet cup of tea. "Why?" she demanded. "Why should you embarrass me in front of my friends?"

"I did not wish to be embarrassing, Constance. I was merely being myself."

"Yourself!" she cried, all the color vanishing from her cheeks. "How can I go back up there and face Lady Sandhurst?"

Why should you want to, he asked himself — but kept his peace. "Tell them the truth," he said: "that you have a husband who is irresponsible and foolish, and that he has no business in the society of righteous people like themselves. Though they — and you, dearest — should bear in mind that the way to Hell is close to the gate of Heaven. And, no doubt, vice versa."

"I am glad you cannot read my thoughts," she said.

"You mustn't make faces like that, darling. What if one of them should stay with you, and you had to go through life looking at me, and all the world, with such contempt?''

She was at the door, and her hand was on it, but she did not open it.

''Connie, it is when I am most difficult that I need you most. It is when I —''

She did not hear the rest. The door slammed shudderingly behind her.

) 9 (

Robbie set the tray of tea things on the rickety table and locked the hotel-room door carefully behind him. ''Have you quite recovered?'' he asked.

''If you could have *seen* me!'' Wilde said, drawing the sheet up to his face like a veil. ''One terrified lion in a den of savage Daniels! A wild-eyed virgin of some sixty winters was determined I should roast in the Inferno — and perhaps she was right.''

''However did you get through it!'' said Robbie, beginning once again to undress.

''I prayed, Robbie. I prayed.''

Despite a slightly moldy odor, the room was unexpectedly pleasant, Wilde was thinking, a far cry from the sordid hideaway he would have expected for the price. The walls were papered in a cheery pattern of marigolds, the grass green carpet was thin but clean, the lace curtains on the windows might have graced a country cottage. Piccadilly hummed somewhere outside, and an occasional coach or wagon rumbled by, yet here, amidst the paper roses and doilies and ghastly framed lithographs, all was permeated by a sense of warmth and cheer, even of safety.

''Tell me, Robbie. Was our 'hostess' suspicious?''

''She was a dream. They're theater people, after all. I intimated that you were a famous writer from the Lake District, called in secretly to work upon a play in Drury Lane. She was *most* impressed.'' Nude, he set the tray on the bed between them. ''Irish soda bread. She made it herself. Or so she insists. Butter. Marmalade. Strawberry jam. Honey. I insisted on the honey. I want to taste it — on your lips.''

''Are you saying my lips are not sweet enough, wretch?'' Wilde rose on an elbow to pour the tea. ''The amazing thing about sin,'' he said, "is how quickly one gets accustomed to it. Still, I can't quite *believe* what we have just done. I am astonished. Fortunately I have always enjoyed astonishing myself."

Two bronze statues, of swordsmen poised to duel, graced the mantelpiece, and Robbie's underpants were hooked on one of their swords. He was smiling at himself in the clouded mirror above the statues, seeming to be quite enjoying his unclothed state. "My dearest Oscar, there is nothing 'sinful' in what we've done."

"Hush, now. I won't have you spoiling it for me. The last thing that interests me is a *simple* emotion. Let me enjoy my guilt, Robbie, while it lasts."

"Come look at me in the mirror."

"Thank you, dear boy, but no. Mirrors have not been very kind to me of late."

Robbie blew him a kiss in the glass. "To me, they are magnanimous. They tell me any lie I wish to believe."

Wilde spread far too much butter on a chunk of the crumbling bread. "It sounds as if they are in love with you." A sudden image of Constance came to him, and his brow knotted. He lay down again, staring up at the shadows on the ceiling made by the breeze-stirred curtains. "The saint always feels like a sinner. And I begin to think that the sinner feels like a saint."

Surreptitiously he glanced at Robbie, once again perplexed by the absolute *oddness* of the boy's looks. And once again charmed by them anew. Still, when all these years he had been secretly longing for Adonis, why had the gods seen fit to send him Puck?

He was so fond of the boy, so fond — and yet he felt a yearning for freedom. What if Robbie grew disillusioned with him? Worse, what if he did not?

"Do you realize that we are criminals, Robbie?" The boy made a scoffing sound. "But, my dear, it is quite true. Haven't you heard that the Criminal Law Amendment Act has just made exquisite dalliances such as ours punishable by two years of hard labor!"

Robbie knelt before him on the bed. "I would accept more punishment than that," he said, "for such an afternoon as this."

Wilde gave him a gentle fond slap upon the cheek, and smiled at him with a mixture of affection and a strange, throbbing loneliness. "Still, it seems unfair. I was speaking to the Queen about it only yesterday, as we strolled among her tulip beds. 'Your Maj-

esty,' I said, 'this new law covers the indiscretions of your mas-
culine subjects. But what about women?' She stared at me in horror a long moment and replied, with barely hidden disapproval:
'But, Mr. Wilde. No woman ever would or ever *could* conceive of
such a thing!' '' He chuckled, an eye on the half loaf remaining
in the wicker basket. He had eaten far too much, but it seemed a
pity to drink another cup of tea without *some* accompaniment.
''There are times,'' he said, with a contented sigh, ''when I would
not exchange all the world's champagne for a bit of orange pe-
koe.''

Columns of sunlight streamed in through the curtains, and Robbie ran to the window and turned so the light shimmered over his
slender body. ''Am I like a statue, Oscar? By one of the Greeks?''

Wilde sighed. ''How curious. To have been so desolate over a
thing that now seems light as thistledown, innocent as — as one of
those sunbeams. I had expected to at least feel a *little* wicked. But
I suppose it is only good people who can manage to do that. No,
Robbie, you are too intelligent to be truly beautiful. Still, how
delightful you are! The curves of your dear little body are like a
lily. You are a Ganymede, rather than an Apollo.''

Robbie began clearing off the bed. ''Apollo is boring, don't you
think?''

''Apollo is insufferable.''

''But what exactly do you think of Ganymede?''

Reluctantly Wilde surrendered the butter dish. ''Ganymede?
Why, I suppose I adore him.''

''True love? Or a caprice?'' said Robbie, crawling under the
covers.

Wilde turned his back on him. ''The only difference between
the two, as far as I can see, is that the caprice usually lasts a little
longer. Robbie! Your naked, must-stained little feet are icy cold!''

Robbie threw his arms around him, and Wilde slowly, almost
reluctantly turned. ''Ganymede loves you! It's true. I really, truly
do, Oscar. Fancy that! A scatterbrain like myself, in love.'' Confronted with Wilde's troubled features, Robbie turned away. ''I
know you can't love me back. I would never expect it . . .''

Wilde thought suddenly of Sarah. The sense, in all her romances, of a curtain going up, or going down . . . He pulled the
sheets over their heads so that the unsettled world outside was shut

away. "Dear boy, I am afraid I am too wise to know a great deal about love." Robbie's skin from the shoulders down was cool, though his neck and face were warm. In a low, conspiratorial voice, Wilde said: "I am expected at the Troubridges'. What if I send them a telegram and explain that I am prevented from coming, in consequence of a subsequent engagement — would that please you, sweet scamp?"

Robbie placed his cheek on Wilde's and held it there. "I wish I were able to understand you. You are a man of mystery."

"More a man of moods."

Robbie pouted. "Moods change."

"That is the charm of them."

"Do you —" Robbie's voice dropped down to barely a whisper. "Do you at least love me more than any other boy?"

Wilde slowly drew the covers from their faces. How strange it was, he thought. Robbie had changed such a lot in these past months. He was no longer a gangling boy, but had become a gracious, witty young man. Whereas Wilde himself had not aged at all, had grown younger — or so, at least, he felt. The image of young Somerset in Frances Richards's studio flickered before his eyes: Somerset in the golden light of late afternoon, and in Frances's portrait. "You have taken my innocence, Robbie. You have turned me into a creature despicable in the world's eyes — if the world, so blind with self-righteousness, can be said to have eyes. You have, in short, made of me a wicked man. How then could I help but love you?"

PART TWO

Child of the Golden Dawn

SHE was determined to make herself into the proper kind of wife.

Day after day she left Cyril to Bridie's care while she sat in the reading room of the British Museum, staring at yellowing volumes about buttonholes and leg-of-mutton sleeves, parasols and necklines, inscribing random notes and more notes, wondering what she was ever going to make of them.

And, of course, she did her best at the same time to pay scrupulous attention to the details of her own wardrobe, loathing every moment of it. It took hours. Every detail must be absolutely perfect before she dared go out. Her undergarments must fit taut to the skin, with not a wrinkle showing; the creamy yellow stockings must appear smooth as flesh; the bodice, examined fearfully in the glass, must neither sag loose nor stretch tight at any point. Finally, she would draw over her head a flowing gown of muslin or light wool, with an artful design of blossoms to it, then call for Bridie to help her attach it in back. And then she would discover a wrinkle at the shoulder or the hip and have to begin the long ordeal again, until at length she stood before the mirror with the pink glow of the fire lighting up her cheeks, as flawless as an etching in a lady's magazine. A length of saffron gauze, then, thrown about the shoulders like clinging mist, and a fine necklace of acanthus leaves in gold, and she would smile at herself doubtfully in the glass, and make an effort at looking like Mrs. Oscar Wilde.

He urged on her more and more lavish and eccentric gowns while his own clothing grew more conservative. The energy he had once devoted to his own wardrobe now seemed to be concentrated on hers.

One day as they were hurrying towards the Embankment, looking for a coach, a grimy-faced lad of perhaps nine years old confronted them — one of the urchins from Paradise Walk. "And 'oo de yer think *you* are, 'Amlet and Ophelia?" he spat out at them.

She was mortified. She wanted to run back to the house and lock herself in.

"Quite right, my lad, that's exactly who we are," said Oscar, already, she was sure, turning the shameful incident into an anecdote to amuse his friends with at that evening's party.

He was so very happy lately, and that was the most worrisome thing of all. Clearly, this elevated mood had nothing whatsoever to do with her. With whom, then? He had always been intrigued by great ladies of the theater. Was he secretly wooing one of them?

But when would he find the time? When the two of them were not out dining in great houses, he was playing host to authors, scientists, poets, politicians — the most interesting figures in London society. They all seemed eager for Oscar Wilde's approval. Young barristers like Frank Lockwood would titillate him with gossip about their cases that had never appeared in the press; the foremost writers of the day would read to him after dinner from their works in progress.

And of course, Oscar had begun writing himself, in the evenings and again in the mornings and, indeed, whenever he could find a free moment. He had little time for dallying; nevertheless, Constance was grateful for his friendship with his new young protégé, Robbie Ross, since that occupied hours when he might have been tempted to seek more alluring companionship.

With herself he was friendlier than he had ever been, and yet too many of the witticisms he fired off so airily in public had begun to focus on the subject of matrimony, and she could not but feel they were aimed subtly but surely at her, that he was using his social prominence to sulk over their marriage in a way he dared not do when they were alone.

"The proper basis for marriage is a mutual misunderstanding," he would say. Or, "The only way a woman can improve a man is by boring him so completely that he loses all interest in life." She never knew how to respond when, after one of these sallies, all faces turned to her, laughing.

"You must learn some small talk, darling," he said at a garden party one spring afternoon when for a moment they were alone. "Then when you're bored, no one will ever know. Now do go over and speak to Lady Lonsdale."

And she tried to converse with Lady Lonsdale, miserably aware of how she must be boring that great lady and, worse, of how she was boring herself.

She began attending afternoon services at Saint James the Elder, finding a strange peace reading the inscriptions in the ancient tombs and monuments banked around the church walls. How many men and women of the parish, their children and their children's children, had found true peace at last. And kneeling there she would remember that other church, its stone walls tinted by the sun shining in through colored panes of glass while she, in the billowing fairy-tale dress Oscar had selected for her, followed the little cousins in their antique costumes up the long, narrow, ruby-red carpet towards the pageant on the flower-banked altar, all the while staring at the glowing white bas-relief above the altar: the Last Supper, the apostles twisting in confusion while Jesus held up a finger as if in warning.

She closed her eyes, remembering that sweet, admonishing white face. *Please . . . please . . . if it be thy will . . . let me once again possess my husband's love.*

The next morning she felt ill, and again the morning after.

"Oscar, I believe — I believe I'm in the family way."

"Nonsense, my dear."

"I recognize the symptoms."

"It is a cold, darling. You are going to have a cold."

And then, little by little, the difficulties evaporated, or if they remained, she had stopped caring about them. This new life was like joy growing within her, joy renewed. It was the answer to her prayer. She no longer felt tongue-tied as he spoke of literature with Robbie Ross, no longer cared if her dresses were drab or dazzling; she abandoned her afternoons at the British Museum.

"I cannot make up my mind," Oscar said, reclining on the Turkish divan in his study, his head in her lap. "Sometimes I think I would prefer a girl cold. Other times a boy cold seems far more suitable, if only as a companion to Cyril. What do *you* think, Connie dear?'' And she would close her eyes and imagine the four of them, a happy family by the fire, chatting or reading aloud from the classics.

Indeed, the weeks and months after Vyvyan's arrival were the happiest she had ever known. Oscar, though she was certain he would have preferred a little girl, seemed utterly happy. And for once, she was certain his happiness was because of her.

Then what was wrong?

''Don't you get lonely all the way up there, all by yourself?'' she asked one evening as he started up the stairs, for he was still sleeping in the room on the top floor, beside the nursery. During his first months there, he had still from time to time come to her room on a little ''visit.'' Whilst she had been waiting for Vyvyan, of course, the visits had ceased. That had been the sensible thing to do. But there was no reason now for him not to resume.

''Lonely, darling? I have my genius to keep me company.''

She was too embarrassed to go any farther into the matter. And yet it was always there between them, unmentionable, unmentioned. And because they could not speak about it, it seemed they could no longer speak about anything at all.

) 2 (

One morning she received a barely legible note from his mother announcing that she was coming to call later in the week, and wished to see Constance alone.

Constance crumpled up the note in terror. It was enough of an ordeal visiting Lady Wilde in Oscar's presence; however would she handle her alone? Thank God at least there were the children to talk about; surely she would have an abiding interest in her grandchildren.

Constance spent two days on her hands and knees with Bridie cleaning every inch of the house, for, casual though Lady Wilde might be about her own soot-blanketed establishment, she was ever ready to report on any speck of dust in the home of someone else.

In the little shop on Bond Street, Constance made Madame Forestier as jittery as herself, trying on dress after dress and finding none that pleased. At first she opted for something elaborate and grand, remembering that Lady Wilde was a great admirer of imposing, theatrical gowns. But it took only one glance at herself, all feathers and furbelows in the full-length glass, to disabuse her of that notion. She decided that simplicity, after all, would be to her best advantage for the momentous interview, and selected a plain, form-fitting dress of green and russet squares, with an unobtrusive sash of a deeper green, gathering about the waist and falling softly down behind in a half train. It made her, she felt, seem taller, statelier.

On the appointed Thursday afternoon she was sitting in the white salon with the baby nestled in a pillow on the sofa and Cyril sulking in his sailor suit. The bell began to ring downstairs and she heard Bridie opening the door to Lady Wilde and then Constance went out to the landing to greet the massive form floating up the stairs.

"Mother, how lovely to —"

"I am exhausted, Constance, exhausted." Swathed in red surah silk, Lady Wilde coursed across the room like a sheet of flame. Tilting her great black ostrich-plumed hat, she scraped its layers of black veiling across Constance's cheek. "I can stay only a short time. I must go on to the Countess of Coventry's birthday ball — an ordeal I have been making ready for with days of prayer and fasting."

"The children have been so anxious to see you. Cyril, give Grandmama a lovely kiss."

The child approached the old woman gingerly and they exchanged a long, measuring look. "Well?" said Lady Wilde. Cyril shrank away.

"The child has no conversation, Constance! Has he begun to read?"

"Mother, he is two years old!" Cyril was clutching at the train of her dress. "What do you say to Grandmama, you rascal? Don't you say hello?"

"Hello, Grandmama."

"When he was your age, dear boy, your father was already making amusing remarks of an innocuous nature." Giving Cyril one last disapproving regard, Lady Wilde now turned the full measure of her attention on Constance. "Yesterday I was subjected to a visit from Lady Holden-Smith — do you know her, my dear? Very much involved with orphanages, ancestral home in Sussex, always dressed plainly with a single strand of suspicious-looking pearls. Well! She went on for what seemed hours about the problems of raising children in modern-day London. Can you imagine anyone speaking to *me* that way? Such talk should be reserved for physicians and those who are paid to listen. Cyril, if you have said all you wish to say, you may go and play somewhere — preferably outside. I feel the vapors coming on, Constance. Do you keep any kind of medicine in the house?''

Constance reached for the bell. ''Bridie makes an excellent Irish punch,'' she said, carrying the baby to the door.

''The very thing!'' said Lady Wilde, looking about the room with disapproval. ''Is it necessary for all the blinds to be open?''

''I will close them, Mother.''

Constance handed the baby to Bridie, instructing her to make both punch and tea, and gently pushed Cyril out the door. Then she went about the room, drawing the shades, conscious of the old woman's eyes upon her as the darkness gathered. At the mantelpiece she turned up the light.

''Not gaslight, Constance! Candles, please.''

''Of course, Mother.'' She reached a taper into the fire and lit one of the candelabras.

''Better!'' said Lady Wilde. ''No woman can keep her allure by gaslight.'' She motioned for Constance to join her on the ivory divan. ''Constance,'' she said, ''you are dressed very tightly.''

''Tightly, Mother?'' Constance's hands went up over her bodice.

''You are keeping your perspiration insensibly and injudiciously confined. There must be free play between the dress and the skin, to gently stimulate the pores. Do you have on a corset, my dear?''

Constance blushed faintly. ''I do.''

''Do you not realize that corsets induce headaches, tuberculosis, apoplexy, dropsy, and whooping cough?''

''No, Mother.''

Lady Wilde rose and turned slowly, demonstrating the looseness of her own gown, which was unbelted and virtually without shape. ''Women have been in thrall for six thousand years, my dear child, fettered and manacled by society. Law, custom, and prejudice have combined to keep us all in abject bondage. We must fight that, and we must begin with our clothes. Let us accept our thraldom to literature, Constance. Apart from that, let us go untrammeled!''

Constance sat next to her, hands folded, staring nervously at the floor. ''Yes, Mother.''

Lady Wilde bent closer, and tilted up Constance's chin with a gloved hand. ''My dear child, you are going to have to learn to speak your mind, and speak it with distinction. You are the wife of Oscar Wilde! Tell me to mind my own business — but do it beautifully.''

Constance managed a little smile. ''Oscar wants me to wear clothes of the eighteenth century! He feels women were more beautiful then.''

''Let *him* wear clothes of the eighteenth century, if he wishes. *You* must look not to the past but to the future. A woman must express herself in any way available to her. For years I was the only woman in all Ireland to wear Bloomers!''

'' 'Rational dress,' Mother?'' Constance glanced at herself in the pier mirror and quickly looked away. ''Oscar would be furious with me.''

''Indeed — and he will adore you for it! You must exaggerate, exaggerate, Constance. Otherwise people will think you shallow. I — the Madame Récamier of Ireland — was once quite shy. I overcame it and taught myself to dress brilliantly. Follow my example, Constance! I tell you this because I am so fond of you. Which is, perhaps, a bad thing.''

Constance's voice was strained. ''Why — would that be a bad thing?''

''The Irish, who are full of strange bits of useless wisdom, say that it is a misfortune for a bride and her husband's mother to be fond of one another.''

Constance stared at the ravaged face with its huge, greedy eyes, which were sweet and subtle, wild and sleepy by turns, and she realized that, yes, it was true, frightened as she might be of this great predatory bird of a woman, she felt a deep affection for her as well. She gave the old withered hand a squeeze, and the warmth of that strange dry parcel of bones beneath her fingers moved her strangely. She pressed her face into Lady Wilde's shoulder, tears spurting from her eyes.

''Now, now, my dearest little girl —''

"Mother — I think — I am losing him . . ."

"Nonsense," said Lady Wilde. "You are the only one who can keep him. But you must work at it, Constance. You see, my darling girl, you have remained a child. It is your childishness, no doubt, that Oscar adored in you. But if you wish to keep him, you must leave childish ways behind. They mock 'strong-minded' women nowadays. Be truthful, Constance: have you ever met a woman who was *not* strong-minded? The disgrace is that so many of us choose to hide our true nature beneath a mask of simpering timidity." She gave Constance a long, meaningful look.

"What of *his* childish ways?"

"Rescue him from them. Or learn to enjoy them. Transcend yourself, Constance! And him! Soar above the miasmas of the commonplace. For both your sakes."

"I think — there is another woman."

Lady Wilde gave her a shake, with a strength surprising in one so old. "And if there were? What difference? Oscar's father was the greatest rake of his age. I could not turn a corner in the whole of Dublin without being wished the top of the morning by one of Sir William's bastards. Did I care? I was proud of it: proud that I was able to surmount it. When he was on his deathbed, a brazen hussy veiled in black came to my door and begged to see him. Can you imagine? What did I do? I led her up the stairs and to his room. Because, dear Constance, no matter how many women might take his eye, only one could hold it. Why? Because I made myself into a source of endless fascination."

Constance frowned. "I am not like you."

"You are! That is why I am so fond of you."

"There is nothing — fascinating about me."

"Forget the drab rules of this convention-shrouded age. Make your own rules. And live by them. Then like will call to like, and you will have him. I know Oscar, my dear. And I know you. If you had wanted some paltry, ordinary romance, you would never have cast an eye in my son's direction. Oscar loves you, Constance. Passionately, I am sure, for like me, he is incapable of anything but the grand emotions. But you must make yourself worthy of such passion."

Bridie entered timidly, carrying a tray. Constance looked up at her miserably. "Your — medicine, Mother." She placed the cup and saucer on a flimsy gilt-dusted table at one end of the divan and took her tea to one of the white chairs facing.

Lady Wilde untied her veils and lifted them a few inches, freeing her red-stained mouth. She stirred the steaming liquid and tried a sip in the spoon. Frowning, she tasted another. "Constance, this is lemonade!"

"It relieves my catarrh, Mother. I take it under doctor's orders."

"Doctor's orders are well and good," said Lady Wilde, moodily sipping at the punch, "provided one never observes them."

The doors flew open and her son came bounding into the room. "Mother! No one told me you were coming today. I would have —"

"Because, my boy, no one wanted you to know."

"I have been at an exhibition at Earl's Court, a most interesting —"

"No tiresome stories, Oscar," said Lady Wilde.

"Oscar has been so busy of late," said Constance quickly. "He is forever scribbling at one thing or another. Really beautiful pieces, some of them."

"It isn't off the grass he licked it," said Lady Wilde. "Another quaint Irish turn of phrase."

"Oscar, read that lovely one about masks."

"Oh, no! Oh, no!" cried Lady Wilde. "I can't be read to, my face would not endure it. It is a little-known fact that the features grow dull and heavy listening to anything but brilliant talk. Forgive me if I sound out of sorts, Oscar, but I arrived here half dead with the vapors, and your wife has served me sugar water!"

Wilde gave Constance a reproving smile and stepped over to the cream-white *japonaiserie* book cabinet, where from a lower shelf he drew out a thick volume that, as it turned out, concealed a bottle of cognac.

"This will surely help."

"Perhaps the smallest drop in my cup," his mother said, untying the veiling and pulling it up farther on her face. And then, with a chilling look at Constance: "It may serve to take away the bitter citrus taste."

"I sometimes get the strange feeling," Constance said when Lady Wilde had left, "that your mother is — imitating you."

"My mother is — what?"

"Again and again, she seems to be trying to talk the way *you* talk, to act the way *you* act."

"My darling Connie." He laughed, tried to stop, laughed all the harder. "You are a great wit, in spite of yourself. You must say such things more often. You will put me to shame!" And he put his arms around her — but almost as quickly pulled them back.

) 3 (

The following day, Constance put away her corsets and crinolines. Later in the week she became a member of the Rational Dress Society.

She had not the courage, of course, to don the divided skirts the society championed: in her eyes they looked far too much like gentlemen's trousers! She compromised by instead wearing a divided petticoat, under skirts of severe pattern and uncompromising fabric — skirts that reached well above the ankle. The astonished looks she inspired in the streets frightened and exhilarated her.

She had expected Oscar to disapprove, but though he made jokes about her new wardrobe, she could see he was impressed — even, she began to suspect, delighted.

The ladies of the Mission Society, though, were far from enthusiastic. Constance began to feel she was wasting precious time at the group's weekly meetings. She began appearing only every other week, and then only once a month.

"Constance," said Gwendolyn Orr one afternoon, as they were getting ready to leave Lady Sandhurst's. "Can I speak to you? In private?"

It was completely unlike Gwendolyn to make such a proposal, and Constance accepted with surprise. They stopped in a tea shop in Bloomsbury and Gwendolyn led her to a table in the back corner, far from anyone who might hear them.

"I have always felt in you a kindred soul, Constance," Gwendolyn said. Studying her pale, dim features, Constance was far from flattered. "I believe you are a very *spiritual* person, Connie. Unusually so." Constance smiled. "And therefore I want to tell you a great, great secret. I think you will understand." She leaned closer, lowering her whispery voice. "Constance. I am a hermetic."

Constance softened her features in sympathy. "Gwendolyn. I'm — *so* sorry."

Gwendolyn blinked her eyes like a startled bird. "Sorry? Why would you be sorry?"

"But — what is a hermetic?"

Gwendolyn looked about her again and grinned slyly. "Connie . . . do you never feel there is far more to this life than what we are privileged to see . . .?"

Fifteen minutes later, Gwendolyn was leading Constance through the columned halls of the British Museum, past the collections of arrowheads, vases, ancient coins. She stopped before an exhibition case of crystal formations. "Here we are, dear Constance. Close your eyes for just a moment. It is necessary to collect oneself."

At the end of the cabinet were several balls of crystal ranging in size from one not much larger than a plum to a great transparent orb greedily drinking in the afternoon light. "Curiously, it is the smallest one that has the most concentrated power." She glanced about to be sure the guards were not watching. "Now Constance, I want you to pass your hand over the top of the cabinet, right over that small crystal, and tell me if you do not feel its vibration throbbing up at you."

Constance hesitated a moment. At last she closed her eyes and reached her hand out over the case.

"Well?"

"I — I believe I *did* feel something. Very — subtle."

"Exactly! The world of spirit is always so terribly, terribly subtle. Isn't it exciting? Would you like to come to a meeting of our group?"

Constance ventured to pat Gwendolyn gently on the shoulder, thanked her ever so kindly for asking, but suggested that with all the trouble of the children, and tending to Oscar, there simply wasn't time.

) 4 (

She arrived home to find that Robbie Ross had been invited to dinner. When it was over they sat in the salon while the two of them imbibed coffee with brandy and she placed bunches of grapes in Madeira, so that they might soak up the sweetness of the wine.

"Is it true, Robbie," she asked, "that Oscar is very fond of Ouida's writing?"

Robbie looked puzzled. "Why — I believe so."

She gave Oscar a reproachful smile, handing him a small cluster of the grapes in a glass saucer. "I always have to ask his friends about his opinions. It's the only way I ever hear them. I myself am reading Mrs. Browning's volume, *Aurora Leigh*."

"Mrs. Browning was a very dear and very good woman, Constance," Oscar suggested, "but it is difficult to take a poet seriously who rhymes *moon* with *table*."

"Where did she do that!" cried Constance, nearly dropping the bowl of wine.

But Oscar did not reply, instead beginning a preposterous tale for Robbie's amusement, obviously making it up as he went along. Sulking, Constance picked up her embroidery and pretended not to be listening.

". . . So the courtesan climbed the snake-infested rocks until she reached the cave of the holy man. And when he saw her approaching he made the sign of the cross, swore anathema, and — instantly became hopelessly enamored of her. Step by seductive step she drew closer, her eyes afire with lust, her —"

"Heavens!" cried Constance, dropping her embroidery hoop. They both turned to her, alarmed.

"Darling, what is the matter?"

"I entirely forgot," she said, blushing. "Cyril's shoes are still at the cobbler's." She had spent the whole afternoon with Gwendolyn Orr and completely forgotten the shoes.

They were staring at her. She looked from Oscar to Robbie, from Robbie to Oscar, confused. "But tomorrow is *Sunday*," she said. "No way to get them then." Her voice began to falter, and this made her angry. "The shoes were ready ages ago!" But the more she tried to extricate herself from her awkward situation, the more tenaciously it seemed to hold her.

"Do finish the story, Oscar," Robbie said, with a tactful chuckle. "The courtesan approaches the holy man, and —?"

"I have forgotten the rest," Oscar said, with a deep sigh. "Or perhaps it has forgotten me."

She started out of the room. At the door she turned back, trembling. "I don't understand you, Oscar!"

He gave her a smile subtle as the Gioconda's. "I am glad to hear it, darling. I live in constant terror of being understood . . ."

) 5 (

"Arthur, if Mr. Wilde should return and ask for me, will you tell him I have gone to Marlborough House?"

The boy held the door open for her. "Marlborough House, ma'am?"

"I am going to study the silks in the Museum of Manufacture. He will understand."

"Thank you, ma'am."

She told the driver to take her to Trafalgar Square. As the cab started off, she found herself staring out into the face of a tattered old woman in black, raddled with age and woe, selling matches. She felt herself going cold. Numbly, as the coach moved up the King's Road, she glanced out at the crowds rushing about the congested streets, and thought of an anthill with its top kicked away. All those unhappy soul-houses sending out their dark vibrations. Indeed, all London seemed a sacrifice to some greedy devouring god, a god of infinite cruelty. It was the cruelty that Jesus, Buddha, all the religious leaders had come to heal. Why did it go on festering? When the coach passed an alleyway, she saw a glassy-eyed mongrel sniffing at a bag of garbage, its stomach caved in with hunger.

Gwendolyn Orr was waiting for her on the steps of Saint Martin-in-the-Fields, and together they took another coach, to Hampstead.

Gwendolyn referred to it as the Isis-Urania Temple, but it was in fact a fine old Georgian house, let to the order by an enthusiastic member. Constance followed Gwendolyn into a large room stuffed with mahogany furniture and filled with people — most either very old or very young. She was introduced to so many of them that their names and faces blurred.

A few stood out. A young man named Heron-Allen, refined, young, handsome, the type of person used as a model in clothing advertisements. An attractive Hindu with piercing blue eyes — or was he an Englishman who had darkened his skin? A woman with the magnificent troubled face of a Madonna, but dressed in a shapeless, shabby gown.

"Don't tell her she's attractive, Constance. She can't bear to hear it!" Gwendolyn was full of stories about everyone in the room. A good many of the members were fond of the mystical properties of hashish, she whispered, which explained the strange sparkle in their eyes. A white-haired clergyman, dozing in an armchair, was known to practice alchemy in the basement of his vicarage. A woman with small owl eyes cast spells on vivisectionists: two prominent Harley Street physicians were recent victims. "She is now after Dr. Pasteur in Paris. He is still living, I understand, but extremely ill."

An attractive, well-dressed man was going from group to group, speaking in a low, soothing voice with a gentle Scottish burr. "That's MacGregor," said Gwendolyn. "He's the leader. What age would you give him, Constance?"

"I would say — thirty-eight. Forty, perhaps."

Gwendolyn again lowered her voice. "He has been alive for over one hundred years! They say he has found the elixir of youth!"

Constance made a little sound that could be interpreted as admiration or as laughter — whichever might be the more appropriate response.

"I have also heard that he is James the Fourth of Scotland — who never died. And others insist he is Cagliostro, come back from the — but here is the Comtesse de Bremont!" A plain young woman draped in furs approached them.

"*Enchantée*," said Constance.

"Oh, I'm not French!" the Comtesse replied in a flat American accent. "I could never twist my poor tongue around those awful French words! My husband and I just make faces at each other, we gave up talking years ago!"

Constance tried without success to say something witty. She heard the gentle voice with the Scottish burr immediately behind her. "You must be Mrs. Wilde."

She turned and met the man's beautiful, cold blue eyes; for a moment she had the absurd feeling that she was going to faint. He was smiling at her cordially, but somehow she knew it was all pretense, facade — and was certain that he knew she knew. He seemed to be unblamingly aware of her own pretenses, to see right through to her soul, and kept studying her in the most piercing, frightening, and yet strangely soothing way.

"A true seeker," he said kindly, smiling a weary smile. "Despite our numbers, we have very few."

"There are — so many women!" she said.

"I believe women are *better* at these arts," he said. "Perhaps that is why they have been prevented all these years from pursuing them! We are most honored to have you here, Mrs. Wilde. It would give us great pleasure if we could be of help to you."

"I — I don't know. I am rather — confused."

"That is the best way to be when undertaking — the Quest." From a pocket he produced a piece of cardboard. On it a symbol was crudely painted: a square in a circle, surrounded by flames and smoke. "Would you care to take part in a little experiment, Mrs. Wilde?"

"I don't think I —"

"Painless, I guarantee. I ask you merely to let me place this card on your forehead. I shall hold it there for a few moments. And then tell me where — if anywhere — it takes you."

She looked at Gwendolyn with embarrassment. Gwendolyn nodded encouragingly. "All right, Mr. MacGregor," Constance said.

"MacGregor is the name. Just MacGregor."

She closed her eyes and as the cardboard touched her forehead, her fists clenched involuntarily. She was conscious of the warmth of his hand pressing the card tight against her. She saw nothing, only the swirling dots and colors of her own darkness. But just as she was about to tell him that the experiment was a failure, a picture came into her mind, or something like a picture, senseless and yet capable of being described in minute detail, like the images in a vividly remembered dream. She saw a clear landscape. A meadow. A child standing in the meadow. "Yes," she said. "There is something there."

"Don't open your eyes, Mrs. Wilde," said MacGregor, sounding excited. "Describe what you see."

"It is a little girl." In fact, it was herself, she thought, herself as a child. Then, "No," she said. "It is a little boy. With golden blond hair. A sweet, trusting face. His expression is — so sweet. Innocent, clear blue eyes. He is standing in a field of grass."

"Is it warm or cold? Day or night?"

"It is warm. Morning. I know because the grass is sparkling with dew."

"Thank you, Mrs. Wilde." He removed the card, and she opened her eyes, again meeting his. They were no longer cold, but seemed at the same time very interested and very concerned.

She laughed lightly. "Now that I have seen it — what have I seen?"

He put his strong hands on her shoulders — a familiarity that surprised but did not disconcert her. "You have met your messenger spirit. Your 'Master,' if you prefer. He is your dearest friend, Mrs. Wilde. He can very easily become your darkest enemy."

"But Mr. MacGregor —"

"MacGregor."

"He could never be evil. He is — the child of the morning!"

MacGregor laughed softly. "Why not — the child of the Golden Dawn? For that is the name of our order."

"But — now that I have found this — this 'Master.' What am I to do with him?"

"Ask him for help. But never invoke him, Mrs. Wilde. All spirits are helpful at first. But even the very best ones turn on us in the end."

Constance felt the need to sit down. Various people came over and spoke to her. She did not know what to make of them. Some few seemed sincere. Most were eccentric in ways she found unsympathetic. Across from her an elderly woman was creating a fuss because, she said, someone had sat upon her astral body, which she claimed was reclining on a leather chair. A small wild-eyed man leaped up and cried: "Someone is walking past this house who murdered his wife!" No one paid attention.

At one moment Constance felt only disgust for the room and the people in it; a moment later she wanted to be part of whatever it was they were doing. She did not know which of the two emotions was the true one. "How," she whispered to Gwendolyn, "does one become a member? I mean, if one decides one wishes to?"

"Only MacGregor can make that decision. And he is very, very difficult."

Biting her lip, Constance looked about the room for MacGregor. Her eyes lit on a rather sinister-looking man with a large black mustache, who was leaning against the wall watching, with a mocking look, the movements of the woman with the lovely Madonna face. Suddenly this woman drew her hair back from her face and walked directly up to him.

"Shall we get it over with?" she said. And she reached up and gave him a slow kiss. Then she stared at him contemptuously. "Now can we concentrate on the work at hand?"

Astonished as the man might be, Constance was more astonished still. And, she feared, suddenly rather ill. "I must — must get back to Chelsea," she whispered to Gwendolyn.

"That is Miss Farr, Constance," said Gwendolyn apologetically. "She is an actress."

"Indeed," said Constance.

As she was putting on her wraps, Miss Farr came up to her in the foyer. "Today was your first time," she said. Constance nodded coldly. "And do you believe it all?"

"I don't know what I believe," Constance answered evenly.

"To me it all seems false. Everything does. Only when I am onstage does anything seem sincere. Don't be hard on me, Mrs. Wilde. I am trying to become real."

Constance noticed that the mustachioed man was searching for his greatcoat. Miss Farr went up to him with that same tired, disgusted look. "Are you not waiting for me?" she said.

Constance shuddered and, without a farewell to anyone, hurried out into the street.

She was trying to hail a coach when she heard footsteps behind her. "Mrs. Wilde — please."

At first she did not recognize him. The handsome young man who looked like a clothing advertisement. In his dark coat he seemed more serious yet every bit as handsome.

Suddenly a coach drew up. She eyed it with annoyance. Now she would have to take it. They looked at each other questioningly. She knew she should step in and wish him a good evening, but she very much wished to speak to him further. She remembered Lady Wilde's injunction to rise above convention. "Would you like me to see you home, Mr. Heron-Allen?" she said with a smile.

) 6 (

In her bed alone that night, she tried to recapture the picture of the golden-haired boy in the meadow.

If it be possible, she said to herself — or to him — *let me, please, even for a little while, know once again the sweetness of my husband's love* . . .

) 7 (

Mr. Heron-Allen became a regular caller at Tite Street — always, as it happened, when Oscar was out of the house. But then, Oscar was out of the house so much of the time.

One evening when he happened to be at home, Constance was mounting the stairs when she paused outside the nursery. Oscar was telling the boys a bedtime story. It was about a statue of a young prince. The prince gives all of himself — his golden plating, the jewels from his eyes — to the poor. Oscar was inventing the story as he went along, as only he could.

She pushed open the door. Vyvyan was asleep in Oscar's arms and Cyril, in bed, was staring up at his father with his lips slightly parted. What a look of admiration and wonder in those lovely child eyes!

Oscar's voice grew softer: " 'Bring me the most precious thing in all the city,' said God to one of His Angels. And the Angel brought Him the prince's leaden heart.

" 'You have chosen rightly,' God told the Angel, 'for in my City of Gold the happy prince shall ever live with me, and praise me . . .' "

She went up behind him. "That's lovely, Oscar," she said, slipping Vyvyan out of his arms.

"Did the happy prince go to Heaven, Papa?" said Cyril, heavy with sleep, but stubbornly holding on to the day — so like his father!

"He did indeed. And now *you* must close your eyes like a good little man and go off to the lovely silvery land of dreams." He gave the child a kiss on the forehead. Vyvyan was now in his crib and Constance embraced Cyril, then lowered the wick in the nursery lamp.

As they started down the steps, she said: "What a godsend Mr. Heron-Allen is for me." When Oscar said nothing in reply, she added: "I feel music has come into my life again. He is an accomplished violinist, you know."

"Wonderful, darling," he said, heading on down to the basement.

She followed. "And such a very *bright* young man!"

"Mmmm. Indeed." In the kitchen he got down the teapot and the caddy.

"Full of talents."

"Mmm."

"I believe I'll have a cup, too — despite the hour." She watched as he poured from the kettle Bridie kept always asimmer on the coal stove; then she got down two of the heavy everyday cups and saucers. "Mr. Heron-Allen is a cheiromantist," she said.

"Mr. Heron-Allen is a what?"

She gave him a cool smile. "He is an expert at reading the lines of the hand. From just the length of the little finger he can tell everything about one there is to know."

Oscar carried the teapot to the table. "If I ever meet him," he said, pouring tea into a cup, "I shall take care to be gloved." The tea was too weak, and he poured it back into the pot.

"You *should* meet him, Oscar. He is a most interesting young man."

Oscar was dipping about in the pantry. He found a morsel of gingerbread and brought it and the butter to the table.

"Shall I invite him to dinner one evening?"

"Of course," he said, giving the tea in the pot a stir to quicken the brewing.

She put her arms around him and gave him a quick hug. "Done, then, darling."

) 8 (

Mr. Heron-Allen was delighted to receive her invitation. She had asked Bridie to prepare a meal especially suited to his tastes. But when dinner was put on the table, no Oscar had shown up.

"Delicious, Mrs. Wilde."

"Bridie is an excellent cook."

"I must ask how she was able to keep the turnips so crunchy in the soup."

"I believe they are carrots, Mr. Heron-Allen. I am sure she will be more than delighted to share her recipe with — ah, I believe that's Oscar now." She felt her body go tense. "How annoyed

he'll be when he realizes he's missed half the meal with such stimulating company."

When Oscar appeared some minutes later, she was somewhat irritated, though not surprised, to see Robbie Ross peeping in behind him. "Robbie, how delightful," she said. "But you are both
late for dinner. And Mr. Heron-Allen has had to settle for boring
women's talk."

"Every word has been utterly fascinating, Mr. Wilde," said
Heron-Allen. "As I hardly need to assure you."

"Heron-Allen?" said Oscar, shaking hands as she made the introductions. "I have heard that name before."

"You remember, Oscar. I told you about Mr. Heron-Allen —
and his many talents."

"Of course!" he said. "What a pleasure, Mr. Heron-Allen. This
is the first time I have met a chiropodist."

"A cheiromantist!" she snapped, then turned smiling to Heron-
Allen. Bridie brought out the main course. She went about heaping rice on each plate as Constance nervously watched.

"Bridie," said Oscar. "You have forgotten the roast."

"No roast tonight," Constance sang. Bridie bowed and stumbled out of the room.

"What *are* we having?" said Oscar with a frown.

"Mr. Heron-Allen is a vegetarian, and I am thinking of becoming one, too. So for a change —"

After a moment, Oscar heaped vegetables on his plate. "Your
diet certainly seems to agree with you, Mr. Heron-Allen," he said.
"You are the picture of health." He chewed on the sprouts, his
nostrils flaring.

"Mr. Heron-Allen was just praising Bridie's cooking," said
Constance pointedly.

"For her iniquities," Oscar replied, "I fully expect Bridie to
one of these days be turned into a pillar of the salt she has never
learned to use properly."

Robbie Ross was watching Heron-Allen with what seemed to
Constance a certain hostility. If only Oscar would do the same!

"Tell us all about your work," Oscar was saying to Heron-
Allen. "I often get severe pains in my feet. Next time I shall certainly ask for your advice."

Heron-Allen laughed. "I can do nothing for your feet, Mr. Wilde.

I merely investigate the lines of the palm — and not very brilliantly, at that.''

Oscar beamed at him. ''I am sure you are too modest.''

''I shall send you a little book I wrote on the subject, *A Manual of Cheirosophy,* which might possibly amuse you,'' said Heron-Allen, with a modest, utterly winning smile.

''Palm-reading!'' said Robbie with distaste.

''My clumsy attempts could only increase your skepticism, Mr. Ross! But there is a true genius practicing the art here in London — on Mortimer Street. Her name is Mrs. Robinson, and if you were to try her, she would leave you with no doubts on the subject.'' He smiled at Oscar again, in his boyish, self-deprecating way.

Robbie was slashing at his sprouts as if determined to do them in.

''Oscar!'' cried Constance. ''Let's go, both of us. Let's do.''

Oscar smiled at her and then at Heron-Allen. ''If so charming an authority as Mr. Heron-Allen recommends her — how could anyone resist?''

) 9 (

Far from the toothless crone the Wildes had anticipated, lurking in some shadowy cave, reading visions in a caldron's rising steam, Mrs. Robinson was a ruddy-faced Yorkshire woman living in a tidy apartment over a silversmith's shop. She seemed better made for milking cows than wrestling with daimons.

''You have a very photogenic dog,'' said Wilde; for over the mantelpiece was a series of photographs of a toy bulldog, mostly out of focus, next to a photograph, also out of focus, of a dour man in a top hat.

''Oh, those aren't Queenie! They're Queenie's mother and grandmother and great-grandmother, rest in peace.''

''And the gentleman?'' said Constance.

''That's *Mr.* Robinson, also rest in peace. Now *do* say hello to Mr. and Mrs. Wilde, Queenie.'' But the dog would not budge from her folded quilt under the window, where she sat meditating.

Mrs. Robinson brought in a tray with cups of tea for the two of them and of hot water for herself, to which she added a splash of milk and a saccharin tablet.

Wilde reached for Constance's hand and thrust it forth. "You *will* be indiscreet, I trust!"

But Constance pulled her hand away. "*Your* palm, Oscar," she said. "I don't want to hear about my own."

Eager as she had been for a reading, something — her messenger spirit, perhaps — now warned her against it.

"Darling, how absurd!"

Mrs. Robinson reached a magnifying glass out of her apron pocket, and drawing Oscar's hand into the harsh light seeping through the curtains, scrutinized the lineaments of the palm, breathing heavily through her mouth.

"Turmoil from the first until the last!" she cried. "A most unusual hand." She reviewed the major incidents of his past life in a few minutes.

"Amazing!" said Constance.

"Has my wife told you all this?" said Wilde, grinning.

Mrs. Robinson gave a hostile look to such a suggestion. "I see a pen and a great deal of writing going on. A star under the mountain of the moon — success. And very soon."

Constance squeezed his arm, knowing how he had been searching for a publisher in recent weeks.

"But you will be working in an office before very long."

Oscar laughed aloud. "Adding up columns of figures?" He gave Constance a surreptitious wink.

"And then the true success. The great success. The world will hear of you, Mr. Wilde."

"Oscar, are you listening? How very exciting!"

"The world has already heard of me, Mrs. Robinson. Perhaps too much of me. But what of our boys? Do you see glad tidings for Cyril and Vyvyan?"

She frowned. "That — is not clear." After a moment, she said: "Your marriage is here, of course. Much happiness." She seemed confused. "Such a delightful wife — you are lucky." She smiled at Constance, and seemed to be debating with herself as to whether to say more. "There are many — friendships."

"Friendships?" said Constance.

"One will be — quite fatal, I fear."

Wilde laughed. "A fatal friendship! That is the one I want to hear about."

"With danger — both on the land and over the sea."

Constance felt her blood had turned to ice. "You mean — another woman?" she demanded, embarrassed at her audacity.

Mrs. Robinson shook her head. "I see no other woman."

"The danger should be easy enough to avoid," Wilde said, laughing. "I shall live in a balloon, and every evening draw up my dinner in a basket!"

Queenie sat up on her blanket and rustled about, barking in a curious way that was rather like a rooster crowing. Then with a long sigh she eased herself back into a prone position.

"She wants her tea," said Mrs. Robinson. "All my dogs loved tea. Queenie's grandmother used to actually *ask* for it. She could speak, you see. She would wag her little tail from side to side and say, 'Woo-woo-*woo*. Woo-woo-*woo*.' That of course meant she wanted a bowl of tea. Would *you* like some more tea, Mr. Wilde?"

He was staring at his palm, spreading the fingers out and closing them again to bring the lines into emphasis.

"A *most* interesting hand, Mr. Wilde. I see a life of brilliance. Quite amazing brilliance. Up to a certain point. And then a wall."

With a smile Wilde closed his hand into a fist. "And what is behind the wall?"

She closed her hand over his and gave him a look of deep compassion. "Nothing, Mr. Wilde. There is nothing behind the wall."

He stared at her for a moment and laughed nervously. "Connie. Your hand."

"No." She was quite determined. "I don't want to know. It's better not to know."

Mrs. Robinson nodded to her gravely. "Perhaps you are the wise one, Mrs. Wilde."

) 10 (

Oscar's talk began to be full of references to life lines and rascettes and the Mound of Venus, and with obvious relish he inserted the vocabulary of palmistry into the fables he invented over coffee and liqueurs when Robbie came to Tite Street for dinner. One tale in particular seemed to fascinate Robbie, of a youth whom a palmist informs that he will commit a murder. Trying to get the deed over with in the least dreadful way possible, the young man makes attempts on the lives of elderly relatives — with no success.

Finally he decides that the one he must murder is the fortune-
teller. He does so — and lives happily ever after.

At Robbie's urging, Wilde wrote the story down, naming it "Lord
Arthur Savile's Crime." To his surprise it was accepted by the
Court and Society Review.

) 11 (

One night Oscar got home late and, rather stunned, announced
that he had been offered the editorship of the *Lady's World*. He
had greeted the offer with bravado, he explained to Constance in
an awed voice, telling them that he would accept only if the name
of the publication were changed. A true lady did not refer to herself as a lady, but as a woman — didn't Constance agree?

"Oscar, what difference does it —"

"They are renaming it the *Woman's World* and I start as editor
next week."

She hesitated a moment. "Working in — an office?"

He did not reply, merely held her close to him in silence.

) 12 (

Happiness at last, she thought. A regular job of this kind would
show him the real, normal world in a way he had never been exposed to it, would drive out of his head some of his excessive ideas
about Art and Beauty. She would never wish him to lose those
interests entirely, of course, but they had a proper time and place.
His family had a proper time and place, as well.

He became completely absorbed in his work, and was soon the
talk of London, a towering success, everything he had ever wanted
to be. Everything — almost everything — she had ever wanted
him to be.

But something was wrong. He did not come scratching at her
door in the night as she had hoped he would. And he began sleeping late in the mornings, going into long, dark moods when he
would not speak to anyone for days. He was eating and drinking
far more than was good for him, and beginning to put on weight.
He went to Bad Homburg for a health cure and came back looking
better than he had in years; but in two weeks he was back to his
bad habits.

Robbie Ross, too, had grown depressed and incommunicative. At the rare dinners when they were together now, they made a somber trio.

It was no longer mere melancholy that she felt. Now she had a dreadful, crippling sense of being totally abandoned — and not even for a person anymore, but for success itself.

She must do something about it, she determined. There had to be some way she could bring him back.

) 13 (

The door was opened by MacGregor himself.

"You won't remember me, I'm sure. I —"

"I have been expecting you, Mrs. Wilde. Come in out of the cold . . ."

He was dressed in kilts, and had a dagger thrust into one of his tan stockings. What beautiful young limbs, she thought, as he led her into his study. It was a large, warm, stuffy room. The walls were of dark taffeta, with a sconce of crystal in every panel. The oil lamps were covered with rose-tinted globes. Before the fire a black bear rug with glaring glass eyes seemed ready to spring up at her.

"I have decided I would like — to be initiated," she said, as she sank into a dusky pink couch of silk plush, embroidered with trailing pink rosebuds. "That is, if I may." Looking into his clean, unlined face she suddenly remembered the story that he was an old, old man. The idea was too preposterous to even think about.

Or was it?

"What has changed your mind, Mrs. Wilde?"

She was certain he could read her thoughts, and had decided not to fabricate. But before she could say anything, he replied for her: "It is because of your husband."

"I want — I want to be able to love him. As before."

A smile brought a surprising softness to his ruddy features. "That is simple enough, Mrs. Wilde. If you want to love him — love him!"

"He won't let me," she said, turning away.

"He cannot stop you! No, I'm afraid what you really want, my dear friend, is for *him* to love *you* — which is something else again. You want to control him. It is the temptation every Adept struggles with: coveting power over what one loves."

She felt as if he had slapped her.

"An initiate must sacrifice all he has and is before he can accomplish the Great Work," MacGregor said. "I think if you join us, Mrs. Wilde, you will learn how contemptible your desire truly is."

"What must one do to be initiated?" she asked, staring at the white teeth of the bear rug, glittering in the firelight.

"Keep the secrets of our order — from everyone. As a sacred trust."

She nodded.

"Swear — total chastity."

She felt she should look shocked, but for some reason she was not. "Total —?"

"We save our energies for — higher things."

Averting her eyes, she whispered: "I don't believe — all your initiates are chaste."

"Miss Farr is a special case." He *could* read her mind! "For some, Mrs. Wilde, lovemaking is a form of self-mortification."

She stared up at him with her lips dry, frightened, thrilled. He placed a hand on her forehead. She remembered the first time he had done so, and the warmth she had felt. Now it was coolness that spread from his hand into her aching brain. "You decided we were charlatans," he said.

Her eyes were closed. "Yes."

"Of all the many hindrances to magical action, the greatest and most fatal, Mrs. Wilde, is unbelief. It checks the very action of the Will! No child could ever learn to walk if he believed it was impossible." She nodded, her eyes still shut. "It is true, Mrs. Wilde: many of us are charlatans. God himself sometimes uses fraud — to make one reach truth."

Her head had begun to pound. She wanted to tell him everything — even things she had hardly told herself. Or was he *forcing* her to tell him? "I married Oscar because — my life was so empty," she said dully. "It is much emptier now."

Before she realized what had happened, MacGregor had slipped the dagger from his stocking and sent it flying across the room — to land with a sickening thud in the very center of a painted triangle tacked upon the wall.

"I am a violent man, Mrs. Wilde. I love nothing more than fighting. My greatest desire would be to go to Africa, join the French

Zouaves, and spend the rest of my life slaughtering all human-kind!'' He drew the dagger from the wall and sent it clattering onto his paper-cluttered desk. ''Upon such unworthy desires I have had to build a new and very different life.''

She allowed herself to smile. How was it she felt so at ease with him? She no longer felt he could read her thoughts, any more than she his — and yet there was some uncanny sympathy between them. She felt she had known him all her life — perhaps in lives before.

''These magical symbols you see around you, Mrs. Wilde. Cir-cles. Triangles. Roses. Serpents. Meaningless in themselves! The important thing is the power in you they may excite. They can focus the Will, Mrs. Wilde. And that is where the magic is.''

''I had expected you would give me — something to hope for,'' she said. ''About — my husband.''

''You wanted me to work 'magic' on you?'' He laughed dryly. ''People come here looking for magic to elevate them beyond the petty considerations of everyday life. But magic is *about* everyday life — and its petty considerations. The things we are doing in the Order of the Golden Dawn are too important to trivialize, Mrs. Wilde. We constantly sift truth from illusion, illusion from truth. Think about what I have told you. For three days. And then make up your mind if you wish to join us.''

She reached for her coat.

''Mrs. Wilde?'' Fearfully she turned back. What was he going to ask of her? She felt there was no way she could refuse him — anything.

''I want you to remember something,'' he said. His voice was melancholy as he replaced the dagger in his stocking. ''Those of us who interest ourselves in the other world — people like yourself and me — can never live contentedly in this one.''

) 14 (

Oscar got home well past midnight and began rummaging about in the kitchen. She drew on her slippers and robe and started down the stairs.

''My darling!'' He was a little drunk, picking at the marmalade pudding left over from the children's dinner. ''You? Up so late?''

''I am picking up *your* bad habits, I'm afraid. I simply couldn't sleep.''

''A few bad habits would do you good, my petal. Come, have a little lager. It calms the nerves.'' He slipped off his overcoat and draped it over her shoulders. ''What, my flower, can be keeping you from the tender ministries of sleep?''

''An organization —'' she began. ''Devoted to philosophy. I am thinking of joining it. It is called the Order of the Golden Dawn.''

He smiled slyly. ''Is that pre- or post-Hegelian philosophy?''

She found a bottle of milk in the icebox, poured some in a pan, and placed it on the hottest part of the stove. ''It is serious, Oscar. I cannot tell you how serious. I shouldn't even be telling you this. I am to take a vow of secrecy.''

''Now that *does* interest me, darling. Do tell me every secret at once. They are the only things worth telling.''

Though the chill was hardly off the milk, she poured it in a cup for herself and shook nutmeg on top. ''I am required to take a vow. To remain — utterly chaste.''

He smoked a moment in silence. ''Yes, I can see how that *would* require a measure of philosophy. All must take this vow? Even those who are lawfully married?''

''All.'' She looked at him now for the first time, his face bloated and weary, and a wave of tenderness went through her. ''Are you — furious, Oscar?''

''Tell me, darling. Is it what you want?''

''What I want?'' She poured water from a pitcher into the empty pan, sponged it listlessly, and left it on the counter to dry. ''If you have any objection, Oscar — even the slightest — I will give the whole thing up. Without another thought.''

He picked up his cape and started for the door. ''I dare not stand in your way.''

''Even — a faint objection.'' She followed him out to the hall. ''You need only tell me, Oscar.''

He was halfway up the stairs. ''I want you to fulfill yourself, my love.'' He looked down at her over the banister. ''And a little chastity — will be good for both of us.''

) 15 (

She was given tasks to do at home. She had to learn the Hebrew alphabet, the symbols of the Zodiac, the Tarot trumps.

Each day she prepared a tea table in a corner of the white salon for her work, setting on it salt in a dish, a triangle of black cardboard, a saucer of incense, and a rose.

She made her own wand from a long dowel she bought in a lumberyard, having it sawed down to exactly two feet in length, then painting one tip black and the other white. She glued on circles of paper in each of the occult colors, and hid it carefully away in a length of white linen.

She was assigned experiments. Once she spent hours trying to make a handkerchief rise in the air. Another day she made an attempt to hypnotize Bridie, and then the cat.

Soon she was ready for the next step: to learn to walk out of her body. This required intense concentration, and the most difficult part was, one could never be certain whether one was succeeding. One afternoon Oscar came into the room in the midst of her practice and, amused, demanded to be told all about it.

"I cannot tell you! I took an oath of secrecy!"

"I am not asking you to betray a confidence, my darling! Only to put this knowledge of yours to the service of art. A little hocus-pocus may help me with the novel I am trying to write."

And because she wanted his admiration, and because she felt sorry for him — he had given up his work at the *Woman's World* and did not seem to know what to do with himself — she weakened. Everything that happened at the weekly meetings of the order, she passed on to him.

"And what are you doing *now,* my petal?" he asked when he came upon her lying stretched out on one of the white carpets one evening.

"I am trying to become invisible."

"But, my darling, that is an art I would say you have already mastered all too well!"

"Oscar, you must learn that this is no joking matter. Really, really you must!"

) 16 (

"I will never learn magic," she told MacGregor.

"But you already know magic! Everyone does. Every time one flies into a rage, it is a means of invoking evil spirits. But that is black magic. We are trying to learn *white* magic here — far deeper, and far more difficult."

He smiled at her discouraged look and assured her he was quite satisfied with her progress. "In fact," he said, "you are among the initiates I have selected to be crucified."

She stared at him, blinking.

"Symbolically. It is a rare and beautiful service. I believe it will change the entire course of your life."

) 17 (

The novel he was working on, Oscar assured her, was to be the culmination of all his life's work. Virtually every morning he would appear at the table in a state of feverish, almost deranged excitement, and give her a garbled report on his progress.

The more he added to the manuscript, it seemed, the more he tore away. Soon the various versions were boiled down into a tale set in their own London and with their own friends as models. It was the story of a youth who cannot grow old, and a painting that ages and withers in his stead.

Oscar kept adding secrets of the Golden Dawn to his manuscript, then altering them, metamorphosing them, so they were barely recognizable — except to her.

"What do you think, Connie?"

"It seems — very interesting to me," she ventured, no longer knowing what she thought, about his novel or about anything else. "Will there — will there be a happy ending?"

He nuzzled her cheek gently. "The bad will suffer. The good will be rewarded. That, darling, is what fiction means."

) 18 (

She was disappointed, when the night of the service arrived, to discover that MacGregor was not going to officiate; had not even made an appearance. Two secondary Adepts took charge, wearing blazing red cloaks over white cassocks, and with metal symbols attached on heavy chains about their necks.

She was given a plain black robe to wear, and made to remove her shoes. Her hands were tied — a bit too tightly — behind her back. She was led down a long, dark hallway to a part of the temple she had never seen before; in front of a closed door she was told to halt. "Inheritor of a dying world," one of the Adepts cried, "why seekest thou to enter our sacred hall?"

She spoke the rehearsed answer in a tiny voice: "My soul wanders in darkness and seeks the light."

The second Adept opened the door to a large room with windows draped in black velvet. It appeared to be a covered courtyard, with a ceiling painted to look like the night sky. A high crucifix of cedar was set up against one wall. More imposing still was a black structure in the middle of the room, like an enormous folding screen, painted all over with gaudy-colored rectangles bearing astrological and alchemical symbols.

The first Adept opened the wings of the screen. "Behold the tomb of Christian Rosenkreutz!" he whispered. In front of an altar covered with a vase of roses, a goblet, a sword, and a whip was a black coffin, draped with a silken cloth embroidered with more delicate versions of the symbols painted on the screen walls. "You are here to gain admission to the Tomb of the Adepti of the Rose of Ruby and the Cross of Gold — a rite practiced in Egypt, Eleusis, Samothrace, Persia, Chaldea, India . . ."

With the sweet fragrance of cedar filling her nostrils, the painted circles and triangles and crescents seemed to flutter and dance before her eyes.

She was hardly aware of them untying her arms and leading her over to the cross. "We bind you to the Cross of Suffering. Despise not sadness, and hate not suffering, for they are the initiators of the heart."

She was bound, tight, by the hands, waist, and feet. The second Adept held up a small black cross; a fresh rose was nailed to it. "Couldst thou ever attain unto the height of a god upon this earth, how small and insignificant wouldst thou be in the presence of God the Vast One."

The goblet was removed from the altar. It was filled with a thick red liquid like blood; slipping a dagger from his belt, the first Adept dipped it into the fluid and made small crosses on Constance's forehead, hands, and feet. Staring at the dripping splotches on her hands, she was certain she was going to be ill. "Will you spiritually bind yourself, as you are bound physically upon the Cross of Suffering, so that you will lead a pure and unselfish life?"

"I will," murmured Constance.

"Repeat these holy words," said the second Adept. "I will keep secret all things connected with the Order and its Sacred Knowledge from the whole world . . ." Constance softly said the words. The Adept went on: "If I break this, my Magical Obligation, I submit myself to a Stream of Power set in motion by the Avenging

Angels . . . so that all the evil in the universe may react on me.''

She felt so dizzy she could hardly get the words out. They untied her and led her — very nearly had to carry her — up to the coffin in front of the altar. ''This is the tomb of Osiris,'' said the first Adept, ''the tomb of Jesus Christ, the tomb of Christian Rosenkreutz, dead for hundreds of years . . .'' He tore the silken covering from the coffin.

The coffin lid was opened with a slow creak. The corpse inside wore an Egyptian headdress, and a withered rose lay upon his veiled face. Constance drew back with fear, but the two Adepts held her firm. Then each of them took one of the cadaver's hands. Slowly they drew it up to a seated position in the coffin. One slipped the veil from the head — to reveal the chalk-white face of Mac-Gregor, eyes staring blindly in front of him.

''I am the Resurrection and the Life,'' MacGregor cried. ''He who believes in me . . .''

But Constance heard no more: she was suspended from the rim of an enormous begemmed chalice, her feet dangling over the swirling, foamy blood inside. Though her cramped, bleeding fingers had no more strength in them, she held on; nothing would ever make her let go, nothing ever, ever, ever . . .

PART THREE

The Unattainable

As Robbie rumpled up the unused second bed, Wilde was fastening his silver and beryl cuff links before the full-length cheval mirror.

He noted the fleshiness about his throat with disapproval, and gave his cheeks a few hard pinches to bring color into them. He had, he was thinking, become a man with something to conceal, a man with a life hidden away from life, an existence incomprehensible to the denizens of the everyday world. So be it. There were times when one had to choose between living one's own life, fully, entirely, completely — or dragging out the false, shallow, degrading existence that the world in its hypocrisy demanded.

Robbie was trudging about the room, sulking. "You *must*," Wilde addressed him in the mirror, "learn to tie a cravat properly. It is the one truly important social grace." He stepped over to help, but Robbie pulled away.

"What difference does it make?" Robbie stalked into the powder-pink salon and threw himself onto the overstuffed sofa. "Where are you today, by the way — in case it should ever come up in conversation with — her?"

"In the north." Wilde sat on the sofa arm. "Reading lurid passages from *Dorian Gray* to the astonished Liverpudlians. That is the terrible thing about marriage, Robbie; it makes a life of absolute deception necessary for both parties. But now I must rush to Lady Hemphill's . . ."

"Both parties?" Robbie said, opening the silver cigarette box and holding it up towards Wilde. "You don't really suspect that Constance is doing anything with that vapid palm-reader!"

Wilde examined the cigarettes with a frown. "At these prices they could have provided better." He took one, all the same. "Robbie, why this sullen mood?" He reached down to touch the boy's cheek, but Robbie darted away.

"What if you were to open that door and see the door opposite opening at the same time, and Constance should come sneaking out, arm in arm with Mr. Harum-Scarum, or whatever he is called?"

Wilde was looking about the room for matches. "I should be the happiest man in London. Robbie, if I could only be jealous of her, it would solve everything!"

Robbie produced the matchbox, which he had been concealing. "You should be patient with her," he said, striking a match. Its fumes made him wince. "She is so innocent . . . and so lovely."

"Yes, lovely," said Wilde, gratefully breathing in the smoke. "That is my wife's tragedy. She is beautiful, but wishes to be merely pretty. She is an Annunciation lily pretending to be a geranium. Now. *What* have I done?"

Robbie still avoided his eyes. "Done? Nothing at all, Oscar."

"And is that why you are angry?"

Robbie said nothing for a long moment. Then: "This is the last time, isn't it."

"The —? What an absurd, morbid idea!"

"Is it because of the book? Is that what has changed everything?"

Now Wilde moved to the window, where the sun over Leicester Square was buried in thick gray clouds. He stared out at the theater marquees, the trees beginning to bud, without interest. He was looking into the crowds, annoyed to be too far away to see anyone clearly — but relieved, as well.

He could no longer gaze on passing youths, telegraph boys, clerks from bookshops, assistants from Swan and Edgar's, without paroxysms of longing. The fact that they were unavailable seemed to make them more attractive; the knowledge that such an adventure was unthinkable made it the more fascinating. The teeming London streets seemed suddenly to be filled with a new kind of beauty, that he would never have noticed, or suffered over, before. And with every graceful form disappearing through the crowds, anguish would slash at his heart with its silver blade.

Beauty in a living male, he had begun to understand, was not the same as beauty in art. Where the one — Botticelli's angelic youths or the injured marble deities of Greece — brought wisdom, repose, the other set off a series of troubled responses in the system like a fire alarm. The painting or statue included one in its serene perfection, its affirmation of all that was good and beautiful. The sight of an attractive young male shut one out, made one feel unbeautiful, inhuman. Which, perversely, made him all the more irresistible. Robbie sidled up next to him.

"Oscar — you have been happy with me. Can you deny it?"

Wilde sat back on the sill and pulled Robbie onto his knees. "I am so very, very fond of you, Robbie." He hugged the boy close, breathing in the warm, familiar scent of his hair. "That is the trouble. One cannot entertain a consuming passion for a person one actually *likes*."

There was an officious knock at the door and Robbie leaped away from Wilde's arms, taking up a stiff pose on the sofa.

An elderly waiter wheeled in a tea cart filled with dishes and silver servers. As Wilde signed the bill, Robbie lifted one silver cover after another.

"You could find no Irish soda bread?" said Robbie.

"Terribly sorry, sir. The chef has never heard of such a thing. French, you know, sir. But there are other things, sir. Russian pumpernickels and German something-or-others. I think you'll be pleased, sir."

"I am supposed to be having tea with Lady Hemphill," Wilde said gloomily when they were alone again. "Half an hour ago."

Robbie poured. "Cheer up, Oscar. *Dorian Gray* is denounced from pulpits. The reviewers accuse you of grubbing in muck heaps. So naturally everyone in London is reading your book. What more could you ask for?"

Wilde shook his head thoughtfully. Certainly his discontent had nothing to do with any of the dreary shades of guilt. How could he accept as a crime against nature a love that had brought his own nature so much peace and happiness? The trouble was that happiness — now that he had tasted it so thoroughly — seemed not to be a very *interesting* thing. Not, certainly, interesting in the way that pleasure was. Pleasure seemed ever fresh, ever innocent — perhaps because ever unattainable. Whereas nothing aged so quickly as happiness. "That is the trouble with success," he said.

"It leaves one feeling so very unsuccessful." He downed the tea in his cup. "And now I really *must* run, dear boy."

Robbie turned his face to hide his eyes, glimmering with tears. "My mistake was in making you happy. I should have been wiser. The best thing is — never to realize. You taught me that. I should have believed you. I should have left you — frustrated and unhappy. Then you would have loved me. That is the way to be loved. To — reject. And turn away."

Wilde pulled Robbie close to him and kissed his forehead, his cheeks, his wet eyes. "Why could we not have been created like the midges, to live but one long summer day of love?" He drew Robbie's face in, tight, to his chest. "Dear boy. Dear, dear boy. Perhaps — perhaps I am merely tired of being happy . . ."

) 2 (

"The Duchess of Harley is obviously based on Margaret Kimbrough," said Lady Hemphill, not realizing that the Duchess of Harley was based on herself. "I recognize *all* the minor characters, Mr. Wilde. But pray tell *who* was the model for Dorian Gray?"

Wilde noticed that George Alexander, the actor, the cynosure of a group of gushing women, was watching him thoughtfully.

"There was none, dear lady. Dorian Gray never existed — except in the tortured imagination of his creator."

Her layers of fat rippled as she rattled a fan in front of her face. "You are being overly discreet, Mr. Wilde. I am certain there is a Dorian Gray. Clever as you are, you could not have invented such a character entirely from the imagination. He fairly *quivers* with reality."

Alexander was detaching himself from his admirers and gesturing to catch Wilde's eye.

"I have never met anyone remotely like Dorian Gray, Lady Hemphill," Wilde replied, edging away from her. "And if I were to, I would quickly turn and walk the other way."

Out of her vast bosom rumbled an arpeggio of raucous laughter. "Let us hope so, Mr. Wilde! Let us hope so for all our sakes."

"George! How lovely to admire you by sunlight instead of limelight."

"Delighted to see you, Wilde." Alexander, completely natural onstage, was exceedingly theatrical in society. "Watching you from across the room, an idea just struck me. Wilde, I want you to write me a play!''

"First of all, if we are not friends we must call each other Mr. Alexander and Mr. Wilde. If we *are* friends, it will be George and Oscar. In either case, my play-writing days are over."

"All you need do is jot down some of the things you say in conversation — Oscar."

Wilde smiled ruefully. "As easy as that! Ah, what curious ideas people have about the fiendishly difficult art of writing prose!"

) 3 (

One drizzling afternoon Wilde was brooding over a brandy and soda amidst the potted aspidistras of the Crown Tavern, glancing over the framed caricatures of theatrical personalities. Next to the grand piano, which was covered with books of cuttings and memorabilia, he spotted one of the "apostles" who had begun clustering around him since the publication of *The Picture of Dorian Gray*.

"Lionel!"

The boy looked up from the bar sleepily, a diminutive, doll-like creature with a blond head that seemed too large and heavy for his small shoulders and spindly frame. He seemed to be having trouble focusing on Wilde. Like most of the others in this new "Wilde Circle," he was clever, literary, attractive — and available.

"Shouldn't you be at Mass, dear boy?" said Wilde — for Lionel was a convert and given to boasting of his religious awakening with tiresome fervor.

"For the moment," Lionel replied, weaving slightly, "I have lost my faith." He told the barman he wanted a lager beer, a glass of milk, and a cognac. He drank down the beer at once, then refilled the glass with milk and dribbled some cognac on top. "But fear not, Oscar, I shall walk among Christ's minions once again, all the stronger for my brief apostasy." He downed the mix, and when he put the glass back on the bar his mouth was ringed with foam. "Now that we are in the nineties, I am determined that we shall all of us become Catholics before the new century begins."

"That we are to be the harbingers of the new century, I think is true," Wilde said. "But by more interesting means, I hope!"

"Oh, *do* find salvation, Oscar. Despite all your talk of wicked-ness, you are a truly, deeply spiritual man. One of that rare kind whom God chooses for his very own —"

"My dear boy, it is two in the afternoon and you are quite, quite drunk." It was impossible, he was thinking, to imagine how Lionel looked in the nude. "Tell me, dear boy: how old *are* you?"

"Twenty-one."

"Really? You look *weeks* younger."

It was difficult to believe that Lionel was one of the brightest of the "apostles," the way he was weaving about, smiling up at Wilde with his lovely gray-blue kitten eyes. "If, by some remote chance, I *were* drunk," he said, "I would have every *reason* to be drunk. I am painfully. Hopelessly. Blissfully. Miserably. Ecstati-cally. Awfully. In love. But I am *not* drunk, Oscar, and you have no right to *say* I am drunk." He ordered himself a hot gin and water.

"But how lovely for you, Lionel," said Wilde, adding his own brandy and soda to the order. "I hope this *grand amour* is a car-dinal, at least."

"More spiritual than any cardinal! And beautiful as — as vir-tue itself. You see, Oscar, I — who am betrothed to the Lord . . . have allowed myself to become enamored of a lower lord. But only a *little* lower. He is a young athlete — though, thank heaven, there is nothing natural about him. It is all a magic mask. The son of the Marquess of Queensberry, of the storied ancient clan of Doug-las."

At the central table of the saloon bar, the usual poets and paint-ers — a few of them quite attractive — were talking their creative energies away, laughing loudly but without amusement, like actors who have been in the same play too long and are no longer able to convince. Wilde rather wished he could join them. "I met the mar-quess once," he said, "and I hope, dear Lionel, that there is no resemblance between father and son. Queensberry put me in mind of one of his own hunting hounds."

"Bosie is godlike!" Lionel cried. "Godlike," he repeated in a lower, more melancholy register. "How delicious blasphemy is! And though Bosie does not, the saints be praised, act like Dorian Gray, I will swear on any Bible that he looks like him! Was it not you, wise Oscar, who said that life imitates art?"

Everyone in the Crown, Wilde felt, was having an amusing conversation but them. Still, he could not ease himself away from Lionel: he felt a certain responsibility for him, as indeed all of Lionel's friends did. And how Lionel depended on that! ''Everyone knows someone who looks like Dorian Gray,'' Wilde said. ''It is the fashion this season.''

Lionel took on a weepy, faraway look. ''Do you know why our friendship lasts, Oscar? Because I have never let you make love to me.''

Wilde laughed. ''That would have been a tragedy for us both!''

''And yet I was in love with you. Yes, for one whole afternoon. Months ago. But since there was a chance that my love might be requited, I abandoned it at once.''

''Naturally.'' Wilde chuckled amiably and gave him a squeeze. ''Whom the gods hate, Lionel, they make young. And overly intelligent.''

''Believe me, Bosie is Greek, Oscar! Truly Greek, not a Roman copy. And full of — of witcheries and secret guiles.''

Yes, he felt a sense of responsibility for the lad, and this was making Lionel very tiresome company. ''When am I to meet this Hellenic marvel?'' Wilde asked without great interest. ''You quite arouse my curiosity.''

Lionel crashed a tiny fist down on the bar. ''Never!'' Glasses jiggled, and he looked about to see what was making the noise. ''P-p-pure. He is pure as the snow. If you were to meet him, Oscar, you would be lost forever — beyond salvation. Even Mother Church could not rescue you then.''

''A peer of the realm and pure? Now I *am* curious! Bring this paragon to Tite Street sometime. Perhaps tomorrow.'' He slipped a card from his pocket and wrote *Tea — 4 p.m.* on it, then dropped it into Lionel's pocket. If he remembered, *tant mieux*.

''Nothing. Absolutely nothing on God's verdant earth. Could persuade me to introduce my poor hapless Bosie. To you.'' Lionel went staggering towards the door of the Crown.

''Lionel, let me hail you a cab. Or at least a passing perambulator . . .''

) 4 (

After he heard the door knocker, Wilde waited in the breakfast room for Arthur to let them in. He could hear their voices in his study. He waited a few minutes, just long enough for them to grow impatient but not bored. In the hallway mirror he gave himself a final inspection, patting down his hair, turning the orchid in his buttonhole a little to the left, yanking down his waistcoat — and then he swept into the study.

"Lionel, how delightful! I didn't know you were here."

"You forgot?"

"Sooner would the lark forget the morn than I a rendezvous with you, dear Lionel. I simply lost track of the hour." He glanced towards the window where a young man was seated, gazing soulfully into an antique book.

Through the panes poured a shaft of golden light, and Wilde caught his breath. Here — here at last —

But then his eyes adjusted to the glow and he got a better look at the gangly youth. Far from the paragon Lionel had boasted of, the boy was flustered, seemed, indeed, to have just been roused from sleep. His eyes were drowsy, his blond hair rumpled, even his clothes looked slept in — wrinkled flannel trousers of a pale gray and a light coat of another gray, neither harmonizing nor contrasting. His shirt bunched up loose at the waist, and his drab tan tie was askew. He appeared a gawky adolescent of not more than thirteen or fourteen. Was this, then, how Lionel saw Dorian Gray!

"Douglas, yes," said Wilde, when Lionel made the introductions. "I know the name well, from *Burke's Peerage*. It is my favorite work of English fiction."

The weary young face looked up at him, uncomprehending. If this was Lionel's idea of a Greek god, one shuddered to imagine the rest of his pantheon! Nevertheless, the young man *was* a Douglas, and the son of a marquess. "Lionel tells me you are a poet, Lord Alfred. You seem far too healthy to be a poet."

"A brilliant poet!" said Lionel. "Only twenty but full of genius."

"To be twenty *is* a kind of genius," said Wilde.

Beaming at the other young man with a hint of mockery, Lionel added: "Bosie is athletic, as well. He rows, and runs, things of that sort."

Wilde reached for the large tin of Egyptian cigarettes on the mantel. "I don't approve. Athletics are quite acceptable for girls, who are so robust. But young men are too delicate for sports." He offered them cigarettes. "You brought some of your poetry, I hope, Lord Alfred?"

The young man, looking paralyzed with fear, shook his head. After all, he was rather attractive; most people would say so, at any rate. A bit empty. There was something willful about his features, and something sad about them, too. *I believe I can have him,* Wilde told himself. *I can tell by that vacant, helpless way he keeps staring at me. Do I want him?*

"What a pity," Wilde said, and struck a dramatic posture at his writing table — a rustic, plain one, polished to a high sheen. "Carlyle wrote *Sartor Resartus* on this table," he said casually, rearranging sheets of Japanese paper.

Looking awed, Bosie reached forth a hand to touch the wood, and Wilde smiled. An English lord. A Douglas, and the son of the Marquess of Queensberry. *Yet there is something about him,* Wilde was thinking, *that I like not at all.* "Tongue-tied and a poet?" he said. "Pity. I am ever on the lookout for fresh talent to plagiarize."

"Was I not right, Oscar?" said Lionel. "Has he not the sort of fatality that seems to dog through history the faltering steps of kings?"

"Quite," said Wilde, watching Lord Alfred Douglas blush scarlet. "Lionel has the exquisite habit of quoting me to myself, Lord Alfred. He knows it is an infallible way to hold my interest. You're staying for tea, of course?"

"Absinthe for me," said Lionel.

"You need nothing more to drink, Lionel," said Lord Alfred Douglas.

"Consider! Not! The need!" roared Lionel, from the depths of his narrow chest.

"Dear Lionel," said Wilde, "you can't be drinking absinthe so early in the day. I never permit myself a drop before five."

"But for me it isn't early in the day! I have been awake since nine last evening, Oscar. I spent all the velvety long hours of darkness reading Saint Augustine. For me *this* is the middle of the night!"

"You will have a brandy and soda, dear boy," Wilde said, ringing for Arthur. "And while the drinks are being prepared, I shall take you on a brief Cook's tour of the establishment." He felt curiously eager to see his rooms through their young eyes — and particularly the eyes of Lord Alfred Douglas.

Just as they were leaving the study, Cyril flew in, and threw his arms about his father's knees.

"Well, young puppy! Don't you know you're forbidden entrance to this room? It is your daddy's *sanctum sanctorum.*"

"I don't care," said Cyril, twisting about to eye the visitors. He had a window cut out of his bangs through which his face peeped, a small pink version of Wilde's own face, with gigantic, glittering blue eyes.

Wilde felt his heart swelling with pleasure and pride. Vyvyan was as yet but unformed flesh, but Cyril had become a little person, an endlessly interesting one — and a friend. He had been a headstrong infant, now he was a bold and persevering child, and he showed it in his every move, even in the way he was handling a small enameled box, making sure everyone saw it and that everyone knew it belonged to him.

Wilde introduced him formally, and Cyril went about shaking hands though his own were sticky from eating fruit. "Do you have any conundrums for us, Cyril? Cyril is a collector of baffling riddles." The child shook his head. "I see. Then are you going to show the gentlemen what you have in the box?"

"No."

"Cyril, how naughty. They should be most interested in a peep at your treasure."

"It's secret."

"I apologize, gentlemen. My son has a large and valuable collection of omnibus ticket stubs, which he picks up each afternoon at the Chelsea terminus when it is swept for the day. He is going to sell them all to keep me when I am an old man. Is that correct, Cyril?"

"Tell me a story."

Wilde hauled him up into his lap, noticing the way Lord Alfred Douglas was staring at the child. "You have heard far too many stories already, my boy. You shall turn into a latter-day Scheherazade, if you're not careful. Would you like that?"

"Tell me a fairy tale, Papa."

"Ah, but you're far too young for fairy tales."

"I'm not."

"I promised your mama no story today as punishment." Grinning at Douglas, he said: "Cyril has been exceptionally naughty all morning, and in this house punishment is to be denied access to great literature." He dandled the lad for a moment in his lap, then lifted him down and gave him a gentle spank on the backside. "If you are very, very good between now and suppertime, I shall tell you the story of a little boy who was naughty and made his mama cry, and the dreadful things that happened to him. Now upstairs with you."

But Cyril hovered in the doorway. "And what dreadful things happen to papas who are naughty and make mamas cry?"

"Out!" Wilde laughed uncomfortably as the boy fled. "Isn't the mind of a child a marvelous thing? Cyril asked the other day if I dreamed, and I told him that of course I did, that it was the first duty of a gentleman to dream. 'What do you dream of?' he demanded, with a child's hunger for facts. Thinking he wanted something picturesque, I told him I dreamed of dragons with gold and silver scales, breathing scarlet flames . . . of thunder-voiced lions . . . of tigers and zebras with barred and spotted coats. I saw that he was utterly bored. 'But what do *you* dream of, Cyril?'' I asked him. He fixed me with his sharp little eyes, and his answer was a revelation. 'I dream of pigs,' he said."

Lord Alfred Douglas threw back his head and laughed joyously — for a moment, utterly spontaneous. Wilde was watching him carefully.

"But you must meet my wife," he said, and led them up the stairs to the salon, where, all in white against the white walls, she sat on the white sofa, embroidering a doily. Vyvyan was lying asleep at her side, like a great plump cat, and on the floor in front of her, Cyril was ignoring his beautiful army of French toy soldiers to play with Vyvyan's rag doll.

"How very beautiful your home is, Mrs. Wilde," said Lord Alfred Douglas.

"But such a dreadful job to take care of," she answered mechanically.

Douglas was examining the furnishings with interest. "You must forgive the wretched condition of that tabletop," said Wilde. "A petal fell from a rose last week and irreparably scratched the surface."

"Don't believe him, Lord Alfred," said Constance. "Not one word. My husband is absolutely incorrigible."

Wilde noted that Douglas was watching her with unconcealed delight. He seemed to drink in from her presence a soft radiance, so that all the vagueness in him dissipated, and he slowly became as beautiful as Lionel had first described him. More beautiful, perhaps. Something stirred in Wilde, a kind of quiet excitement unlike anything he had felt before. *Morte moriemur, guida videmus Dominum,* he remembered — *We shall surely die, for we have seen God* . . . And yet there was something deeply troubling about this strange, cold beauty, in which the soul with all its maladies seemed absent.

At the door, seeing them out, Wilde said: "You've already read my book, I suppose?"

"I've been — meaning to," said Lord Alfred Douglas apologetically.

Wilde stopped in the study for a copy of *The Picture of Dorian Gray.* He opened the cover and scrawled a quick inscription. "The young must be exposed to the classics," he said. "It is our only hope for the future."

He shook Lord Alfred's hand, and noticed Lionel's worried look. "We must see each other again, Lord Alfred."

"I should be honored."

Wilde held his hand an instant longer than was proper. "I go up to Oxford quite often. I shall certainly stop by to see you. For I think we are going to be friends, Lord Alfred. I think we are friends already . . ."

) 5 (

Was it true? Was he bored with being happy? Now that magazines were filled with his essays and articles, Wilde lost all desire to write others. He seemed to have lost all desire to write anything. It was so much more pleasant to bask in a café or restaurant and criticize literature than to actually create any.

And yet he kept thinking of George Alexander and his suggestion to write a play. Actors. The tawdry world of theater, so glittering and false. It repelled him very near as much as it attracted him.

Nevertheless, he began jotting down thoughts in hansoms or

during the rare moments when he was alone. His previous plays had been serious dramas — melodramas, even, as they now seemed, in retrospect — set in exotic places. What if he were to write something about the world he was living in, with all its charm and all its triviality . . .?

During an arid spell he sent a telegram to Lord Alfred Douglas announcing that he would be visiting Oxford the following Saturday. Would Lord Alfred give him the pleasure of lunching with him at the Carlton?

) 6 (

"Eating Camembert," Wilde said, "would be the most thrilling experience known to man — if it were a sin."

Their table was screened off by velvet curtains, so they could see only one corner of the room. The sunny day outside was muted by the windows' dark-tinted panes of thickly leaded glass, and candlelight created shadowy coves where other diners whispered to each other. Lord Alfred Douglas, in a suit of palest beige, sat close to the table with his eyes fixed steadily on Wilde. His blond hair was brushed beautifully back and the aroma of *lavande ambrée* emanated from his pale, clean-shaven cheeks.

They had selected the finest dishes from the Carlton's kitchen: a clear turtle soup followed by ortolans wrapped in crinkled Sicilian vine leaves, accompanied by a Lazard Frères 1880 Pouilly-Fuissé — two bottles of it. And now, as the cheeses were removed, the waiter — a cadaverous Frenchman with fagot-ends of an unkempt mustache bristling from his nostrils — brought a plate of maraschino-flavored pineapples and Seville oranges.

"We should like some Extra Fine Reserve with our coffee, and some of your heavenly chocolate mints," said Wilde. "And perhaps — a strawberry or two."

"*Très bien, monsieur.*"

"I have already had too much to drink!" said Bosie.

"Too much, dear boy, is a feast. You *must* let me read your work. I'm certain it is full of passion and strange music. I have been laboring all week over my play — one of those modern drawing-room things with pink lampshades. It would be refreshing to delve into something truly deep."

"I could never show my amateur efforts to you, Mr. Wilde! Ah, no, I should die of shame. I have no confidence in my work. My father —'' His voice died away.

The brandy appeared with tiny cups of scalding mocha coffee. Bosie pulled his chair out slightly and crossed his legs before attacking the dessert. ''You know my father, of course?''

''I know *of* him. We met once, years ago. I was but a callow youth.''

A golden bowl of mints, a silver one of berries were deposited in front of them. Wilde made a writing motion on the air, and the waiter hurried off again.

''I barely know him myself. He is more the Marquess of Queensberry to me than Papa.''

Despite the heat of the coffee, Wilde sipped with evident relish. ''When you speak of your father, a strange dreamy light comes into your eyes. I envy him for that.'' He lit a pale violet cigarette at one of the candles, drew deeply, and, over their heads, exhaled a cloud of smoke. ''It is the perfect type of a perfect pleasure, a cigarette : it is exquisite, and it leaves one unsatisfied.'' The smoke, catching light from the candles, created a veil between them. He gave Alfred Douglas a bemused look. ''Whether you knew your father or not, you have grown up quite beautifully, Lord Alfred.''

''Bosie.'' To cool his coffee, Bosie poured brandy into it. ''It was Boysie originally. Mother called me that. My brothers soon corrupted it to Bosie. It's the name my friends use.'' He hesitated, blushing. ''I should like to think of you as my friend. I long for those strawberries — but I am too full!''

''Take them with you in a napkin. Some pleasures — can be postponed.'' Wilde's voice lowered. ''I sympathize with your brothers. Something in you invites — corrupting.'' Reaching for his glass, his hand brushed against the boy's.

Bosie froze. He snatched his hand away.

''Wasn't the hock delightful?'' Wilde said, as if nothing had happened. ''Yellow wine is my favorite. Everyone insists on referring to it as white wine, but as you see, it is quite yellow.''

He toasted Bosie, not removing his eyes from the sweep of blond hair above his high forehead. ''Such a distinguished name, 'Lord Alfred Douglas.' It sounds like a winning blossom at the Royal Hospital Flower Show. And I *adore* historical names; so much nicer than 'Robinson' or 'Jones,' don't you think?''

The waiter's shoes creaked as he traversed the carpet, bearing the bill of account in a saucer. Wilde reached into an inner pocket for a pen of gold.

Bosie grinned. "I suppose you've heard about his renowned atheism?" And when Wilde looked puzzled, he added: "My father."

"I know he made some dreadful scene at Tennyson's play. Didn't he deliver a speech attacking it? On opening night?"

Bosie chuckled. "My father simply cannot *bear* the mention of God," he said proudly. "Awful, awful man."

"I shall certainly leave poor God out of my own efforts, in that case," Wilde said, handing the bill to the waiter without bothering to check over the figures. "I should hate the Marquess of Queensberry to make a fuss at *my* premiere."

"What would you do, Oscar? If he were to insult you? Challenge him to a duel?"

Wilde shrugged. "Fall in love with him, probably."

Bosie frowned and lowered his eyes.

The waiter glanced approvingly at the bill, then gave Bosie a mournful smile, touching the ends of his bristling mustache. "*C'est votre papa?*"

Bosie stared at him, uncomprehending, then exploded with laughter. "*Mais non! C'est un ami!*" When the waiter left, he could not stop laughing.

"Are you ready to leave, dear boy?" Wilde said, with some irritation. "I should like you to show me Oxford — *your* Oxford. I want to see it all through your eyes — 'Oxford, with the sun upon her towers . . .' — fresh and new."

) 7 (

But it was Wilde who conducted them on a sorcerer's tour of the town, while Bosie followed like a bewitched child. The rolling spire-topped panorama of the city had the detached, unreal quality of a magic-lantern show, and its domes and turrets, spires and facades looked like pictures cut out of some dusty book of engravings, recomposed by a fanciful child. Bells began to chime from behind All Souls' towers. The proctors patrolling the slow, sun-warmed streets in gowns and mortarboards took on the harsh dignity of medieval saints. The tarnished gold colleges, caught in the shadows of time, with their quadrangle lawns "soft as an adoles-

cent's cheek," as Wilde put it, seemed all at once unbearably lovely
to him.

"Alas, we won't have time to search out the Dodo in the University Museum," he said. "It seems all the most interesting trea-
sures of Oxford are kept locked away."

After the blinding sunlight dancing over the ivy-covered towers
of Magdalen College, with all its carved knights and dragons, the
long dark cloister seemed dank and cheerless. They crept up the
winding stairway next to the kitchens, where plates being washed
set up a steady clatter, and Wilde stopped before a landing with
an oak door, reflecting a moment, saying a silent prayer, before he
tapped. The door swung open and a young man stepped out into
the landing.

Might they spend a moment inside, Wilde asked, explaining who
he was and adding that, back in the dear, dead past, these had
been his rooms.

The suggestion amused the young man. "Perhaps one day I will
be doing the same thing myself!"

Wilde chatted all the while he walked through the rooms, and
yet he was profoundly moved. How odd it was, he thought, that
such a bitterly painful time should in the memory appear so sweet.
"I learned so many, many things in this room," he said. "On that
mantelpiece I kept my collection of rare plates. It was the talk of
Oxford. The vicar of Saint Mary's preached a sermon against my
blue china!" He pointed out to Bosie a pane in the window where
he had scratched a crude drawing of a fellow student. Then he
looked out past the stone gargoyles and griffins and cherubs' heads
at the willows hanging over the waters of the Cherwell. The hollow
pop pop of a tennis ball punctuated the silence.

"Our young barbarians, all at play," Wilde said sadly. "I would
like Cyril to come to Oxford one day. I would like him to have
this very room . . ."

Melancholy had hold of him, and he said nothing crunching along
the gravel path leading to Magdalen Bridge.

Would he, Bosie asked timidly, find punting along the Cherwell
too banal for words?

"A little banality, dear Bosie, is precisely what this dangerously
lovely afternoon most needs."

And so they rented a boat beneath the bridge, where clattering coaches made the only sound in the sleepy sunlight, and drifted far along the river's drowsy undulating banks, past low-hanging willows, fig trees, and acacias, past thick-clustered fruit trees, mulberries, elms. High overhead, banks of blinding silvery clouds sailed slower than they. Young men sat on the grass reading books or newspapers in the shade, still as figures in a wax museum.

"You are so silent," said Bosie, poking the black-green waters with a bamboo pole as they ambled past a dozing swan. The broad straw hat shaded his eyes but left lips and chin glowing in the sun.

"Seeing you in this strange, dreamy light," Wilde replied, "I am seized with a longing to do a strange, dreamy thing. What would all Oxford think if I were to reach over and — touch your cheek?"

Bosie was suddenly sober. "More important, Mr. Wilde, what would I think?"

A cloud trailed slowly across the sky like a bride. "Surely ours is not doomed to remain a Platonic sort of friendship?" Wilde said at last.

"Precisely! We shall be like Socrates and Alcibiades, only in reverse. With us it will be bold Alcibiades who counsels purity and discretion, as he sits at the feet of wise, wonderful Socrates, adoring, praising, learning. And just as nothing vicious ever sullied that beautiful friendship, nothing will blemish ours!" Laughing, Bosie reached the napkin of strawberries out of his pocket and began to eat.

Bees were mumbling around the pistils of a cluster of irises, purple and white. Wilde lay back, meditating, letting a hand trail through the water. "Still," he said, almost to himself, "how very immoral nature is." Bosie was leaning over the side, peering into the water where goldfish, just beneath the surface, appeared and reappeared, trembling and darting away.

"You have looked much in mirrors, dear boy," Wilde said. "Therefore I am going to tell you a story." He watched the reflections along the edge of the shore, then said in a low voice: "When Narcissus died, the nymphs, stricken with grief, hurried to his pool, hoping they might bring comfort. 'Ah,' said the pool, 'if all my drops of water were tears, I should not have enough to weep for Narcissus. For I loved him dear.' 'We do not wonder that you weep for Narcissus,' sang the nymphs, 'for he indeed was beautiful.' 'But was Narcissus beautiful?' said the pool. 'And who should know better than yourself?' the nymphs replied. 'Us he ever passed by, and sought for you, and would lie on your banks and stare down at his beauty in the mirror of your waters.''' Wilde paused, modulating his voice to a darker shade. "'But I loved Narcissus,' the pool answered, 'because while he looked down at me, I saw my own beauty mirrored in his eyes.'''

Bosie had reached a clump of daisies on the shore. He plucked one, and meditatively sat brushing it over his upper lip. The berries had stained his mouth a vivid crimson. "How wonderful to be here, listening to you, Mr. Wilde. You make all life a fairy tale." After a moment, he added: "Tell me: are you a very bad influence?" The soft rose of his cheeks, the clearness of his eyes, were as much emblems of health and virtue as the beauty of the wildflowers all around him.

"I have heard that question somewhere before, surely?" said Wilde, as they slid away from under a willow.

"Dorian asks it. Of Sir Henry." Bosie began pulling the petals from the daisy and dropping them into the water.

Wilde shielded his eyes from the sun. "Then I must tell you what Sir Henry told Dorian: there is no such thing as a good influence." He looked questioningly at Bosie, who had removed his straw hat and was turning his face to the left and right, to catch the sun. "You see, dear Bosie, to influence someone is to give him your soul. Whoever, outside of fiction, would consent to such a plunder?"

Bosie turned to watch the uneven line of petals floating in the water, his thick lashes adding a wealth of darkness, a mystery of meaning to his full, frank blue eyes. "Who indeed?" he said.

) 8 (

Wilde had an appointment, he announced, to call on the greatest living master of English prose, and he wanted Bosie to accompany him. It would, he promised, be one of the highlights of Bosie's education. Walter Pater was the teacher who had done the most to mold Wilde's own raw talent when he was Bosie's age. "It was Pater, the dear man, who taught my generation to burn with a hard, gemlike flame. I, needless to say, was his most unqualified success."

As they reached the rather ordinary-looking cottage near Brasenose College, Wilde said: "You are going to have to keep your ears peeled. Pater plays upon his voice as upon a flute. The result is a series of exquisite whispery modulations, virtually impossible to make out. One does not hear Pater: one overhears him."

"Mr. Wilde . . ." whispered the great man at the door of his home. The rooms — practically bare of furnishings, even of books, and reeking with the stench of cats — were a disappointment. Pater himself was a small man with a chalk-white face that all but disappeared behind a bushy military mustache. His rheumy eyes kept staring up over one's head or down under one's chin. "Did you see . . . the cricket players?" he asked, looking from Wilde's hair to Bosie's, and running his fingers delicately along his mustache as if making a count of its bristles.

"The cricket players, Professor?"

Pater sighed wearily. "Wonderful . . . young . . . animals." A heavy old gray cat leaped into his lap and rolled into a ball, sulking. "I am afraid I do not . . . feel . . . well this evening," Pater whispered, fondling the cat's ears.

"*Cher maître!*" cried Wilde. "Is there something we can do?"

"Like all things . . . fair personalities . . . fine forms . . . like life itself . . . it shall pass."

He spied with his cautious little eyes Bosie admiring a bust of a broad-shouldered Hercules, which, with a few bleak etchings of male nudes after Michelangelo and Ingres, provided the room's only ornament. Hugging the cat to him, Pater stepped over to the statue and reached out a trembling hand as if to touch it. "Is it not . . . wonderfully . . . inexpressive?" The cat gave him a reprimanding look. Pater regained his seat, his face recomposing itself into a bored attentiveness.

"When did this malaise overtake you, Professor?"

Repositioning the cat, Pater slowly crossed one short dark-trousered leg over the other with exquisite deliberation. "There are too many . . . flowers . . . in bloom. They so affect my . . . imagination . . . as to actually give pain. I admire . . . the frank . . . sensual . . . abandon . . . of the musk rose. But this afternoon there is . . . perhaps . . . too much beauty . . . in Oxford. Nature . . . in England . . . does everything . . . in excess. She has . . . much to account for."

"I have often thought," said Wilde, "that nothing succeeds like excess."

Pater stared at him for a long, silent moment. Then slowly, painfully, a small smile creased his lips, making his cheeks web over with wrinkles. "You have not . . . changed, Oscar. Well, well. I don't mind . . . what you say. So long as you say it . . . beautifully."

) 9 (

"And then," Wilde said, summarizing the interview an hour later at the Mitre, "Pater looked away from me. And then he looked away from Bosie. And then he looked away from both of us. And then, solitary prisoner in this dream of a world, his noble head weighed down by perfectly formed thoughts of, perhaps, too great an intensity, he reflected for a long, long while — a good twenty minutes, at least — and said, or rather whispered: 'I beg . . . your pardon, Lord Alfred, but . . . are those . . . cork soles . . . you are wearing on your shoes?'"

Max, the most intelligent of the apostles and the most formidable, laughed uproariously, and Lionel — wearing a mortarboard and black gown that made him look an inquisitor — joined in, though halfheartedly. Reggie hardly laughed at all, but then Reggie was, as always, in love. With whom this time, Wilde wondered. Max? Bosie? Himself?

"I, for one," said Max, "have no reverence for the prose of Walter Pater. He does not write English, he embalms it."

"Yes," Wilde said, "dear Pater has written the most exquisite sentences in the language, telling us how to live beautifully — and seems to be devoting his entire existence to refuting them. Nevertheless, I adore him. He is Oxford's greatest poet, a kind of Presbyterian Verlaine, as delicately sensuous as his French counterpart and, alas, as ugly." He flushed slightly, fearing that Reggie, who was so homely himself, might take offense.

But no. "Too true!" Reggie said, clearly untouched by the remark. He was watching Lionel, who had produced a bottle of *eau de Cologne* from his gown and was splashing it liberally into his stein of porter.

"I have not been to church in two days," Lionel announced. "I have decided that Nirvana is the same as lying in bed — only more so." He guzzled down the beer.

Oscar frowned at him tolerantly and turned back to Max: "And do you approve of Oxford, Max?"

Max shrugged, brushing an imaginary crumb from his beautifully tailored dark blazer. "It is like a corner of Manchester through which Apollo once passed," he said with a sigh. "But I endure it. What were *you* like as a student, Oscar? Did Oxford have a great influence on you?"

"I believe I had a far greater influence on Oxford!"

Lionel suddenly rose to his feet and in a dreamy voice announced: "Anyone who does not believe in eternal damnation is unspeakably vulgar!"

"Oscar," said Bosie a moment later, drawing him aside, "did you mean it when you said you wanted to see my hopeless attempts at poetry?"

"I did indeed."

"We could — go to my rooms."

A wave of excitement throbbed through Wilde, which, he recognized, had in it a strong element of fear. "Your rooms?"

"They're on the High Street. Only a few minutes from here."

"Dear boy." He smiled at the others almost imploringly, as if wanting them to keep him there. "Nothing could be more delightful . . ."

) 10 (

Darkness had intensified the scent of earth and flowers, and as they walked up the steps of the old house, the air was full of fragrance, ravishing for an instant, then numbing, suffocating.

When Bosie opened the door, a young man inside leaped up, startling them both. He had been sitting with his feet up on the table.

Bosie frowned. "Still here, Mason?" The room was filled with smoke, and Mason — a tall, wiry youth with frightened eyes — had the butt of a cigar in his mouth. "You needn't finish up, Mason. You can go."

"Go?" said Mason.

"This is my servant," Bosie explained to Wilde, smiling apologetically. "Go, Mason. I won't need you for the rest of the evening."

The young man reached his hat off the back of the door and, nodding at Wilde in a surly, suspicious way, left the flat.

"Servants are so difficult to find up here," said Bosie.

"Really? In my day they were easy enough." Wilde was examining the rooms, typical quarters for an Oxford undergraduate of good family — but untypically messy. Amidst the wicker chairs and Indian throws were piles of books, the usual student favorites: *Atalanta in Calydon, The Plays of Marlowe, Ars Amatoria, Les Fleurs du mal.* They seemed to have been accumulating at random for months. The windows were streaky, the carpet dirty and wrinkled, a pile of soiled dishes rested on the floor beside a table burned with cigarettes.

"Your Mr. Mason isn't terribly efficient, Bosie!"

Bosie grinned bashfully. "I don't care about such things, really."

Along with the usual mezzotints of the Sistine Madonna and the Enchanting of Merlyn hung a series of photographs, which Wilde scrutinized. "A mute testimony to your love for beauty," he said. "All these photographs are of yourself." He looked from one of the pictures back to Bosie. "Like all true beauty, of course, yours is not immediately evident. It has to be worked for."

Bosie knelt on the floor and dug amidst papers, accumulating a small sheaf. "Do you know, you have made me a better poet?" he said. "My work in the few weeks since we met has taken on a new character . . ." He handed the pages to Wilde.

Wilde read in silence, just long enough to glance over the poems and compose a flattering critique. "Excellent, my boy, very fine, indeed."

"You are mocking me."

"A poet as well as a prince. I never doubted it."

"They're rubbish, I know. I can hardly believe I've actually shown them to you! Or that you had the patience to read them through."

Wilde leafed through the pages once again, courteously. "I know the worst thing one can do for genius is to help it. Still, you might find a better turn of phrase than 'pleasant fields.' That, I would say, is a little trite. You see, a literary composition is nothing but a bundle of ideas tied together, with the edges trimmed off. I believe your poems could stand more trimming. Or even —''

"Trite!" Gripping the back of a chair, Bosie's hand was white.

"Ever so slightly. Not to mention a vague but unpleasant echo of Milton you occasionally evoke."

Bosie snatched back the poems. He tore the pages into halves, and into halves again. He threw the pieces over his shoulder.

"Bosie! You mustn't — mustn't destroy your lovely work! Of course it is not perfect. How tiresome perfection would be, and in a young poet, worse still! But even to cut hair, one must learn *how*. Do you think one writes flawless verse *by nature?*"

"I *said* it was rubbish." Bosie looked as if he were going to weep, and Wilde felt a tightening of the heart.

"My rose-leaf and ivory boy . . ." he said, almost to himself. "What you said after luncheon was wise. We must walk in the footsteps of Plato, and create a friendship he would approve of."

"I need a friend," Bosie said. "I have — no one."

Wilde could hardly bear to look at him, so moved was he. "Perhaps we might seal our friendship with — a kiss."

"Oscar!"

"A kiss good-night — as I kiss Cyril and Vyvyan. Surely that would compromise neither of us."

Bosie shook his head solemnly. Wilde opened the door. The blackness of the corridor outside looked to him like the jaws of hell. He looked round at Bosie questioningly.

"You don't really see me, Oscar. Not the way Lord Henry saw Dorian. When first our eyes met, you did not in the least grow pale. No look of terror came over you. There was no chance — none — that my personality could ever so fascinate you that it would absorb all your nature, all your art, all your — soul." He gave Wilde a tragic smile. "Good night. Good night, dear friend."

"You are right, of course," said Wilde, entering the darkness. "One kiss would lead to — chaos." As the door began to close he reached up a hand to stop it. "Bosie — will you never, ever belong to me?"

"You must not talk that way, Mr. Wilde. It upsets me. I shall be — your best friend. If you like." He started to close the door

and then giggled. "What did the waiter say? *'C'est votre papa?'*
Wasn't that amusing?"

"Terribly amusing."

Bosie smiled at him shyly and closed the door.

Wilde made his way slowly down the winding stairs in the darkness — and then there was light again from above. "Oscar?"

He bounded up the stairs. The door was open only a few inches
yet the light seemed blinding. "Yes, dear boy?"

Bosie was smiling strangely. "Didn't Alcibiades say that Socrates — if he had really willed it — could have made him do
anything?"

"Bosie!" Wilde moved towards the door — to have it gently
close. Behind it there was silence. And then Bosie's muffled voice:
"Good night, Papa!"

) 11 (

Back in London, Wilde found it impossible to get Bosie out of
his mind. Such a pure young man he seemed, such a *good* young
man, fresh, eager, and unspoiled. At moments Wilde felt himself
unworthy of such a friendship.

He wrote to Bosie, over and over — but only an occasional letter
was mailed. What if Bosie should divine the true extent of his
feelings! — for it seemed that, from the first instant he had gazed
upon that glad young face, peace had forsaken his pillow.

He began to channel some of this passion into the notes for
Alexander's play. Memories of Bosie would flesh out disparate
characters and scenes. "We are all in the gutter, but some of us
are looking at the stars," he wrote — and he was thinking of himself gazing up at Bosie.

"How long could you love a woman who didn't love you?" he
had one character ask another, and the answer was his own secret
oath to Bosie: "Oh, all my life!"

> DUMBY: Experience is the name everyone gives to their mis-
> takes.
> CECIL GRAHAM: One shouldn't commit any.
> DUMBY: Life would be very dull without them.
> CECIL GRAHAM: Of course you are quite faithful to this woman
> you are in love with, Darlington, to this good woman?
> LORD DARLINGTON: Cecil, if one really loves a woman, all other

women in the world become absolutely meaningless to one. Love changes one — I am changed.

Love *had* changed him. He *was* changed. And, unable even to imagine dallying with anyone else whilst this pure passion burned so beautifully in his breast, he stayed faithful to Bosie — even though Bosie could neither know nor care.

It began to seem to him that his previous life had been corrupt, empty, meaningless. He had been sick with that *ennui*, that *taedium vitae*, that comes on those to whom life denies nothing.

But life had, after all, denied him one thing: the adoration of an ideal, of a person too pure, too idealistic, for him ever to dream of possessing. And the hunger for that impossible ideal would, Wilde felt certain, lift him to a higher plane of being.

Bosie, in all innocence, had enslaved him. And he shuddered at the thought of being free.

The play spilled out of him in a matter of weeks, without effort, almost without thought — so spontaneously, in fact, that he was afraid to show it to Alexander. Afraid it might be nothing but romantic claptrap and drivel. He had it delivered with a casual note and waited nervously for a reply.

Alexander himself appeared at Tite Street that same evening. "I am willing to give you a thousand pounds," he said. "I want to buy the play outright."

Wilde pondered a moment. "George, you are the shrewdest manager in the West End. I have absolute confidence in your good judgment. If you think my play is good enough to buy outright, I would be mad to sell it to you!"

They came to terms on a royalty fee, and set a date for rehearsals to begin.

) 12 (

Bosie came to London on occasional weekends, and they ate at the Albemarle and Claridge's, Wilde in a state of deep anguish approaching ecstasy.

"How wise you were, Bosie, to impose chastity on me. I have never written so beautifully. I have never worked so well . . ."

And Bosie would say very little, listening, brooding, smiling sorrowfully, and with every painful evening they spent together the boy seemed more innocent, more beautiful.

) 13 (

"What is this I hear," Lady Wilde demanded on one of her rare visits to Tite Street, "that your new play is to be entitled *A Good Woman*. Is that correct?"

"That is my intention, Mother."

"You must be mad! In the whole of London do you think there is a single soul who would put down a farthing to see a play about a good woman? You must change the title at once."

She was mistaken, he told her; she would change her mind when she saw the play and realized how fitting was the title; nevertheless, by the time the actors went into rehearsal, he was referring to the work as *Lady Windermere's Fan*.

) 14 (

The rehearsals were painful for everyone concerned. George Alexander wanted to change the emphasis of the key scenes, and Wilde was adamant about keeping them exactly as written.

"Perhaps I shall abandon the production," he said to a number of the apostles in the Crown one afternoon. "I am seriously thinking of having it staged for puppets. Think of the advantages of working with puppets! No arguments about lengthening or shortening speeches. No tiresome theories of art and dramaturgy. No temper tantrums."

As a respite, he took a holiday in Paris, staying in a suite of the Grand Hotel that looked out over the boulevards and the green-shingled rooftops circling the Opéra. Perhaps in reaction to the contemporary setting of *Lady Windermere's Fan*, he scribbled a short biblical melodrama in French based on the legend of Salomé, hoping he could persuade Sarah to star in it. But before he was able to finish the arrangements, he had to be back in London for more rehearsals.

"You do not understand the nature of drama, Oscar. All you care about is making people laugh! I assure you, there is more to comedy than that. The trouble is, you are not an actor: you cannot see things from the inside."

"My dear George," Wilde said evenly, "anyone can act. Most people in England do nothing else." He was at least as nervous about the play as Alexander, but was determined that no one should know it. It became ever easier to calm himself with an extra brandy and soda at luncheon, or a sip of Irish whiskey in midafternoon. And always with him would be the memory of that shy young face at Oxford, glancing mournfully at its own image in the Cherwell's shimmering waters.

) 15 (

"Oh, I would never sneer at any superstition!" Lady Queensberry was saying with a little tremolo in her time-darkened voice.

Wilde was watching her intently, the fact that she was Bosie's mother lending enchantment to her every move. She had a way of holding her head slightly forward, as if it were a painful but noble burden imposed on her by a difficult world, and her clear blue eyes — the exact pale periwinkle of Bosie's — seemed always to be regarding something very, very far away.

She was poised on the edge of the Louis XV settee, making even her nervousness seem a rare accomplishment, and Bosie crouched on the carpet at her feet, hugging his knees, looking from her to Wilde, bestowing the same visionary, almost beatific expression on the one as on the other.

"Oh, yes," she went on, "if I were to spy a crack in that mirror, I can tell you I should feel very, very anxious indeed."

Wilde's eyes turned, as if at a command, to the great mirror from Venice on the far wall with its wonderful warped glass that looked like still water with a breeze blowing over it, water of a Venice lagoon, and in its cloudy depths the four of them seemed captured in some stage drawing room of flickering candlelight and camellias, ever so much lovelier than the real world, with not a hint of the stains of Sussex damp he felt creeping over the house's ancient walls, or of the wing closed off for lack of servants, or the cruel cold drafts that had kept him awake the previous night, coursing through the corridors like vengeful, wailing ghosts.

"But you *should* sneer at superstition," said Constance, not about to let *that* subject drop. In a downy white evening dress with puffed sleeves and a trellising of pearls about the wrists, she was quite billowy, a visitor from another century, with the elegance of a swan and a swan's ineffable air of sadness. She had abandoned her brief flirtation with "rational" dress, and Wilde rather regretted it. Once again she was dressing to please him, and somehow that did not please him. "For superstition is only ignorance," Constance went on. "What *I* was referring to is occultism, a very different matter. Occultism is knowledge, and the very opposite of superstition."

"How very interesting," said Lady Queensberry impatiently. "Don't you think so, Mr. Wilde?" She was wearing face powder — rather too much — and the flesh had caved in slightly around her mouth, creasing her upper lip.

"You must excuse me, Lady Queensberry, but I am locked on the horns of a dilemma. My practice is to listen to brilliant women, and to look at beautiful ones. This evening, faced with yourself and my dear wife, I confess I am utterly at a loss as to which course to follow."

It was not flattery pure and simple: there was indeed something beautiful about Lady Queensberry, with her fragile porcelain skin and her wispy lavender gown. Her fine hair, drawn up and caught in two ornate combs, fought loose of them, and silvery tendrils swirled about, catching the light and forming a soft halo about her face. She looked, he decided, rather like a deluxe edition of a French novel.

Clearly she did not shy away from praise. "Oh, there was a time when I wasn't too bad. '*Vieillesse felonne et fiere, pourquoi m'as si tôt abattue?*' or however the thing goes. Every eye used to follow when I'd stroll through the Row — men and women both. Even the horses seemed to be staring! But of course, *he* turned me into the apparition you see before you now . . ."

"Damus!" cried Bosie. "Leave him out of it, please! Not tonight. You only fatigue yourself."

She nodded tragically, turning to the windows with their moonlit views of the autumn-muted lawn — like so many bad paintings. Ripe mulberries dropped from the trees with soft popping sounds. As if on cue, a bird throbbed in the shrubbery.

"The cuckoo," she said despondently. "I have been waiting for him. He has become a dear friend." She looked at Wilde and then at Constance, as if to gauge the full effect of her remark. They listened politely to the bird's song.

"He is doing a nearly perfect imitation of Haydn's 'Toy' Symphony!" said Wilde. Bosie giggled — and tried to suppress it.

"Magic is not vague, foolish mumbo jumbo," said Constance,

bright-eyed with excitement. "It is scientific and precise. The body, you see, is only the house of the soul. Oh, it *seems* to have its own identity, but it is a false one! For the body is built of atoms from countless ancestors, atoms that have survived their own poor bodies' destruction. But remember, Lady Queensberry: our house of flesh must perish — and yield up its debt to the future."

"My wife," said Wilde, with a certain measure of pride, "is a mystic."

"And right to be," said Lady Queensberry, sighing, studying her rings.

"Principles have been isolated called 'yin' and 'yang' to describe the conflicting pulls that govern everything in —"

"I think you have sufficiently enlightened us, my dear," said Wilde, stepping behind his wife's wing chair and reaching down to fondle the dark curls gathered about her ears.

She stared up at him with a piqued, almost defiant air, then with a crestfallen look turned towards the harp in the corner of the room, with its rusted strings.

Lady Queensberry sat on the arm of Constance's chair, and with a sweet smile took her hands. "Is it true, Mrs. Wilde, that you are an amateur of music?" she asked kindly. "For I am one of those dreadful hostesses who force their guests to sing for their supper. You are to sit at that pianoforte this very minute. I insist."

That seemed to cheer Constance somewhat, despite her protestations, and with many twirls of the piano stool they got her seated before the keys, whilst Bosie lit the candles on either side of the piano. She massaged her fingers for a few moments, then picked out a series of melancholy chords. Then she began to sing in a breathy, childish voice:

> *"Take back the heart that thou gavest*
> *What is my anguish to thee?*
> *Take back the freedom thou cravest,*
> *Leaving the fetters to me . . ."*

She seemed to forget herself entirely in the performance and looked up startled at the applause as if she had been surprised in an indiscretion. As Constance regained her chair across from Wilde, Lady Queensberry positioned herself leaning on the back of the sofa, so her head was well above all the others in the room. Wilde had noticed that whenever anyone stood, she — seeming hardly even to think about it — would slide into a chair, or move to the far corner, so they would all have to turn to face her. "We had better go in now," she said. "The servants get cross if we keep them waiting . . ."

Her silk dress was slightly crumpled now, making her look like a wilting spray of lilacs. Smoothing it, she glanced at the walls with their jury of family portraits, then extended her arm. "Mr. Wilde?"

As they strolled towards the dining room, she airily suggested that they might later have a game of croquet in the moonlight. "Would that amuse you, Mr. Wilde?"

"Ah, no, Lady Queensberry," he said. "I abhor violent sports."

The sullen-faced servants at the dining-room doors grudgingly slid them open. She gave them a look of contemptuous acknowledgment. "But surely you take some exercise, Mr. Wilde?" she said, pausing before sweeping into the room.

"I played dominoes once. On a spring evening, outside a French café. I found the experience both morally and physically exhausting."

She laughed her thin, aching laugh. "How very wicked you are to mock me, Mr. Wilde," she said, carefully glancing over the arrangement of plates. "I beg you to accompany me on a walk in the garden, at least. After dinner. I would like the rare pleasure of talking to someone who, Bosie assures me, is Literature's great hope! You will sit here on my right, dear Mrs. Wilde. And you, Mr. Wilde, on my left. Bosie —"

"Damus, darling!" he said. "Why not place Oscar at the far end, for all to admire?"

She stared down the table to where the great chair, engraved with the Queensberry coronet, dominated the table like a throne. "Mr. Wilde would be embarrassed if we asked him to take the marquess's chair."

"I should not be embarrassed, dear lady, if you asked me to take Pope Leo's chair! But I should certainly struggle against being relegated to a position so desolately far from the hostess — when the hostess is as lovely as you. Besides," he continued, "I wouldn't want you all to have to strain to hear me. I am feeling wonderfully amusing tonight."

Constance leaned closer. "You will soon get used to my husband," she said. "He is incorrigible — but endearing."

Lady Queensberry was coldly watching the butler as he served the soup with sarcastic gravity. "I am used to him already," she said. She dipped her spoon in the soup — but hesitated. "My son has begun to echo you, Mr. Wilde. Most unsuccessfully, I fear."

"But an echo," said Bosie, "is often as beautiful as the voice it imitates."

"Not always," she replied, giving him a stony look.

Wilde sat back with calm beatitude. "You really mustn't be brilliant at meals, Bosie. It diverts the appetite."

At last Constance ventured to say something: "How very like you are, Lady Queensberry — you and your son."

"Ah, no," she answered, with an interested smile. "Alfred has entirely too much of his father in him."

"Damus and I have the same features," Bosie said, "but unlike me, she leads a life of rectitude. It has aged her dreadfully."

"Bosie!" she cried.

He was flushed with excitement. "That is the worst thing about virtue," he said. "One cannot conceal it."

Wilde tried to put on a disapproving look, but could not hide his amusement.

"You couldn't have said it better yourself, Mr. Wilde," said Lady Queensberry, glowering. "Though I rather suspect you did . . ."

) 16 (

From inside, the sky had seemed cloudless; now, however, as Lady Queensberry led Wilde through the rose garden behind the house, the full white moon was blurred by mist, and clouds from the horizon were slowly moving towards it. The barn, the poultry house, the granary looked derelict in the moonlight; even the stables, which still sheltered a few horses, had a forlorn, deserted look.

"Autumn!" she said. "Such a melancholy season. Thank you so much, Mr. Wilde, for coming to bring us some cheer."

"It is for Mrs. Wilde and me to thank *you*, Lady Queensberry. A weekend away from London is always —"

"Especially in the midst of all the excitement of producing a

play, it must seem lethal to you up here.'' Beyond the garden the
house seemed unreal, theatrical, its vast chimney-potted roof sil-
vered over with moonlight. The countryside, all heath and pine,
was like a crude drawing in blue pastel. ''I often wonder how
you get any work done on your play with Bosie forever at your
heels . . .''

Ah, so that was it. ''He is a delightful companion,'' Wilde said.
''An inspiration, even.''

''You can't be serious. For Bosie's part, of course, you are the
answer to a hundred prayers — his own and, of course, mine. I
have tried so hard to instill some reverence for poetry and the arts
in the boy — despite his father's leanings in a very different direction.''

No roses remained on the bushes and the strange, sprawling house,
with most of its windows dark, loomed over the empty garden and
the almost naked trees in a way that made one apprehensive. It
was like a huge, stuffed animal of prey that seemed still to contain
some secret source of dangerous life.

Lady Queensberry stopped to examine a bush that was nothing
but thorns. ''I suppose Bosie has told you about his father and
myself ?''

Wilde hummed noncommittally.

She strolled ahead of him in silence: it was like stumbling into
Lammermoor and finding Lucia, poised amidst silhouettes of cy-
presses, ready to sing a melancholy air. ''Do you believe, Mr. Wilde,
that one can be drawn to a person simply *because* they are ill-
matched? Looking back, I ask myself if I was bewitched. I, who
cared for nothing but beauty, gentility, art, for someone like myself to marry such a man as — forgive me, Mr. Wilde.''

He remembered the curiously dreamy way Bosie looked, whenever he spoke of his father. There was in Lady Queensberry's scorn
for her former husband a similar kind of pride, almost a fascination for the very things she most berated in him. Wilde realized
with interest that she was still in love with the marquess. ''Forgive
me for my sordid memories,'' she said, with a morose little sigh.
''In any case, I have tried to bring up my children with some sense
of beauty. Not always with success, I fear.''

''How wrong you are !'' he said.

''So you can imagine how delighted I was when I heard that

Bosie had bagged *you* as a friend, Mr. Wilde! What a tremendous lot he can learn from you. And what a towering opportunity for a boy of his age.''

''It is Bosie who is teaching me, Lady Queensberry,'' Wilde said uneasily.

''And yet I wonder . . .'' she went on.

''You wonder, dear lady?''

''I ask myself if it isn't a bit — overwhelming for him. Bosie is — so very young, after all. He is only twenty.''

''Twenty-one, I believe,'' Wilde said gently.

Her mouth twisted in a crooked smile; how beautiful her smile must once have been, he thought. ''Do you remember being twenty-one, Mr. Wilde?'' she asked, with a look of reproach.

''It is the only thing I *do* remember.''

''One thinks one knows so very much about the world and its ways. And yet how very, very innocent one is. But then, you have children of your own, Mr. Wilde. So you know the responsibility they represent.''

They had left the terrace, and now were walking towards the rear of the house, where the colonnaded staircase was in bad repair, the shrubbery was unkempt, the ground was thick with piles of untended leaves.

''Oh, they are a constant source of anxiety, Lady Queensberry! My elder boy will have nothing to do with poetry and books and sneaks off to play cricket at every opportunity. I shudder to think what the future holds for him.''

She sighed deeply. ''Bosie is more innocent than most boys. I have overcompensated for his father's indifference by being perhaps too protective. He knows nothing of life, Mr. Wilde. Nothing.''

''Don't you realize, Lady Queensberry, that his innocence is the most priceless gift you have given him? It is at the very heart of his personality, shining through his every act. He is an inspiration to all — to his friends and colleagues, surely to his teachers. To yourself, no doubt — and, I do not hesitate to add — to me.''

She was silent for a moment. ''You are so much older than Bosie. And *so* much wiser.''

''Older, yes,'' said Wilde.

''You can — help him, perhaps. In a way I no longer can.''

"Help him, Lady Queensberry?"

"Protect him, Mr. Wilde. From himself, if need be."

They were almost at the door. The moon, which had been hidden by thick clouds, now peeped out for a moment, but was almost instantly obscured.

"Protect him?" Wilde said dully.

She stopped and fixed him with her cool blue eyes. "From anything that might change him. Or spoil him. Or corrupt him in any way," she said. "Anything — or anyone."

) 17 (

Bosie was invited to the premiere, and Robbie, and all the apostles. He asked each of them to wear a green carnation as a buttonhole that evening. Of course he knew that there was no such thing as a green carnation. That was the charm of it! A florist in Birdcage Walk was devising one for Lord Darlington in the play, and Wilde thought it would be amusing for all his special friends to wear one, too.

Arriving at Saint James's in his green suede and fur coat, he was pleased to find the theater abloom with green carnations in black satin lapels. Constance was on his arm, in a brocaded gown dripping with lace and pearls, with an underdress of silk moiré puffing out through slashed sleeves, copied from a picture by Sir Joshua Reynolds. She might have materialized from another century. His taut nerves were helping him to carry the evening off with bravado; it was Constance who seemed close to a faint.

He leaned forward in the box and picked Bosie out in the crowd, sitting next to Reggie Turner, the homeliness of the one making the other all the more beautiful, and vice versa. Hesitantly, he waved, and they excitedly waved back. Bosie stood and bowed, his face lighting up. Then Wilde sat back, giving Constance's hand a reassuring squeeze, and waited for the lights to dim and the curtain to rise. There was applause for the setting and then the dialogue began. With the first waves of laughter, Wilde relaxed, knowing it was going to work, was going to be wonderful. And, leaning over the edge of the box, he gazed down at that blond head gleaming in the darkness and thought: *For you, my darling . . . all for you . . .*

) 18 (

He was surrounded at the bar during the entr'acte — by the apostles and anyone else who could get near. "You were dreadfully unkind to me in your book," he was saying to Richard Le Gallienne, gangling over the others with his head of frizzy red hair.

"Oscar, I never mentioned you in my book!"

"And what could be unkinder than that? Bosie! Reggie! Come and meet everyone. Do you know Robbie Ross?"

"I have never seen a theater filled with so many attractive people," said Reggie, pretending to be annoyed. "I am the only one here who is not beautiful."

"More champagne, Richard?" said Wilde.

"Yes — for temptation is the one thing I cannot resist," replied Le Gallienne, with a wink.

"I am surprised to hear a poet misquoting one of my lines," Wilde said. "I thought that was a privilege reserved for actors."

"And the green carnations!" Robbie cried. "I never saw one before tonight — and tonight I see nothing else."

"My instructions were to dye them the color of absinthe. Carnations will soon grow that way, of course. Nature will imitate our green carnations, as she imitates everything else, being naturally uninventive."

"Tell me, Oscar," said Reggie, with mock petulance. "Am I truly the ugliest person in the theater tonight?"

"In all of London, Reggie," said Wilde. "In all of London." And he threw his arms about the young man and gave him a great hug — a familiarity he would not dream of indulging with any other man in England. But as he did it, his eyes never left Bosie's face.

He waited in the wings during the last few moments of the play, and after the applause began and the actors were taking their bows, lit one of his violet cigarettes. At last he heard the cries of "Author! Author!" He arranged his green coat carelessly over his shoulders and sauntered out onto the stage, puffing at the cigarette as casually as if he were in his smoking room at home.

"Smoking!" whispered one shocked voice after another in the audience. "Smoking a cigarette."

"Insolent."

"Outrageous."

"*Marvelous.*"

He raised a hand for silence. "Ladies and gentlemen, I have enjoyed this evening *immensely,*" he said. "The actors have given us a *charming* rendition of a *delightful* play, and your appreciation has been most intelligent! I congratulate you on the great success of your performance, which persuades me that you think *almost* as highly of the play as I do myself."

The applause, mixed with laughter and shouts of delight, was like a vast roll of thunder. In the midst of a bow, Wilde caught Bosie's eyes. He straightened, and for an instant faltered. Quizzically, almost apologetically, he smiled. *Do you accept it?* he asked with his eyes. *Do you accept me?*

People in the stalls were standing, and others began getting to their feet. Most of the theater was standing, clapping, cheering. Then Bosie rose, his eyes on Wilde's, making no effort to hide the tears pouring out of them.

Wilde stared down into all the faces below him, smiling at them, blowing kisses. His head began to reel, and he had to grasp for the curtains. It was as if something were sucking him towards them, a profound magnetic force, violently pulling at him, as if trying to make him fall.

) 19 (

In Willis's Rooms, his joy over the play's success had already diminished perceptibly. The conversation and laughter he had to sustain seemed to Wilde like labor forced upon him; he wanted only to be alone with Bosie. But that was not possible.

Bosie, too, seemed discontent. "I must get home," he said. "I promised my mother . . . I want to thank you for the most thrilling evening of my life."

"Your life thus far."

"No one can have loved your play as much as I did. I felt as if all the words were being spoken — just to me."

Wilde stared at him miserably. After a moment, he said: "There will be greater thrills, let us hope — for both of us."

"Oscar!" cried Robbie Ross at the far end of the table. "Come hear this."

Wilde bent closer to Bosie. "We will arrange another premiere," he said, his voice hoarse. "A premiere for just the two of us. Can you see the play again on Wednesday evening?"

"I can't possibly." Bosie smiled radiantly. "But I shall! If you wish me to." He winked — a startling flash of vulgarity in that pure, sweet face — and left the restaurant without a further word.

) 20 (

"It's over," Constance said the next morning. She was preparing to go to Ireland with the children, to visit her aunt. "Can you take no pleasure in it?"

"I am delighted, Constance. Does it not show?" And indeed, since he had met Lord Alfred Douglas, life was richer than ever before, at once more deeply sensuous and more deeply ideal. But far more melancholy, too.

"Your friends are so happy for you," she said. "If only you could be happy for yourself."

He chuckled softly. "I am fortunate in my friends. Anyone can remain faithful when things are going badly, but it takes courage for friends to hang on when things are going well."

She looked down at him pityingly, then put her arms around his shoulders. "Poor darling," she said. "It is a good thing they don't see you as I do."

He frowned up at her, indignant. "Whatever do you mean, Connie?"

She pressed her cheek into his hair. "It is not an easy thing to be Oscar Wilde," she said.

He reached up her hands to his face, inhaling the sweet scent of them, kissing first one palm, then the other. "Nor Mrs. Oscar Wilde, either," he said.

) 21 (

Their meal after the play the following Wednesday sparkled with gaiety and gleamed with silences. Then suddenly they were alone in the dining room, with the waiters fussing about pretending to clear off tables that had been cleared hours before.

"It is a tragic thing," said Wilde, "that in England one is forbidden to eat strawberries after midnight."

"I hate for things to end," said Bosie.

A cab was waiting outside the restaurant, in the biting cold. Bosie started into it, but Wilde pulled him back. "Not that one. The horse is white — bad luck. We'll wait for another."

"Oscar! In cold like this?" He mounted into the cab. "We'll make our own luck, you and I!" Wilde hesitated, then followed.

"Now, my good man," he said to the driver, "what exorbitant price will you charge us to get to Cadogan Square?"

"No," said Bosie. "For once let *me* drop *you*. I'm in the mood for a long, long drive." Wilde gave the driver the Tite Street address and they agreed on a fee.

As the hansom coursed southward, they were silent, and the horse's hooves clattered in the hushed streets. A cold haze covered all of London, and the houses seemed white with hoarfrost, the gaslit byways glimmering like fairy grots.

Wilde abruptly began to speak: about his children, actors, Shakespeare, his French play, which Sarah Bernhardt would be doing in London in the spring. Then he once again withdrew into silence.

The coach turned into Buckingham Palace Road and Bosie craned at the window, wiping off the mist. "My father lives there," he said.

Wilde nodded. For a time they were both silent again.

"What is it, Oscar? I have never seen you like this."

"I am feeling a twinge of exquisite melancholy."

"Melancholy?"

"Getting what one wants is rather a dreadful thing."

The boy shifted in his seat: warmth rose out of him as from a stove. "Surely you haven't everything you want?"

"I believe I have. Like Alexander, I gaze upon the vast empire of my triumphs — and can only weep."

They passed the Royal Hospital, a few squares of yellow light in the haze. "It shouldn't be difficult to find new things to desire. Someone so — imaginative as you."

"I believe, *hélas*, that I am content." He lifted the latch as the cab drew up to the house. "Forgive me for my dreariness." But Bosie preceded him out of the cab, and held the door open for him, grinning.

Wilde glanced down towards the river, where the gaslights on either side blinked and flickered in the clean air. The night seemed to be sighing a plaintive melody, like a series of ghostly thirds on an out-of-tune piano. "It is late. The huntsmen are up in America, and they are already past their first sleep in Persia." He turned back to Bosie with a smile. "Your being part of all this has been the brightest ornament to my success. But we must not stand in the dark and cold. Good night, dear Bosie." He reached for his keys.

Bosie laughed: "Is it dark? Is it cold?" He opened the coach door again but hesitated. "Have you any champagne inside?"

"Champagne? Of course. The servants love it so."

"Let us drink one final cup. To the melancholy of — not wanting anything."

"Kindly wait," Wilde instructed the driver. "Lord Alfred will be out in —"

"No," said Bosie. "Pay him, Oscar. I'll want to walk a bit. I'll want to clear my head."

"In this cold?" Wilde paid and the cab jingled off.

The fire in the study was banked low; a little probing with the poker started it blazing. Wilde went into the kitchen for the wine. Arthur was out of bed and dressing. "No need, dear boy. I can take care of everything. Go back to sleep."

Bosie was reclining on the settee, and the books and papers that had been piled upon it were scattered all over the study floor. He was turning the pages of a manuscript.

"How naughty you are to read private papers without asking permission!"

"It's your French play. It's wonderful! *'Je baiserai ta bouche, Iokanaan!'* Thrilling! The words are like honey on my lips."

"Have you read enough to be astonished?"

"Enough to make me shiver."

Wilde placed a glass on the table next to Bosie. "Good. In literature the shiver is the only thing that counts."

"As in love."

Wilde laughed. "What do you know of love!" He seized the bottle between his thighs and opened it, muffling the sound. "Can you think of anything more vulgar than the popping of a champagne cork?" He poured wine into Bosie's glass and was reaching for his own when —

"From the one chalice we must drink!" said Bosie, stopping his hand. He sipped from the glass and turned the rim smudged by his lips towards Wilde.

Wilde stared down into the bubbling wine. Hesitantly he reached it to his mouth, and — downed every drop. Their eyes met.

"A little too dark," he said, bounding across the room to turn up the oil lamp on Carlyle's table. He made a few alterations in the bowl of roses. "These will be more beautiful tomorrow, when they are embrowned a little, as roses ought to be."

"I hope you will not ask for anything, Oscar. You mustn't. On such a night as this I would feel a monster to refuse."

"Yes," said Wilde, pouring more wine. His hand was trembling. "It would be — wrong."

"On such a night wise Socrates might tempt foolish Alcibiades — almost beyond endurance."

Wilde eased himself into his downy wing chair. "Never mind, dear boy. On such a night old Socrates is quite content — just as he is. One mustn't tempt the gods."

Bosie rose to his feet unsteadily. "How does Salomé say '*Je baiserai ta bouche*,' Oscar? Lustfully? Naively?" He hovered over Wilde, his young face flushed.

Wilde stared up at him, viscera tightening. "That will be for Sarah to decide." He moved away; Bosie followed, making a sign to him to turn back. Wilde disobeyed; but only for an instant. "You will have to meet Sarah, Bosie, she —"

"Come," said Bosie. He was at Wilde's side, and the glass was quite full. Wilde looked into his face beseechingly, trying to understand. That face was so calm, so beneficent, so beautiful! Bosie lowered his head, tasted of the champagne, and gave it to Wilde.

"You have been right all along, Bosie. We must not. It would be —"

"*Je baiserai ta bouche*, Oscar. *Je baiserai ta bouche*." A warm glow emanated from him, as he drew Wilde to his feet.

"Bosie, no." Wilde wanted to pull away, to run from the room, hurry upstairs and hide himself — in the empty nursery, perhaps. "It would be wicked. It would be — a sin."

Bosie threw back his head, locking his arms around Wilde's neck. "Let us sin then, Oscar," he said, laughing. "Let us sin."

PART FOUR

A Flaw in the Crystal

) 1 (

THEY could have crept to the theater faster than the coach was taking them. Rain had congested traffic all along Piccadilly, and though the sun was out again the streets were filled with mud and pools of brown water.

"There will be braziers of perfume," Wilde was saying. "Scented clouds will rise from them, veiling the stage with different fragrances for each of the play's emotions."

"Interesting," Robbie said.

"What do you mean, interesting? *Overwhelming.*"

It had been ages since they had spent any time alone with each other, and there was so much not to say; thus the luncheon at the Albemarle had been long. Robbie now wore a fine, thin mustache and a bowler hat, as if to suggest that in spite of his continuing boyish looks, he was someone to take seriously. "Are you excited to be seeing Sarah again?"

"Very," said Robbie quietly. The dear boy had determined to make a career in the arts, but since he had no great talents — except his enduring one for friendship — he kept wandering from one endeavor to another, researching books for authors, studying paintings with an eye to dealing in them, copying manuscripts. "Don't you think we'd better get out and walk, Oscar? The rehearsal started an hour ago, and if you remember, 'Madame Sarah' doesn't like people to be late."

The cab had halted, and the driver was flinging curses in all directions. Wilde tapped at the window, handed up the fee, and eased himself out after Robbie. "I did not realize it was to be such an *athletic* undertaking," he said.

They walked past the new fountain planted in the center of Piccadilly Circus, with its sleek bronze Eros. Prostitutes were sunning themselves around it as water trickled down with a motion so unchanging from hour to hour that it counted, in this bustling place, as an image of unalterable rest. Wilde led Robbie through the jumble of immobile coaches, their horns blaring, and the two men picked their way through dung-scented puddles into Shaftesbury Avenue. The street criers were trying to best each other, the "Chairs to mend" tenor outshrieking the "Brooms, brushes" basso profundo, while a hurdy-gurdy man drowned out both with the teeth-stinging clink-a-link of "Love's Old Sweet Song."

"I would like you to tell me what is wrong, Robbie. Where is your old fire and mischief? Are you ill?"

Robbie said nothing.

"You are angry with me. But why?"

"Is it not the prerogative of the favorite? Once deposed?"

Wilde dismissed this with airy laughter — obviously insincere. "Depose my tenth muse? You shall always be the favorite, Robbie. I have never entertained the slightest doubt that you and I shall remain friends forever."

"That is my curse," said Robbie with a smirk. "I am everybody's friend." He stopped abruptly and looked up at Wilde. "You are in love with Lord Alfred Douglas." He wavered. "Are you not?"

"Bosie?" said Wilde, walking ahead. "What a mad, romantic notion, Robbie! Oh, I suppose I don't — hate him. Bosie has had the droll idea of translating my play from the French. He just may be able to do so, with my help — though, frankly, I fear to make it any more accessible to the English. Can you imagine what would happen if they were actually to understand *Salomé?* I shudder at the very —"

"Don't change the subject, Oscar, please!"

They crossed Greek Street, and the red stone palace of the new opera house came into view. "Robbie, I am willing to discuss any subject with you but two: novels in Scottish dialect and my feelings for Lord Alfred Douglas. Is that agreed?"

Robbie's little marionette face was sulky. "I feel like a rag doll — fit to play with for a time, then tossed aside once it begins to wear a little in the seams." He darted in front of Wilde, trying to make him stop. "Am I to believe that it is only words that bind him to you?" Robbie said sarcastically, though Wilde knew he was longing to believe it.

With a wave of his hand, Wilde relegated the subject to oblivion. "Bosie is spirit, pure spirit. He hardly knows the *meaning* of flesh." Entering the stage door, he avoided Robbie's searching gaze; but just before they entered the wings, he stopped and turned to address him in a low, serious voice: "I assure you, dear boy, nothing can ever come between yourself and me."

They climbed up a narrow metal staircase, and their footsteps resounded as they crossed the wooden floor, past flats and pulleys, ladders and rolled-up sets. "How surprised all the tattletales will be," Robbie said, "when they hear that this straw-headed shadow of yours is nothing but your — translator!"

"Shhh!" hissed the stage manager. He had been growing increasingly testy, Wilde decided; since Sarah had been peopling the wings with French supernumeraries, the stage manager had very little, in fact, to do. "The lady is rehearsin'," he told Wilde. "Or somethin' like."

"She began without me!" Wilde lumbered down the side steps to the orchestra, Robbie following. "But Sarah knows I am always late!"

The stage was crammed with rows of lotus columns, palm trees, black cat goddesses and sphinxes, all of papier-mâché. Sarah appeared in the theater each evening in her production of *Cleopatra*, in which she had toured half the world, and for economy's sake she had decided that the same settings, with a touch of legerdemain, could be used for the court of Herod in Wilde's play.

It was difficult to imagine what the final results would be like. In the sunshine streaming down from open skylights, the back wall of Cleopatra's palace, with its patterning of hieroglyphs, looked hopelessly unreal. Palm trees were stacked together, waiting for final positioning. A pyramid on wheels was being painted a brighter gold. Cleopatra's throne — now Herod's — took up the center of the stage, covered with a length of gold-shot silk. A kitchen chair beside it represented the companion throne of Herodias, still being constructed in the wings.

An upright piano had been wheeled in under one of the palm trees, and a gray little lady sat before it pounding out arpeggios.

Towards the center of the stage an open-shirted John the Baptist was perched on a wooden stool, script open in his lap, puffing at a cigar. Pacing around him in an irregular circle, reading from a binder of patterned gold, was Sarah Bernhardt.

Despite the theater's stuffiness, she was shrouded in heavy dark velvet. A collar of mink encased her throat, her arms were sheathed in gloves of black leather, and her face peered out anxiously from beneath a many-tiered hat of bristling fur and feathers. All irritation forgotten, Wilde sat next to Robbie, tensely grasping his hand.

It was his white body she loved, Sarah crooned to the cigar-smoking young man. His body was as white, she sighed, as a field lily that the reaper had never reaped.

No, she growled, it was not his body — his hideously white body, white like a leper's — it was his hair that she loved, his hair like black grapes hanging from vines in the land of the Edomites.

Then no, she giggled, her voice modulating into a cool song, it was not his hair, his hair covered with mud and dust. His hair was loathsome on his forehead as a crown of thorns. It was his mouth she loved — his mouth like a band of scarlet on an ivory tower . . .

In the darkness, Wilde sighed audibly.

"*Je baiserai ta bouche, Iokanaan,*" Sarah moaned. "*Je baiserai ta bouche . . .*"

Then, barking instructions in a staccato French, she began peeling off her gloves. A young man appeared from the wings, furiously scribbling notes into a crocodile-lined notebook.

"*Très bien!*" groaned the director, in the front aisle. He had been watching half asleep.

It was terrible! she informed him.

"*Oui, Sarah.*"

Each word, she said, would have to fall like a pearl upon a dish of silver.

"*Oui, Sarah.*"

No one must move rapidly, she went on; each gesture must be stylized. They must create, not so much a painting as a bas-relief.

"*Oui, Sarah.*"

"Sarah, you are divine!" cried Wilde, applauding. "You are creating sins for my Salomé that even *I* have never dreamed of !"

She swept about to face him, feigning surprise. "My Oscar!"

she whispered — and crumpled down into a deep curtsy, blowing him kisses.

"You make the play more and more divine!" he said.

"Your *Salomé,* she is *magnifique!* I love this play! But we will have many work before that we are finish." She had some kind of capsule in her hands, which she crushed : then smeared scarlet over her mouth. She rubbed her hands clean in a handkerchief, and tossed it behind her; the little woman at the piano ran to pick it up and breathed deeply of it, her eyes closed.

"One thing, my darling Oscar. Hérodiade cannot have blue hairs."

"Sarah! Hérodiade *must* have blue hair. It is one of the loveliest things in the production."

"It is *I* who must have the blue hairs!"

Wilde sank back in his seat. "You, Sarah?"

Just then, Bosie appeared in the wings. The stage-door man pointed to the orchestra steps, and he descended them slowly, seeming strangely forlorn.

"Dear boy!" whispered Wilde, as Bosie took the seat at his right. "I am so glad you could come." A perceptible chill came over Robbie. He nodded at Bosie with a tight smile.

They would work on one more scene, Sarah informed the director. Had the moonlight been perfected yet?

The technicians were still working on the moonlight, the director told her. But they were ready for a run-through of the dance, if she wished.

"The dance?" whispered Robbie. "Won't she get a young ballerina to substitute?"

Covering his mouth with a hand, Wilde tittered. "Sarah? Give someone else the Dance of the Seven Veils?"

She had drawn on her gloves again and stood poised before theunfinished pyramid. The stage manager was assigned as stand-in for Herod, and he took his place on the throne, making it clear that he did not approve of the proceedings at all. Shades were drawn over the skylights, and darkness slowly gathered about the stage. A soft blue light spilled over the mass of clutter, giving the columns and figures of papier-mâché the eerie significance of objects in a nightmare. After three gloomy chords, the pianist struck up a languid *danse orientale.*

Sarah moved slightly, twitched, rotated her head. Prowling forward, she circled the throne, step by slow little step. She paused, reflected, her features chilling over with contempt. Her back arched, and her arms reached up as if to capture the confines of throne room, palace, desert, sky, in a slow gesture of ownership. Her body seemed to be burdened, as if by the awkwardness of veils — and then suddenly the tight dress of velvet seemed to disappear, along with the gloves, and the feathered hat, and she *was* wreathed in veils, long veils, tinted veils, veils of many lengths wrapped about her limbs and face.

She allowed one to dislodge, drew it back, let go, drew it back — and cast it to the floor. The remaining veils she hugged close to her undulating body.

Then she leaped to the platform and leaned her back on the throne, rubbing sinuously against the armrest, her mouth slowly falling open. She grasped one of the throne's twisting finials, her fingers fondling its curves and fissures, as she stared into the eyes of the stage manager, who drew back. She tossed a veil over his head, and he blinked. Even in the dim false moonlight his blush was visible.

"Isn't she sweltering in all that fur?" said Bosie.

"Fur?" Wilde said. "The poor darling is all but nude!"

One veil after another was released, and Sarah's body conjured up a catalogue of lewd movements, shocking yet strangely beautiful. For a moment she hesitated, assuming the elongated grace of a saint carved in a cathedral doorway; and then she was dancing faster, gyrating and recoiling as if trying to exorcise some demon that had her in its grip. She twisted. She froze. She skipped. She leaped. She sprang.

"How old *is* she?" whispered Robbie.

"Hush," said Wilde.

Weary then, Sarah staggered towards the throne. Her shoulders shuddered as she sank drooping to the floor. Twisting in a languorous slow yawn, she stretched out her long, lean body and coiled, hardly moving, nearly asleep, staring up at the clouds as if in them she had discovered a veil more beautiful than any she might possess. Slowly, an arm lifted away the last of her veils, and descended with it wearily, sorrowfully to the floor.

There was a moment's silence. All were staring at the stage, stunned.

Then everyone in the wings and orchestra was applauding, shrieking, weeping. Everyone but Bosie, who merely stared up at the stage. "Saints preserve us!" murmured a stagehand in a seat behind them.

Wilde was hurrying up to the stage, Robbie behind him and Bosie following farther back. "Goddess!" he cried, kneeling next to where she still lay sprawled out on the stage. "You have out-done yourself!"

She sat up, staring at him confused, a little shocked. She drew the cloth of gold from the throne and held it over her body.

"You have made of my *ingénue* a Saint Teresa who worships not Christ but the moon!"

She seemed to be regaining consciousness of who he was, who she was. She smiled at him shyly and began to respond to the voices around her, the hugs, the flattery. In a moment she was laughing.

She marched over to the little gray woman and berated her sentimental rendition of the music. She herself banged out a little cakewalk on the keys. The music must be faster, she insisted — and cold, ice-cold.

"Yes, but you danced it differently this time, madame!"

"I dance it differently every time!"

"But madame does not follow the music!"

"The music, she must follow me!" Sarah said, dissolving with laughter.

"My dearest Sarah, I should like you to meet one of my closest friends, a young English lord who, if I do not introduce him to you, threatens to destroy himself."

She was enchanted, she said, allowing Bosie to kiss the dragonfly ring on one hand while with the other she stuffed chocolate bonbons into her mouth, at the same time asking Wilde if he didn't think Herod's speech about jewels was a little too long and in any case would be more interesting if *she* delivered it? Wilde demurred, but she was not listening: she was dictating a letter to her dressmaker in Paris ordering a cloak of monkey fur, while her frail recording angel took down every word.

) 2 (

Dusk was falling as Wilde led Bosie out of the stage door. Robbie had left earlier, and Wilde had been sorry to find himself relieved to see him go.

"I am shattered, Bosie," he was saying. "I doubt if even a dinner of ortolans could revive me!" Bosie said not a word. "I see you too are overcome, dear boy. But then, everyone in London is utterly devastated by her. Did you know that the llamas at the Royal Zoo have been trying to imitate Sarah's smile?"

"If I am overcome," Bosie said, "it is not by Sarah Bernhardt's smile."

They walked in silence for a moment. "How strange it is, Bosie. Since we have become so — very close, I feel you far away. Farther than ever you used to be."

"*Will* you sermonize?"

Shocked by his tone, Wilde stopped abruptly, but Bosie went hurrying on across Charing Cross Road, and Wilde nearly had to run to catch up with him. "It is hardly a sermon, darling boy. I only wish I might have back a little of the you I — used to have. But where are we going in such a hurry?"

"Who cares?" said Bosie. "Anywhere." His lips twisted in a sneer. "Since childhood I have longed to know Sarah Bernhardt. For me she has always been the perfect woman — the most beautiful, the most sensual, the wisest. And now I have met her. I have touched her hand."

"Indeed, Bosie, you have come closer to a goddess than most ever do. But you seem dissatisfied."

They passed the old opera house. A number of young roughs were playing a game of cricket in front, using coats for wickets and a broomstick for a bat. Bosie looked them over but turned away without interest. "Sarah Bernhardt is old," he said. "Sarah Bernhardt is scrawny as a witch, and hard-eyed, and ugly!"

Wilde walked in silence for a moment. "I'm ashamed of you, Bosie. How *dare* you see Sarah as she really is? The whole *point* of Bernhardt is that in her presence, nothing is as it really is. She, least of all. To those with eyes to see, she *is* the most beautiful woman in the world. To the blind — to those like yourself at this moment, dear Bosie — she is an aging Paris waif, steely-eyed and homely. But that waif can conjure up the living presence of Cleopatra, of la Tosca, of the lady of the camellias, as no other woman ever has or ever will."

"Illusion," Bosie said, spitting out the word. On the steps of

Covent Garden Theatre, shoeless girls were tying up bundles of drooping violets. ''Can we have something to drink? In some quiet place? Where no one knows us?''

''There is no such place in all London, I hope,'' said Wilde, ducking as a pear was tossed from one porter to another. The streets of the market were carpeted in sawdust, and carts were piled high with cabbages and turnips, potatoes and leeks. Business was ending for the day, and the vendors were tidying up, their faces weary. The air was heavy with the stench of rotting fruits and flowers. ''Please, Bosie — don't walk so quickly!''

They passed a tall blind man, standing next to a fishmonger's stand. He had a thick head of snarled white hair and kept shifting his weight from foot to foot. His battered hat rested on the cobblestones, askew, with a few neatly sharpened pencils in it, and two or three pennies. He was staring up at the sky — no doubt, Wilde thought, imagining it as being far more beautiful than it really was. Wilde slipped a pound note into the dusty hat.

Bosie had stopped at a brick building curved round like a Celtic tower. ''This will do,'' he said. A pub, small and dismal, took up the better part of the building's facade. Through the filthy windowpanes, the shadowy figures inside were like sorcerers gathered together in some evil conclave.

Bosie flung open the door and led the way, past a few elderly men in a corner playing chess, their pipe smoke blending into smells of wood shavings and stagnant ale. While Bosie ordered at the bar, Wilde repaired to a secluded round table near the unused stove. He faced a Lillie Langtry poster of several seasons past. On the cold stove a yellowing aspidistra languished.

''They have no brandy and soda, Oscar. We'll just have to be satisfied with lager.''

''Lager!'' Wilde took a sip from the stein Bosie handed him and made a face. ''Who could drink so foul an elixir?'' he said — but went on drinking. ''Now — what has happened?''

''I'm ashamed to look at you.''

''Ashamed? Bosie, whatever of?''

The young man's drawn features relaxed, softened. ''I have been tricked. Misused. Abused.'' Tears were spilling down his cheeks and he was dabbing at them with the heel of his hand and laughing unhappily. ''I am disgraced. I have made a fool of myself. I've

brought shame on my family, on my name, on — on our friendship.''

With a jingle the pub door opened, letting in the market's nox-
ious evening air, and with it the white-haired blind man.

''Bosie, tell me what you have done!''

''What has been done *to me.*'' He stared down at his hands,
clasped in his lap, as if he had never seen them before. ''It was
a — vile creature. At Oxford.''

The blind man, with slow, measured steps, reached a table at the
far end of the saloon bar.

''A vile creature, you say?'' He gave Bosie a cigarette and lit
it.

''A young man,'' Bosie said, exhaling smoke. ''A young — lout.''

A sting of anxiety tightened Wilde's entrails. ''A young man —
from the university?''

''Ah, if he had been! Then there might have been some trace of
decency in him. A tough. A drifter. A worthless young — criminal. Whom I tried to help. I believe you met him, Oscar. Mason.
My servant.''

Wilde frowned. ''The young man with his feet up on your dining-room table.'' Revolting as the ale tasted, he swallowed all of it
down, then carried the empty steins to the bar and had them refilled. ''Enlighten me quickly, Bosie,'' he said, back at the table,
''for I fear I may be ill.''

''I knew he was worthless as a servant. But I hadn't the heart
to fire him. You see, I've always been an easy mark. I'm too soft.
My father always laughed at the way I would bring sick kittens
home! I cannot listen to the farthest-fetched hard-luck story without wanting, somehow, to help. I thought a decent job might give
Mason a chance at a better life. Fool that I was! One night, before
I knew what was happening, he began to make — advances to me.''

''Advances?''

Bosie stubbed out the cigarette as if it had insulted him, jam-
ming it down again and again, long after its embers had blackened. ''He babbled the same nonsense they all go on with: your
eyes are so blue, you're so terribly handsome. As if I weren't quite
aware how empty all that talk is!''

The blind man had a small pile of coins in front of him and

Wilde watched him arranging them — by feel, no doubt — into neat stacks. "Your servant — made advances to you?"

"I was of course appalled. I told him to get out at once. He refused. He threatened me. I was frightened. Mason is — quite strong."

Wilde kept returning to the gaudy lithograph of Lillie Langtry's face. It gave her a tawdry beauty that was not hers at all, whilst of her true loveliness it made not the least suggestion. With scorpions devouring his innards, why should he be fascinated by something so absurd? "Exactly what sort of — advances — did Mason make?"

"I shall not embarrass you, going into details. He wanted to — touch me."

"To touch you."

"He was unnaturally excited. I had allowed him to finish a bottle of my wine — another mistake! It went to his head."

"He wanted to touch you."

"He — put his hands on me. I was terrified. He was frenzied, an animal. He tore at my clothes . . . ." Bosie buried his head in his hands.

Through the grimy pub windows Wilde stared at the darkness coming on. *The days of June are, in fact, shorter than the days of February,* he was thinking. *And how long the nights.*

"And now the cur is threatening to blackmail me!"

"Blackmail? But Bosie, how absurd!" From the vantage point of darkness, all memories of light, of spring, of loveliness, must appear fatuous, insubstantial. Death, Wilde thought, must be very much like night. "You will have him arrested at once, of course."

"Can't you see, Oscar? He will tell the police any lie he wants to. He's of their own class. They'll naturally choose to believe him. They'd be overjoyed to be able to drag a name like mine into the mud. I cannot go to the police."

"But this is monstrous! You must not be intimidated in this way."

Bosie looked strangely cold, as if hardened by his terrible experience. "I am not intimidated! Oscar, if you are going to be hysterical, you are useless to me. I am looking for advice, that is all."

Wilde gulped down the lager. The blind man, now smoking a

cigar, had the *Evening Standard* spread out before him and was bent over its columns.

"George Lewis will know what to do," Wilde said in a strained voice. "There is no wiser solicitor in London, and fortunately, he is a very dear friend." He brushed a hand over his forehead: it was moist. "Still — I hesitate. A case of this kind —"

One of Bosie's eyebrows flickered above the other. "A case of this kind?"

"It is so terribly — delicate."

Bosie's mug crashed down upon the table, splashing beer about. "Do you think I have done something too shameful to mention to this great friend of yours? Why do you look away from me? Are you afraid?"

Everyone in the room was staring, the blind man among them. Indifferent to their eyes, Wilde returned Bosie's gaze, closing a hand over his. "Yes, I was afraid to look at you. Afraid you might see how much love is in my heart for you at this moment, and blanch, and turn away . . ."

) 3 (

"Pay what he asks," said George Lewis.

"Unthinkable!" cried Bosie. The look of sweetness vanished from his face — but instantly reappeared. "That would be supporting crime!"

The window looked out on the severe aristocratic houses of Ely Place, irreproachably correct in every way.

"Be realistic, Lord Alfred. The man must be kept silent at any cost." Seated sideways at his desk, Lewis seemed to be occupied with some far-off aspiration. Behind the protection of thick gray whiskers, his face had the hurt, resentful look of a disappointed child's. He had seen much in his long career; evidently much of it haunted him still. "If you permit the least publicity about this matter, young man, your name, I need hardly tell you, is mud."

The office walls were a time-stained dun color, like old sheets scorched by much ironing. It was a large, well-appointed office, Wilde thought, but a small one to work a life away in. All these cases filled with thick, beautifully bound volumes contained, he was certain, not one book of poetry, for though George Lewis was a connoisseur of the arts, he did not mix business and pleasure.

"Don't forget, George," he said, "Lord Alfred is the wounded party."

Lewis had the look of one who has seen too much; or perhaps merely eaten too much. "Do you think it makes a difference?" He was so accustomed to veiling his emotions professionally that he no longer seemed to have any, though in fact he was the most sentimental of men, easily moved to tears by a good symphony or a good meal. "Did you offer this person ready cash?" he now asked.

Bosie stiffened in his chair. "*Pay* for infamy? Encourage viciousness? Not, I, sir. I could never compromise myself in such a fashion."

"Living," said Lewis dryly, "is all about compromising oneself. You would not be 'paying for infamy,' Lord Alfred — but to shake yourself free. Hmm. What can he prove against you? Anything? Anything whatsoever?"

Bosie, face red, rose to his feet. "What are you suggesting, Mr. Lewis?"

"Could he, in a court of law, prove justification in any way?"

"George!" Wilde's voice was faint. "How can you even ask such questions?"

Despite his look of world-weariness, there was still a flame flickering in those tired brown eyes. "My business is to ask such questions. Could he, Lord Alfred?" His eyes narrowed as if he were studying a brief. "Or couldn't he?"

Bosie was at the window, glaring at the houses across the way. "It is *I* who shall take him to court. I don't care about scandal. Why should I? I have done nothing."

George Lewis was holding himself as if he were posing for a bronze portrait by David d'Angers. "Do that, young man. If your goal is to be ruined forever."

"Ruined? Not when I am exonerated!"

Lewis swiveled to face the other direction, striking precisely the same pose, strong, thoughtful, unbending. "In such cases even the innocent are tainted. An unpleasant odor hangs about everyone involved — for years. Sometimes forever."

"George?" said Wilde, feeling suddenly like a stranger before his old friend. "What shall we do?"

There was no interpreting the meaning of the look that Lewis gave him; yet it made Wilde wince. "How much did this man ask for?" Lewis demanded of Bosie.

Bosie hesitated. "One hundred pounds."

"Pay him the hundred pounds."

"Never! Anyway, I haven't *got* a hundred pounds. And no way to get it. I could hardly, under such conditions, ask my poor mother for such a sum! And my father —" He laughed bitterly. "He would rather see me dead . . . ."

"George! I shall send a check at once, if that is what you think must be done."

Another penetrating look. How curious it was, Wilde was thinking, that this most courtly and elegant of English gentlemen was, in fact, self-made and a Jew. "Send it through me, then," Lewis said. "If he sees it is coming from a solicitor, he will perhaps believe Lord Alfred is not to be intimidated any further. Perhaps. That is the only advice I can give."

"You — don't mind it going out under your name?" said Wilde.

"Mind?" said Bosie, frowning. "Why should he mind?"

Lewis regarded him thoughtfully. For all his worldly success he had the look, Wilde decided, of a man whom life has betrayed. "I don't mind, Oscar," Lewis said.

Wilde reached out his hand, relieved when the older man took it with something of his old warmth. "How am I to thank you, George? You are the only man I know who is kind and wise, and still good company."

The smile on Lewis's lips dimmed when he glanced up at Bosie, who was holding open the door while a draft blew in, rustling papers on the desk and tables.

"Learn a lesson from all this, Oscar," said Lewis, pursuing a sheet of foolscap across the floor. He retrieved it and, with a discreet frown at Bosie, placed it carefully inside a notebook. "Be careful of the company you keep."

) 4 (

Wilde was in his dressing room at Tite Street putting the final touches to his *toilette,* trying to think of witty things he might say to the journalist downstairs. But vipers were crawling through his brain.

He patted a little talcum into his cheeks and pressed a pearl-tipped pin into the knot of his dusky pink cravat. Alas, the mirror gods were being hostile. Was he reduced to this, then: a man of a certain age, fleshly and all too mortal, staring with despair into a mocking pool of silver?

That, he told himself, was not the way Bosie saw him. In Bosie's eyes, his heaviness was merely evidence of a life too richly lived, and the slight thickness of his features lent character, gravity to his face. In Bosie's eyes he was imposing, handsome, verging on the divine.

Wasn't he?

But a blackmailer! He kept feeling that there must be some factor in his relationship with the boy that, if brought into the light, would explain all, forgive all, free him from this new sorrow that threatened to engulf him — so things might be as they had been, only days before. Then he would be able once more to share with the boy only amusement, only joy, without these doubts, suspicions, second thoughts.

It was not, he feared, a friendship that could support much suffering.

Since their talk in the dreadful bar in Covent Garden Market, Wilde had been reviewing every moment they had spent together, seeking for some new clue to shadings of sentiment he might have missed at the time, some proof that, after all, Bosie did not genuinely care for him or — just as difficult to ascertain — genuinely did. He was tortured with uncertainties that *must* be resolved; yet at no time was he able to think the whole thing out, so busy was he doing other things, or pretending to do them, or looking for other things to do.

The anonymous note he had received the previous day, for example, stating that an actor named Brookfield had written a parody of *Lady Windermere's Fan* and was hoping to have it produced in the West End. Should he take action to stop the production? But he rather suspected that the more people were exposed to Oscar Wilde, the better, even if through mockery — provided it were the right kind of mockery. And in any case it generated some excitement, some confusion, and he seemed to require more and more of both.

But who was this Brookfield? He had the troubling sense that he knew him, and that there was something menacing about the man — though he could not even remember what he looked like.

A blackmailer.

Was Oscar in love with Lord Alfred Douglas, Robbie had demanded. He thought not — not really. Genuine love, he suspected, was a far milder emotion than this.

Though conceivably he might be in love with Bosie's being in love with him; for he had to have admiration, he could not live without it. He flourished in admiration like an orchid in jungle heat. And Bosie was a Douglas, and a peer of the realm, with the noblest blood in England coursing through his veins.

Bosie might be moody, evanescent, impossible to fathom; yet how haunting were those dreamlike hours they had known together, heated by the warm breath of passion and its spasms of delight! Even the boy's sulks and hostilities might merely be a reaction to too powerful an attraction. Bosie loved him, of that Wilde felt sure — or almost sure. And yet he could recall nothing in his life that he had desired so feverishly, and nothing that had left him so unsatisfied.

He needed to be alone to think — and yet this balmy July morning when he might be confronting the question of Bosie with a clear eye, he was instead preparing for an interview with a journalist he detested from a newspaper he detested, en route to Kettner's for a preposterous "mauve luncheon" he no longer wished to give.

"You yourself once worked for the press, Mr. Wilde, if I'm not mistaken," said the newspaperman, as the cab made a slow turn into Kemble Street. He was middle-aged, dry, conscientious with, as far as Wilde could see, not a single redeeming vice. "Would you consider returning to journalism?"

"Heavens, no. Nothing is farther from literature than journalism."

"Can you tell me the secret of your genius, Mr. Wilde?" He had arrived with a seemingly endless list of questions, and was apparently determined to get through every one.

"There is no secret. It entails having something to say. And then saying it."

The coach drew up to Kettner's, its wheels scraping against the curb. ''But why do you only write about the upper classes, Mr. Wilde?''

Wilde stepped out and searched through his wallet for a pound note. ''What would you have me write about?'' he said. ''Blackmailers?''

''It seems to me, Mr. Wilde, that your plays are about trivial people leading trivial lives. Have you no interest in the drama of everyday existence?''

The driver thanked Wilde profusely for his tip and snapped his whip, and the coach pulled away. ''I am afraid that to me, everyday existence says very little. Nothing of any dramatic significance would be suggested to me, for example, if a journalist were to be run over by a four-wheeler on the Tottenham Court Road — an incident that I regret to say I have never witnessed. And now I must bid you a good afternoon.'' At the entrance to the alleyway beside the restaurant he noticed a foul-looking beggar sitting in a pile of rags. He averted his eyes and turned back to the journalist with a tired smile. ''I am relying on you to misrepresent me.''

But his heart clutched at him as a liveried porter held open the door. ''One moment,'' he said, and stepped over to the alleyway.

The beggar was grasping tight the lapels of his shabby coat. He was unshaven, and a smell of rot rose from his soiled clothes. ''Spare a penny or two, sir? For a crust of bread? I been out of work goin' on two months, sir.''

Wilde countered a feeling of disgust with bravado: ''Work?'' he said. ''But why ever should you want to work? And surely there are better things to eat than bread?''

The beggar covered his face with his gnarled, dirty hands.

Wilde's voice grew gentle: ''If you had said to me that you had work to do but could not dream of working, and you have bread to eat but could not dream of eating bread, I would gladly have given you two pennies.'' He reached into his pocket with a smile. ''Instead I give you — half a crown.''

As he held forth the coin the man gaped up at him with strange, wild eyes. Suddenly he grasped the hand with the coin in it, pulling Wilde closer. Wilde tried to draw back, but the beggar was stronger than he looked. For a moment Wilde feared he wanted to pull him off his feet and force him down into the rags with him, but the man merely whispered, ''God bless you!'' and let go.

Shaken, Wilde paused in the restaurant foyer to study himself in a baroque mirror with a twisting mirrored frame. Could he face them, these clever young men with their many facets all asparkle, using him as the chief source of illumination? He wanted to be lonely, to sit somewhere and brood about the beggar and the absurdity of life and this strange sordid affair between Bosie and a servant. There were depths of sorrow attached to all of it that wanted to swallow him up, that something in him longed to be swallowed up by. Could he heave himself up from them and make himself shimmer once more? He stopped at the half-empty bar and asked the deaf old bartender for a brandy.

"I feel a cold coming on, Martin," he said, moving his lips carefully, so they could be read. Then, after downing half the glass: "The artistic life, Martin, is nothing but a long, exquisite suicide."

"Indeed, it must be difficult, Mr. Wilde."

"Ah, no — it is delightful."

The cheers when he entered the dining room buoyed him up more surely than the brandy had done, or the hock and water he had been sipping earlier in the morning, before the odious *Express* reporter had arrived. The table was splendid with its cloth and candles and plates all tinted mauve. At once he felt relieved, light, even carefree, carried by the waves of laughter and enthusiasm.

Max, the cleverest of the young thurifers, was also invariably the best dressed, and today he was turned out magnificently in a lounge suit of gray with a mauve handkerchief spilling from the pocket. But Max was small and tidy, and clothes took to him well. Reggie, at his side, looked like an upturned laundry hamper. Lionel Johnson was very nearly as bad in his double-breasted blazer of navy blue, spattered over with stains from forgotten meals and libations. Richard Le Gallienne strove to appear aesthetic but only looked funereal, and Aubrey, in a suit of gray silk, seemed faintly vulgar.

"What is life?" said Lionel. "Life is the sunsets we worship, the books we read, the faces we love."

"Lionel," said Bosie impatiently, "you are quite drunk."

"Don't bend brows of reproach at me, dearest Bosie. I am neither drunk, nor addled, nor flutterpated, nor woozy." He downed his brandy and soda and then drank down Bosie's as well.

Max was full of talk about *Salomé*. Why, he wanted to know, didn't Wilde rewrite all the rest of the Bible while he was at it?

"I intend to, Max! The Archbishop of Canterbury has requested me to prepare a new version, leaving out all the tiresome religious and inartistic parts. I plan to begin work at once," Wilde said, inhaling the bouquet of mauve roses in the center of the table. Lovely as they were, they had no more fragrance than a lettuce leaf. "And I am going to give you the first copy of *Salomé* when they publish it. If they ever dare to do so. They are speaking of putting off printing it till the twentieth century, when the times may be riper for such a work."

"Its publication in *any* century would be premature," said Max.

"I hope you are not serving us absinthe, Oscar," said Lionel. "We are all bored with it. I am expecting hellebore at the very least. Though I might settle for mandragora."

The others, Wilde noticed, had gradually, and probably unwittingly, drawn away from his end of the table and were leaning towards Bosie at the other end — towards youth.

Lionel was arguing that "The Hound of Heaven" was irreverent rubbish.

"I know what you mean, Lionel," said Wilde. "It makes me yearn for damnation, in the same way Wordsworth's 'Ode to Solitude' fills me with the wildest passion for society. Nevertheless, I regard Thompson as one of our greatest poets."

"*Minor* poets," Bosie corrected — clearly feeling that the conversation should be centered on *his* poems, the appearance of the first volume of which was the cause for this afternoon's *fête*.

Wilde beamed at him. "Let us be grateful for minor poets, dear boy. I should hate to be left entirely to the mercy of geniuses!" A thrill of pleasure went through him at Bosie's faint pout. "Isn't Bosie handsome in periwinkle blue?" he said to the others. The answering chorus of compliments lifted Bosie's spirits somewhat.

And he seemed delighted with his luncheon, with its mauve wine, mauve meat, mauve vegetables — even the rice was tinted.

"So there was Sarah," Wilde was saying, "the greatest Cleopatra London has ever seen, shrieking out her golden lungs and throwing things about, slapping poor Charmian and Iras black and blue, stabbing the luckless servant who brought the unhappy tidings about Marc Antony.'' Wilde cupped his hand to his mouth to stifle his giggles. ''And in the seat behind me I heard a matronly British voice saying, 'Hmmm. How different from the home life of our *own* dear Queen.' Wasn't that too, too heavenly?''

''We have heard the story, Oscar,'' Bosie said. ''Oscar is like the thrush: he tells his stories twice over, lest we should fail to capture their first fine careful rapture. And now he is annoyed with me. Would you like me to leave, Oscar? 'In a marked manner'?'' Giggling, he took a few loping steps from his chair. ''Have you ever noticed that in Oscar's writings, people always leave the room 'in a marked manner'?''

Reggie rescued the company from the awkward silence this inspired by suggesting that Bosie read one of his poems. With a little smile, Bosie accepted, reaching a copy of the *Spirit Lamp* out of his pocket. In a breathless, singsong fashion he read a long ballad about a prince who changes places with a peasant.

All applauded when it was finished, none more heartily than Wilde, who compared it with Chaucer at his best.

''Oscar,'' said Max, drawing him aside. ''I should like to speak with you about something — in private.''

Wilde stepped over to a table in an alcove, covered with desserts. ''Have some strawberries, Max. I understand Mr. Kettner brings them from his own garden.''

Max held his cigarette tilted at an elegant angle from his lips. ''Why did you tell me, Oscar! I always find that fruits from the garden lack that little *je ne sais quoi* of ones from the market, don't you?''

Wilde roared. ''The days are numbered, dear Max, when you and I can attend the same parties! I *adore* that!''

''You are free to borrow it if you wish. I would be flattered.''

Wilde looked shocked. ''Max! A true artist never borrows. He steals outright.'' He threw an arm around the younger man as light streaming in the stained-glass iris window tinted their shirtfronts. ''Now what is this 'private' matter you wish to speak about? Something dreadful, I hope?''

''I merely wondered, Oscar — is anything wrong?''

''Wrong, dear Max?''

''To be candid, you are drinking such a great deal these days . . .''

"Max, I am blind sober!"

"And eating such a great deal, for that matter. Do I seem a scold?"

Wilde returned to the table for their glasses. "Max, the gods have bestowed on you the gift of perpetual old age! I believe it is our *duty* to indulge ourselves. For all too soon we will be able to indulge ourselves no more."

Max held up his glass as Wilde filled it with champagne that was more or less mauve in color. "I don't understand you, Oscar."

"Good. The moment we begin to understand someone, our affection for that person spreads its wings, preparatory to flying out of the window." Taking a sip from his glass, he glanced over at Bosie, and the tight smile on his lips dwindled away. "Yes, Max," he said softly, "we love best only what we cannot understand . . ."

) 5 (

Charles Brookfield arrived at Tite Street late one afternoon.

He was an intelligent and ambitious-looking man of thirty, with bold chiseled features that many would have called attractive, women especially. Wilde found him strangely repellent, his smile too practiced, his large greedy eyes too interested, too alert. "But I know you from somewhere, Brookfield, do I not?"

"You have seen me many times," Brookfield said in a measured, resonant voice. "Through many rehearsals at the Saint James I have sat in a shadowy side aisle, listening, learning . . ." He might have been reading from a script.

"How very flattering! Only — how did you get into rehearsals at the Saint James?"

A trill of stage laughter made Wilde's hackles rise. "I am an actor, Mr. Wilde. I call every stage manager in the West End by his first name." For all his polish, there was some innate shabbiness of spirit about Charles Brookfield, Wilde decided. It poked through everything about the man, his manner, his voice, his attitude.

"I see. Well, I am *dying* to find out how you have massacred poor Lady Windermere. I hope you've left something of the unfortunate woman intact. A wishbone, perhaps."

"She is entirely unimpaired, Mr. Wilde! For all its naughtiness, my little lampoon is a work of great reverence and adulation. You see, I am one of your greatest admirers.'' He lingered over his words as unctuously as if he were sucking on dried apricots.

''I congratulate you on your taste, Brookfield. If there is a wittier man in London than the author of *Lady Windermere's Fan*, I can't imagine who he might be. But may we get on with the reading? I am *breathless* with curiosity.''

Brookfield handed him the manuscript in an ostrich-skin binding — rather ostentatious, Wilde thought, for a beginning playwright. A few minutes' perusal revealed the work for what it was: a paltry, uninspired burlesque of Wilde's style, heaping paradox upon paradox with never a flash of fire, never a glimmer of true wit. Imitation, he had always held, was the compliment mediocrity pays to genius, but *The Poet and the Puppets* went beyond imitation to an ugly kind of malevolence.

''Delightful!'' he said, returning the manuscript. ''Utterly charming. I feel I have been — how does one say — delightfully 'spoofed.' But I do think it's cutting a little too near the bone to call your protagonist Oscar. For good reasons or ill, the name Oscar has become a household word for the English public. Do find another name for your hero, won't you?''

''Your middle name, O'Flahertie. You couldn't object to my using that?'' An ugly smile played over Brookfield's ugly lips. ''That surely isn't a household word.''

Beneath his smiles and simpers, there was something troubling about Brookfield's manner: he held himself with an arrogance, a kind of recklessness softened by effeminacy, that gave Wilde the unsettling sensation of looking into a distorting mirror. ''But how did you know I had O'Flahertie in my name?''

''Ah, Mr. Wilde, there is precious little about you I don't know!''

Wilde regarded him closely, trying to see something behind the affable smile. ''Well, I suppose that would be all right,'' he said, leading Brookfield out of the study. ''Yes, call him O'Flahertie, if you will. And I wish you the best of O'Flahertie and your play and all your future endeavors.''

He saw Brookfield out and in the hall encountered Cyril, who insisted on being allowed to sit upon his knee. Holding the child that way, Wilde returned to work on the manuscript of *Salomé*, but even an hour later, when Cyril was fast asleep on his chest, he was unable to free himself of a sense of unease Brookfield had inspired, a sense of danger.

) 6 (

Wilde sat in the bar of the swimming bath, alone, waiting for Bosie to tire of the water. He skimmed over rather than read the copy of the *Observer* spread out before him.

The waiter had found him a wedge of cheddar to nibble on with his brandy and soda — his third this morning. He was determined to cut down. Tomorrow.

He could not stop thinking about money and how quickly it was going. The profits from the first month of *Salomé* were already spent, and it was not even certain the play would be successful.

He wondered if he would ever write another play. Never another comedy, he felt sure. All the humor seemed to be drained out of him.

Bosie rushed in, dripping wet, followed by two other young men. "Look whom I discovered beneath the waves!" he cried. "Oscar Wilde, I want to present my two brothers, Francis and Percy."

"Your brothers!" Anything connected with Bosie seemed to throb with a strange magic all its own; and the sight of these strapping young males, smiling at him like two shy Tritons, with water dripping down their nearly nude bodies, had an unsettling effect.

The eldest, Francis, stepped forward, extending his hand. "It is like coming face-to-face with a legend," he said. "Our brother never ceases talking about the great Oscar Wilde."

"Francie has just come back from several months at Devonshire," said Bosie.

"Looking so healthy?" Wilde replied. "People usually deteriorate in the country air. But what a delightful place to meet you both — an oasis of Hellenism in our dreary London."

As they made small talk, Wilde compared the three brothers, trying to decide how fortune had meted out her gifts — and her curses — to each.

Where Bosie had some of the beauty of a head by Phidias, without the firmness of character, Francis had the Phidian character, but without the beauty. Years in the Coldstream Guards had given him an aura of authority, of responsibility, but while he seemed to have left childhood behind, one felt a yearning in those soft gray eyes to turn round for one last look.

Percy was as different from the other two as it was possible to be: playful, earthy, a bit ungainly, more peasantlike than any peasant. As well as Wilde was able to recall the features of the Marquess of Queensberry, Percy resembled him. How odd it was, he thought, that so many peasants looked like aristocrats, while so many aristocrats looked, unfortunately, like Percy and his father.

"Are you not coming in for a swim, Mr. Wilde?" said Percy.

"Heavens, no. The only form of strenuous activity I approve of is talking." He accompanied Percy and Francis as far as the terrace. "Good heavens! Isn't that Lord Arthur Hargreave doing the trudgen stroke? Whatever must the water think of him!"

Bosie had ordered champagne. "Oh, do let me have a glass of that, dear boy," said Wilde, back at the table. "My mouth is as dry as a volume of sermons."

"Aren't they dreadful?" Bosie said, and drank down a glassful of the wine as if it were water. "Which is the greater philistine?"

"They are charming young men, both of them."

"And which would you rather make love with?"

"Be serious, dear boy."

"I saw the way you eyed Francie. Do you think he would do it? I'm sure he would! Though perhaps not with you! I think he does it all the time. And then acts sanctimonious."

The barman presented the bill for the champagne — to Wilde. With a rueful grin, he signed for it. "He seems an extremely sensitive young man, your older brother. Perhaps — too sensitive."

"Never mind," said Bosie, laughing. "I'm not jealous. There's a lifeguard here who could make me quite forget all *my* cares — at least for an hour or so."

"Bosie, I *hate* for you to talk that way." Moodily, he settled back into the sofa, staring up at the arched ceiling with its painted sailing galleons.

"Why shouldn't I talk that way? Or any way I please?"

Wilde closed his eyes. "I am remembering you as you were that first day at Oxford. What a vision you seemed to me then. A vision of — the greatest purity."

"How very boring! And now — ?"

There was still a morsel of the cheese left in a saucer; Wilde offered it to Bosie, who refused. "And now you have the more — interesting beauty that comes with a sin or two."

Bosie laughed a hard little laugh. "None of that blackmail business would have happened if I hadn't met you. Do you think I would have been defending my virtue before your smug solicitor friend if you hadn't shown me what a — what a *millstone* virtue is around the neck of any young man? In your cursed book you had Dorian experiment with every 'exquisite' sin. Why should I not do the same?"

Sir Nigel Drew walked past in a big, baggy swimming costume and nodded to them both. Bosie's face immediately softened, regained its seraphic look.

"Bosie, you are speaking of a work of fiction."

"Life itself is a work of fiction. You taught me that! Now you are jealous because I am living it more brilliantly than you! But Oscar, you made a grave mistake with Dorian Gray." He blinked his eyes and opened his mouth slightly, affecting innocence. "After each of Dorian's acts, the picture ought to have grown more sweet, more saintly in expression!"

Bosie's eyes narrowed, assessing a bather strolling by on the terrace. Wilde looked away. Was it jealousy he felt — or shame? Shame for Bosie? For himself? "Goethe said he had to live his romances so he could write about them," said Wilde with a sigh. "I wrote my romance first. Now I am forced to live it." He made himself smile. "Do you realize how I dote on you, dear boy?"

Thinking he had an admirer in a bearded gentleman of a certain age imbibing a glass of wine across the way, Bosie stretched out his moist body provocatively, but the man looked away. "Do you know how boring it is to be doted on?" Bosie said sullenly. "I thought you were an artist of life. It is all an act! You are tiresome. Sentimental. Do you have any idea how — very boring you are, Oscar? Worse than that. Conventional! Do you think I regret the things I did with Mason? He was bold, and young, and beautiful in his fascinating, ugly way. We did strange, secret things together —"

Wilde feared he hadn't the strength to lift his glass to his lips. "Secret things?"

"Things I would never do with you!"

Youths were descending the steps from the roof, blotched red from lying in the sun. Bosie watched them hungrily.

"Is it my gilt and ivory boy — saying these terrible things?" He raised the glass, and drained it. "I thought — I had the idea — you loved me."

Bosie made a mirthless laughing sound. "I loved you. For a brief, foolish while. The way you were on the Saint James stage that night. The world at your feet, screaming its adoration, and you high above, showing nothing but contempt. You were as a god that night."

"I should imagine even God finds it difficult to be godlike twenty-four hours a day."

"Must I get the ungodlike hours?" Bosie stretched his body back languidly in the chair, the damp bathing suit tight as skin. "Yes, look at me closely, Oscar. You are seeing me at last."

Wilde picked up his silver-topped walking stick from the far side of the table. "I am seeing a phantom," he said. And then added, more to himself than Bosie: "Perhaps that is all I ever saw."

He started for the door, praying Bosie would call him back, praying he would not. If he could make it to the door, he would be free. He could find himself again, be whole again — so long as Bosie did not call him back.

He reached the door. Bosie did not call him back.

) 7 (

Sunday. It seemed now always to be Sunday, London's impossible Sunday, the long, gray Sabbath of despair.

He had awakened shuddering after a triptych of evil dreams — all dreams of Bosie. And yet how awful to leave the land of sleep. *We term it a death*, he thought, *and yet it is waking that kills us . . .*

He spent the morning trying to amuse himself at home, but it was impossible. Constance was depressed over some revelation in the Tarot cards. Cyril was learning new ways to laugh, practicing giggly trills. Vyvyan cried.

Wilde wandered about the steamy, fog-yellowed streets of Chelsea. Alone, he felt less lonely — for a time. The shops were shut, the streets almost deserted; Chelsea was like a forlorn, neat cemetery that no one would ever come to visit. A small rain came down, filling the streets with mud and brown puddles. The rain was so faint that it might never stop; there seemed water enough to drizzle down forever.

He dawdled along the Embankment, staring at the moss-covered trees, their leaves sticking together from the rain. A sickly brown willow drooped over the river, fragile as a fern one might find pressed in a forgotten book of poems.

For long moments he would not think of Bosie, would become interested in some new project, some aspect of the landscape that cried out for description. And then all the sweet, cruel memories would come flooding back, stronger and more anguishing for the hiatus.

He walked out to the middle of the new Battersea Bridge and studied the river, a pewter thoroughfare parting the city in two. In the distance vaporous domes and towers quivered and shrugged away into the mist.

With bitterness he remembered his words of praise for the mysterious loveliness of fog. There was nothing lovely about it now, these poisonous copper-colored clouds rolling over the river, stealing over streets and buildings, suffocating any flicker of life, of hope . . .

Underneath, currents of bleak water flowed faster and faster, as if trying to outrace each other, and curled against the bridge's pillars in gray breakers, whirling back into the water's shivering stream.

Fathomless those waters seemed, the waters of Lethe, shrouded in mist. How easy it must be to answer their call, he thought: to plunge downwards into the bottomless fascination of the abyss.

He took a coach to the Brompton Oratory and heard part of a Mass. It was a new experience to listen to a sung Gloria with a bruised heart: never had the ears of his spirit been more attentive. And yet the music spoke to him, not of hope and resurrection, but of endless winding corridors and empty rooms.

He walked about the slimy brown streets of Belgravia, streets he had once loved. They were like a mausoleum. His eyes seemed attuned to the color blue, and he kept focusing on awnings, flowers in shop windows, the cloaks of passing women, all in the same melancholy tone of blue.

The blue of Bosie's eyes.

He decided to dine alone at Kettner's, scene of so many happy trysts. But when he arrived, he could not make himself go in. The restaurant, which had only a few days before seemed so festive and radiant with life, now appeared gaudy, grim, pretentious. He was ashamed of ever having cared for it, for anything connected with Bosie.

Yet anything not connected with Bosie seemed empty of any tremor of meaning.

It was over. The small fire that had warmed his life — for how short a time — extinguished. He was not sorry. When so fair an edifice could harbor such dark specters, it was better to be free. Bosie was incapable of respecting him even enough to tell the truth, if he knew what truth was. Whatsoever is harmonically composed delights in harmony: Bosie preferred chaos. He was crude, and attracted to what was crude, as uncultivated and tasteless as any of his lordly peers. He lacked even humor: he would miss the point of a brilliant epigram but cackle mindlessly over the tiresome drawings in *Punch*. And self-satisfied!

There would be others. As wonderful as Bosie. More wonderful. And yet Wilde was afraid. Afraid of the terrible power creatures got over him the moment he knew he held them fascinated; for he was able to resist those he was attracted to, but not those who were attracted to him.

And to what were they drawn? They loved the myth of Oscar Wilde he had created, and neither knew nor cared to know the real person buried within. No one — not even Constance — was able to love that hungry, frightened, hidden Oscar Wilde. They wanted the performance, the pose.

He passed a bent-over vendor, huddled in a doorway, turning chestnuts with tongs, looking in the red glow from his charcoal fire like a medieval torturer. A handkerchief was jammed into his back pocket: a soft periwinkle blue.

Perhaps, after all, love demands that one transcend oneself continually, that one die and be reborn, again and again. This then was the failure of his love and Bosie's: there had been no rebirths.

Deaths only. He had been flax, mere flax, and Bosie flames of fire.

The fog rose, thinned, thickened. It had its own seven veils, and seventy times seven. It reeked of coal fumes, sulfur, brimstone, soot — all the devil's stenches. For an instant, in the midst of it, he beheld a brown disk, glowing like a new penny — and realized with a pang that it was the sun.

He would think no more of Lord Alfred Douglas. He was sorry for the boy, sorry — how vain it sounded! — that Bosie would now have to live without the excess of love that only one so excessive as himself could offer. The boy so desperately needed it.

At the same time, he feared that Bosie's real tragedy was that he was not unhappy!

And he felt, as far off steamers on the river wailed and moaned and people hurried past like spirits stealing from their graves, that it was not just the loss of love that was tragic, but love's very existence, its fragile, ever-optimistic trembling on the brink of new possibilities, when life — real life — was nothing but a continual parting, a continual *adieu*.

) 8 (

Working on the play was difficult. Sarah was drawing *Salomé* ever closer to herself, twisting it more and more into her own creation. He hadn't the will to stop her. He had hardly even the inclination.

She was dredging up from her depths far too much melodrama, becoming cloying in the process, coarsening the role. His lines contained sensuality enough: that element if anything required underplaying. His delicate, perverse drama of the shadows was being transformed into a maudlin puppet show, and he could not bring himself to care. He seemed, in fact, to be fascinated, hypnotized, watching the slow, exquisite destruction of his play.

) 9 (

"Cyril has become impossible!" Constance cried. The rain had been humming its endless dirge all the afternoon.

Wilde put down his pen and went to embrace her, but she pulled away. "He needs a father's touch, and his father is never in the house."

"I am in the house now, Constance," he said softly.

"Working on your play. Is nothing else of importance to you but scribbling?" She had given up all interest in clothes, and now went about in fatuous dresses that would look provincial in Manchester. She had given up her interest in the Golden Dawn as well, or so it seemed. She would not speak to him on the subject anymore.

"What has Cyril done this time?" he said carefully.

"Tortured his brother, beaten him, kicked him about like a rag doll. Poor Vyvyan! It is a dreadful thing to see. Cyril has a vicious streak, which he certainly never got from me! I try to tell him to pray for it to be removed. He refuses point-blank! And that, Oscar, is your doing. With all your mockery of morals and faith. Cyril will be an atheist one day, I am sure of it — if he isn't one already."

There would be no more work done on *Salomé* this afternoon. It had been a mistake to try to write at home. He wished he might be anywhere in London but here. He thought of the pubs around Saint James's Theatre, the ones off Charing Cross Road. But it would be terrible if Bosie suddenly appeared. And terrible if he did not. "Perhaps Cyril has stumbled upon some deeper spiritual truth. 'Unless ye become as little children . . .'"

"Stop mocking me!"

"Darling, I was doing nothing of the —"

"Perhaps the child needs *guidance,* Oscar. Of a kind only a father can provide. One who is home in the evening every once in a while!" Her body suddenly relaxed, seemed almost to collapse upon her. "I'm sorry," she said, her voice dull. "I am turning into a foul-tempered old harridan." She looked at him questioningly. "It's true, isn't it! I have become an impossible person to live with. Why? Why is this happening?"

But he was unable to answer. "I am going to speak to that young hellion," he said, starting for the door.

The nursery was bordered with a gigantic alphabet and papered with a Morris print of tree limbs and pomegranates. A tall cabinet held books and toys, and high at the top of it were objects the boys must "aspire to": gifts, mostly from his mother, they were not yet ready for. One was a fat stuffed partridge on a wheeled board, with a long red pull-rope. It had not been difficult keeping the toy from the children, since they were both terrified of it. On the same shelf was a copy of De Quincey's *Confessions of an English Opium-Eater* in jeweled leather, given to Cyril on his fourth birthday ("A child is never too young to be exposed to fine prose," Lady Wilde had explained).

Hanging on the walls were framed pictures from fairy-tale books, and in the dim afternoon light the castles and forests, elves and medieval queens had an aura of deep melancholy: Wilde wondered if the children felt it. Cyril was seated at the window, staring out at the soft, steady rain in his navy blue knickers and jacket, white shirt, and navy blue tie. In a bowl next to him postage stamps glued to bits of envelopes were soaking in water.

"Now, my little man, what is this I hear about your brother and yourself?"

"Don't have any brother." Cyril reached into a box and produced a battered clock.

"You most certainly do have a brother, and you are going to have to learn to treat him properly."

Cyril pried off the back of the clock and studied the cogs and wheels inside. When Constance had first given him the broken old clock, he had taken it apart and somehow managed to put it all together again. To everyone's astonishment, the clock had begun ticking. In the storm of congratulations, however, Cyril had decided to demonstrate how he had perpetrated this miracle by undoing the clock once more, and it had never ticked again.

He looked up at his father with a pose that was becoming increasingly characteristic, one eye closed and his lower lip jutting out. "Mama says the missions in Africa need people most awfully. Why can't we send Vyvyan?"

Wilde lifted the boy, taller, heavier than just a few weeks before, up onto his knee. "To Africa! Dear, dear, your mama and I would miss Vyvyan terribly if he were to go all the way to Africa. And so, you little scoundrel, would you."

Cyril leaned his face back on his father's shoulder, a smaller, more perfect version of Wilde's own face. He was frowning with the effort to solve the Vyvyan problem for good. "Then why don't we throw him in the Thames? To teach him a lesson. Then he wouldn't be crying all the time and riding other people's bicycles and falling off. Vyvyan doesn't *belong* with us. He isn't strong or clever or *anything*."

He refused to take any pleasure in Wilde's dandling him; the matter was too serious for such levity.

"Vyvyan," said Wilde, "happens to be a *very* clever little boy. It is a different kind of cleverness from yours. Surely you wouldn't want him to be another little Cyril?"

The child had a better idea. "Why don't we give him to Miss Grahame? Miss Grahame needs a little boy."

Wilde was studying the shining wet leaves in the backyard trees, remembering his own childhood's endless rainy afternoons. "You have been very wicked with Vyvyan and, more important, you have been very wicked with your mother. You have made her cross and unhappy. Now I want you to kneel down at once and ask God to forgive you and do his best to turn you into a good little boy."

"Miss Grahame would *love* a little boy like Vyvyan instead of all those cats. Why don't we give Vyvyan to Miss Grahame for just a few weeks?"

"Cyril?"

Turning on his father a murderous scowl, the child slipped to his knees. "OurFatherwhichartinheavenhallowedbeThyname . . ." He crossed himself and rose.

"Is that all?" said Wilde. "Isn't there something you are forgetting to ask God to do for you?"

Cyril sighed from his very depths. "Will he do what I ask?"

"He might."

Cyril's eyes were closed, his face squeezed tight with concentration. Wilde was pressing his lips tight together to keep from laughing. There was a long silence. At last Cyril crossed himself again and scrambled to his feet.

"Well!" said his father. "Do you feel better now?"

"Much better, Papa." He dug in a drawer for an old perfume bottle of Constance's.

"You asked for God's help, I presume?"

"Yes, Papa. Let me show you a magic trick." He held up the bottle for a moment, then, after passing it behind his back, produced it once again, without its glass top. The top skittered across the floor.

"Astonishing! But what exactly was your prayer, if I may ask?"

Cyril smiled craftily. "I prayed with all my heart that God would make Vyvyan a good boy."

"But that's the problem exactly!" cried Constance, when Wilde repeated the story to her over tea. "The child has no sense of reverence whatsoever. How can you laugh, Oscar! There is nothing amusing about it."

Though he had promised himself only one scone, Wilde reached for a second, and lavished butter upon it. "Cyril is wiser than any of us," he said with a sigh. "Instinctively he knows that there is no way to have the thorn in one's side removed. One might as well pray to have it removed from someone else . . ."

) 10 (

When Wilde entered the saloon bar of the Crown, he was pleased to see so many familiar faces — but pained, and relieved, that Bosie's was not one of them.

He threw his arms about Max and Reggie, standing at the bar. "My dears, I have just learned of a new Gospel that has been discovered in the Holy Land, as a result of which I am going to have to change the ending of *Salomé*."

He knew nothing of this Gospel, Max confessed.

"It seems that after Salomé won the head of the Baptist, she brought it to a Nubian philosopher in homage, for the young man was as young and fair to look upon as he was wise. Smiling, the young philosopher said: 'There is only one thing I truly desire, my beloved. And that is your own head.' At this the lovely dancer turned pale and withdrew. That same evening a slave presented the philosopher with a golden dish on which rested a severed head with solemn, lovelorn eyes. The beautiful wise young man glanced at it, exclaimed, 'Take this disgusting bloodstained thing away!' — and went on with his reading of Plato."

"Lovely, Oscar," said Reggie. "I hope you have written this 'new Gospel' down."

At every sound of the door opening, Wilde's eyes darted towards it. "I was unable to, Reggie. I had far too much time."

"Is it true, Oscar," said Max, "that you have stolen most of your paradoxes from Chuang-tzu?"

"All of them, dear boy. And in return, Chuang-tzu is translating *Dorian Gray* into Mandarin and claiming it as —" He drew back, startled, when a child darted in front of him. But it was not a child.

"Are you quite, quite satisfied, Oscar?" said Lionel Johnson, standing hands on hips, weaving slightly.

He seemed to have become smaller, paler, more fragile, and his gray eyes were sunken and weary. Wilde frowned. "Dear boy, it is hardly three in the afternoon: early for you to be up, isn't it?"

"Do you not in the least regret what you have done?"

Embarrassed, Wilde smiled at the others. "My only regret, Lionel, is for what I have *not* done. But whatever are you talking about?"

Lionel was pouting like an infant on the verge of tears. "What I once thought your strength, I now see is your weakness. What I thought was your virtue has changed into your vice." He raised his glass aloft, like a torch. "A toast, gentlemen," he cried, turning in a slow circle. He stopped in front of Wilde. "To the destroyer of a soul." He tipped the glass to his lips and, finding it empty, blinked in surprise.

"Hush, Lionel," said Reggie.

"I will *not* hush. Until this fiend got hold of him, he was the dearest, most innocent boy I ever knew."

"I take it," Wilde said, his cheeks catching fire, "that you are referring to Lord Alfred Douglas."

Lionel lurched before him, barely reaching to the knot of Wilde's cravat. "I would kill you for what you have done, Oscar! Only I fear divine retribution. Think of it: an eternity in Hell. Next to you!"

Razors seemed to be slicing through Wilde's entrails. "Lionel, you are drunk!" he said.

Lionel raised himself up on tiptoe, as tall as he could, as if trying to match Wilde's height. But he only leaned farther and farther backwards. Reaching the extremity of imbalance his spine would allow, he remained poised for a moment, gave Wilde a ferocious scowl, and at the top of his lungs shouted: "I believe in the Holy! Roman! Catholic! Church!" Then he crashed to the floor.

Wilde was so shaken he could barely lift him. "Max! Reggie!" He carried the astonishingly light body to a chair; Lionel opened his eyes and tried to stand. Le Gallienne was in a corner with Dowson, but they were both too drunk to be of any use.

Max took charge: Lionel was only a little smaller than he, and he was able to hold him comfortably propped against a column. "I will get him to his bed," said Max. "Coming, Reggie?"

"Keep him outside a moment," Reggie said. "The air will do him good." Once Max was out of earshot, he clasped Wilde by the shoulders. "Oscar. Pay no heed to Lionel."

"I know, dear boy," said Wilde, looking away. "Dear Lionel. He is rarely rational, but he is never dull." He nodded to the barman for a drink. "There is always something so vicious and yet so impotent about the violence of literary people. No matter how righteous they proclaim their cause to be, it is really always a question of rhetoric."

"I cannot bear to see you hurt, Oscar," Reggie said. "You who are so careful never to hurt anyone else."

Wilde laughed bitterly. "You see kindness in everyone, Reggie, because there is so much kindness in you."

An old man at the bar was showing off his mongrel dog, little more than a puppy. He was a strange old man, overeager to please, with a sly boyish face, and he held a lump of sugar over the puppy's head. Reggie turned away, chewing his lip. "But I think — Oscar, I fear I must hurt you even more."

Wilde gave him a questioning look.

"I pray I am doing the right thing, telling you this, Oscar. I only hope the truth — will set you free."

Wilde downed his brandy and soda. "The truth?"

The mongrel puppy was walking frantically about on its hind legs; the lump of sugar was always higher than it could reach. Reggie lowered his voice: "That whole business between Bosie and Mason —"

"Mason? Bosie's servant?"

"No." Reggie was in an agony trying to phrase the words. "Mason was Bosie's — lover."

Wilde merely stared.

"One of his lovers," Reggie went on. "There have been — many."

The dog was thrown the lump of sugar, and immediately began pawing the old man's leg for more. "Mason, Bosie's *lover?* But that is impossible." No one appeared very interested in the puppy's dancing, and the old man looked downcast. "When I met Bosie he was as chaste as the icicle! He could never — Mason! Someone as contemptible as that!"

Beads of sweat dotted Reggie's brow. "Mason was the best of them, Oscar! Bosie always picked the vilest, most dissolute specimens he could find. Telegraph boys. Grooms. Racing touts. Worse.

The more disreputable they appeared, the more they fascinated him. He has repeatedly been beaten, robbed, vandalized. It has only made him avid for more.''

''Reggie, please, I don't wish to —'' He could not finish the sentence.

Reggie fell silent, mopping his brow with a silken handkerchief. He did not smoke usually, but now he accepted one of Wilde's cigarettes. The man with the dog had requested a saucer from the barman, and now filled it with lager.

''Bosie — and Mason?'' Wilde said, his eyes closed tight.

''Mason was honest, at least. He turned on Bosie because of the brutal, inhuman way he was treated. Like a —'' He glanced down at the floor, where the mongrel puppy was lapping at the saucer of beer. ''Like a stray dog, affection lavished on him one moment, every kind of humiliation the next.''

The Crown's stucco walls seemed to be shrinking and expanding, shrinking and expanding, as if the room were gasping for breath. Hatred for Reggie welled up in Wilde. Why was he saying false, revolting things? He was jealous — of Bosie's beauty, of Bosie's charm. He was trying to make Bosie appear as ugly as himself in the only way possible to him: through lies. Vile, detestable lies.

He knew they were not lies. He despised himself for allowing such thoughts to pass through his mind. Reggie was of all the young men he knew the kindest, the most generous, the best.

''When?'' Wilde said. ''When did this all begin?'' He was hoping, absurdly, that it was his friendship with Bosie that had caused this vile behavior, so that at least to that extent there would have been a meaningful connection between them — even if it must be a sordid one.

''As long as I've known him. A year at least. As long as he's been at Oxford. And probably before.''

When he saw that no one remained long interested in his dog's antics, the young-old man grew sullen, staring down at the dog with hostility. Wilde's hand clung tight to the bar. ''But Lionel is Bosie's closest friend. He must have known all this. Why would he insist that it was I —?''

Reggie buttoned up his coat. ''Lionel is like a child, with a child's narrowness of vision and a child's hardness of heart. Lionel sees what he wants to see. And alcohol helps him to see nothing more.''

Wilde called for another drink, but when the barman began carefully pouring, he snatched the brandy bottle from him. "Why — why did you tell me, Reggie?" he said, filling his glass. "It is necessary to know. I am glad to know. And yet — how sweet it would be to believe as I did one hour ago.''

"I must go, Oscar. Max is waiting. I pray I have done the right thing.''

"One hour ago — I thought I was unhappy!'' The man with the mongrel opened the barroom door and kicked the worried-looking puppy out into the street; then he himself stalked out, slamming the door.

Reggie stared in that direction distastefully. "Please, Oscar — never mention this conversation to Bosie. I am afraid of him. Afraid of what he might do to me.'' He smiled bitterly. "Bosie is always in search of new people to hate. He *needs* them. Sometimes I think he pursues friendships merely as a way of recruiting future enemies!''

Wilde looked away. "Bosie spells Friendship — like Love — with a capital *I*.'' He put an arm on Reggie's shoulder. "No power on earth — no power in Heaven, for that matter — could ever make me speak to that —'' He shook his head solemnly from side to side. "I swear to you, Reggie, if I ever cross Lord Alfred Douglas's path again, I will turn and walk the other way . . .''

) 11 (

On the bare stage of the theater, he sat at a table smoking a cigarette, fanning himself with the pages of script he was supposed to be correcting. It was urgent that he work out a way of getting Iokanaan moved from his cistern to the stage, but in fact he was permitting — even inviting — one dark-colored fantasy after another to distract him.

He heard a commotion in the wings and then the stage manager appeared, followed by a tall individual in a heavy black coat, walking with all the gravity of a pallbearer.

"Mr. Wilde,'' said the stage manager apologetically. "This gentleman is from the Lord Chamberlain's office. He says he must see you.''

"I don't know the Lord Chamberlain," said Wilde, wearily taking on the role of himself.

"My name is Pigott," the man said, removing his coat and folding it neatly on the back of one of the folding chairs. "I am the Lord Chamberlain's Examiner of Plays."

"Ah! You I am familiar with, Mr. Pigott, in action if not in person." He shook the man's cold, thin hand and bade him sit, trying not to act on an impulse to wipe his hand clean. "I have long been aware of your chastening presence in the theater — lurking in the wings, as it were."

"Why, thank you, Mr. Wilde." In his dull brown suit Pigott looked, Wilde thought, like a boiled potato turning dark with age. "We try to do our best, Mr. Wilde — for playwrights and public both." He smiled his hearty mortician's smile and rubbed his hands. "I have the duty of informing you, Mr. Wilde, that this — um — play of yours —" He opened his pigskin case, which for some reason appeared to be moist, even slimy, and reached out a dossier. "Yes, a play by Mr. Oscar Wilde with the title *Salomé*."

Wilde gently corrected his pronunciation. "The play is about a princess of a foreign land, Mr. Pigott, not a length of sausage."

"Now," said Pigott, squinting at a page of notes copied in a prim, narrow hand, "by the rights invested in His Excellency the Lord Chamberlain, Sir Nigel Orme, by Her Majesty the Queen, the play *Salomé* by one Oscar Fingal O'Flahertie Wills Wilde is denied a production license and may not under penalty of law be produced in England, Scotland, Wales, or Ireland."

Wilde was watching Pigott with such fascinated distaste that he had only half been listening to his words. "My dear man, whatever are you saying?"

"It's all quite clear, sir — clear as I can make it," said Pigott, chuckling. "The play, in this case at least, cannot go on."

"Let me see that." Wilde snatched the document from him and glanced over the crabbed lines. "Kindly tell me the author of this rather tiresome joke so I may congratulate him on his lack of taste."

Pigott peered at him with his tiny, red-rimmed Peeping Tom eyes. "His Honor the Lord Chamberlain, Sir Nigel Orme, sir. It was him who sent me. By the rights invested in him by Her Majesty the —"

"You have read my play, presumably? You're not going to tell

me there's anything in it that could be called indecent? It couldn't
be more moral!''

Pigott read down the paragraphs of his document, shaking his
head from side to side. ''Nothing here about indecency, no, sir.''
Then he glanced about the theater to see if anyone might be close
enough to hear. Lowering his voice, he said: ''I thought it was
thrilling, sir.'' Then he screwed up one eye into a hideous, con-
torted wink, at the same time releasing from his thin lips a long,
purple tongue covered with froth.

Wilde shuddered. ''If you agree it is not indecent, then whatever reason can there be to ban my play?''

''The Bible's not permitted, sir.''

''The   what?''

Pigott giggled. ''The Bible. It cannot be presented on the English stage. As being disrespectful. Nothing personal, Mr. Wilde.''

''You're joking,'' said Wilde. ''You have to be. The only really
artistic subjects are all B.C.''

Oh, no, sir. A French gentleman a while back wanted to put on
an opera here, all about Samson and Delilah. *Very* exciting, that!''
He looked about and twisted his face into another terrible wink,
giving Wilde a nudge with his shoulder. ''A great deal of sensuality! But we couldn't grant him a license for it, oh, no, sir. The
Bible, you see.''

''There can be no such law. I refuse to believe it.''

Pigott's mouth twisted into a cold, gray smile. ''But there is,
sir. A jolly old law, at that. It's dated —'' He glanced once again
into the pages of the dossier. ''Dated fifteen thirty-nine, sir. Why,
the Magna Charta itself can't be much older.''

''My play is to be banned because it is about an incident from
the Bible? Yet you are willing to license every kind of frivolity,
every kind of vulgarity! A dreadful piece by a Mr. Charles Brookfield recently appeared, mocking me and one of my finest works,
in the most amateurish and despicable fashion. Fortunately it closed
almost immediately. Still, you didn't hesitate to license *that*, which
was indeed an affront to morals. Why should you object to *Salomé*, which like everything I write is beautiful, uplifting, and
therefore utterly moral?''

Pigott seemed to be having a good time, warming himself at
Wilde's wrath. ''It's not my doing, sir. If it was up to me, now,

I'd say give us all the indecency you like! But, sir, it's the law.
I'm here to uphold the law, that's my job."

"The law?" said Wilde, grasping for his green suede coat, thrown
carelessly over a carpenter's horse. "Then we are going to have to
change the law!"

) 12 (

But the law, to Wilde's chagrin, was not to be changed. Not a
word of it. To official after official he fulminated, able to impress
not a one of them with his literary standing, with the requirements
of art, with common sense. The law would not be changed — for
him, for anyone.

Was this, then, all the respect his fame had earned him? How
little power, after all, the bitch goddess wielded! For once, he could
not wheedle, he could not coax, he could not charm. And as much
as the banning of the play grieved him, this humiliating sense of
his own impotency was more painful still.

Striding through the fog-laden streets he found himself again
and again close to tears. Everything he had been living for was
vanishing. His world — the world of imagination and drama he
had created for himself — was sliding away from his grasp, turning into an ordinary, tedious, dreary place. The loss of Bosie had
created a maelstrom, and everything beautiful and meaningful was
being sucked down into it.

The most dreadful thing to consider was how to tell Sarah. After
her great expenditure of time on *Salomé*, the considerable amount
of money she had put into it, and — most critical for Sarah — the
huge store of emotional energy she had invested, how would she
react to the play's abortion?

He journeyed with mixed hope and dread to the villa she had
rented in Saint John's Wood. He, after all, was the party most
wounded. She might very well be flooded with compassion for him
in his loss. On the other hand —

The maid led him through rooms filled with trunks and boxes,
statues, caged animals, lengths of fantastic tissues sprawling across
the floors. She opened the door to a large drawing room, and a
fragrance of flowers and animal hide enveloped him.

A handsome young boy was sitting on a high stool in a shaft of
sunlight, reading a letter. He wore a loose white costume like a

clown's and held a long silver leash in one hand, at the end of which a thin black monkey was secured. At the boy's feet were piles of unopened mail.

"*Cher!*" cried the boy, leaping off the stool and rushing over to kiss Wilde on the cheek. "No matter how many letters of admiration I get, there are never enough!" Even when he realized the laughing Pierrot was in fact Sarah Bernhardt, Wilde went on seeing her as a boy.

The monkey, she explained, was the gift of an unimportant Rhodesian king. The Archbishop of Paris had promised to baptize him for her, and she was going to name him Charles Darwin. Would Oscar care to be one of the godfathers?

"I should like nothing better," he said. Glancing at her slender rump, he wondered if there might be truth in the rumor that Sarah was not a woman at all.

But why was he looking so serious, she demanded, on such a heavenly day? She was delighted he had come, she told him, falling backwards into a Turkish corner of pillows covered with silks and skins. Now they could talk about rewriting Herod's speech about the jewels so that *she* could speak those rhythmic, those perfumed, those wickedly wonderful words. In her white hand she clutched a cambric handkerchief trimmed with pearls.

He slipped down onto a zebra skin across from her. Everywhere he looked he seemed to see the face or paws of some dead beast. "I'm afraid I have something very, very disagreeable to tell you," he said, the smell of rose and mimosa making him feel close to nausea.

But nothing could be so disagreeable as all that, she insisted. He must be like her: philosophical. Anyone who had to endure the torments of a passionate heart, as she did, was not going to take any of life's lesser agonies with great seriousness.

"I am so glad you feel that way, dear Sarah!"

With a twisting gold brooch — a lizard with gleaming emerald eyes — she fastened a sprig of gardenia to her breast. "When you have existed such a long time as I, Oscar, you will also be indifferent to the little stupidities of Fate."

He outlined the details of the decision from the Lord Chamberlain's office.

She nodded, laughed heartily at his description of Pigott. "Ah, well," she said, and pondered deeply. There was a silence. Had she understood correctly? This man Pigott, he was able to prevent her from playing Salomé? He had that power? Is that what Oscar was trying to say?

Yes, alas, it was.

Sarah nodded. She exchanged Charles Darwin's leash for a collar of fat baroque pearls, to which she attached another leash of smaller pearls, and led the monkey hopping across the room. "Elisabeth!" she called at the door, and her golden voice echoed through the corridors of the house. Sarah gave the monkey a kiss on the mouth and tossed him into the arms of the arriving maid, who ran off shrieking. Sarah closed the door and leaned against it, her head bowed, her arms folded primly together.

Suddenly she was staggering across the room. "I cannot breathe! I cannot breathe!"

Wilde rushed to her assistance, but Sarah flung him away. She came to rest at an ormolu chest covered with Chinese vases and alabaster urns. With a movement of slow, deliberate finesse her hand brushed blindly over the articles on the chest. It stopped at a Ming vase, a cool apple green.

The vase hurtled across the room. Inches above Wilde's head it shattered into a wall-to-ceiling mirror, which it cracked, sending bits of porcelain flying in all directions.

"Sarah!"

Object after object came flying towards him, vases exploding in the air like rockets. She flew to the curtains, ripping them down over her. "I suffocate! I must have air!"

In a matter of seconds the room was wrecked. Wilde cowered on a sofa, terrified to move. The walls began to reverberate. Sarah was screaming, her voice so shrill as to be barely audible.

"Sarah! Calm yourself!"

She turned on him then, one hand spread wide before her like the clawed limb of an animal. He backed up, stumbling over yards of velvet, staring at her fingernails with their red lacquer the color of fresh blood. She advanced, her eyes wild, her lips drawn back over sharp white teeth. The sound she made was something between a hiss and a snarl. On a narrow inlaid table heaped with papers and books lay a long, curved Turkish knife. Sarah's eyes lit on it. Then the knife was in her hand.

"Sarah, we must be sensible!" Over a bolt of gold-shot velvet he tripped, and landed supine on a leopard skin. She was on top of him, teeth clenched, panting. She raised the knife high.

"Sarah!"

The knife came down on his chest with a hideous thud. He cried out, closed his eyes. The pain was so intense it went beyond feeling. He felt nothing, nothing at all.

Darkness.

But surely he should feel some little sting?

He opened his eyes at Sarah's shouts — shouts of laughter. She was holding high the dagger, pressing a button and making the blade appear and disappear. *"Mon cher Oscar!"* she cried, when she was able to speak again. "I have given you the great fear, no?"

"Sarah, what a — what a dreadful thing to do."

Screaming with laughter, she stumbled across the debris to the door and shouted to Elisabeth to bring champagne. Extending her hands to Wilde, she hauled him to his feet.

By the time the maid arrived, they were seated, laughing with each other, on either end of a long, S-shaped sofa covered with tiger and wildebeest skins. In her lap Sarah was dandling Satan, the snake she used for her death scene in Cleopatra, easing a ruby bracelet up the creature's middle. The maid betrayed not the slightest surprise at the room's condition, simply deposited the champagne and glasses on the chased copper table in front of them and fled.

"There are two people who will never be old, Oscar. You and I. Because we are, both of us, actors. We are all the time on the stage. Even when we are all alone, we are playing that we are all alone. A thing can move us very much, *very* much, but still we are acting. And always we are superb, because we are not acting for *them.*" With a contemptuous wave she indicated all the world outside the chaos of that room. "We are the actors. But we are the spectators, as well. We are acting for us — for ourselves."

"That is our glory," said Wilde, raising his glass in a toast.

She looked about the debris of the room and for an instant a tremor of disgust seemed to go through her. "That is our trag-edy," she replied.

Their glasses clinked.

) 13 (

"But you *can't* move to France, Oscar," said Frank Harris, puffing on his fat cigar. "London would be so dull without you."

From their corner table at the Café Royal, amidst the tarnished cupids and caryatids of the Domino Room, they commanded a view of the entranceway, bordered by palm trees, and of the vestibule beyond, where women — most of them in the latest fashions — wandered in and out of the newspaper shop as if they were doing something they ought not to be.

"Oh, can't I!" said Wilde. The band had been playing "Partir est mourir un peu" and now swept into "The Teddy Bear's Picnic"; Wilde looked as if he might take out all his rancor on the violinist. "The most outrageous thing is that not a single *actor* complains."

"Yes, Oscar." Harris was clearly impatient to return to the great literature of the ages, a subject about which he knew too little and spoke too much, but Wilde was not to be pacified. "It is an insult to their art as much as mine, yet they remain silent! Even Irving, who is forever prating about the grandeur of the actor's —" A waiter passed, uneasily balancing a glass and bottle on a silver tray. He was about seventeen, with blond hair tight-curling like lamb's wool and a face filled with all the flushed, hopeful sweetness of youth. "Look, Frank!" whispered Wilde. "Don't you think —"

"No, Oscar. I see no resemblance whatsoever between that fresh young face and the tight mean features of Lord Alfred Douglas."

"Frank! I was going to compare him to that statue on the Acropolis — the youth carrying a heifer or a lamb or whatever it is," said Wilde, blushing. He turned to the clouded mirror behind them, in which the crowded room was transformed into a hall in a sultan's palace, hung with veils of costly incense. In it he saw someone approaching their table, a rather plain young man whom he seemed to recognize from somewhere.

"Oscar — ?"

"What a coincidence!" said Frank Harris in his most unctuous voice.

Wilde turned slowly, fearfully. It was a moment before he could equate the small, pale, nervous youth standing before him with the creature who had been the constant companion of his thoughts these past weeks, months. "Dear boy," he whispered hoarsely.

"I heard about your play. I wanted to tell you how terribly sorry I am."

Hands trembling, Wilde reached for his cigarette case. "I have endured greater losses. Frank, you know Lord Alfred Douglas, of course?" No — he was not going to succumb. A door in him had shut against Bosie forever.

"Is it true you are going to live in France?" said Bosie, never glancing at Harris.

Wilde's voice sounded alien to him. "In this benighted country, some preposterous archaic law is considered more important than the dignity of an artist. If you could *see* Her Majesty's censor, the aptly named Mr. Pigott. It can only have been by some oversight that a person so ignorant and incapable was not made Prime Minister. Yes, Bosie, I plan to become a citizen of France. A poet is appreciated there."

"The fools!" said Bosie, smiling a shy, pleading smile.

"The older you get, Lord Alfred, the more you resemble your father," said Frank Harris mellifluously, relighting his cigar.

Bosie stared at him a moment, frowning, then turned back to Wilde. "Oscar, I've missed you. Terribly."

Wilde had to look away. The tears frozen in him all these cruel weeks now threatened to melt. "Bosie," he said tentatively. If a door in him had shut, a window seemed to be opening in its stead. "Our first true quarrel. And our last. Dinner? At the Connaught?"

"Oscar —" said Harris, looking troubled.

"Nothing could give me greater pleasure!" Bosie said.

"Will you excuse us, Frank?" said Wilde, rising. "I hear the horses of Apollo pawing at the gate — or is it only a waiting coach? Lord Alfred and I are going to spend the evening itemizing all the laws of God and man. I am determined that we shall break them, one by one . . . ."

PART FIVE

In Praise of Shame

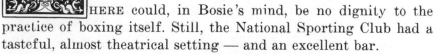

THERE could, in Bosie's mind, be no dignity to the practice of boxing itself. Still, the National Sporting Club had a tasteful, almost theatrical setting — and an excellent bar.

How very like his father, then, to eschew the club and come to a place like this instead — if, indeed, he *was* here. The night attendant had only just come on duty and was not certain which part of the premises the marquess might be found in, but he advised Bosie to stroll about until he found him.

Bosie stopped first in the small gymnasium, where at a pair of hanging leather bags men in tights and bare to the waist were lined up, watching silently as two of their number, plump and hairy as weary old bruins in the zoo, attacked the bags with idiot determination, their boots sliding over the sawdust floor. And no sign of his father anywhere. The smells of flesh, fat, sweat were as powerful as ammonia; he wanted to hold a handkerchief to his nostrils, but was afraid that the men might laugh.

Sheets serving as curtains were stretched over the entranceway to the bathing rooms, and he peered into one cubicle after another, but his father was nowhere amidst the clouds of steam.

He felt young and fresh in his new lounge suit for the fall, a sandy silk with legs as tight as on a jockey's uniform. His ivory shirt made a muted background for the superb cravat of red moiré silk Oscar Wilde had brought him from Paris, and he wore his greatcoat of camel hair hanging from the shoulders like a cape. It amused him to be dressed so brilliantly in such a setting, and he wished some friend might appear and see him; but it was hardly the kind of place people of his circle would patronize.

He was keyed up. There was invariably the sense, before any rendezvous with his father, of something important, something exciting in the air.

He crossed through the gymnasium leading to the boxing room, delighted with the astonished glances he inspired. This room, larger than the other gymnasium, had a highly polished wood floor covered with mats of black leather upon which sweating males, alone or in small groups, performed calisthenics of various kinds. Against the far wall stood a yellowing copy of the Apollo Belvedere, its sublime form making mockery of all the overfed carcasses writhing about the floor.

Bosie was about to move on to the ring, but stopped. In a corner of the room, being lectured to by a garishly dressed Turk or Arab of some sort, was a tall, nude, wonderfully muscled young man. His body was as fine as the Belvedere's — finer, because pink and warm and throbbing with life. Surely this, Bosie decided in a rush of enthusiasm, was one of the most perfect creatures he had ever laid eyes on. Slender but powerful, he was Bosie's own age, perhaps younger, and was standing hand on hip, one leg slightly askew, in the stance of the David of Donatello.

For all his casualness, though, there was something ineffably sad about the young man's beautifully carved face, something in it of gentleness and frustrated sensuality — something, Bosie thought, so perfect as to approach sanctity.

He sucked in his breath. *If we could change places, he and I!*

He inched closer so that he might overhear the conversation. The young man spoke with a thick Irish brogue and was bargaining over a fee. The marvelous dignity of his nude body removed any suggestion of coarseness from his speech, made it seem for the moment the idiom of some messenger of the gods. The swarthy man refused the requested sum. They argued. Was it possible this slender deity was one of the out-of-work Irish laborers who hung about the clubs, knowing nothing about boxing but willing to take on professionals for a copper or two, enough for a meal? To imagine so made Bosie feel ill.

And then another thought came to him: *He needs money. I can buy him!*

The older man beckoned to a skeletal figure seated on a bench, reading the *Evening Standard*. A doctor, it appeared; at least he had a stethoscope about his neck. The doctor made a cursory examination of the superb body. The police must have insisted on this precaution since the recent death of a young boxer who, as it turned out, had entered the ring in an advanced state of starvation.

The doctor was nodding, and the dark, flamboyant man handed over a pair of tights, which the beautiful youth slipped into. They were a dirty gray and far too large for him. Then he walked out proudly into the boxing ring next door. The dark man followed. Cheers greeted their entrance. Bosie, with an ache of excitement close to nausea, took a step towards the door.

The room was far smaller than he would have expected. The ring in the center virtually filled it: there was barely room left over for two rows of benches on all sides. These were packed with spectators, shouting obscenities at the young Irishman. They were from all classes: many looked shabby and poor, but he recognized several gentlemen in their midst. His father was, for once, correct: boxing was indeed the great leveler.

Through the clouds of cigar smoke he could barely make out the face of the surly Mediterranean in tights, leaning against the ropes. He was sweating, the spectators were sweating, the very walls seemed to be sweating. The Mediterranean smiled with contempt as the Irishman slipped in through the ropes. A boy carrying a pan of jellied eels maneuvered through the crowd: "Any toff want a bit o' jelly, six or three?"

"Alfred! I've been trying to find you." His father, stripped to the waist and in loose brown tights, was striding across the room towards him, toweling his face. "The porter told me you were somewhere about." He was followed by his drunken crony, Tuzzer Williams.

"Papa!" Bosie cried, backing away from the door, feeling a strain of hysteria rising in him. Had his father noticed him staring after the beautiful young Celt? As they stood before each other Bosie felt they were going to — had to —

No: his father shrank from the embrace as much as he himself did. Strange, every time they met, it was always the same surprise. *He is so short!* Bosie thought. His father was forever riding or hunting or boxing, yet exuded no aura of physical strength or power; if anything, he seemed as nervous and raddled as an over-

worked banker or accountant. He had the instinctive fearful look
of an animal, but without an animal's grace; with his long arms
reaching down to his knees there was something almost simian about
him. Nevertheless, Bosie was, as always, strangely touched by his
father's presence. Studying the aging, wind-roughened head, with
its deepening lines of disappointment about the cheeks and eyes,
its tight hair dulling into gray, he thought: poor tragic man, I
have never once seen you laugh with joy, or smile with content-
ment. Perhaps you are above such petty emotions.

"Three rounds! Two minutes each!" barked a voice from the
ring. "Our own 'Jewey' Lavine from Hammersmith and a new-
comer, Patsy Gallagher from county Cork in Ireland." The walls
vibrated with cheers.

His father extended a thick, stubby-fingered hand. Bosie went
as if to take it — but up over his face the hand flew and into his
hair, tousling, hurting. "Time you had a haircut, isn't it?"

His retort was instant: "I haven't the money for a haircut. You
haven't sent my allowance. That's why I am here."

His father laughed uneasily, his tobacco-colored eyes glittering,
and glanced over at Tuzzer. Then he took Bosie's chin in one hand
and tilted his face up towards the unshaded chandelier. "Why are
you so sickly pale? Do they give no exercise at Oxford these days?"

Tuzzer chortled, embarrassed. He had a herculean body that was
going to fat, especially in the belly, and he was dressed in the same
loose tights as the marquess, but with a flannelette shirt to absorb
sweat. It was hard to assign an age to Tuzzer, or even a face. His
own was so battered, with the nose broken, one of the ears curled
in on itself, and so many streaks and gashes across forehead, cheeks,
and chin, that it had become a mask of scar tissue. And yet,
strangely, Bosie found something vaguely attractive about Tuzzer.
Indeed, he might once have been a beauty, and that not too long
ago.

"Don't worry, Tuzzer, we'll have the ring to ourselves as soon
as those imbeciles in there are through. Which should be a matter
of minutes. I'll be in shortly. This so-called son of mine has come
to bleed me dry." Tuzzer gave him a shy smile and moved out the
door to the ring.

Bosie was angry. "You have only to put some money into my
account, Papa: then I shall happily stop bothering you!"

His father glanced out the door to be sure Tuzzer was gone. "Don't speak of money matters in front of Tuzzer. I don't trust him."

Bosie laughed. "Tuzzer is your great friend! Your only friend, as far as I can see!"

"It's a lucky man that knows his friends, Alfred." A sound of cheers rose from the arena.

"Why do you keep staring at me, Papa?"

"Have I not the right? You're my son, as far as I know."

"What is there to stare at?"

"I was thinking of —" He did not pursue his thought. "I see no traces of my own ugly mug in yours — lucky for you. You're not such a terrible-looking mongrel, after all. And what is she up to, your mother?"

"Damus?" After a moment's consideration, Bosie said: "She needs money. Badly."

"Your mother always needs money." A rope was hanging from the ceiling and Queensberry grasped it, slowly ascending it, arm on arm. "Have you heard that Francis has been offered the title of Lord Drumlanrig?"

"I've heard," said Bosie, surprised: he had expected his father to be annoyed at the news; instead, he seemed quite pleased.

"At least *one* of my sons may amount to something," said his father, panting. He slipped his feet into the rings. "Perhaps after all I will not have failed *utterly* as a father." He let go of the rope and hung by his feet. Then he lifted himself again and swung free, landing with a crash on the floor. "But my dear Alfred, I have a crow to pick with you." He wiped his face with the towel. "A person who asked me not to reveal his name has given me some information about you. Something I must say I didn't like to hear."

Bosie's scalp prickled. "And what — what might that have been?" He was besieged by a host of dreadful possibilities.

"He saw you in the company of a certain Oscar Wilde."

Bosie gasped with relief, and turned it into laughter.

"I am told he is a man of the theater. Is that true?"

"A man of literature, Papa! Yes, I am proud to say Oscar Wilde is a friend of mine. He is my best friend, in fact, and I am his."

Now his father was standing before the parallel bars. Clutching them, he pulled up his body until he was poised high in the air.

"The man is — twice your age. As old as myself! You —" He swung himself up, and his legs caught. "You are still only a boy."

"Oscar Wilde is younger than you! And he happens to be a great admirer of my work."

Queensberry's head was hanging just a few inches from the floor. "You *do* no work!"

"My friendship with Oscar is a literary one. You, of course, would have no knowledge of such things."

His father leaped back to his feet. Massaging his shoulders, he glanced around the room, to be certain they were alone. Then, watching Bosie with a faint smile, he let out a great explosion of a fart.

Bosie winced and turned away.

"Disgusted, are you?" said his father, chuckling. "Good. A bit of disgusting is what you need. I have seen this Oscar Wilde strutting about the West End. His manner does not please me. Not one iota. I don't know what impression he wishes to give the public at large, but I for one find him — loathsome. It is not suitable for you to be seen with such a person."

There were more cheers from the ring. "How very old-fashioned you are, dear Papa!"

"Old-fashioned enough to spank that little behind of yours, Alfred, if you're not careful."

"You are not equipped to understand a person like Oscar Wilde. He is a man of fashion — the most fashionable man in London. All society adores him. He is looked up to by peasants and princes alike. And he admires me! He believes I am a very great poet."

"Fashionable!" his father spat out. The door to the boxing arena flew open and two men staggered in carrying a limp, broken figure, spattered with blood.

Bosie stared down at it a moment, then reeled backwards, crashing into his father.

Queensberry laughed. "I suppose *that* offends your poetic sensibilities!"

Only by the oversize tights, now torn and stained, could Bosie identify this battered relic as the young Irishman. Nothing about his face or body was recognizable. The skin was scraped raw like meat in a butcher's. All the bones in his body seemed to be broken.

As they carried him past, he stared up beyond Bosie, one eye closed, the other filled with blood, and from his shattered lips strings of red saliva slavered to the floor.

Hand stuffed in his mouth like a child's, Bosie turned away, shuddering with horror, with disgust. He closed his eyes, tight, and dove into his father's arms.

But Queensberry pushed him away. "What you need, my fine bucko, is toughening up!" He shouldered Bosie ahead of him into the adjoining room.

Many in the crowd had left, but a few men remained on the wooden benches, discussing the match. Tuzzer, in the ring, was shadowboxing. Bosie was still too stunned, too horrified to resist as Queensberry led him to the ring.

Queensberry slipped Bosie's camel-hair coat from his shoulders, and then his jacket. "This lad needs a lesson about life," he said, unbuttoning Bosie's shirt.

Tuzzer leaned over the ropes, nodding vaguely. "Anythin' Your Lordship says." He stepped out of the ring and jogged to Queensberry's side.

Only as the boots were slipping from his feet, and the trousers being drawn down from his legs, did Bosie make any effort to understand.

"Papa!"

"You'll thank me for this one day, Alfred. Won't he, Tuzzer?" When the red cravat would not untie under Queensberry's small, thick fingers, he yanked it over Bosie's head, tearing the silk in the process. As he pulled off the shirt, two buttons popped. Bosie, in underpants now, tried to yank free of his father's grip.

"Help me get him up there, Tuzzer!" his father cried, hardly able to speak for laughing. The men remaining on the benches were watching now, getting interested.

Then Bosie was in the ring, and Tuzzer was holding him while his father slid a glove over one hand, then the other. Bosie just stared, mesmerized, no longer resisting.

"We don't want that lovely porcelain face damaged now, do we, Tuzzer!" said Queensberry.

Bosie was staring down at the canvas, spattered with dried brown blood. His father released him then, and gave him a hard push into the far corner of the ring. Bosie hurtled into the ropes, and lost his balance. Crouching on his knees, he looked about for a means of escape.

"Fight!" his father shouted. "Act like a man for once in your life!" He slipped out of the ropes and took a seat.

"Fight!" shouted one of the spectators, brandishing a fist. Others picked up the cry. "Fight! Fight!" They began stamping in rhythm, jeering, whistling.

Tuzzer was standing before Bosie, looking apologetic, but rotating his fists dangerously. Bosie circled away from him, but the battered giant followed his every move, like a figure in a mirror.

Bosie's nostrils filled with the stench of sweat and cigar smoke. He tried to look superior to all of it, but he was trembling uncontrollably.

For an instant he saw rockets of light and, just after, spasms went through his head. He stared at Tuzzer in a fury. He had dared to strike him! Looking embarrassed, Tuzzer gave him another tap on the ear. It felt like a spear going through his head.

Enraged, Bosie swung back and fired the hardest punch he could at Tuzzer's cheek. Tuzzer just grinned at him in his foolish, friendly way.

"Fight!" the filthy animals — led by his father — kept shouting. "Fight, you little poof! Fight!"

A crunching blow to the shoulder knocked him clear to the other end of the ring, where he stumbled over a tray of sawdust. "Good man, Tuzzer!" his father yelled.

He tried to crawl out under the rope, but his father was in the ring and pulling him to his feet. He was hurled back into the center.

Tuzzer, with one hand behind his back, delivered a series of hard, delicate jabs to the ribs. Bosie shrieked with pain. Crying and determined not to, he flailed about, his arms feeling weak, boneless. Tuzzer was firing crackling punches to his face, making his head jerk back. Bosie was unable to parry a single one. His eye seemed to be puffing up. He reached up to touch it but could feel nothing for the glove.

"Try to look like a Douglas, for Christ's sweet sake!" screamed his father, his eyes popping from his head. But all Bosie could think of was that Tuzzer's gloves were wet, shiny with blood. *His* blood.

Tuzzer was waiting, his hands turning slowly, but Bosie backed away from him and lunged towards his father instead. He battered at his face with all the strength he could find. "I hate you! Hate you, hate you!" And then, with the face of a crazed beast, his father was punching him. Bosie cowered against the corner ropes, hands raised before his eyes to fend off the blows. Tuzzer was trying to pull Queensberry away. "Easy, Your Lordship, easy. You'll kill the lad!"

The pain had blended into one piercing ache, then stopped. He was afloat now, beyond pain. Feeling nothing, nothing at all. The air had coagulated in some way, and he was dissolving into it. The lights became heavenly bodies. The screaming voices transmogrified into a children's choir. He was lost in clouds, and through the clouds a presence approached, a deity. But the clouds were steam. And the deity was —

"Papa?"

He was back in childhood, in infancy, and his father was leaning over him with an expression of love and pride. There was such a lot of love in that face, so much caring, if Bosie could only find the way to deserve it. "Papa? Papa?"

He was stretched out in a cubicle, next to a tub of steaming water. A sheet hung over the entranceway. He was covered with another sheet, and with a heavy coat — his father's. It had his father's good smell.

But everything was moving, and he could not catch up with it.

"Darling boy, how sorry I am," his father was saying. He reached over a hand — hard, callused — and touched Bosie's cheek. That touch started up once again the layers of pain — so much pain. When he tried to turn, every muscle in his body seemed to cry out.

"Life, Alfred, is hard, so hard. I did it for your own good. I want you fit. I want you strong. It was never my intention to hurt you, nor any man. You must understand that, Alfred. I could never hurt you."

Bosie closed his eyes. There was no way to stop the images racing by.

"You were always my favorite, Alfred," his father said, and placed a firm hand on Bosie's shoulder.

"It . . . hurts. Papa, it . . . hurts."

His father did not remove the terrible squeezing hand, but knelt,

smiling down on him tragically. How beautiful his face was, loving, strong. If only for a moment he would stay still.

"My poor dear Alfred! If anyone were ever to touch you, I
would kill him. With these bare hands. I would never let anybody
cause you the least pain, Alfred. Believe that, my boy, if you never
believe anything else. I care for you so deeply. More than you can
ever know." And again the thick, small hand began to squeeze.

) 2 (

As they got out of the coach in front of the Royal, Bosie groaned
faintly. "Still in pain, dear boy?"

Bosie shook his head. The wounds, in fact, had all healed over
the past month — the outer ones, at least — though a certain stiff-
ness came into his limbs when he sat without moving for any length
of time. To compensate, he strode into the Royal with an unusually
jaunty step, as Wilde hung behind to pay the driver.

"You seem almost proud of the way he —"

"Please," said Bosie harshly, "let's leave my father out of it,
shall we? In any case, Oscar, it was entirely because of you." In
the lobby he stopped to glance at the new books from Paris. "My
father insisted I never see you again," he said, fingering a yellow-
covered volume. "He accused you of corrupting me. Of introducing me to disreputable people. Naturally I stood up for you." He
tossed the book back on the shelf and peered into the smoke-filled
galerie des glaces of the Domino Room. "Let's eat upstairs for a
change. The people down here look boring."

Wilde followed him up the carpeted stairs. "To which 'disreputable' people was he referring? Whistler? Sarah Bernhardt?"

Bosie surrendered his greatcoat to the little German woman at
the desk, and opened a button of his Norfolk jacket. "He says
you're a sham — common and vulgar." With a little smile, he
added: "You see, Oscar, my father is a dreadful snob!" He had
to get his coat back to retrieve the sonnet he was writing from the
inner pocket.

"We have no reservation," Wilde was saying to the maître d'hôtel.

"Perfectly all right, Monsieur Wilde."

Following him across the room, Wilde said: "I would like you
to remind the marquess that *my* father was knighted by Her Majesty for the excellency of his work in the field of optical surgery.

Whereas his own father, if I am not mistaken, never in his life did any useful thing other than to blow out his own — forgive me, Bosie.''

But Bosie was more amused than rankled as he slid into the chair the maître d'hôtel held out for him. Half the restaurant was deep in shadow, the other columned with bright noontime light streaming in the windows overlooking Regent Street, and their table, banked by potted palms, was near one of these. Bosie spread out the pages of his poem on the tablecloth. It was written on gray paper with the Savoy Hotel's monogram. '' 'I am Shame,' '' he read aloud,

> *'That walks with Love. I am most loath to turn*
> *Cold lips and limbs to fire; therefore discern*
> *And see my loveliness, and praise my name.'*

What do you think, Oscar? I can't decide whether to make it a sonnet or work it up into a ballad.''

''It outglitters Keats,'' Wilde said absentmindedly. ''I like it. Yes, I like it very much.''

The fumes rising from plates of food combined with the flames of chafing dishes and clouds of cigar and cigarette smoke to make a fragrance that was the Royal's own. The crowd was a typical London gathering, well mannered and buzzing with excitement, and composed almost entirely of attractive foreigners.

'' 'Outglitters Keats,' indeed!'' said Bosie, tearing at a piece of French bread. ''You weren't even listening.''

''Forgive me, dear boy. I am unable to clear my mind of last night's — adventure.'' He looked relieved when the waiter arrived with their drinks; he snatched his brandy and soda from the tray.

''You were shocked, I suppose? I hope so. You see, Oscar, my soul has its West End — but its Whitechapel, as well. And then there was that wonderful bit of melodrama when the maid came in this morning!'' he said, tittering into his cupped hand. ''I watched from my bath. It was exactly like a scene in a French farce — a second-rate one.''

''Whatever must she have thought! The young man was still in — your bed.''

''Who cares what a maid thinks?'' Bosie threw open the menu and glanced over the day's featured dishes. *Suprême de volaille à la Patti. Sole Beaumanoir. Turbotin paysanne.* "Everything sounds tiresome."

"It was not you who had to meet the poor woman's horrified eyes," said Wilde moodily. "Not that I blame her for being horrified."

"You're not going to start moralizing, Oscar, I hope? For if you do, I will simply get up and —" Suddenly, Bosie fell back in his chair, gasping.

"Dear boy! Whatever is wrong?"

Bosie stared, eyes agog in a waxen face, down the length of the restaurant. A tall waiter was conducting his father to a table directly across the room from them. They passed swiftly from darkness to light to darkness . . .

"Are you ill, dear boy?"

Queensberry frowned disapprovingly at the table he was assigned to, but at last shrugged and plumped himself down. He had not seen them. There was still a chance of escape.

"Oscar!" Bosie whispered. "We've got to get out of here!"

"Dear boy, I have no intention of forgoing the *saumon poché hollandaise* for anything on earth. Why ever should we?"

Bosie's voice was barely audible. "The man at the far table over there — who just sat down —"

"Is your father. Yes, I recognized the marquess at once. Regarding him from so close, I must confess I see no justification for the great awe you invest in him."

Bosie leaned over into the shadow. "He mustn't see us! Oscar, he warned me. There's no telling what he'll — you don't know how insane he is! How violent. And he detests you!"

Wilde reached a gold-tipped cigarette from his case. "I am quite capable of defending myself."

With a snort, Bosie said: "He could destroy you with a single tap!"

Wilde struck a match, and stared at him coldly in its flame. "Go over to that table at once, and invite the marquess to join us," he said, and lit his cigarette.

"You're even madder than he!"

Wilde's drink was gone, after only two swallows. "If you don't, Bosie, I shall. And that would not appear well-bred."

Smirking at Wilde, Bosie sprang to his feet. Through the shafts of sunlight he traversed the room. His father's table leaned against a banquette supporting a great urn of coppery chrysanthemums and bright green leaves. In France, Bosie thought wildly, it might be a funeral bouquet.

He stared down at his father coldly for a moment. At last, with a sigh, he said: "I would not have come over except that I was sent."

"I am not surprised to hear it." His father too was wearing a Norfolk jacket, in a dark muddy brown, that looked two sizes too big for him. The only thing it had in common with Bosie's beautifully cut one was that they were both badly in need of pressing.

"Mr. Oscar Wilde wishes me to introduce him to you."

"The last person I intend to meet."

Bosie leaned over the table and lowered his voice. "Perhaps you are afraid?"

Upper lip curling back like a wolf's, the marquess stared at Wilde's table with narrowed eyes. "Afraid?" He got to his feet.

Wilde was exhaling a long, slow puff of his cigarette when they arrived at the table.

"Father, I would like you to meet —"

"But we know each other, the marquess and I!" said Wilde, rising to his feet. "We met at least a decade ago. I have never forgotten." With a sweeping gesture, he proffered his hand. "I have been longing to run into you, my dear Queensberry. For you are certainly the only man who can help me."

"Is that so."

"Sit down, sit down." Wilde glanced at the surrounding tables secretively. "I have decided, Queensberry," he said, lowering his voice, "to become an atheist. Only I don't know how! From what I have heard, no one could be more helpful to me in my plight than you. If you will pardon an ill-chosen phrase, you are a godsend!"

"You know of my 'campaign' then," said Queensberry, his voice gruff. "If I can give it so grandiose a name."

"It is more than a campaign, Queensberry, it is a crusade, and a thankless but sublime one. You must accept your own heroism, my friend. Humility is for the hypocrite, modesty for the incompetent. That marvelous speech you made in the House of Lords — against God! How breathtaking. How courageous. I'm sure God himself was most impressed."

"Heard about that, have you?"

"Hasn't everyone? Most people disapprove, of course, but that is because they are Christians. And quite sincere — though their sincerity is little more than stereotyped stupidity."

"A good way to describe them!"

"I once knew a woman who found a live mouse in the pocket of her gown, Queensberry. She fell down dead on the spot. If I were to find generosity of spirit in any practicing Christian, the same thing would happen to me! That is why I was so thrilled to hear that you attacked them on *their own ground*. It is no exaggeration to say I was positively *dazed* with admiration. I wanted to write to you at the time, since I have always been fascinated at the typically English way in which great ideas are handled — or rather, mishandled. We are living in an age when only the dull are treated seriously. So naturally people like yourself are continually in danger of being misunderstood. I shall not go into the injustice I suffered because of my play *Salomé*."

The far wall, Bosie noted, was lined with antique mirrors, which reflected bits and patches of the diners like a brackish pond. He tried to see himself but could not.

Queensberry shifted in his seat. "A letter to me would have been wasted. I am not a literary man."

"But such an original one! I believe that to disagree with three-fourths of the English public is the hallmark of a truly original mind. What amazes me is that, despite all your iconoclastic ideas, you appear to be something of a deity among so many Londoners. It is no doubt because of what you have done for boxing, a sport about which, I must confess, I understand nothing."

Queensberry accepted a cigarette, only pausing for an instant to regard the golden tip. "And what about boxing do you not understand?"

"It seems so — brutal."

"It breeds pluck. And courage. And it is well to remember, Mr. Wilde, that in countries where boxing is unknown, the knife, the dagger, and the stiletto usually take the place of fists!"

Bosie had never before seen Wilde give such a performance; he would be asking the marquess for an autograph next!

"Of course, they are incapable of truly understanding their outstanding men, the English. They have such a talent for turning wine into water! Being Irish I can catch the nuances of English behavior far better than a native. Don't you find it a dreadful thing, being noteworthy, Queensberry? The only thing worse than being talked about, as I'm sure you've noticed, is not being talked about. You'll be my guest for luncheon, of course."

Bosie wanted to laugh out loud at the absurdity of it all. Did Wilde think his father was an out-and-out imbecile to succumb to such cheap flattery? Much as he feared and dreaded what was coming, he felt that Wilde deserved it, that just such a comeuppance was what he most needed.

"Don't mind if I do," his father said. Bosie stared at him as if he were a total stranger.

"As if in your honor," Wilde went on, "the *pièce de résistance* is salmon, rushed in this morning from a Tyneside loch." He snapped his fingers and instructed the waiter to set a fresh place at the table. "And we will begin with steamed mussels, which are quite enormous here. And perhaps a dusty bottle of Château le Tertre . . ."

To his astonishment, Bosie heard his father say: "I've heard some contradictory things about you, as well."

"All of them no doubt true. People have been going about London spreading scandalous rumors about me, with not a *trace* of falsehood in them."

The waiter set a dish of fat mussels in a buttery wine sauce before each of them. "Your plays are doing quite well, I understand," said Queensberry.

"Mr. Beerbohm Tree is directing one of them now. He is a most difficult taskmaster, alas! He asked me to cut an entire scene the other day. I was quite upset. I told him that from his point of view, what he was asking me to suppress might seem only a simple scene in a play, but for me it represented the labor of at least five minutes."

Queensberry began to chuckle. "You really sweat, do you?"

Bosie gaped at him — at both of them. How long it had been since he'd seen his father's angry face relaxed, amused, smiling. It took years off, made him recall the father of his childhood. And yet, for some reason, this upset him, made him sullen and silent.

The mussels had no taste for him, and he let his mind wander; he listened idly to the voices at the bordering tables, all with American accents. When his attention returned to Wilde and his father, they were talking about religion as the salmon arrived in a great silver salver, circled by blue flame. It took long savory moments for the waiter to extinguish the conflagration with spoon upon spoon of heavy cream.

"Are you opposed to Jesus, too?" Wilde said. "Or is it only God who meets with your disapproval?"

"I hate the whole blasted lot of biblical mucky-mucks. It's all a pack of nonsense."

Wilde looked hurt. "But Jesus is so very amusing, don't you think?"

Bosie held up his glass to catch a sunbeam's light. "Look at the marvelous clear amber glow," he said, looking rapt — but neither of them paid the slightest attention.

And then Queensberry himself began to tell stories, and not the coarse smoking-room variety he usually brandished. Bosie was surprised to find him quite apt with words. He had Wilde chortling with laughter and he himself was laughing openly, spontaneously — for the first time in Bosie's memory.

"But Nero *had* to do something about the Christians," Wilde was saying. "There he was, with everything going along quite smoothly and splendidly, when one day two provincials with the unheard-of names Peter and Paul arrived, collecting crowds and blocking traffic in the very center of Rome. Can you imagine waking up in the Golden Palace, looking out the window, and seeing your back garden cluttered up with a whole lot of *miracles?* More salmon, Queensberry, I insist. Don't you find it as lovely as the curving mouth of the Gioconda?"

His father started off on *his* ideas about Nero and the early Church, but Bosie could bear no more. "I'm going to Cadogan Square," he said. "I have studying to do."

"Admirable," said Wilde. "Your son is planning to spend his Christmas holidays working."

"About time he'd do some work," said his father, back in character.

Wilde extended his hand to Bosie in the most gentlemanly fashion imaginable. Bosie felt like spitting on it.

"This then will be a rather long *au revoir,* dear boy. I shall be going down to Torquay tonight, most probably, with my wife and children. But I do hope to be back in London for a day or so around Christmas. We must have a meal together.'' And then, to Queensberry: "Do you know Torquay? Lovely place. You will have to come and stay with Constance and me some weekend.''

Bosie bowed, first to Wilde and then to his father. Somehow he made it to the lavatory before he threw up all his lunch.

) 3 (

Bosie felt so weak in the knees and light-headed as he crossed the Regent Street Quadrant that he wondered if the food might have been poisoned. He approached the rank of waiting hansoms, but hesitated. He had no desire to go to Cadogan Square and an empty house.

He knew that his feeling of illness was related to the excesses of the night before. He knew, too, that he only wanted more — more of the same. *Wanted* was not the word. He *must* have more.

Every face he passed had something in it that made him ache with discontent. The always startling, always inevitable lineaments of the beautiful filled him, as ever, with despair, but even in the comfortable features of the less favored some smug, reproachful evidence of the hand of God seemed to be visible, seemed to be shining out from every face, indeed, but his. The mediocrities had their blessed ignorance that let them get through their tedious days without forever questioning wherefore, why. The beautiful ones seemed to have been vouchsafed some deep, special knowledge of their own significance, that he had somehow been born without.

He turned through a narrow dark *cul de sac* that stank of urine, then slipped down the four twisting steps at the corner. From his earliest days he had suffered from this sense that all the others — his older brothers, the children he played with, even the servants' brats — knew some rich, magical secret about the meaning of their lives, about all life, that he knew not. Oh, he was aware that he had gifts: position, talent, a conventional cast of feature that was regarded by most as handsome. But without that baffling touch of all-hallowing grace, granted to the most common but denied to him, all the rest counted for little, counted for nothing.

He hurried past Half-Moon Alley's shadowy doorways down a tunnel cut through the houses and strolled into Leicester Square. The theaters glowed in the early winter dusk with the light of a thousand electric bulbs. The Empire and the Alhambra were decked with Christmas garlands and flashing lights of red and green. He wanted to expunge from memory the image of his father and Oscar Wilde seated across from each other, chatting amiably like two consummate hypocrites. Much as they might pretend in their dissembling ways that he was of primary importance to them, he knew that neither the one nor the other had any true sense of who he was. He peered in the window of the Wheatsheaf. Desolate. He moved on to the Brown Bear.

The pub itself was crowded with the usual types, most of them literary. The last thing he wanted was to discuss literature! He was about to leave, but glanced in through the door of the saloon bar. This room spread out around a large fireplace with a black iron fender placed importantly in front of it. There, sitting cross-legged on a settee and wafting a gauzy violet handkerchief before his nostrils, was an expensively dressed fop a few years beyond his youth's first bloom — a *grande dame* in everything but gender. More important, someone was sitting across from him, listening silently to the cascades of chatter, who looked very interesting indeed.

"Haven't we met?" said Bosie, slipping onto the settee.

The fop drew back, as if expecting to be insulted, or struck. "I would hardly have forgotten, my dear," he said, trembling into a different pose, head tilted high, lips pursed in an aristocratic smile. "I am Lord Alfred Douglas."

The other man's eyebrows arched: "What a great, great pleasure, Lord Alfred," he said in his breathless voice. "My name is Alfred Taylor — perhaps you've heard of me?" He might have been wearing a silvery Pompadour wig, the way he kept primping at his woolly red hair; and the way he kept fussing at the sleeves and pockets and cuffs of his tight fawn-colored suit, it might have been an endlessly complicated evening dress by Worth. His face, though, was not in the least delicate or effeminate: it was craggy and coarse, with a flat nose and bushy ginger brows.

"I am most pleased to meet you, Mr. Taylor," said Bosie — but his eyes were on the youth sitting silent across from them.

"But *do* call me Alfred, Lord Alfred," said Taylor. "And — *que le monde est petit!* — we have another Alfred here, as well! This is my newest '*protégé*,' Mr. Alfred Wood. Heavens, how confusing all this is getting!"

Alfred Wood, with his large eyes and rueful mouth, was watching Bosie carefully. He seemed no more than sixteen, and for all the rude health beaming in his cheeks, looked somehow underfed. His unruly blond hair flew out in cowlicks and wondrous curlicues over a high, narrow brow. His face, all bone and sinew, was bordered by large pink cup-handle ears, and he kept chewing at his moist, sensuous lower lip. "Impressive, isn't he, Lord Alfred? One would say a youthful Viking, just off his longboat."

"Too thin to be a Viking," Bosie said, his heart accelerating. Wood's greasy jacket and cheap trousers were small for him, and his wrists and ankles jutted out. When Bosie took his hand, it was large and callused, and the grip was firm, almost too firm. For a long moment, Bosie held on, flushed at his own daring.

The tables nearer the wall were pushed up against high carved wooden benches, like bishops' chairs in a cathedral; the walls and ceiling were timbered, the plaster darkened with soot from the fire. "Oh, I *do* feel the cold," said Alfred Taylor, huddling closer to the embers. "They make something here called a Tonsil Tease, Lord Alfred. Will I order you one?" He turned his large white hands this way and that, examining the carefully manicured fingernails mirroring the firelight, and added: "I imagine Mr. Wood here knows some interesting ways to tease the tonsils, if he puts his mind to it."

Wood smiled bashfully and moved his chair closer to Bosie. "Ever been to the States?" The voice was a shock. From such a throat should have emanated tones of gold; in fact, Wood spoke in the hoarse, cracked, discordant twang of the East End. But with such a face, what did it matter?

"Never," Bosie replied, not taking his eyes from Wood's.

"Our young wanderer is determined to set sail for the New World," said Taylor, "and won't London be the poorer!"

That, said Bosie, called for a celebration. He stepped over to the bar, which was illuminated by a cluster of globes held in place by a scarlet-robed plaster blackamoor. When the waiter found a bottle of Dagonet 1880, Bosie said: "Put it on Mr. Oscar Wilde's account, if you please."

There was much fuss over the opening of the bottle, Taylor holding his hands before his face, claiming that the popping of champagne corks terrified him. Bosie snatched the bottle away from the waiter and handed it to Alfred Wood, who, despite being ''unfamiliar with dear things,'' as he said, handled the task with a certain finesse.

Just then a tall sailor well into his cups entered the saloon bar and staggered towards the stairs leading to the Gent's. ''My *dears!*'' said Taylor. He exhaled a cloud of smoke from his pink-tinted mouth, and then drew it in again through his nostrils. ''I believe I hear the call of nature.'' He drew himself to his feet and carefully adjusted his necktie.

''Will you find your way back?'' said Bosie, laughing.

''*Moi?* Never fear, Lord Alfred!'' And he hobbled towards the stairs, pausing on the top step to blow a kiss in Bosie's direction.

''Have you plans for the evening?'' Bosie said, refilling Wood's glass.

''Don't know as yet, sir.'' The boy was proud, and held his head erect and his square chin forward, no expression in that wide, delicious mouth. Yet the look of deep sorrow never left him, Bosie noted: this boy had shed tears, had known renunciations.

Bosie glanced about to see if anyone might be close enough to eavesdrop. ''My family is away. I want you to come with me.''

''I don't know, sir.''

Bosie grinned. ''I won't play cat and mouse. I am interested in you. You're the kind of person I like best.''

The eyes mirrored the square of sky to be seen through the Brown Bear's cut-glass window. ''What type of person would that be, sir?'' They were framed, those dreamy eyes, with astonishingly dark lashes, clear, wet, shining . . .

''The kind who will — astonish me.'' Bosie downed his wine. Wood did the same. Bosie rose, Wood rose. They placed their empty glasses next to Alfred Taylor's half-full one, and Wood followed Bosie out into the early winter dusk.

) 4 (

In the morning Bosie padded down to the kitchen and told old Whittaker, poring over the *Observer* with a magnifying glass, to make chocolate for him and his young schoolmate.

''I will serve you breakfast in your rooms, sir.''

''I will take it up myself, Whittaker.''

He carried the *petit déjeuner* up the stairs, past the guest room

— during the night he had stopped in and deliberately rumpled the bed — and into his own bedroom.

"Breakfast," he said.

For all Damus's efforts to reproduce, here at Cadogan Square, the atmosphere of the nursery at Kenmount where he had spent his childhood, she had never, to Bosie's tastes, succeeded. Oh, the toys from generations past were here, neatly piled on shelves, the soldiers and dollhouses and books were all in place, the cabinets held their collections of stones and eggs and glimmering butter-flies. There were quite as many nooks and hiding places and pi-geonholes and secret doors. Yet it was not his own true playroom, and he would forever mourn the loss of that laboratory for young alchemists, that gremlin's workshop, in a house now far away.

" 'Morning," said Wood with a yawn, rubbing his eyes, pulling the blue satin comforter up over his narrow shoulders. He seemed to be having trouble remembering where he was.

Bosie sat on the bed, staring at him in awe. He had never in his life, he told himself, been victim of so violent an attraction: the force of it humbled him, frightened him. This was not like any of the others. This might be forever. "Please — kiss me," he whis-pered.

"Oh, I couldn't do anything like that, sir! The other little fa-miliarities were all right, just a bit of muckin' about. But I couldn't give you no kiss, I couldn't."

Bosie stared at the wide mouth, dry now, and thought he might weep with desire. "You are so incredibly beautiful!"

"Don't be tellin' me things like that or you'll be turnin' my 'ead," Wood answered in his dreadful voice. "Not that you're so bad yourself, sir."

Bosie placed a hand on his shoulder, carefully rubbing his fin-gertips into the skin. "Did I shock you last night?"

"I wouldn't say shocked, sir. I was a bit taken aback, maybe. A gentleman like yourself . . . ."

Bosie smoothed down a place on the bed to set the tray. "I hate it, all this 'gentleman' talk. I want to be — what you are."

They were in the process of devouring the buttered, toasted bread when there was a knock. Wood looked frightened. Bosie knotted his dressing gown and tiptoed to the door. "Yes, Whittaker?"

"A letter, sir. Your father's hand, if I am not mistaken."

Bosie opened the door a few inches and reached out for the letter. ''Thank you, Whittaker.'' Sitting before the fire, he tore open
the envelope.

He felt a tremor of excitement seeing the paragraphs in his
father's tight script. But the letter was only about Oscar Wilde.
He had been entirely mistaken about the man, Queensberry declared: he was a delight to be with. No wonder Bosie sought him
out. He —

Bosie crumpled up the page and threw it into the embers of the
fire, picking at them with a poker.

''Bad news?'' said Wood.

''Only my father.''

''Not very respectful to your father!'' Wood said, plumping up
his pillow.

'' 'Not very respectful to your father!' '' Bosie mimicked,
laughing. Much as he mocked cockney accents, though, they excited him. He slipped a cold hand under the blanket. ''If I'm respectful to you, what do you care?''

When Wood shrieked, Bosie hummed with pleasure. He yanked
the bedclothes away. Then, staring at the long, white, freckle-dusted
body, he was once again close to tears. ''Alfred Wood, I adore you.
I dare not tell you how much. I am not going to Sarum Close
today, I've decided. I want to stay right here, with you.'' Wood
pulled the blanket back over his shivering pale body, and Bosie
knelt over him. It was like staring into a country pond and seeing
a different self. He kept wanting to see Wood's profile when he
was looking at him head-on, and to see him head-on when he was
looking at his profile. ''Different as we are, we are alike,'' he said.
''Two jewels. Side by side. In a crown . . .''

''Oh, my!'' said Alfred Wood, reaching a hand out from the
covers to give one of Bosie's nipples a pinch.

Two jewels in a crown, Bosie thought, drawing away. Words
rushed into his head. He frowned and snatched up a writing pad
from the small student desk next to the bed.

''I do 'ope you're not writing about last night in your diary!''
said Alfred Wood coquettishly. ''That *would* be naughty.''

''Don't act the ponce with me,'' Bosie said, scribbling away. ''I
don't like it.'' The words were coming harder. His burning soul.
Salisbury and its Gothic things. Love — love not letting him part.

"It's a lot warmer in 'ere under the covers," said Wood.

"Hush." Bosie spent the better part of an hour working and reworking the phrases until he had a sonnet.

> *Tired of passion and the love that brings*
> *Satiety's unrest, and failing sands*
> *Of life, I thought to cool my burning hands*
> *In this calm twilight of gray Gothic things:*
> *But love has laughed, and, spreading swifter wings*
> *Than my poor pinions, once again with bands*
> *Of silken strength my fainting heart commands,*
> *And once again he plays on passionate strings.*
>
> *But thou, my love, my flower, my jewel, set*
> *In a fair setting, help me, or I die,*
> *To bear Love's burden; for that load to share*
> *Is sweet and pleasant, but if lonely I*
> *Must love unloved, 'tis pain; shine we, my fair,*
> *Two neighbour jewels in Love's coronet.*

It was excellent. Or was it? Only one person could tell him for sure. He wrote a quick letter to Wilde enclosing the sonnet and saying that he had decided to stay in London a little longer, since the empty house was so peaceful and pleasant to work in. He would be going to his mother, in Salisbury, in a day or two. Perhaps, he added in a postscript, he might visit Oscar in Torquay en route. For an instant he thought of making some comment to Wilde about his night with Alfred Wood — just enough to tantalize him. He decided not to. He placed the letter on the discolored brass door handle, so he would not forget to give it to Whittaker to mail.

Then he stepped over to the fire, where Alfred Wood, with a sheet wrapped about him, was staging a battle with toy soldiers on the rug. "Who are you backing, Bonaparte or Wellington?"

"They're the same to me, sir."

Bosie's hand stole over to Wood's bare feet. He ran a thumb around the ankles, the toes. "I picture you with your feet stained with trodden grass and cowslips. Daphnis in the Attic sun. You don't know who Daphnis is, of course. I'm glad you don't! Stand up, Alfred Wood. Let me see you."

Reluctantly, Wood got to his feet. Bosie knelt before him. "I have never seen anyone so beautiful, I swear it on God's name,"

he said. "You are a prince — a god — in the body of —" He
yanked the sheet away. "You have me enslaved, Alfred Wood! Do
you understand what I am telling you, my love, my flower, my
jewel? You are my king! My god! You can make me do anything
you want!"

Wood smiled foolishly. "A bit cold in 'ere, sir."

"I am common. Ordinary. Dirt under your feet. Tell me what I
must do, my lord. Command me — oh, command me!"

) 5 (

By week's end, Bosie was wondering how much more conversation he could bear on the subjects of money and the United States.

"Another suit?" Wood was saying, watching from the bed as
Bosie tried for the second time to knot his necktie properly. "And
where did you buy that one, Alfie?"

" 'Alfred' will do nicely, thank you." Wood was like a piece of
Slavonic music: the very thing one found so affecting in it on first
hearing was what grew cloying and hateful. For a time, the growing irritation Wood inspired had acted as a kind of aphrodisiac;
now even that failed.

"You don't mind 'Alfie' when we're doin' you-know-what," Wood
snapped, his color rising. He mastered his anger, however, and became purringly affectionate again — little realizing that this was
what Bosie couldn't stand in him. "I must admit it's a lovely suit
of clothes, that. I certainly wouldn't mind 'avin' me one like it."

"I'm quite certain they have others at Peele's. Why don't you
go and see? They're open till seven."

" 'Ow much would it cost, that kind of a suit?"

"I'm sure I don't recall, they —" There was a light tap at the
door.

"A letter, sir," said the butler, reaching forth a silver salver.

"Thank you, Whittaker."

Glancing at the Babbacombe postmark, Bosie tore the envelope
open.

> My Own Boy,
>   Your sonnet is quite lovely, and it is a marvel that those red
> rose-leaf lips of yours should have been made no less for music
> of song than for madness of kisses. Your slim gilt soul walks

between passion and poetry. I know Hyacinthus, whom Apollo loved so madly, was you in Greek days.

Why are you alone in London, and when do you go to Salisbury? Do go there to cool your hands in the grey twilight of Gothic things and come here whenever you like. It is a lovely place, and only lacks you; but go to Salisbury first.

Always, with undying love, yours

Oscar

Bosie kept all Wilde's letters in the top desk drawer, and now he tossed this one in and slammed the drawer shut.

"Your father again?" said Wood.

Bosie stared at him as if he had never seen him before. "A man who is one of the greatest and most important persons in England. You, of course, have never heard of him." He lit a cigarette, neglecting to offer Wood one. Then he again slipped open the desk drawer and snatched back the letter, along with one or two others. Not bothering to kick off his boots, Bosie lay back on the bed reading the letters over as if Wood were invisible, from time to time flicking ashes on the rug.

He was trying to find some evidence, some clue in the wording that would convince him Wilde truly admired his work. This last letter was meaningless. Effusive as it might be, there was not a single word of genuine appreciation for the poem. However was he expected to construe a phrase like "quite lovely"?

Like a dog waiting to be stroked, Wood crept over to the bed. Bosie did not stroke him. Wood sat cross-legged on the floor, smiling what he no doubt thought was a seductive smile.

"A suit like that," Wood said, "would make a lad feel like a new person."

With an impatient sigh, Bosie stuffed the letters in a pocket. He walked past Wood without even glancing at him. Kneeling before the fire, prodding with the twisted old poker a log that had failed to ignite, he said: "What would you do for it?"

"Do for it? The thing is, Alfie, a suit like that could 'elp me get a decent job. In America."

Bosie held the poker in the coals, watching it glow red. "You'll never get to America," he said. "You talk about it too much."

"Oh, I'll get there. And things'll change. I won't need to be 'angin' round with the likes of Alfred Taylor in America, I can tell you that!''

Bosie spread his legs wide, savoring the heat of the fire on his thighs. ''That pretty face of yours,'' he said. ''It means a lot to you, doesn't it.''

''Sir?''

''If I were to take this —'' he held the poker up before him like an archangel's glimmering sword — ''and give you the least little scar? Say — across the cheek?''

Wood laughed nervously. ''I wouldn't like it, sir.''

''If I were to — pay you for the privilege? Say, a hundred pounds? And into the bargain let you have this suit you like so well? Would you do it? Would you let me — ruin that pretty face of yours?''

Wood's lake-blue eyes were confused, fearful. ''No, sir. I wouldn't let you do that.''

Bosie moved closer, holding the poker in back of him. ''Kiss me,'' he said.

Hesitating a moment, Wood did as he was told. His lips were dry.

''A suit like that,'' Wood said, backing away. ''It'd 'elp a lad get started.''

''My clothes won't fit you,'' Bosie said, his voice husky. ''You're too big around the backside.'' He began unbuttoning his trousers.

''You're a caution, you are, Alfie,'' Wood said, watching Bosie eagerly. He took the trousers from him and pulled them on. They were clearly too small for him. ''I could 'ave them let out. No trouble doin' that. And I'd pay you back, Alfie, word of honor. My first pay envelope in America, I'd mail you the money.''

Bosie was studying Wood's trousers: cheap, worn, dirty. For a moment he thought of slipping them on. Instead, he tossed them to the floor.

Wood was admiring himself in the closet-door mirror. ''When I get me a decent job, Alfie, I intend to wear suits like this all the time. Doesn't look like much without the coat, of course . . .''

''You bloody renter,'' said Bosie in a low, excited voice. He tossed the jacket to Wood and moved to the fireplace.

Wood was offended. ''I'm no renter, sir.''

Bosie was on his knees, thoughtfully prodding the logs. Ashes fell in gray heaps through the grate. He got to his feet, holding the poker tight.

Wood was too busy studying himself in the glass to pay any attention to Bosie coming up behind him. He held one sleeve up to the light, brushing his fingers lovingly along the weave. He struck first one pose, then another, a rapt, faraway look in his eyes. He did not see Bosie's arm slowly rise.

The mirror shattered in pieces as the poker crashed into it. Wood flew back, stumbling across the room. Bosie staggered over to the wing chair and collapsed into it, laughing helplessly. He tossed the poker back into the fireplace.

Wood's face was ivory white. "Shouldn't 'ave done that, sir!" he said. "That's — that's seven years' bad luck."

Bosie laughed all the louder. "No, 'Alfie,' " he said. "*You* were the one looking so intently in the glass. The seven years' bad luck are yours . . ."

) 6 (

"I wonder," said Wilde, "how my boys are spending Christmas. Ireland seems so very far away."

"I want more caviar," Bosie said, snapping his fingers for the servant.

"It is a loathsome imitation," Wilde replied, glancing about to make sure no one had overheard. Large as the room was, the number of laughing, boisterous men crowded together in groupings of French chairs made it appear much smaller. The windows were covered with flounced velvet draperies over Austrian curtains embroidered with red and yellow roses; one curtain was only half drawn, and beneath it a plain black shade blocked out any chink of natural light. The ceiling gaslights were screened by clusters of Japanese parasols.

"Do you think people come here for the food?"

"Ta-ra-ra-*boom*-dee-ay!" the crowd was singing. The center of the highly polished parquet floor was serving as a stage, set off from the rest of the room by a circle of candlesticks representing footlights. A mustachioed figure was kicking his petticoats about in a cancan. There seemed to be two age groups, late adolescents and men in their forties. Many of the guests had stopped in a dressing room near the entrance foyer to plaster their faces with makeup and change into dresses or costumes. Crinolines and parasols and picture hats were everywhere in evidence, and here and there a Japanese maiden in a kimono jostled a portly Thaïs or a giggling Marie Antoinette. Even the men who were not in costume seemed somehow to be wearing masks.

"Why are we here?" Wilde said. "And on Christmas! We would be welcome at the brightest, most delightful tables in London." He fanned himself with his napkin: the sour tobacco scent was mingling with fragrances from wilting bouquets, colognes, and Oriental perfumes burning in lotus-shaped *encensoirs*. Lowering his voice Wilde added, with a pleading look: "Why do we seek the bread of life among the dead?"

"You, I suppose, would prefer the Christmas pantomime in Drury Lane." The caviar arrived, delivered by a wispy youth in a Greek peplum. Bosie tried a spoonful and decided he did not care for it, after all. "And how *are* your 'darling boys'?" he said. "How is the beautiful, bold Cyril? You don't like to talk about him in front of me. I suppose I am not good enough."

The guests were pressed so close together that all conversation seemed virtually communal. "What *I've* always wanted to know," said a man nearby wearing an elaborate Pompadour wig, "is how a woman could possibly perform the act with a swan?"

"Never mind how," said his companion, a young man sitting on a huge pillow made of a priest's stole, "just tell me *why!*"

"I am always impatient for them to go on holiday," said Wilde. "And when they are gone for a few hours, I feel that all the good of life has gone with them." He tried a little of the wine and made a face. "They have served us *eau de Javel!* Cyril?" he went on, with the air of not wishing to talk about the sacred in a setting of this kind. "As delightful and incorrigible as ever."

"Let me introduce you to our hostess," said Bosie, smirking. Alfred Taylor came wandering through the crowd, stopping to kiss some guests on the cheek. He was wearing an evening dress of scarlet brocaded silk, decked with chiffon and strewn with roses, a copy of the gown Julia Neilson had worn in the second act of *Hypatia*.

Bosie presented Taylor to Wilde. "*Enchanté*, to say the least," Taylor said, extending a hand in a red glove that stretched up nearly to the shoulder. "What an honor for my little home!"

"The honor is mine," said Wilde, bending his lips to the limp hand. "It is quite splendid, this apricot-colored palace of yours."

"It's a far cry from the ancestral halls Lord Alfred must be used to, but I've tried to make it cozy." He gestured vaguely to a sofa nearby. "Have you met George, and Alfie, and Tom?"

"I'm not Alfie," said a hard-eyed young blond on the sofa. He was wearing the uniform of a telegraph boy. "I'm Eddie."

"Eddie!" Taylor said. "And a fine old name it is." He bent towards Wilde, lowering his voice. "It's a little hobby of mine, introducing nice people to each other. In this wonderful, terrible London of ours, there are so many lonely souls! People were meant to share things with each other. I'm alone myself, of course. But you know, Mr. Wilde, hope springs eternal in the human breast."

"That," said Wilde, "is one of the great fallacies of this melancholy age."

"Oh, Mr. Wilde, your vivid witticisms! They leave me weak! Now, *do* enjoy the festivities, or I am going to be very cross with you both." And he wafted through the crowd.

The next volunteer was imitating Jenny Lind singing an aria from *Robert le Diable*. The pianist, a giant of a man with rolls of fat wobbling about his face, proved to be rather accomplished. Then a nervous youth did a lackluster imitation of Happy Fanny Fields whooping out a German song. And then a handsome man in his prime, dressed in business attire, sang in piercing falsetto a song about a young angel from the Angel at Islington who had four little angels at home.

"I wish my father could see all this!" Bosie crowed.

"Your father," said Wilde, frowning. "Must we always invite him to the party?" He touched Bosie's foot with his own. "I have thought of a Christmas gift I should very much like to have."

Bosie yawned. "Have I not given you enough already?"

Alfred Taylor, standing at the piano, was demanding more applause for the singers than the spectators were willing to give.

"Look at me, Bosie, please? You never look at me anymore. You have cast me out into an unmirrored world." But Bosie kept his eyes on the stage. "Yes, you have given me a great deal. But kept the one thing without which the rest is — insignificant. You have allowed me to find no place of harbor. In your soul."

"Be quiet, Oscar, please."

The pianist was playing slow Strauss waltzes, and some of the men got up to dance. Bosie drew Wilde to his feet. They launched into a slow, formless waltz, Bosie's cheek on Wilde's lapel, breathing in the smell of tobacco and *héliotrope blanc*. With a little smile, Bosie said: "You want me to declare my undying love. And what would you give in return, Oscar?"

"Anything I had it in my power to give."

Raising his eyebrows slightly, Bosie said: "Would you let me have — Cyril?"

For a moment Wilde stopped dancing, as if he had turned to stone. Then he shuddered and once again began to waltz, his eyes closed tight. "I have never understood your humor, Bosie. You lack all subtlety. You would laugh at a man sliding on a fruit peel."

Bosie was carefully studying everyone around them, imagining himself in the arms of each in turn. "It is *you* who have no humor," he said. "Why are you always so *gloomy?*"

"Forgive me, dear boy. Amidst all these painted, overmerry masks I seem to keep seeing the face of — of Banquo. And in sepulchral tones he says to me: 'This is not what your life was meant to be.'"

"Really," said Bosie, exasperated. He moved back to their chairs.

"And I am worried about my work." Then, when Bosie frowned with impatience: "Bosie, you so admire my finished plays, my first nights. But you refuse to recognize the amount of sheer *labor* the Muse demands before she vouchsafes one tiny glimmer of genius."

The second waiter, tall and splendidly built, was clearing off the table next to them. "Then why don't you go home and work?" Bosie said. The waiter wore nothing but a loincloth pulled tight around his muscled thighs. His eyes glittered behind a black domino mask, and his bare feet were black from the floors. Bosie watched as a man at a neighboring table slipped a pound note slowly down inside the loincloth.

"I looked through *The Picture of Dorian Gray* the other day," Wilde said.

"Oh? Did you recognize me?"

"I did indeed! I am only beginning to understand my novel. Yes, you have become Dorian — or Dorian has become you. And I?" He poured more of the terrible champagne. "I am the portrait itself! While you skip, ever young and fresh, through your wicked life, I grow more and more unsightly, absorbing the stains and ugliness of those sins that seem to leave you more beautiful than before!''

Bosie had been hungrily studying a young boy seated nearby; now the boy returned his gaze, and suddenly stopped being attractive. ''My sins? How very self-righteous you are, Oscar.''

In the center of the floor someone was doing a coarse imitation of Queen Victoria, and Wilde laughed in spite of himself. Then he seemed to grow more depressed for the moment of levity.

''The thing you cannot admit,'' said Bosie, ''is that I have brought meaning to your life. And you are enjoying every minute of it.''

Wilde turned slowly, gazing at all the tables, the rollicking couples, the shadowy corners of the room. Suddenly he said: ''I want to be free, Bosie. Will you release me? *Can* you release me?''

Bosie forced himself to look grave. ''But you *are* free.''

''When you said that dreadful thing — about Cyril. Do you know what my first reaction was? Before any sense of horror froze my blood, I for a terrible instant was — flattered. Flattered that you should desire him, and he my son.''

The pianist started up a tremolo rendition of ''Adeste Fideles.'' Alfred Taylor swooped to the center of the floor. ''Ladies and gentlemen!'' he cried. ''I do hope that no one among us is too sophisticated to remember the true meaning of Christmas! And if anyone *is* so hard-hearted, then I must ask him to avert his eyes from our next little *tableau vivant*.'' He strode over to the green velvet portieres blocking off the next room and yanked them open, revealing a Nativity scene: one of the guests, swathed in blue veils, holding a doll, while the muscular waiter, blanketed over, leaned on a broomstick and solemnly watched. He was still, Bosie noticed, wearing his mask.

Loud applause greeted this. Some in the room were giggling, looking about uncertainly, but others were in tears. ''Isn't it lovely?'' shouted Taylor. ''I have never seen anything so touching in all *ma vie!*'' All voices rose in the carol — all but Oscar Wilde's.

''Old sobersides,'' Bosie said.

''I was thinking of another Joseph. Joseph of Arimathea, and of the way darkness came over the earth, and he passed into the Valley of Desolation . . .''

''Oscar, please. Not a parable. Not on Christmas.''

"And Joseph lighted a torch of pinewood. And a young man was there, naked and weeping. He had torn at his body with thorns, and on his head of golden hair he had placed ashes for a crown. 'I do not wonder that you weep,' Joseph said to him. 'For surely they have killed a just man.' And the young man replied: 'But it is not for Him I am weeping. I weep for myself. For I too changed water into wine. I healed the leper, and gave sight to the blind. I walked upon the waters and cast out devils. All the things that this man did, I have done as well.' " Wilde wet his lips with wine and sagged back in the chair. " 'And yet they have not crucified me.' "

"Some money, please," said Bosie. "I am tired of your dreary tales."

Wilde tossed his billfold on the table. Bosie reached out a pound note. The masked waiter was resuming his duties, and Bosie summoned him. Giggling, Bosie stuffed the note into the loincloth. The waiter remained immobile, unsmiling. Then he strolled away without a word.

"I want him," Bosie whispered. "A Christmas gift. Get him for me, Oscar."

Wilde emptied his glass.

"And you shall have *your* gift, Oscar. Just as you wished. My undying love. Are you satisfied? I love you, Oscar. Now — will you cheer up?"

Everyone seemed to be dancing now, the great hoop skirts pressing up against each other amidst titters of laughter.

"You think you're humoring me," Wilde said. "But it is true. You belong to me, Bosie. In a way you do."

But Bosie could not keep his eyes from the masked waiter, leaning against a column and watching the dancers with a look of disgust. Alfred Taylor was standing there, too, and blew kisses to them and to all the dancers with both hands. "Well, Oscar? If I belong to you, does that not make you happy?"

Wilde stared at him, his face bloated and heavy, flushed with wine. "I feel," he said, "as if someone had just walked over my grave . . ."

PART SIX

The Letter

OB CLIBBURN might appear carefree as he sauntered among the shops and doorways of Fleet Street, yet he was in fact appraising every passing face in the jostling crowd.

It was evident that his person cost him no more trouble than an old glove; yet some innate elegance of manner made this seem mere eccentricity, as if he might be a rich man down on his luck. Though Clibburn was well below thirty, all the youth had long been drained from his long, glum face, and he had the despairing look of one who thought about things too deeply. His knobby head was bald in the center, fringed round with thin ginger hair, which added to his unworldly aura, giving him the look of a doubt-haunted monk.

Back and forth he paced in the unseasonably warm January sunshine, crossing from the cool shadows of Saint Bride's to the stationer's across the road, sweating in his ill-fitting old suit. At last he spotted his man.

Singleton was trudging down Ludgate Hill, anxious and ashen-faced, dragging his body along past the halting drays and omnibuses. Rob smirked. The great stallion of two nights before had turned into a lifeless gelding! Concealed behind a newspaper stand, Rob waited till Singleton reached the front gate of the church, grasping it as if for support, looking as if he hadn't enough spunk in him to take another step. No, Rob decided, there would be no detective following. With a firm clip he weaved in and out of the stalled coaches.

"I 'ope you brought what I axed you," he said to Singleton. "We been at this off and on for days now. My patience is pretty near run out."

Singleton was dressed in drab grays that harmonized with his steely hair. He gave Rob a look meant, no doubt, to be pitiful. "I *beg* you to reconsider, Mr. Clibburn. You seem an intelligent chap. You must have some sense of decency, of fairness. For a sum of this amount I have to work an entire year!" In a few days' time the man had aged decades, Clibburn thought with amusement. "My wife is not well, Mr. Clibburn. She needs —"

"Your wife?" Clibburn smiled, revealing teeth the same yellowish color as his skin. He had the patient but sharp look of a fox that has been caught not once but many times — but has always escaped. "You weren't thinkin' of no wife when you was makin' indecent proposals to an innocent lad like my brother," he said menacingly. "You weren't worryin' about '*is* 'ealth, neither. I shouldn't wonder if poor Alfie isn't roont. That kind of thing leaves an uncommon severe scar on a young lad — maybe for life! And Alfie is little more'n a child. When we got 'ome he had a dreadful swole face from cryin'."

"But it was your brother who approached *me*."

"Our Alfie? If you don't speak civil, Mr. Singleton, I'll 'ave no recourse but to ask for a more decent capital expenditure from you. So just keep things all fair and aboveboard, as they ought to be, and no slanderin' of the innocent. I certainly don't think that wife of yours would enjoy too much 'earin' all the unsavory details of the matter, neither. Then she'd really 'ave somethin' to feel sick about."

With a look of loathing that he was unable to disguise but seemed afraid to entirely reveal, Singleton removed from an inside pocket of his coat a bulging brown envelope. Clibburn grinned and tore the envelope open. "Surely you're not going to count it!" said Singleton, looking frantically about. "Not in Ludgate Circus!"

Clibburn showed his teeth again in silent laughter as he leafed through the ten-pound notes. "Aren't we delicate, though!" he said, raising his voice so all the passersby could hear. "You wasn't so delicate when you jeopardized the morals of my poor little brother in the gents' lavvy in Tottenham Court Road . . ."

) 2 (

Despite the harsh beating sound of the rain tapping on the old house's loose tin shingles, winter in the rambling Southwark streets was keeping mild. Still, it was damp and agonizing cold down here in the cellar room — to Willie's mind at least. The walls were pitted and scabby, as if the room were afflicted with some kind of nasty, wasting illness, and the mean little fire in the grate only seemed to give off a few inches of heat. Rob, of course, was the kind that didn't care too much about comfort.

"You know what I likes, Rob?" Willie said, wrapping the torn blanket tighter around him and pushing his wooden chair a bit closer to the fire. "I likes magic. I'd like for *everything* to be magic."

Rob said nothing. Moving his chess pieces around, he seemed uncommonly cheerful. He had no blanket around him, not even a sweater, and his almond-shaped eyes were heavy-lidded, which gave him a sleepy look, though as far as Willie could tell, Rob was always wide-awake. He was sipping whiskey from a dirty glass.

"Know what we could do tomorrow, Rob? Go to the 'orse races," Willie went on, trying to pat down his hair, still wet from the rain and shooting out from his head like the quills of a hedgehog. Though Willie's skin was white, his nose and ears were a bright red from the cold. "I feel like I been locked up in this 'ole all the winter long." He was feeling bad. Here he was sporting a whole new wardrobe of clothes — new boots, a stunning flash waistcoat of blue corduroy that buttoned right up to the throat, a red handkerchief tied around his neck. But Rob hadn't even noticed.

"Don't care about gamblin'," Rob said. "I only likes certain wins." The last thing Rob himself would ever buy was clothes; he always looked halfway to the ragshop. No, he preferred spending his cut on books and the like. He was a thinker, Rob was — even if he'd been in no schools. Perhaps too much of a thinker. The only thing in the room he appeared to really care about was his hip tub, pushed to the side of the fire, out of the way. It was made of real tin and was so large he could very nearly lie down in it. The thing had cost Rob a pretty penny and he liked to think it was as good as the tub of any gentleman in the whole of London.

"Chess is gamblin', ain't it?" said Willie, sulking. Rob wasn't friendly with him the way he used to be. The trouble was, Rob had a taste for nice looks as bad as any gal's, and that went for women and men alike. Willie wasn't so fetching to look at anymore. He was getting a belly on him, and Rob had never cared for his oversize hands and feet. And it wasn't just Rob. Even the old parties weren't as easy to win over as before.

"Chess develops the secret powers of the mind," said Rob. He moved one of his knights abruptly, then loped around to the other side of the table to study the board fresh. ''And when a body only plays against 'imself, how can 'e lose?''

The place reeked of cat pee, burnt meat, cabbage: you could never get rid of the smells in an old place like this. The pictures Rob had tacked on the wall did little to take the curse off : mostly black-and-white photogravures from the newspapers, and mostly of men on trial. All the criminals of London were heroes to Rob. In their midst, looking most uncomfortable, was Her Majesty the Queen in a headdress of white lace.

''Couldn't we at least go out someplace and spend a few browns on a decent bit of food? Now that we're in clover? I'm starved, Rob. I 'aven't 'ad me a decent —''

There were three sharp raps on the door, then two soft ones. Willie scrambled up the rickety steps and opened to Alfred Wood in a rain slicker, dripping wet. ''So for once little Alfie is on time,'' said Willie.

''Bugger yourself,'' murmured Alfred Wood, stepping past him without a smile. Making his way down the steps, Wood held tight to the banister. He looked about the room for a place to sit, touching the only empty chair to be sure it was not dusty.

''I'm really sorry, Alfie,'' said Rob, without looking up from the chess pieces. ''We made you come out in all this rain — and for nothin'.''

''For nothin'?'' Though water was dripping down his boyish face, he did not use the towel hanging on the doorknob: perhaps it was too soiled for his fastidious tastes. ''What're you sayin', Rob?'' Frowning, he threw his slicker over a closet door.

''Sorry, Alfie,'' Rob said. ''Any'ow, no rain can get at you down 'ere.''

''Sorry, Alfie!'' echoed Willie. ''You'll just 'ave to sell some of those precious silk 'andkerchiefs of yours.''

Wood tried to make his voice threatening: ''Why do you say I came out for nothin', Rob? What's goin' on?''

Rob slowly moved one of his knights, then darted around to the other side of the table. ''Singleton. 'E changed his mind. After all our trouble, the old geezer said 'e wouldn't give us a shillin'.''

Wood fell into one of the chairs, looking as if he might burst into tears. ''Jesus,'' he whispered.

Rob was staring at Willie, his almond eyes crinkling; suddenly he began roaring with laughter. ''Alfie! If you could only see your face!'' Still laughing, he turned to a stack of books on the kitchen table, reaching inside of one for an envelope.

''What's the bloody joke?'' demanded Wood. ''Did the bloke come acrost with the money or did he not? And what're *you* laughin' about, Willie? It's none of your affair.''

Rob threw a pile of notes on the table. ''Beginner's luck, Alfie! The old bugger bled out three 'undred sweet pounds!'' Almost purring with satisfaction he leaned back till the chair touched the wall. ''We finally got ourselves a rum old party — a real gentleman, *very* genteel, with a conscience and all that goes along with it. Most of these chaps don't give a rabbit's arse what they do, long as they get their pleasure. They're immoral, the lot of 'em. But old Singleton, now, there's a true gentleman, if ever you want to see one.'' Looking faintly bored, he began counting out the money. ''Anyway, them as is so greedy after makin' money ought to be made to spend some. Why should they 'ave all of it and us none?''

''By rights I ought to get more than the two of you,'' said Wood uncertainly. ''It was me 'ad to get in bed with the old bloke.''

''You'd think you didn't enjoy it!'' cried Willie.

Rob gave Wood a serious, studying look. ''That, Alfie, was only because you're the pretty one. But I'm the smart one. And in this cruel world of ours, it's always the smart ones as gets the lion's share. Remember that.''

''He loved every minute of it!'' Willie crowed. ''Wasn't 'e disappointed when we broke in earlier than we was supposed! Afore the toff had a chance to *really* stick the old wand in 'im.''

Leaping across the room, Wood grasped Willie by the collar. ''Look, you, if you ever accuse me of a thing like that, it'll be you're the one that gets buggered.'' He glanced over to Rob, embarrassed at the violence of his outburst. Willie scurried away, making an obscene gesture.

''Fightin', fightin', fightin','' said Rob moodily, almost to himself. ''Isn't the world violent enough? Must we be violent with ourselves?'' He handed Wood his share of bank notes.

Wood rubbed them between his fingers, smelled them, kissed them. ''You chaps won't be seein' me round this miserable city for long,'' he said. ''First I'm goin' to get me some new cotton shirts. Do you think I could get a tailor to sew a little stripe up the sides of these trousers 'ere? I 'asn't clothes as is fit for the U.S.A. I want to show those Yanks that I'm somebody to take serious.''

"I'd say our Alfie makes a stunnin' good ponce," said Willie, mincing across the floor, waggling his hips.

"Bugger off," said Wood. "You 'ave no taste but in your mouth — where you take in those old boys' willies. That's why you're called Willie, isn't it?'' He removed a small yellow packet from an inner pocket, checked to be sure it had not been dampened by the rain, and tossed it on the table. "What can I get for these, Rob? They was presented to me by a certain gentleman — though 'e don't realize 'e give 'em! A peer o' the realm, no less, 'as took a real fancy to yours truly. This suit I'm wearin', in fact, is a token of 'is 'igh regard!'' He lowered his voice, as if there might be someone in the room besides themselves. "But I warn you, 'e is one dangerous toff, 'e is. I wouldn't trust that bugger with my back turned.''

Rob had undone the elastic band and was glancing over the letters. "You're learnin' the trade fast," he said admiringly.

"Oh, 'e thought I was peaches an' cream, Lord Alfred did,'' Wood went on dreamily. " 'E was a real swell, and it was another swell as wrote 'im these letters.''

" 'Red rose-leaf lips,' Rob read. " 'Madness of kisses.' Oh, I say, says I! Sounds like this Oscar is ever so sweet on 'is 'darling boy,' now, don't it! Tell us, Alfie, who is Oscar?''

"If I knew that, I wouldn't need the likes of *you* blokes," said Wood. "Somebody 'igh up, I believe. One of the most important men in England.''

Rob put his chessboard away on the dresser top and set the four letters out carefully on the table, pressing down the wrinkles. " 'Ave a look, Willie.''

"You know I don't read," Willie said. "Not much, any'ow." To Wood he added defensively: "I could read when I was a child. But I can't now. For want of practice.''

"This 'peer of the realm' of yours,'' said Rob. " 'Ow well off is this 'darling Bosie'?''

Wood was glowing from all the attention. " 'E's no pauper, that one. 'Ad a ring on his finger with a stone in it big as a boiled fish eye. 'E took me to the Savoy, what's a grand restaurant with all the swells in London eatin' there. We 'ad all kinds of strange vittles, things I couldn't guess the name of, they was so Frenchified. But in the bedroom, the cove turned into a real animal. Bitin' and slappin', and teeth like little saws. I don't mind tellin' you, I'm scared o' that one.''

Willie was picking at his toenails sulkily. "You gave 'im every satisfaction, I'll bet.''

"I must get me to the ablutions place," said Rob. He started towards the steps, but halfway up he stopped. " 'Ow much can you bleed 'im for, do you think, this great swell of yours, to get the letters back?''

Wood was preening from Rob's new admiration for him. "I s'pose I'll start 'igh and work down," he said cockily.

"You 'ave to be delicate about it, Alfie," Rob said, leaning his arms on the banister. "Tell 'im you'd 'ate to 'ave to tell old Oscar the things that went on between 'im and yourself, but you just might 'ave to. See what *that* does to 'is peace o' mind.''

Willie, who had taken Rob's empty chair, was brooding at being excluded from the conversation.

"Oh, that would never work," said Wood. "The old fella's onto it.''

Pointing down to Willie's back, Rob gave Wood a wink, as he unbuttoned his trousers. Suddenly a stream of silver went arching down over Willie.

"Gawblimey!" Willie cried, leaping up from the chair. He began shrieking and slapping at himself. "Oh, you filthy whoremonger, Rob. My good new clothes! I'll bastardwell kill you for that. Stop laughing, you bastard's get! I'll get quit of you and this place yet.''

Rob, convulsed with laughter, came stumbling down the steps over to where Wood was standing. He gave him an affectionate slap in the face. " 'Ow old is this lord of yours?''

"Just twenty. Maybe twenty-one.''

"Ha!" said Willie, drying himself with a sheet of newspaper. "You didn't mind givin' yourself to *that*, did you!''

"I'll tear your face off, Willie!" Rob screamed, the tendons in his neck taut. "Our Alfie 'ere is smart as a terrier, and you're not to give 'im any more of your back chat." He smiled warmly at Wood. "Mustn't mind wee Willie 'ere. 'E'd throw rocks at the

Crystal Palace, if you'd let 'im — but 'e's got a 'eart of solid gold. And you, Alfie, you're a young man of talents. It's up to we lads to 'elp you develop them . . .''

) 3 (

The following Friday, Wood was back. ''I did as you said, Rob, duly and truly. But it was a right stinkin' idea.''

Rob, who had been pouring water from the kettle into his tub, now situated directly in front of the fireplace, looked offended. ''What kind of a way is that to talk?'' he said. ''A little respect is in order, wouldn't you say?''

''I wrote to Douglas, like you said. And look: 'e went right to the other bloke and told 'im everything.'' Wood slammed a telegram down on the table. Rob glanced at it with heavy eyes, as if the thing were hardly worth the effort of picking up.

YOU CAN DISCUSS LETTERS WITH MR OSCAR WILDE IN
TAP ROOM OF CAFE ROYAL PICCADILLY ON THURSDAY FEBRUARY
SECOND NINE PM HE WILL BE WEARING GREEN CARNATION
LORD ALFRED DOUGLAS

''Good,'' said Rob. He carried a box of Dr. Tidman's Sea Salt over to the tub and poured a good quantity into the steaming water. ''Good, good, good.''

''What's good about it!''

Rob unbuttoned his shirt. ''I imagine this Oscar is a deal better off than your twenty-year-old peer of the realm. 'E can buy anything that takes 'is fancy, I'll bet. Wouldn't you say so, Alfie?''

Wood tried not to stare as Rob unbuckled his pants and drew them off. ''It's a trap. The blessed place'll be filled with crushers.''

With the firelight flashing over his slim body, Rob stood before Wood a long moment, a slight grin dancing on his lips. Then he eased himself slowly into the tub, groaning with pleasure. ''What could they pin on you, Alfie? You're just tryin' to find out what's on Oscar's mind.''

''Send Willie.''

Rob laughed his dry, tired laugh. ''Willie used to be middlin' pretty, three years ago or so.'' He soaped a large yellow sea sponge and rubbed it under his arms. ''But believe you me, Alfie, 'e'd never make a patch on your arse. When old Oscar gets a look at *your* sweet face, 'e's sure to tumble. Listen, Alfie, you're doin' famous, as far as Rob is concerned." He squeezed the sponge high over his head and let the water trickle down his back. "London is a mean, mean place. I saw that when I was only a lad, that this 'ere city is filled with 'ard, wicked people. I soon learned to take care of old Rob . . ."

"By makin' yourself one of the mean, wicked people?"

Rob stood, with water cascading down his body, and gave Wood a brooding smile. "Soap my back, Alfie. If you don't mind gettin' your 'ands wet." Wood hesitated a moment, then reached for the cake of brown soap on the floor beside the tub. "You're a very innocent boy, Alfie. And London is 'ard on innocent boys. You need somebody what'll look after you — somebody strong. But you 'ave to trust that person. You 'ave to do everything you're told." Suddenly he turned and grasped Wood's arm. "I'm not sure you could do that."

Wood gaped at him, trying to hide the shudder that was coursing through him. "I — I could, Rob."

"Could you?" Rob said, and pulled Wood's trembling body towards him.

) 4 (

The warm scent of lilacs seeped through the evening air, as if the city had bypassed the end of winter entirely. All along the Quadrant's curve, striped awnings were drawn over the shop windows, and Wood was pretending to study the displays of cravats and shirtfronts in Allison's, then in Swan and Edgar's, then back to Allison's as if deciding which window was arranged more artfully, all the while stealing backwards glimpses of the Café Royal across the way. Sweat was trickling down his neck and chest and private parts.

At length he whispered a prayer about Jesus Meek and Jesus Mild, remembered from childhood, and shot across the road as the carriages slowed down, without permitting himself the luxury of thinking it over.

He strutted under the glowing glass globes past the entrance columns, through the swinging doors with their gleaming brass handles, and straight into the lobby, not daring to look left or right. At the sight of the butler or majordomo or whatever the gink was, standing so fierce next to the newspaper office, Wood hesitated for an instant, afraid to smile and afraid not to. His clothes, which on taking leave of Langham Place he had thought so smart, began to feel like the cheapest rags off a handcart. Even his looks seemed to be deserting him: he felt himself growing ugly.

At any moment the trembling on the inside might start showing on the outside, so without another thought he walked right into the taproom and barked a quick "Good evening" to the chucker-out standing, arms folded, at the door.

He caught his breath. The ceiling was covered with paintings he could not make out for the clouds of blue smoke rising like incense in a church, pictures of angels and women with their clothes half off and heavenly landscapes of all descriptions. The walls were lined with bare-breasted goddesses of painted gold. Jesus! The Royal, he decided, was his kind of place. Definitely. In the city's many rubbishy precincts, Alfie Wood was always ill at ease; grandeur, however, made him feel right at home.

Waves of conversation, measured and sweet, rose up on all sides like snatches of song. These were the sort of men and ladies he had always felt he belonged with, well dressed, soft-spoken, polite.

But there was no green carnation anywhere to be seen.

"Help you, sir?" said the young barman. He was almost too courteous: might it be some kind of mockery? "I want a whiskey and soda water," Wood replied, as gruffly as he could.

Yes, he had always felt that some great mistake had been made somewhere, him getting born into that shabby pigsty in Spital-fields, where he never for one minute felt that he belonged. He ran his eyes around the swells chatting at the bar and leaning over to whisper to each other at the tables. He wanted to give the impression that he was as good as any of them but, if they should want to get to know him, he was willing. Still, if anyone looked in his direction, he flushed and turned away.

Where was the bloody carnation? Was it a trick of some kind? Or a joke? Was Lord Alfred Douglas sitting in that grand house of his this very minute, laughing to beat the band? He could put up with almost anything, Wood told himself, but not being laughed at by a degenerate toff like that one.

From a table in the corner of the room a heavyset bloke swooped down from the platform and hurried across to the bar, extending a large white hand.

"You, my dear young man, must be Alfred Wood," he said with a slight smile. In his lapel was pinned a dark pink orchid.

"I'm a bit late," Wood said stiffly, glancing about the room. "Sorry about that, Mr. Wilde."

"How wise of you! Punctuality, I always say, is the thief of time." He took a step backwards. "But you are — perfection! The face of a young athlete in a Roman statue of the decadence — all innocence and wonder. Mr. Wood, you are quite poisonously beautiful!"

Wood was a little dazed; Wilde seemed not to care who overheard. Just then the barman served the whiskey, with a small glass pitcher of soda water. Wilde instructed him to put the drink on his bill, and led Wood to his table in amongst the palm trees. Crossing the room, Wood kept catching images of himself in the smoked mirrors, walking in all directions at once.

"Whiskey," Wilde said. "Such a lovely virile drink."

Wood accepted the chair Wilde pointed to, right next to his own. The man was far too sure of himself; all this bluster wasn't natural. It was surely a trap. "You were to be wearing a green carnation," Wood said reproachfully.

"And where would the pleasure have been, if you were expecting it? I wanted to surprise you, Alfred! Besides, they've become so common. I understand the Prince of Wales himself is seen everywhere these days with a green carnation for his buttonhole — poor unimaginative Bertie. You don't despise me for resorting to a humble orchid instead?"

The woman at the next table was wearing a hat and feathered boa of black, making her look like a perched raven. Wood forced himself to stop staring at her and drank down half the whiskey smartly, the way he imagined swells must do. As it hit his belly, he felt himself soar with a sense of amplitude, and decided he didn't care what might happen next, just so long as he'd had the chance to come to the Café Royal.

Wilde's talk was so smooth and high-class, it was a treat just to sit and listen, even when Wood couldn't always follow the meaning. "That's a genuine pearl you've got stuck in your tie, ain't it," he said with a bashful smile. "You can always tell."

Wilde opened a silver case of cigarettes and passed it over. He lit a match and held it up for a moment before Wood's face. "Yes, I see you as quite definitely Roman. Even though Lord Alfred Douglas told me you were of a Grecian cast."

"Oh, I'm English, Mr. Wilde. Or should I say, a real limey."

"*Do* say 'a real limey'! You are indeed English, through and through, Mr. Wood — and very, very naughty."

Wood, preening with pleasure, suddenly caught sight of his new cuff links. In the pawn shop they had looked like diamonds. Now he pulled his arms in tight to his sides, certain Wilde would instantly spot the things as glass.

"But have you never been to Rome, Alfred?"

"I never been any further than Ladbroke Grove, Mr. Wilde! In a omnibus! Rome may be in Timbuktu for anything I may know, Rome may be."

Wilde bent close at every phrase, listening attentively as if Wood were the greatest talker in London. "Now, what is this about your having letters of mine to Lord Alfred Douglas?" he said, his voice lowering, his eyes squinting with mirth. "I adore jokes of any kind, but they must have a point. As you can imagine, I am *most* eager to learn the point of this one."

Wood squirmed in the chair, playing with the glass in a way he hoped looked classy. "It's no joke, I'm afraid, Mr. Wilde."

"Oscar, if you don't mind," said Wilde, snapping his fingers for the waiter. "And I am going to call you Alfred, because I think we're going to be great friends."

Wood looked to the highly polished floor, where the lavender and green and gold of the walls blurred into a darker version of themselves. "I can't talk fancy the way the swells in this place does."

"Nonsense," said Wilde, signing the bill. "Every time you drop an *h*, the entire room tingles with excitement. How fascinating it must have been for Bosie — Lord Alfred — to contemplate you."

"'E never complained."

"Your face is like a more perfect version of his own!" Wilde tamped out his cigarette sadly, and added, as if to himself : "How the gods must be laughing at us all. You'll dine with me, Alfred, of course?"

Wood scrutinized Wilde's face, still fearing he was being mocked. "I don't mind."

"Only not here." Wilde led him past the close-packed tables, nodding to people smiling up at him or catching outstretched hands as they passed. "The Royal is for old friends who wish to renew their acquaintance. We require a place where new friends can — get to know each other better."

) 5 (

They crossed Leicester Square, past the line of cabs in front of Jimmy's, where women shimmering with gems were trying to be seen by as many people as possible before being whisked inside. A street singer chanted about his home in Australia, far away, adding a brief shiver of melancholy to the unseasonably warm night air, and they moved through an alley where dim-lit shops displayed naughty books, on to a courtyard lined with foreign restaurants. A tiny Japanese was leading two disreputable-looking ladies of the evening into the Rupert, but the three of them were so drunk they could not negotiate the door.

The restaurant had many rooms on many floors, and Wilde led Wood to a cozy private cubicle at the very top, perfumed with the fragrances of forgotten meals. Color lithographs of Rome and Venice covered the white-plastered walls, and the rafters were hung with wine bottles in baskets and bouquets of garlic and onions.

"You haven't told me, Alfred," Wilde said, after the champagne had arrived and the red-cheeked waiter was prying it open, "how you became a hardened criminal at such an early age."

"I'm no criminal, Oscar!"

"Don't disillusion me so quickly, dear boy." The cork finally popped and Wilde stared at the bottle reprovingly. "To wickedness," he said, raising his glass in a toast. "How curious that you should bear such a marked resemblance to that other Alfred who so perspicaciously introduced us. You might indeed be cousin to Lord Alfred Douglas himself."

Wood drank the champagne down as if it were soda water. "Wish I 'ad a bit of 'is money! Then I could dress myself up fancy the way Lord Alfred does. I'm not a tailor, but I understands about clothes, and 'is is top quality. I likes things uncommon good and excellent myself. Like that pearl you're wearin' in your cravat!"

Wilde was staring at him coyly over the rim of his glass. "What a pleasure it must have been for him to look into your fresh young face and see virtually the reflection of his own! You have the cold,

unreasoning look of an unformed Augustus Caesar. I like that.''
A bowl of fruits rested on a sideboard next to their table, and
Wilde reached for a grape, placing it in his teeth. Suddenly he
brought his mouth up against Wood's, crushing the grape against
the young man's lips. Laughing, he drew away. ''Was Lord Alfred
— gentle with you?'' he asked.

''You're a regular Nosy Parker, Oscar!'' said Wood, rubbing
his napkin over his mouth. ''I thought we was supposed to be dis-
cussin' a certain parcel of letters.''

Wilde cupped the young face in a big soft hand. ''Extraordinary eyes . . . glowing and flickering like blue vigil candles. How
many letters do you have?''

The sound of singing floated up the stairs, an impassioned tenor
in a sensuous, romantic aria. ''Four,'' said Wood.

''And you took them from Lord Alfred Douglas, you scoundrel?''

''They were in a suit of clothes 'e gave me.''

Into the room walked a guitarist and the tenor, who was short
and very fat. ''Yes, Lord Alfred always treats the classics with
irreverence — it is part of his charm,'' said Wilde, over the din of
the music. ''But I don't wish to discuss commerce now. We must
order our dinner . . .''

Much later, Wilde was pouring from the third bottle of champagne. ''Is the apricot soufflé to your liking, Alfred?''

''Elegant, Oscar! Not that I knows much about these foreign-
eering dishes. But the stuff slips down like — like soapsuds down
a gullyhole.''

Wilde sighed. ''I suppose we really do have to discuss those letters. How tiresome. Incorrigible that you are, dear Alfred, you
expect me to pay you money to get my own letters back! It seems
to me that you are utterly cynical, immoral, and ruthless. In fact,
you have all the makings of a business tycoon. I think you should
come home to Chelsea with me.''

Wood frowned, suspicious. ''What's in Chelsea?''

''Chelsea is where I live.'' Wilde poured more champagne in
their glasses. ''But we would have to be ever so quiet, Alfred. I
wouldn't wish to waken my wife. Nor my darling children . . .''

''Wouldn't that be a bit — dangerous? Your 'ome?''

Wilde reached for the bell to summon the waiter. ''Terribly

dangerous,'' he said, and rang. He stretched over and brushed his lips against Alfred Wood's small pink ear. "That is what will make it so exciting . . ."

) 6 (

They woke many times during the night, with the dim pink embers glowing through the fire screen, sending crisscross reflections over the walls and floors and the white goatskin bedspread. Chelsea outside was silent as a city of the dead. Towards dawn, though, cocks began to crow, and finally Wilde rose, grumbling, and wrapped himself in a robe of blue silk. He stopped for a moment before the oval toilet mirror of satinwood, patting down ends of hairs and shuddering, then stood before the filigree screens at the windows and stared out at the rose-streaked sky.

"And now, dear boy," he said at last, "you must tell me exactly what you expect for those letters."

Wood took his time dressing, pretending to be searching for a shoe from one end of the room to the other. Then he sat naked on the bed, slowly drawing on his dark hose. "I don't 'ave the letters, Oscar."

Wilde lit a cigarette from an ember in the grate and stood leaning against the window frame. He said nothing.

"They was stolen from me. By two disreputable acquaintances." Wearing only his dark stockings, he stood, hands on hips, in front of Wilde. "That's what I wanted to tell you earlier, Oscar. But you seemed in no mood to listen."

Wilde studied his cigarette thoughtfully. "The letters were stolen from you?"

Wood reached a hand up to caress Wilde's shoulder. "Splendid robe, Oscar. Real silk — finest quality. You are a man of —"

"Did you say they were stolen, Alfred?"

"These acquaintances — they want a great deal of money to return the letters, is what they told me. And they're real disreputable types."

"How much?"

"They said — fifty pounds."

Wilde laughed dryly and extinguished the cigarette in a glass ashtray on the mantelpiece. "For my whole book of poems I received thirty-five."

"And of course, I'd 'ave to pay a detective to find the blokes . . ."

"Alfred, Alfred, Alfred," Wilde said, almost to himself. He poured water from a ewer into a bowl and dipped in his fingertips, splashing his cheeks and forehead. "We'll put it this way, my boy. Do what you must to get the letters back. If you can take care of all your expenses and turn a slight profit for, say, ten pounds, I shall give you the ten pounds." He poked through the closet and came up with a towel as large as a bedsheet to dry his face with. "If not, let these dastardly 'acquaintances' keep the letters. Perhaps they ought to keep them in any case. I understand exposure to great art can go a long way to reforming the criminal mind."

Wood drew on his trousers, shivering at the feel of the rough wool against his legs. "I don't think they'll accept ten pounds, Oscar."

"I do hope they will. I should hate to see you go to so very much effort — a detective and everything! — and end up with nothing for all your pains. And now we must spirit you out of here."

When Wood finished dressing, Wilde led him down the stairs, shushing him repeatedly. In the vestibule they whispered plans for a meeting one evening later in the week, in a German beer garden in Glasshouse Street, and then Wilde gave Wood a quick kiss on the forehead.

It was colder than it had been. Wood pulled his jacket up about his neck. A market cart was rolling slowly along the Embankment, and the houses were tinged pink from the light of the rising sun. "You sure got cautious awful sudden-like, Oscar," Wood said, shivering with the cold. "You wasn't very cautious last night."

"Madness possessed me," Wilde said, with a yawn. "Still," he added, stuffing a pound note into a pocket of Wood's trousers as a coach appeared from the direction of the Royal Hospital, "from time to time genius *requires* a little madness — to stay sane."

) 7 (

When the evening of their rendezvous arrived, Wood was late — but Wilde was not there at all. The pub was full of rosy-cheeked Germans smoking pipes, and Wood was catching the eye of man and woman alike. The bowler hat he had bought that afternoon made him feel uncommonly handsome.

"Dear boy," said Wilde in the doorway, "do remove that dreadful hat." It was sinful, he said, for Wood to cover his honey-colored hair.

"I never did taste 'oney," Wood said, with a soulful look. "I've 'eard it's like sugar and butter mixed. Is that true, Oscar?"

"It is indeed," said Wilde, regarding the others at the bar. In the back room, a crowd of diners began to sing a German song. When his stein of black beer arrived, Wilde sipped it hesitantly, as if it might contain poison.

"They won't 'ear of anythin' less than fifty pounds, Oscar," Wood said, his face full of sorrow despite its roseate glow.

"What a pity," said Wilde, sipping at his beer and seeming to quite enjoy it. "But we won't let that worry *us*, Alfred, will we?" And no more was said about the letters that night.

) 8 (

Wilde was in love again — though not with Alfred Wood. It was the sweetness of spring that had captured his heart, and Wood was merely the beneficiary of an ancient infatuation, once again renewed.

The days grew longer, the air balmier, and they had many meetings. These were usually in the Savoy, now Wilde's favorite hotel — and Wood's, as well. Wilde was only too happy to drink and laugh and talk for hours on any subject imaginable — any subject except the letters.

Wood didn't mind. He was enjoying himself. He felt he could spend the rest of his days in the Connaught or the Savoy. But late in April the matter of the letters was brought up once again.

They were in Wood's room in Langham Place, having tea.

"I ran into them two blokes, quite by accident," Wood said, passing Wilde a soggy crumpet. "The ones as 'as your letters."

"Ah," said Wilde. He had not, Wood noted with annoyance, said a single word about the decor. Wood had made the room quite fancy, with lace curtains and Greek-type plaster statuettes and every kind of tasteful knickknack. "I wish you would realize, Alfred, that no one could possibly be interested in those letters other than a student of fine prose. And he could easily find far more accomplished works of mine at any bookseller's."

Wood was sulking. He had even bought the *Criterion* and the

Pall Mall Gazette to give the impression that he was a reading person. But Wilde seemed not in the least impressed. "Oscar, I believe there are certain people who would be very interested in those —" And suddenly Wood's head was on the table, and he was sobbing, rattling the cheap teacups in their saucers. "You think I'm somethin' loathsome, Oscar." Wilde stared at him, astonished. "I'm somethin' you wouldn't want to sweep your floors with, ain't I! I've always 'ad bad luck, that's the Gord's truth. But I'm not a bad boy, Oscar. I never was that. They never gave me a chance, was all. At 'ome, we was shockin' 'ard up. If I was to tell you the way things was, you wouldn't blame me for a thing. Mother used to be up and out very early washin' in families. She'd work from six in the mornin' till ten at night, which was a bloody long time for a little child's belly to 'old out. And Dad was no good for nothin' but suckin' on an old bottle of gin. I tried workin'. I was a errand boy, runnin' off me backside twelve hours a day for 'alf a shillin' a week. Luck was against me. I fell into bad ways, I'm the first to admit it. I met up with bad companions. I've tried to get away, Oscar, but they won't let me. This Rob Clibburn, 'e has a 'olt on me and I can't get loose. You don't know 'ow much I 'ates people like 'im. And Taylor."

"And me?" said Wilde, moved. "You must hate me as well."

"You're a man as 'as some respect for a person, Oscar. You listen. Like you're listenin' to me right now. You care for me a little, I believe. Do you think I could talk this way to any of those other bastards' gets?"

Wilde came up behind and gently massaged his neck and shoulders. "Dear boy, I believe you care for me a little, too."

Delicately, Wood ran a hand over his running nose. "If I could get me on a ship and sail to America . . ."

"Why would you do better in America than here? Don't you realize that — no. I was going to say something brilliant and witty, and like most brilliant and witty things, utterly untrue. America sounds a splendid idea. I think that is exactly what you must do, Alfred. Start afresh."

Wood was at the mirror, an elaborate one with a gold-painted frame, dabbing at his face with a towel. "I makes a first-rate appearance, Oscar. I know that. Even though I wasn't brought up to no trade, I can be a stunnin' good workman when the mind takes me. I work like sticks on fire, given 'alf a chance. To get me to America wouldn't take much. Thirty pounds'd buy me a ticket. And I could start all over.''

Wilde was sitting on the sagging bed. "Thirty pounds, Alfred, is a great deal of money.''

Wood lowered his eyes. "There's some as would say I was worth it, Oscar.''

"Indeed, Alfred," said Wilde, with a melancholy smile, "if all the poor had profiles like your own, the problem of poverty in London would vanish overnight.''

"All I ask is a fresh start. Get me a good job. They likes us English lads in America. We can write our own tickets there.''

Wilde gripped him by the arm. "I am starting a Society for the Reformation of Good-looking Young Roughnecks. You shall be my first great success. You shall have your thirty pounds, Alfred. And, I hope, a whole new life. Meet me tomorrow at the Regent and we will have one last delightful lunch together.''

Weeping again, the boy threw his arms about Wilde. "Oscar, I'm ever so grateful. Truly I am.''

Wilde took Wood's face in his hands and gave each of the tear-dampened eyes a kiss. "All I am interested in, Alfred, is your happiness," he said, and collected his hat and gloves. Just before he opened the door to leave, he paused. "You won't, though, neglect to bring them this time, Alfred? Those wicked, wonderful letters that first brought us together — and are now so inexorably tearing us apart?''

) 9 (

"You get ten pounds of it," Wood was telling Rob. "With the other twenty and my savin's, I'm off to the U.S.A.''

The coffee stall was directly across from Mudie's Library, and fifteen or twenty people were huddled about it — cabbies, prostitutes, guardsmen off duty and looking for company, a hooligan or two — holding saucers and sipping from steaming cups. It was after midnight and the passing police regarded them all with suspicion. "Anythin' you say, Alfie," murmured Rob.

Wood looked puzzled. "Aren't you goin' to try to keep me in London?''

When he smiled it was as if the thin skin of Rob's face became transparent, revealing the bone and cartilage beneath. "You'll come back," he said.

"Don't depend on it, Rob."

One of the women shouldered past them and banged her fist on the counter. " 'Ere, give us a couple of 'ard-boiled, and look lively. We ain't goin' to spend the whole bloomin' night 'ere."

"You'll get awful lonely in America, Alfie. You'll soon get to thinkin' of old Rob, wishin' you could come back." He gave Wood a mock punch in the jaw. "Hey, you're not givin' the old boy *all* the letters, are you?"

Wood was blowing on his coffee, unable to drink it hot, though Rob had long finished his. " 'E won't give me the money 'less I do."

" 'E'd never miss one letter. Let us 'ave just one of 'em, as a goin' away present. Somethin' to remember dear Alfie by. The one about the 'madness of kisses.' That one's 'ot enough to get old Rob a few pounds when you're off rollin' in the 'aystacks with some big Yank."

Wood forced himself to down a mouthful of the coffee, squinching up his face with the effort. "I couldn't do that, Rob."

"One letter, Alfie. Old Oscar won't never miss it. At least, not until it's too late."

) 10 (

"I have grown inordinately fond of you, Alfred," said Wilde. He spread a spoonful of caviar on a thin slice of bread. "Knowing you has been a thrilling experience." He popped the bread in his mouth and hummed with pleasure.

"Ditto, Oscar. I shall miss you, as well. If everybody in this town carried as good a face as you, a lad wouldn't 'ave to worry about a thing."

Wilde offered him a spoonful of caviar, but Wood shook his head violently.

"But Alfred, whatever will you do once you *get* to America? If you were wise, of course, the moment you arrived you would take the next boat back to England. But you are not wise, I fear. And thirty pounds — it isn't really a great deal to conquer a whole new *continent* with. I am going to send you a little more once you get there — four or five pounds to get you started."

"You are very genteel, Oscar. You truly are."

Then, with a slow smile, Wilde said: "And the letters? You did bring them?"

Avoiding Wilde's gaze, Wood tossed the small packet on the table. Wilde slipped it into a pocket of his green velvet coat. "To crime," he said, raising his glass.

They parted like two City bankers after negotiating a mutually profitable deal. It was not until he was back at Tite Street late that afternoon that Wilde removed the letters from his pocket and read them.

They brought a sting of melancholy, those words of his, as he remembered the agonies of fondness that had inspired them, the feigned and real affection that had rounded every phrase. They also brought shame, at the thought of the alien eyes that had gluttoned over these pages.

And now that the danger was past, he was flooded with remorse. Oh, the unsavory paths his attraction to Bosie had led him into! Bosie. How weary he was of adoring him.

From upstairs came a sweet, faltering melody, picked out uncertainly on keys in need of tuning. What a long time since there had been music in the house. Without even being aware of its absence, he had missed it.

The fragile tune, made more poignant by the stumbling way it was played, seemed to deepen his concern over the cesspool that in recent months he had been sinking down into. Consorting with blackmailers and prostitutes, and why? To impress Bosie? To shock himself? Remembering Alfred Wood strutting about right here in this very house, as Connie and the children slept, he cringed at the power of his own perversity. He was afraid of himself, of the dark forces slyly battling in his soul.

Something in the phrases of music seemed to be speaking to him, imparting a message subtler than words. There was good left in him: if not, the music's message of hope would have passed unobserved.

Three letters. Had not Wood said four? What difference. He tore them into small pieces, bitterly recalling how little these pages had meant to the one they were written for. Bosie had not even suggested he might want them back: that was what hurt most. Wilde dropped the scraps into a large glass bowl he used for an ashtray, and lit a gold-tipped match.

He watched the fragments curl and blacken. His foolish lovely words going up in smoke. As his youth was. As his very life was. He emptied the ashtray into the dead embers of the fireplace.

Her quilted dressing gown was embroidered with an intricate pattern of roses and lily of the valley, and she was staring down at the keys with gloomy, dark-circled eyes.

"A lovely melody," he said.

She stared up at him quizzically. "Home so early?"

"Don't stop. Please."

She closed the piano lid softly. "If I'd known you were in the house, I should never have attempted Chopin." She stood at the window, brushing the edges of the curtains, then slipped onto the white sofa. Her hair was wrapped up clumsily around two tortoise-shell combs, and her face looked pale and confused, as if she had just been awakened from sleep. And yet she had a curious loveliness he had never seen in her before, the cool, self-absorbed look of a child. "I used to play rather well," she said, more to herself than him.

He was seeing the room with fresh eyes. He was tired of it, tired of its elegance and all the effort necessary to maintain that elegance. Did they dare to throw out all the costly furnishings and start again? "Used to, Connie?"

"I loved it so, everything about it, even the five-finger exercises. Yet whenever I felt myself making any progress, I — drew back. As if I were afraid to — accomplish anything."

Perching himself on an arm of the sofa, he dug in his pocket for a cigarette. He felt shy with her, he realized. "You were wise, Connie. Accomplishment is the last resource of those who have forgotten how to dream."

She stared at him coldly, making herself even more beautiful. "The Golden Dawn, too. I loved it — and let it go. Our home. This room —"

"You never liked this room."

"I did. Even if I chaffed you about it, I felt this room was ours, this house was ours . . . I loved everything about it. And I have abandoned it. It is Bridie's room now! Whenever I love anything too much, I — I have to let it go."

He slid down next to her on the sofa. "Are you going to let me go?"

She moved away from him, but he pulled her back. Reaching a hand up to tuck in ends of hair, she gave him a thoughtful look. "How odd for us to be alone," she said.

"We should be alone more often."

She shrugged. "I hardly know what to say to you." She drew away slightly, shuddering, though the room was warm. "I keep expecting Lord Alfred Douglas to come creeping out of the shadows."

Wilde was staring at her pouting lips. "In some ways, we hardly know each other, you and I."

She smiled in spite of herself. "I know you too well, Oscar."

"Do you?" He placed his warm, moist hand over her cool, dry one; she stiffened but did not pull away. "Then it is only fair that I know you as well, Connie. Tell me about yourself."

She released a small peal of laughter — breathy and harsh. "I am Mrs. Oscar Wilde."

"And who *is* Mrs. Oscar Wilde? What does she think about? What does she truly want?"

She sat at the piano again, and after a moment opened it and stared down at the keys. "If you were able to enjoy being at home once in a while, Oscar. If you could only —"

"You are speaking of me again, Connie," he said, coming up behind her and resting his hands gently on her shoulders. "*My* happiness. What of yours?"

She picked out the opening bars of the same Chopin piece. "I suppose I should like to be — the kind of woman you — you need."

"Connie! Stop thinking of what I need. What do *you* need?"

Turning her hands into claws, she crashed them down upon the keys. Her face was flushed with anger and frustration, and she got up from the piano and started towards the door. But he yanked her back.

She tripped on the carpet and, falling, pulled him down with her. They fell sideways, muffling each other's impact on the floor. She laughed halfheartedly, but stopped. Her dressing gown had flown open: she tried to adjust it, but he was pressing close to her, pulling her in tight to him. His mouth was on hers, his hands cupped about her head. She was paralyzed, and then her hands were at his shoulders, pushing him away.

He would not be pushed. He was tearing at her robe, his hands rushing over her body, his lips greedy and moist. She flung herself from him, and stumbled across the room onto the sofa. Gasping for breath, she held a cushion before her for protection.

"Connie, can't we change?" he begged, kneeling before her. "Can't we start again?"

She thrust the cushion into his face. "Don't, Oscar! Dear God, please — leave me alone."

"I thought —"

"Leave me!" she said, sobbing. "Please — please leave me alone."

) 11 (

A tall man in a worn gray sweater sat with his chair propped up beside the stage door in the warm afternoon light. His face was youthful and handsome, but his hair was white, and he was reading the *Evening Standard* through small, round, wire-rimmed spectacles. Willie Allen stood patting down the spikes of his hair, waiting to be noticed.

"Deadish, ain't it," Willie finally said. "Don't seem like spring nohow." The man went on reading.

Willie didn't give up: "I understand a Mr. Oscar Wilde does business in this place, is that right?"

The doorman would not give him the satisfaction of looking up from his paper. "Who wants to know?"

Willie reached forth the folded letter. "I've got a certain little billet-doux 'ere that ought to be of great interest to the gentleman. Let me see the bloke and I shouldn't wonder if 'e'd give you a nice tip."

The newspaper rattled. "Mr. Wilde is havin' an uncommon long lunch, I would say. Anything as you wants 'im to 'ave, you just leave it with me."

Willie studied the letter a moment, pretending to be reading it with deep interest. "All right," he said, sliding it down in front of the page the doorman was reading. "Tell 'im this is from Mr. William Allen, Esquire. And I will be on this same spot tomorrow at four p.m." Without putting down the newspaper, the doorman stuffed the letter in a bottom drawer of the desk just inside the door. "I 'as relations in the theater myself, y'know," Willie said grandly. No reaction. "By the way, you can tell Mr. Wilde I know the whereabouts of the original of that letter, if 'e 'appens to be interested. You hear that? The original article.''

"Mr. Wilde will receive the message," the doorman murmured. At that instant a man in a greatcoat with a high fur collar came hurrying down the alley, leading a beautiful, giggling woman. A clump of bright red hair jutted out from under his top hat. The doorman got up to make way.

"Back for more?" he said. "Aren't you worn out, sir?''

The man flashed a great smile. ''I'm radiant as always, Shelby. Radiant as always.'' He led the woman in the stage door, leaving it ajar.

"Gawblimey," said Willie, "what a coat! That wouldn't be Mr. Wilde, would it?''

Shutting the door carefully, the doorman appraised Willie as if he were some species of rodent. "That, if you must know, is Mr. Tree. Star and manager.''

"Manager, is it? Seems a tip-top gent, 'e does.''

The doorman unfurled his paper, leaning his chair against the door. "Best director in the West End, they tells me. I never 'ad the honor to be invited to one of 'is productions.''

"'Ere, tell you what. Give us back that letter. You wouldn't allow us to 'ave just a few words with Mr. Tree? I think 'e might be very interested in 'avin' a look at this 'ere letter.''

Without removing his eyes from the newspaper the doorman rummaged a hand about the desk, pulling open the bottom drawer. "Mr. Tree? 'E's a very busy man.''

"Well, then, 'ow's about *you* givin' 'im the letter? And write my address on the back.''

"Write it yourself.''

"I never 'ad me no time to be bothered learnin' to write," Willie said. "You write it. Then, in case the bloke is interested in findin' out more, 'e knows where to go . . .''

) 12 (

Over the stage the technicians were spreading a false lawn, while on the wire-mesh shrubbery two of them touched up paper roses with pink gouache paint. Grasping his script, Beerbohm Tree scratched a cross in chalk on the spot where his wife, smiling coolly at Rose Leclerq, was waiting for her cue.

"All right, darlings, once again," Tree said.

Rose Leclerq drew an imaginary scarf before her nostrils. "Well," she said, "from *whatever* source her large fortune came, I have a great esteem for Miss Worsley." She took a few steps in front of Mrs. Tree. "She dresses exceedingly well. All Americans *do* dress well. They get their clothes in Paris."

Mrs. Tree opened an invisible parasol, upstaging Rose Leclerq. "They say, Lady Hunstanton, that when good Americans die they go to Paris."

"Indeed?" said Rose Leclerq, strolling in front of Mrs. Tree. "And when bad Americans die, where do *they* go to?"

Beerbohm Tree rose from his chair and faced the empty orchestra. "Oh, they go to America."

"No, no, no, no, no," came a voice from the back of the theater. Oscar Wilde came bounding down the aisle. "You mustn't be so *prim*, Herbert. The line is a delicate bubble of fancy, not an obituary notice. I want the play to be at least a *little* less vulgar than reality."

Tree stiffened. "Lord Illingsworth must at least *appear* to take his comments seriously, Oscar."

"Exactly not. He must toss them off as if they are lovely bits of gossamer he is weaving in the air."

"That is *not* the way people talk, Oscar," Tree said in an agitated voice. "I am trying to add some *depth* to Lord Illingsworth's character."

"If I ever sink to writing the way people actually *talk*, Herbert, I will consider my artistic career at an end."

Tree stared down at him like an outraged deity regarding a supplicant who has committed some impious act. "You wish the play to be absurd, then?"

"Precisely," said Wilde, starting back up the aisle again. "As in life itself, all the poetry is in the absurdity."

"Speaking of poetry, Oscar," said Tree, with difficulty mastering his anger. "I have something to show you." His soft beautiful voice was a study in calm. "Take a break, darlings." As the others left the stage, he reached for the billfold in his waistcoat pocket and produced a scrap of paper. "A young man left this with the doorman the other day. I believe it's a letter of yours."

With a sigh of impatience, Wilde reached up for the letter. He held it away from him as if it emitted an unpleasant odor. "A letter of mine?" he said, laughing. "This is the handwriting of an illiterate."

"The letter has been copied, Oscar. Read it."

Wilde sank into the plush of a front seat and read the page. He sat for a long while in silence.

"Well, Oscar?" said Tree.

Wilde smiled slightly. "If it were in verse, I would call it a delightful poem."

Tree smiled, too. "But it is not in verse, Oscar."

"The only thing keeping it from *The Golden Treasury of Poetry*." He reached into an inner pocket for a narrow silver cylinder and from it took a quick swig.

"I spoke to the bearer, Oscar," said Tree, glancing about to be certain no one was within hearing distance. "He is attempting to sell the original of that letter."

Wilde glanced down at the page. "I didn't realize I'd attained the level of the popular press."

"He claims it was written to Lord Alfred Douglas. Did you write the letter, Oscar? Not that it is my affair . . ."

Wilde had put on a good deal of weight in recent months, and when, as now, he grew excited, his face became bloated and almost purple. "I wrote a kind of poem in prose once that this is a crude copy of, yes. And yes, I believe I dedicated that poem to Lord Alfred Douglas. And yes, it was sent in letter form. But for heaven's sake, *why*, Tree? Whatever difference can it make?"

For all the obvious satisfaction Tree was deriving from the conversation, it was clear that he was also deeply concerned — unless it was only another of his performances. "People might put a — wrong construction on the letter. That is all."

"Thank you for telling me, Tree. May I keep this? I have a scrapbook of highlights from the world's great poetry. This should fit in nicely. And now, shall we get back to the second act, which I am hoping to see played with just a *little* less reality this time?"

) 13 (

Neither Wilde nor Tree noticed the figure in the balcony stealing silently to a rear door. He sprang down the steps, several at a time, and made for the back door of the theater.

"Shelby!" he said.

The doorman, cleaning a pipe out in a dustbin, looked up with a smile. "Here again today, Mr. Brookfield? Don't you never get tired watching Mr. Wilde?"

"He grows ever more interesting! So long as he doesn't catch me."

"I should think 'e'd be flattered, sir."

"Shelby — did someone give you a letter yesterday? Perhaps the day before?" He sat on the stage-door desk, staring intensely down at the doorman. "To give to Mr. Tree?"

"Someone did indeed, sir." He filled the clean pipe with coarse leaves of blackish tobacco. "Unsavory-lookin' little squint, I don't mind sayin'."

"You didn't by any chance read that letter?"

Shelby was offended. "Certainly not, sir!"

Brookfield looked desperate. "The unsavory-looking squint — did he by any chance leave his name?"

"That 'e did, sir. Allen Williams, it was." He lit the pipe and a cloud of sweet smoke perfumed the alley. "Or was it William Allen? Blimey, first one sounds right, then the other does. Anyhow, it was one o' them names. 'E left 'is address, as well. Number eleven, Plunkett Road. Funny, that stands out in my memory clear as a bell!"

"Brilliant, Shelby!" said Brookfield, scrawling the address on an envelope. "Another clue to the puzzle of Oscar Wilde!"

Shelby chuckled, digging in the bowl of the pipe with a key. "You study that man as serious as if 'e was a part you was goin' to do in some play."

"We are all playing parts," said Brookfield, adjusting his tie in a chipped, frameless mirror over the desk.

"P'r'aps, sir."

"But Oscar Wilde is hardly the role *I'd* choose, Shelby! Do you actually see *me* playing the fool?"

) 14 (

Bosie told the cab to wait for them while they dined: a new extravagance he had adopted — though Wilde, of course, would be expected to pay.

All conversation seemed to stop as they entered the restaurant.

Wilde followed the waiter, Bosie followed him, and everyone in the room turned towards them — though not as in the past. The faces no longer betrayed amused interest: rather, they were filled with hostility, or with disgust.

The waiter pointed to a table in a far corner of the room, near the kitchen. "This is where you're seating *us?*" cried Bosie.

"It's the only table as is left," said the young waiter, glancing nervously towards the maître d'hôtel.

"You're joking!" Bosie snapped.

"Hush, Bosie," said Wilde, taking a seat and smiling at the waiter. "He is only following instructions."

Bosie pulled his chair far out from the table and sat staring at everyone around them, glowering. "We were always given the best table in the room!" he hissed.

"Wherever I am seated *is* the best table in the room."

"I take this as an insult."

"Dear boy, you take everything as an insult." He looked at Bosie fondly, trying to disguise the pain he felt. Bosie's mother had arranged for him to spend some time in Egypt, hoping he would take to the Foreign Service, and that the Foreign Service would take to him, and this was in the nature of a farewell dinner.

In a way Wilde was eager for Bosie to be gone, so he could once again submit himself to the agonizing pleasure of serious work. At the same time he had already begun to miss his darling boy, who seemed to grow ever more precious as his sailing date approached. "You can hardly blame them, Bosie. No one would charge us with being overly discreet of late . . ."

"Discretion is for little people," said Bosie, shuddering as if the restaurant were covered with cobwebs. His indignation dissolved, however, in his excitement over the news he was bursting to convey. His older brother Francie, it appeared, was vacationing in Homburg with his employer, Lord Rosebery. "And my father followed them there — carrying a horsewhip!"

"Bosie, I don't wish to —"

"A horsewhip! For Lord Rosebery! Remember last year, when Francie was made an English lord? Until the day it happened, my father seemed to be delighted. But from the moment Francie was officially named Lord Drumlanrig, the old fool began to absolutely *boil* with jealousy! Can you imagine? But Oscar — *guess* the reason for the horsewhip!'' Bosie seemed to be addressing the silent couple at the next table rather than Wilde.

''I cannot guess.''

''It seems my father got a brainstorm and decided that Rosebery is — listen to this — that Rosebery is *buggering* my brother!'' Laughing harshly, he looked about to be certain everyone around was listening. ''Is it not too, too amusing? Francie? And Lord Rosebery? Can you even *picture* such a thing? I only hope it's true, don't you? He's mad,'' Bosie cried joyously. ''My father is mad!''

And then the food arrived, and while Wilde was enchanted with the way the partridge was prepared, Bosie insisted that there was too much Hungarian curry on it — reason enough to start a heated row. Secluded though the table was, soon everyone in Kettner's was aware that they were in the room, and battling. Wilde spent the rest of the meal in a poisonous silence.

As they were leaving, once again running the gantlet of staring faces, Bosie's gaiety revived. He grasped Wilde's arm and gave him a radiant smile:

''I want everyone in this restaurant to stare,'' he announced in a loud voice, as they passed the maître d'hôtel. ''I want them to say, 'Look — there goes Oscar Wilde with his young minion, his catamite, his whore!' Nothing could give me greater pleasure!''

Entering the restaurant was Sir Wilfred Oakes, a friend of Wilde's from Oxford days. Brightening, Wilde moved to greet him — but Oakes's face turned cold and empty as a marble bust. He turned and strode away in the opposite direction.

''Who was that pompous slug?'' demanded Bosie.

''I saw nothing,'' Wilde said, and marched out to the row of cabs waiting in front.

) 15 (

In his study, Wilde was quietly sipping brandy from a water goblet, leafing through an old notebook given him long ago by Robbie Ross. The balmy summer weather had subsided as summer itself approached; strangely, it seemed to grow cooler every day.

He was dreading the thought of being separated from Bosie, even though he had encouraged Lady Queensberry in every way to send him off to Egypt. He knew it was the only hope for Bosie, and the only way he himself would ever again do any work. Wilde needed to make a good deal of money quickly. Funds were disappearing, especially in recent weeks. Bosie used the excuse of his final days in London to demand more pleasures and surprises than ever before, and more expensive ones. And how could Wilde deny him? What pleasures were there going to be in Egypt?

He must write a new play. It was the surest investment for his time and talent. There was a single dreadful problem, however: he was drained of ideas — drained dry. He felt, indeed, as if he could never write a play again; that as an artist, he had ceased to exist.

Art had been the first and deepest passion of his life: yet he had traduced the artist in him in every way so that he might make people laugh, knowing that the more extravagantly they laughed, the more lavishly they were willing to pay. Pigs, he had noticed, became extremely impatient for one to cast pearls before them. Only it was becoming ever more difficult to do.

Robbie had made him a present of this notebook, a kind of anthology of Wilde's conversational sallies — mostly nonsensical. In their first months together, the boy had carefully noted down virtually everything Wilde had said. Only find some fragment of a plot to hang these quotations onto, Robbie insisted, and Wilde would have his best and most brilliant play.

He turned the crinkling pages skeptically, picking out here and there a remark that amused him. He paused often for a sip of brandy: he could hardly be expected to do anything artistic while thoroughly sober. Dear Robbie. A creature of boundless faith, perhaps because he was a creature of boundless love.

"Lady Effingham was quite altered by her husband's death," he read. "She looks twenty years younger. In fact, her hair has turned quite gold from grief."

"In married life, three's company, two's a crowd."

"I like to carry my diary when I travel; one should always have something sensational to read in the train."

"Ignorance is like an exotic fruit; touch it and the bloom is gone."

"Novels that end happily invariably leave one feeling depressed."

He tried to recall the occasions that had inspired these thoughts, and on the whole they saddened more than amused him: reminding him, when he was able to remember some specific incident, of how his life was rushing by — and of how his memory was failing, when he could not.

"A — a person to see you, sir," said Arthur, who was growing out of his uniform.

"A person, Arthur? What do you mean, a person?"

"A Mr. Allen — that's the name he says. He says to tell you it's about a certain letter, sir, and that you'll understand."

Wilde closed his eyes a moment. "Give me a few minutes, Arthur. Then show this Mr. Allen in."

When Arthur was gone Wilde reached a bottle of Gordon's gin out from the bottom drawer of his ebony chest, and slugged a mouthful down. The sting made him gasp and choke, but he welcomed the very harshness of it. He lit a cigarette then and poised himself on the edge of the wing chair.

The cigarette was almost finished when the youth came edging into the room. He had a sickly air about him, and was grasping in his hands a greasy-looking hat of straw. It had left his hair standing straight up like porcupine quills. Not a very attractive specimen, Wilde noted, though he probably once had been. Pity.

He puffed thoughtfully on the cigarette. "I suppose you've come about the beautiful letter I wrote a few months ago to Lord Alfred Douglas."

"I 'ave, Mr. Wilde, sir. I've got it 'ere — the original article. And I'm willin' to let you 'ave it. Right cheap."

Wilde poured two glasses of sherry and handed one to Allen, who accepted doubtfully, as if the glass might break in his enormous, clumsy fingers. "Much obliged, sir."

"Are you employed, Mr. Allen?"

"Used to be, sir. Father was a dredger, and grandfather afore 'im. I tried it, too, but the work was gallows 'ard. I got sick of it."

Wilde nodded; how was it possible to stay hostile to anyone, once you knew a little about them? "If you hadn't been so foolish as to give a copy of that letter to Mr. Beerbohm Tree, in your abortive attempt to embarrass me, I just might have considered buying it from you. After all, I consider it to be a work of art."

"Oh, it surely is, sir. Only there are persons who might think it an uncommon strange letter for one gentleman to be writin' to another."

"Might they!" Allen was younger than he looked; how had the poor lad gotten embroiled in such a life? "Well," Wilde said, "I suppose art is rarely intelligible to the criminal classes."

"There's a certain party what 'as offered me sixty pounds for it."

Wilde blew a cloud of smoke high over Allen's head. "Splendid!" he said, conclusively. "That will be the first time so slight an effort of mine will have received such a fee. I hope it becomes a prototype, Mr. Allen! And now I must wish you a good evening." He threw open the study door.

Allen looked bewildered. In a weak voice he said: "You can call me Willie if you like, sir."

Wilde laughed kindly. "If you take my advice, Mr. Allen, you will accept that certain party's offer — and at once."

The *Times* was lying folded on a side table, and Allen carefully rested his half-empty glass on it. "The party — 'appens to be out of town at the moment."

"You must go to see him immediately upon his return. For he's likely to lose all interest in the letter when he learns it's to be published in one of our better literary magazines."

"Published?" said Allen, frowning.

Wilde reached for Allen's hat on the desk, lifting it by the very outmost edge of the brim. "As a poem — which, of course, is what it is." He had to smile, remembering his frantic telegram to Pierre Louÿs in Paris, begging him to translate the letter into a *poème en prose*. "If you'll leave your address, Mr. Allen, I shall be happy to send you a copy." He handed Allen his hat. In return, Allen gave him the empty sherry glass, looking disappointed when Wilde did not offer to refill it.

"Look, Mr. Wilde, I'm awful 'ard up," said Allen, crossing to the far side of the room. "It's not for myself I need the money, but poor Mother 'as to 'ave a eye operation. It's real serious-like, and I'm the one 'as to arrange everything. I don't know what to do."

"You must inform your dear mother that for precisely such desperate cases, Her Majesty has established several very generous charitable institutions. I, unfortunately, am not one of them."

Allen reached the letter from his pocket and began unfolding it carefully. "You can 'ave it for just ten pounds."

Wilde closed the door, but not entirely. "You have no appreciation of literature, Mr. Allen. If you'd asked for sixty pounds, as you did with that 'certain party' you mentioned, I might have given it to you! However, I have no need of the letter. It will soon be in print, and I already have a sufficient number of the author's original manuscripts to satisfy even *my* enthusiasm for his work." He motioned for Allen to follow him out.

"Give us a few pounds at least, Mr. Wilde. I'm truly desp'rate."

With a sigh, Wilde reached in his pocket and produced a half sovereign. "I must wish you a good evening, Mr. Allen." He led the way out through the vestibule and held open the outside door.

Allen turned in the street to wave good-night, but the door was closed. Tipping his straw hat down over his eyes, he slunk down Tite Street towards the river.

The Battersea Bridge stretched over the Thames under a sky brown as cough medicine, and along the Embankment the lamp-posts twinkled in the mist. Rob was leaning against a tree, staring disgustedly at the fog clinging in patches over the black water. "Well?" he said, flipping his cigarette into the river.

"Didn't work. 'E only laughed at me."

"You got nothing at all?"

"All the same 'e's a rum old party, this Wilde is. The letter's to appear in some magazine or other, 'e says. Give me a 'alf quid to be rid of me." He pulled the letter from his pocket. "Doesn't even *want* the bloody thing. Should I chuck it in the river?"

Rob lit another cigarette. "Give it 'ere." He stuffed the letter in his pocket and, hands behind his back, started off towards Tite Street. "I'll pay the bastard a little call."

"No use, Rob," Allen called after him. "We'll never see any money from that one."

Arthur was nervously refusing Rob entrance, despite his tale of having urgent business with Mr. Wilde, when Wilde himself appeared in the doorway, and said he would handle the matter.

"Listen, young man, I have a great deal of work to do. I cannot be bothered with foolishness of this kind."

Rob reached forth the letter. "We've decided to let you 'ave the blessed thing."

Suspicious, Wilde examined the letter front and back. "Why?" he said. "Why are you giving me this?"

Rob withdrew his hands and concealed them behind his back, as if only just realizing how filthy the fingernails were. "My butty says you're a right decent gentleman, says 'e, and there's no use tryin' to rent you. You only laugh at us, 'e says."

"You haven't taken very good care of my lovely letter," Wilde said, delicately folding it. "Very well, then, I'll accept it. After all, it *is* an original manuscript by Oscar Wilde."

"Sorry if it's in bad condition, sir. The letter 'as, as they say, been around."

"Indeed it has," said Wilde, chuckling ruefully. He handed Rob a sovereign with a smile that bordered on admiration. "You look as if you should be a monk," he said. "Have you ever considered taking Holy Orders?"

"No, sir."

"But what a wicked life you are leading!"

"There's good and bad in every one of us," said Rob.

"A born philosopher," said Wilde, laughing, and reached forth his hand. "I wish you well, whoever you are." With a wave of farewell, he closed the door.

) 16 (

A few days later, Charles Brookfield entered the lobby of Carter's Hotel, in Albemarle Street.

"The Marquess of Queensberry is living here at the moment, is he not?" The old man at the desk looked up sleepily and nodded. Brookfield presented his card. "Can you let me have the marquess's room number, please?"

PART SEVEN

Rule 1 — To be a fair stand-up boxing match in a 24-foot ring, or as near that size as practicable.

Marquess of Queensberry rules

WHEN Queensberry woke, he was lying on the floor and his mouth was full of death. A bottle of Hennessy brandy, nearly full, rested beside him, and an empty one lay on its side before the cold ashes in the fireplace.

He half rose; his back ached so badly he collapsed and had to try again. The room did not seem familiar to him. It was filled with oversize pieces in black mahogany. Glass ovals in the doors of an enormous cabinet revealed the books inside: mostly thick, superannuated volumes on accounting, left by a former tenant. The only sound was the old clock on the mantel, its scythelike pendulum swaying back and forth with a gloomy sigh. Six twenty-five. Morning or evening? Through the liver-colored draperies at the windows, the dismal blue gathering about the rooftops might be dawn or dusk. He carried the brandy bottle to the fireplace, where on a tattered bear rug a stiff chair hard as a church pew faced a bulky rocker. He selected the hard chair and sat waiting, sipping at the brandy. If it got lighter outside, it would be morning; if darker, night.

He grasped the sides of the chair. Someone was in the room with him. A ghostly shape was bunched up on the leather sofa, staring at him with menacing eyes.

In a shimmer of nausea and regret, the incidents of the night before returned to him. But the staring, menacing eyes were only in his imagination: the girl was asleep.

He knelt before her frail lovely body, filled with a yearning to protect her — from the cold, from life, from himself.

"Oh, Gord," she said, wriggling beneath the threadbare blanket.

"You're in safe hands, lass." Things they had done the night before kept coming back: he did not wish to remember them in their entirety. She was neither as pretty nor as young as she had seemed to be; yet she was an attractive enough little doxy. Except for her coarse, reddened hands.

"Got to be movin' me arse," she said. She pushed the blanket from her; he tried unsuccessfully to make her take it back. She shuddered: "Rotten time for a body to go out in the cold streets, ain't it." She was wearing a corset and black stockings.

"Stay, lass. We can have a bit of breakfast. I'll take you anyplace you like."

"My man is goin' to kill me," she said, yawning, scratching her thigh.

Queensberry carried the bottles into the kitchen and took a silent pull at the full one. Her dress was on, and she was standing at the window, staring out at the houses etched against the crumbling indigo sky. Pity about her hands, he thought.

"Why would you live in a place like this if you're really a baron?" she said, tightening the elastic on one of her stockings and making a knot in it.

"A marquess." He took the other bit of elastic from her and carefully knotted it in place. "I live all over. I don't tie myself down." She was too proud to ask for help hooking up the blouse and he was too shy with her to offer.

"You have no family?"

"None."

"That's a misfortune, I should say. A man your age —"

"I don't need anyone," he said, turning away. "People need me. Finish up now. I have things to do."

She threw her cheap coat of red wool over her shoulders and he counted out the money they had agreed on the night before: with all the rest a blur, he clearly remembered the sum.

When he handed her the coins, she counted them, too. "You wouldn't make a body walk home at this hour, would you? A gentleman like yourself?"

"I am short of funds . . ."

"Make it twenty instead of fifteen, whyn't you? I worked bloody hard last night."

"Go."

"After all, *you* were incapable. If you're always like that, I can see why you have no family."

He was holding open the door. "Get out of here. At once."

She pressed a long pin into her straw hat, and adjusted it at an angle. Then, grinning crookedly, she sidled over to him as slowly as she could. She pressed out her lips as if to kiss him good-bye, then slowly stuck out her tongue. "You're a small man, my lord," she said, starting for the stairs. "Small in every way."

Queensberry slammed the door and crumpled against it, all atremble. He tried to laugh. Angry at a little baggage like that? In the grate he lit a small fire, then went to the kitchen to shave himself, his hands still unsteady. A cracked mirror was set at an angle to the window, but in the meager gaslight he could hardly bear the sight of his ravaged face.

He changed his clothes. Every garment was unpressed. Blasted MacTavish would simply have to be let go. He was too old, too confused. Over the years he had gotten progressively less capable, and now he seemed to expect special consideration because of his age!

To distract himself, Queensberry sat before the fire and leafed through the *Times* of the day before, trying to concentrate on items of news in which he had no interest. Suddenly a name leaped out from the page.

MR OSCAR WILDE ON HIS NEW PLAY — AMONG OTHER TRIVIAL TOPICS

Queensberry's eyes danced through the article, lighting on random paragraphs:

'What is your play about, Mr Wilde?'

'It has its philosophy: That we should treat all the trivial things of life very seriously, and all the serious things with sincere and studied triviality.'

'Is it only in deference to the imperious mandate of the public that you appear before them after all your plays?'

'Yes, I have always been very good-natured about that. The public has always been so appreciative of my work I felt it would be a pity to spoil its evening . . . '

Queensberry crushed the newspaper into a heap and began tearing at it furiously. Kicking at the bits of paper, he went about snatching them up and flinging them one by one into the flames.

) 2 (

Keen for lunch, Queensberry strolled into the Café Royal, intending to dine in the upstairs restaurant. Something made him pause at the Domino Room entrance.

The place was full and boisterous, as always at midday, and through a veil of tobacco smoke he saw familiars hobnobbing with the very dregs of society, writers, painters, God knew what all, most of them ne'er-do-wells who owned nothing but the ostentatious clothes upon their backs.

He was turning to leave when suddenly, in the depths of one of the mirrors, he saw them. He backed behind a clump of palms, whence he might watch unseen. Several small tables had been pushed together to form one long one, and the two of them held court in the very center, surrounded by a crowd of chattering admirers. It was, Queensberry decided, rather like a travesty of the Last Supper, a fat, purple-faced Jesus and next to him the simpering beloved disciple. So Bosie was back from his abortive honeymoon with the Foreign Service. Naturally he had never thought to let his father know.

Queensberry wanted to go over and drag this imbecile son of his from the table. He remembered the letter given to him by the actor Brookfield. But who could take an actor seriously? It might be part of some aesthetic trick they were all trying to play, hoping to make a fool of old Queensberry. He would show them he was not so easy a mark.

But certainly something unnatural was going on. Bosie would whisper something to Wilde, then turn to the man on his other side, blinking his eyes like a schoolgirl, and then they would both shriek with laughter, and Wilde would join in.

Queensberry was shaking with anger, and yet something forced him to stay, watching. Observing people who did not know they were being observed gave him a pleasant feeling of power over them. At last he turned away. All appetite was gone; he felt ill, in fact. He left the Royal, certain that he would choke up the least bite of food. A few brandies would serve him just as well.

) 3 (

The letter would be calm, even cordial. "Dear Alfred," he wrote — and anger stabbed through him. He forced himself to be calm, and gently pointed out the shabby future his son was preparing for himself by loafing about instead of finding some means of earning a living. Then, with a rush of something like pleasure, he brought up the intimacy with Oscar Wilde:

> I am not going to try and analyse this intimacy, and make no charge; but to my mind to pose as a thing is as bad as to be it. With my own eyes I saw you with the most loathsome and disgusting relationship as expressed by your manner and expression. Never in all my experience have I ever seen such a sight as that in your horrible features. No wonder people are talking as they are. Now I hear that Wilde's wife is going to divorce him. Is this true, or do you not know of it? If I thought the actual thing was true, and it became public property, I should be quite justified in shooting him at sight.
>
> These christian English cowards and men, as they call themselves, want waking up.
>
> Your disgusted so-called father,
Queensberry

After he posted the letter, his mood improved. At the Jockey he engaged in chat about the last meet at Windsor, where his old friend Lord Roxdale's horse was said to have been drugged. Even if it turned out to be false, the rumor itself would ruin Roxdale as a sportsman, perhaps forever. Queensberry roared with laughter and remained in high spirits for the rest of the evening.

Two days later, MacTavish brought in two pieces of mail. "I've been thinking over your request," Queensberry said to the old man. "You may have Saturday evening free to visit your sister, if it's absolutely necessary."

"Thank you, sir."

The old faker must learn that Queensberry was not an employer to be gulled with tales of family illnesses and the like. Nevertheless, Queensberry planned to be at Ascot for the weekend, so it little mattered. He opened the telegram first, feeling a slight bristle of excitement.

WHAT A FUNNY LITTLE MAN YOU ARE.
ALFRED DOUGLAS

"Will that be all, sir?"

Queensberry whirled on the stooped old man as if he might knock him down. "I have changed my mind. I will require you to be here all the weekend."

"All the — all the weekend, sir?" MacTavish looked stunned; for a moment it seemed he might fall to the floor. "Very — very good, sir," he said, and left the room.

Queensberry tore open the letter. It was from a firm of solicitors — one of the most respected in London.

It had been brought to the attention of their client, Oscar Wilde, Esquire, that the Marquess of Queensberry had written a letter insulting Mr. and Mrs. Wilde. Accordingly, Mr. Wilde was expecting an immediate apology.

"MacTavish! MacTavish!" When the old man shuffled back into the room, Queensberry was at the fireside. "I want you to take a message to Henry Drummond. At once." His voice was shaking. "Tell him I will not be able to join them for lunch. No explanation."

The old man bowed. "Very good, sir."

More to himself than to MacTavish, Queensberry grumbled: "I have more important things to do. Not that the bastards care much whether I come or not . . ."

) 4 (

Clive Merriam's "offices" were in fact a run-down flat over an apothecary shop in the Edgeware Road. He was a small, tidy man with hair streaked gray, and as he conducted Queensberry into a small room that smelled of sausages and bacon — it no doubt served as the dining room when he had no clients — he kept his hands clasped together like a curate.

"I want you to track down all the information you can about the person who wrote the original version of this," Queensberry said, tossing the soiled, wrinkled copy of Wilde's "madness of kisses'' letter onto the drop-leaf table. File boxes were piled up on a sideboard, and in front of them rested a large glass punch bowl, very dusty. Expensive brandy bottles were lined up, all empty: souvenirs, no doubt, of more prosperous times. Merriam was said to have been forced to retire from the police for reasons of corruption. To Queensberry he did not appear very corrupt; nevertheless, he would have to do. ''He is a man of the theater,'' Queensberry went on, ''a mountebank who goes by the name of Oscar Wilde.''

From Merriam's lazy, peaceful look, he would have been retired from the exigencies of active departmental life for a good decade or more. ''I know the name well,'' he said.

Queensberry scowled at him. ''Any leads you find, get them to inform you of other leads. You can pay them for their help. I'm making five hundred pounds available in a private account, Merriam. You see, the recipient of the original copy of this masterpiece was — my son.''

''Well, well,'' said Merriam, studying the letter with a crafty look, as if trying to prove that, despite his timid country-bumpkin face, he was a bona fide detective. He turned the page over, felt of the paper, crackled it at his ear. Gazing at Queensberry over his spectacles, he said: ''Well, well.''

''I want evidence on the pair of them. At any cost, on Wilde.''

''Aren't you afraid, sir, you'll be tarring your son with the same brush?''

In the midst of the brown photographs on the wall, depicting children in various stages of growth, were an old blunderbuss, a certificate or diploma of some kind, an engraving of the Queen. ''My son is in with Wilde. And it's essential that I know exactly what he's up to. I want a report on his *every action*.''

''But not legal evidence?'' said Merriam, seeming to look straight at Queensberry over the rimless lenses but in fact staring a little higher, at his eyebrows or perhaps his forehead. ''That is, in the case of your son — it isn't 'evidence' you want against him? Not of a legal nature?''

''Why is it not?''

''You are trying to prove your son's innocence, Lord Queensberry, not his —'' Merriam pondered a moment. ''This investigation is for the purpose of protecting your son, not proving that he is a —'' The detective smiled at his new client in confusion. ''Please correct me if I am wrong, sir.''

''Evidence,'' Queensberry snapped, slamming a hand on the table. ''Any kind of evidence.''

''But you would not wish me to find evidence that your son is — a poof!''

Queensberry looked as if he might turn over the table in his rage. ''You damned fool!'' he cried, his eyes bulging. ''Don't you see I'm trying to save him from being one!''

) 5 (

''Look, Your Lordship,'' said Tuzzer Williams amiably. ''Would it not be better if I just grabbed the bloke by the collar and gave him a right good punch beneath the ear? You know the way I does it — soft and gentle, so they never knows what hit 'em.''

''Stop babbling,'' cried Queensberry, furious that Tuzzer had been drinking, though it was Queensberry himself who had offered him the first whiskey, as a reward for staying dry for so many months. All the way across Belgravia in the hansom, Tuzzer had been pestering him with suggestions, and Queensberry had lapsed into a meditative sulk. ''Scare the piss out of the cur,'' he said. ''That's all. We don't want to be facing any prison term for the likes of that scoundrel. Stand behind me, Tuzzer, and do nothing at all. Just *look* menacing, that will be quite enough for a coward like Wilde.''

The coach jiggled along the Sloane Street cobblestones, and Tuzzer's hat was knocked off. He had some difficulty picking it up from below the dashboard. ''Menacing, Your Lordship? Now, tell us, do I look more menacing like this —'' He narrowed his big oily eyes into slits. ''Or p'r'aps like this?'' He curled back his lips to expose broken, crooked teeth.

''You look a bloody idiot either way. Keep yourself in the background and stay mum.'' The cab rumbled to a halt on Tite Street. Queensberry hopped out and paid the driver without, for once, negotiating the fee. He checked the address in his pocket and turned the door chime. To the youth who opened he said: ''Mr. Oscar Wilde, please. Tell him it's the Marquess of Queensberry — and friend.''

Wilde came lumbering down the stairway in a flamboyant green velvet smoking jacket, looking more purple-veined and unhealthy than he had in the Café Royal — but taller, as well. Clutching his walking stick, Queensberry stood firm.

Wilde made no effort to be sociable. "Come in the study," he drawled, glancing with distaste at Tuzzer Williams. He led them into a small crowded room off the entrance foyer, where the sunlight was filtering in through tinted panes over vases of flowers and naked statues.

As the door closed, Queensberry pivoted abruptly. "Sit down, you," he snapped, staring up at Wilde's blubbery face.

Wilde tightened the belt of his smoking jacket. Expressionless, he said: "I don't allow anyone to talk to me in that tone."

Queensberry looked to Tuzzer, but the ass was merely staring at Wilde with an admiring smile.

Wilde had reached for a silver cigarette box on the mantelpiece, which proved to be empty. He shouted to the servant to bring cigarettes. "I suppose you've come to apologize for the terrible statements you made about my wife and myself?" he said. "You are aware, Queensberry, that for such remarks I could prosecute you any day I chose."

"I am free to say anything to Alfred I like — about you or anyone else. A letter from a father to his son is privileged." Queensberry glowered at a nude male statue. "I am certainly free to advise him to stay away from the likes of *you*."

"Tell me, Queensberry," Wilde said, folding his arms before his chest. "*Why* do you wish to believe dreadful things about your son and me?"

"You were both thrown bodily out of the Savoy Hotel for your disgusting conduct! Or should have been!"

Wilde threw his head back in a despairing little laugh. "A lie! Someone is telling you an absurd set of lies about your son and me. Why do you choose to *believe* such absurd stories?"

Wilde was obviously nervous, and Queensberry made right for the belly. "Are you going to deny that you were thoroughly well blackmailed for a disgusting letter you wrote to my son?"

Perspiration beaded Wilde's forehead, which did not for an instant take away his look of insolence. "I am aware of the letter in question," he said. "It is a work of great beauty — written for publication. It has appeared in a literary magazine, in the form of a poem in prose translated into the French language." The footman appeared with a cigarette packet, and Wilde tore it open. He lit a cigarette with unsteady fingers, then broke into a smile. "Lord Queensberry," he said, in his normal voice, friendly now: "Are you seriously accusing your son and me of improper conduct?"

Queensberry held himself as tall and threatening as he was able, but something in him backed off. His voice went hoarse: "I don't say you *are* it, Wilde. But you look it, you *pose* as it. That is just as bad." Hearing something whining and apologetic in his tone, he sprang across the room next to Tuzzer Williams. "Listen, you bastard, I am making you a warning, and here is my witness. If I catch you with that weak-headed son of mine in any public restaurant, I will personally thrash you. I will have you arrested and committed to a lifetime of penal servitude — or worse." He held his fists up tight before his face.

Wilde stamped out his cigarette and crossed the study, flinging open the door. "Leave my house at once. I don't know what the Marquess of Queensberry rules are, but the Oscar Wilde rule is to shoot on sight."

Queensberry backed up so he was leaning on Tuzzer, who was watching Wilde with his mouth agape. "Who is going to make me leave?"

"The police." He called down the corridor: "Arthur?"

Queensberry started out the door, motioning for Tuzzer Williams to follow. "You and my bloody so-called son are a scandal," he hissed, passing Wilde in the vestibule.

"*You* are the author of the scandal. No one else is." On the house steps, Queensberry began to shout threats at Wilde in the foulest language he could think of. "Arthur," cried Wilde, "I want you to remember this man's face. He is the Marquess of Queensberry, the most infamous brute in London. You are never to allow him to enter my house again."

The door slammed violently shut: it was miraculous that the glass panes on either side did not shatter into slivers. Queensberry skipped out into the center of Tite Street, where he grabbed at Tuzzer William's arm with a cry of triumph, looking as if he might suddenly start waltzing him through the silent Chelsea streets.

) 6 (

There were several letters and telegrams from Bosie in the following months. Queensberry longed to open them, but preferred to frustrate his son by sending them back unread.

As he was looking through the illustrations in an American sporting magazine, MacTavish entered the room. "A postcard for you, sir."

"A postcard!" Queensberry edged his chair closer to the open window.

> As you return my letters unopened, I am obliged to write on this. Ever since your exhibition at O.W.'s house, I have made a point of appearing with him at The Berkeley, Willis's Rooms, the Café Royal, etc., and I shall continue to go to these places whenever I choose and with whom I choose. I am of age and my own master. You have no right over me, either legal or moral. If O.W. was to prosecute you in the Central Criminal Court for libel, you would get seven years' penal servitude for your outrageous libels. Much as I detest you, I am anxious to avoid this for the sake of the family; but if you try to assault me, I shall defend myself with a loaded revolver, which I always carry; and if I shoot you or if he shoots you, we shall be completely justified, as we shall be acting in self-defence against a violent and dangerous rough, and I think if you were dead not many people would miss you.

Queensberry read the postcard several times over; then he began to laugh. Rich, harsh bellows of laughter thundered out of him, rocking his body; he was filled for a moment with purest joy.

He stopped, and as suddenly was stricken with a sorrow that seemed to have no bottom. After a time he reached up a hand to draw the curtains shut. He sank back in the chair, feeling stiff and tight and old as he stared into the gathering shadows of the bleak, cheerless room, which seemed to be getting smaller all the time.

) 7 (

As the summer lapsed into a chilly, gray autumn, with the sun hidden for days on end, Queensberry's waking moments were plagued with fantasies. He could not stop picturing Francie and

Lord Rosebery, Bosie and Oscar Wilde, in salacious animal pos-
tures, indulging their unnatural appetites to the full. He had no
peace at night, either, when sweating nightmares about the lot of
them would torment him.

He would awake each morning with the familiar horror of finding himself once again with• a whole long day to fill. And then
would begin the tormenting suspicions about his sons. At least they
were powerful enough to fill the emptiness.

Nevertheless, there were hours when no amount of concern could
occupy his thoughts, when he would grow tired of the boxing club
and of the games of whist and bridge, grow tired of the talk of
horses at the Jockey, and he would be haunted by all the old disappointments, by memories of all the people who had rejected or
hurt him. Their numbers, God knew, were legion. He would
halfheartedly seek some means of diversion from these memories,
and yet — painful as they were — they had a certain fullness, an
inevitability, a siren fascination.

On one such afternoon he took an omnibus to an abandoned
church in the East End. The pews had been removed from the
ground floor and replaced by an improvised dirt track, and spectator seats were being sold for the balcony and choir loft. Queensberry stared down as a scurvy-looking type and his three equally
unsavory young sons — Italians, they looked like — released baskets of captive rats into the ''ring,'' and then threw in a starved
terrier to hunt them down. The scrawny arms of the three lads
were covered with rat bites, and they were kept hopping, knocking
the terrified rats down from the walls back into the dirt.

Before Queensberry's eyes that afternoon over forty rats were
torn to bits, but still he could not shake the gloom that was pursuing him.

Back in Buckingham Palace Road, he leaned before the mean
little fire, trying to warm himself. He regretted having let Mac-
Tavish go, especially since he was unable to find a replacement.
Without a job, what might the old fool be doing? The sense of his
importance in the life of another human being, however insignificant, brought a moment's warmth that all too soon was dispelled.

Amidst the family pictures on the mantelpiece was a small one
of Francie and Bosie together, taken five or six years before. They
were wearing new spring suits with sprigs of flowers in their la-

pels. Two sons with no interest in life but to defy and mock the father who had given them life and sustained them through all their years.

He recalled all too vividly how much he had once adored their mother, and the agonies of doubt the passion had engendered. How little she had appreciated the depths of his love for her — how shallow she was! Never for an instant had he believed she was faithful to him, anyone so beautiful, so elegant as she. She must desire other men, he had always believed, and by the same token she must despise him.

Continually he had questioned her, followed her about, tried to trick admissions from her friends. At least he had proved himself right about one thing: she admitted she had come to despise him.

He stared at his sons in the photograph, and then at himself in the silver depths of the pier mirror. There was something in their overdelicate, pampered features, something mocking and effeminate — hardly the features of the Douglas clan — that he had begun to detect in his own!

He frowned at Francie's simpering face — Lord Drumlanrig, indeed! — and swiped the picture from the mantelpiece. It crashed to the floor. The broken glass splintered in a pattern around Francie, making it look as if he himself had shattered. The strange effect made Queensberry laugh.

The clock sounded, startling him. Four times the harsh bells chimed. Chuckling dryly at his taut nerves, he replaced the damaged picture amongst the others and, unable to think of any place he wanted to go or anything he wanted to do, he decided on another evening exploring pubs.

In the morning an insistent pounding throbbed through the caverns of his aching brain. When he tried to ignore it the noise grew louder, more demanding. Cursing as he crossed the ice-cold floor in his nightshirt, Queensberry opened the door a careful crack. Bosie, a tired ghost, stood weaving in the corridor shadows. Queensberry's first reaction was one of fear. Was Bosie armed?

But no, everything in his son's manner expressed sorrow, even contrition.

"Alfred?" The sight of him there, looking so frail, so defeated, made Queensberry melt. He longed to embrace this son of his, fondle him, shower him with luxury and love, tell him the truth he

had been hiding so carefully, that all their enmity had been merely
a test of endurance, and Bosie had passed the test at last.

"Papa — let me come in, for God's sake."

The door had hardly closed when the boy began weeping; his
great racking sobs tore at Queensberry's very soul. Were they to
be father and son once more, was life at last going to fall into
place, would everything finally make sense? Queensberry felt tears
rise in himself as well. He wanted to throw his arms about this
impossible boy of his, the one most like himself — but he had to
be sure. And as his son collapsed into the rocking chair before the
fire, weeping like a child, Queensberry made resolutions. Bosie would
see, finally, what a perfect, forgiving, loving father he had.

The sobbing ceased long enough for Bosie to form a few words:
"Have they — told you?"

"Told me, Alfred?"

"About Francie?"

"I have seen no one. For days. Weeks. Since you saw fit to abandon me, I —"

"Francie is dead."

Queensberry stared at him.

"Shot. With a hunting rifle. By his own hand. Almost on the
eve of his marriage." He began once again to choke with tears.
"Twenty-four," he sobbed. "Francie was only twenty-four."

Then Queensberry was seated by the fire, not knowing how he
had got there. Was it a moment ago that Bosie had told him the
ghastly words, or days past? Was it his son he was hearing about,
or his father? He had never accepted the news in his childhood,
had pushed it away, pretended nothing whatsoever had happened,
and now it was back, banging on the doors of his awareness, insisting that he let it in at last.

"Alfred, what — what is this all about? You must tell me what
has happened." This other son, the one he loved best, was bent
over in the chair opposite, sobbing. "Francie could not have done
such a —"

"Don't you realize we're mad, the lot of us?" Bosie screamed.
"Look at your father —"

"Shut up, Alfred!"

"Look at your brother. Poor mad Uncle James, slashing his own
throat in the Euston Hotel. Oh, what a heritage you've given me!"

"Francie had everything to live for!"

"Do you not realize, little man, that he was the laughingstock of the Foreign Service? Because of you? Picture your eldest son — brilliant, sensitive. Now picture his reaction on hearing that his father has come to beat the Foreign Secretary, a member of the Prime Minister's cabinet and his own beloved employer — with a horsewhip! Do you think a person like Francie could endure such a humiliation? And the vices you have been accusing him of! Picture his reaction to such filthy accusations. Can you see all that, little man? Can you? Can you understand?"

Queensberry felt the room swimming around him; he must swim faster, or be drowned. "How — how dare you speak to me in that tone of voice, reptile!"

"Will you say it wasn't you that killed him? As surely as if you'd pulled the trigger? You are without feelings! You destroyed Francie! As you destroyed my mother! As you're trying to destroy me!"

"Without feelings? I?" Queensberry rose unsteadily from the chair. He tried to take a step, spun towards the wall, afraid of keeling over. "Get out of here, cur," he said, his voice low and guttural. "Out! Or I will surely strangle you."

Bosie, face twisted in loathing, backed up towards the door. "You're the one who should be strangled, little man. How I would love to do it! You'll get it. And soon! You'll get it — in such a way that all the world will see you for the monstrous wretch you are!"

) 8 (

The piper stood before the fireplace, his red cheeks puffing up as he filled the bag with air. He was gasping for breath when the sweet whine started up again.

"Some other tune, sir?" he said, when the song was finished.

"The same. 'Highland Mary,' " said Queensberry, sitting up stiff in the hard chair, staring at the photograph of Francie and Bosie with tears streaming down his cheeks. His fingers were bleeding from where bits of the frame's broken glass had lacerated them.

The young piper was wearing the blue and green tartan of the Black Watch regiment, with black wool stockings up to his knobby knees. " 'Highland Mary' again, sir!"

"Again, you bloody imbecile — until I tell you otherwise!"

And once again the pipes droned out the mournful song while Queensberry sat before the small, crackling fire and stared at the image of his sons behind the shattered glass.

) 9 (

The short dim days of November flashed by. It had never been colder in London. The coachmen wore three or four coats and often the alleys were littered with frozen dogs and cats. Queensberry would go out and feel the cold gripping him at the throat, under the ears, and he would stiffen, hating to move the least bit lest he admit any of the biting wind into his warm parts, hating the touch of his greatcoat's harsh edges scraping against his body.

No amount of coal would warm the little flat on Buckingham Palace Road, so he left it for a hotel, which proved too expensive, and then another, which proved unclean.

Then the holidays began, with the city putting on its weary masquerade of cheer. In the night the worn-out carols, sung by reedy voices, would echo through the cold streets, or groups of revelers would dance in drunken chains down Piccadilly.

By the new year Queensberry was quite himself again. The hideous incident of Francie's death seemed to have slipped away from awareness entirely, to hide itself behind that same secret locked door where all the other horrors and obscenities, from his father's mystery-cloaked death onwards, were stored — still, perhaps, rankling and festering, but out of immediate view. What did it matter how dreadful memories might be, so long as one was always able to find ways to keep from looking at them?

When the opening of *The Importance of Being Earnest* was announced in the newspapers, Queensberry was among the very first in the ticket queue. He reserved two seats for the opening night, as close to the stage as he could get.

He had his maneuver carefully prepared. He was going to arrive at the premiere carrying a "bouquet" for the author — of turnips and carrots and onions. Then, when the brute walked to the footlights to make one of his notorious curtain speeches, Queensberry would hurl the vegetables up at him, climb onto the stage, and make a little speech of his own. All those muckling worshipers would learn some harsh truths about this posturing false god of theirs. And if any applause was to be given, it would go to the one who had exposed the scum for what he was.

He thrived on this scene, played and replayed it through the black winter nights. He thought of nothing else, lived for nothing else. It was as if all the disappointments of his life were to be wiped away in this one triumph, all his past pains justified, even glorified. He memorized and then continually revised in his mind every word of his speech. He sent notes to select acquaintances, begging them to come and see the spectacle he was planning.

The morning of the premiere, snow began lightly powdering the streets. It was falling heavily by the time the children were hurrying to school, wrapped in sweaters and scarves, and it muffled their laughter. By noon London had become a toy city of spun sugar. The street hawkers built fires in rubbish tins and warmed their hands while snowflakes gathered in their hair. The horses could barely budge the carriages by late afternoon. Soon the streets were banked high and people were stamping slowly through the soft white mass, their voices seeming to come from far away.

Queensberry could not remember time ever moving so slowly. The faster the snow flew, the slower the day seemed to pass. He was continually checking the old silver watch in his pocket, finding it two when it should have been three thirty, three thirty when it should have been five.

When he went out, it took a good five minutes to trudge from his hotel to the corner through the hillocks of snow. As he inched down Saint James's Place, en route to the pub near the theater where he was to meet Tuzzer Williams, he was shaking from the excitement and the cold.

In the pub men were complaining about the snow, or standing about the stove stamping their feet like Highland dancers. "Where I prefer to go is the music halls," said Tuzzer. "But I don't mind a little educatin', either, I do not."

"You're starting at the top, then, Tuzzer," said Queensberry with disgust. "This cur is the most fashionable author on the English stage. Which says little for the state of the English stage."

They left the pub and started across the street to Saint James's Theatre. Queensberry felt strangely light, as if he had taken leave of his body entirely. Twice he stumbled in the snow, and Tuzzer caught him and held him with a massive arm.

Protected by the marquee, the crowds in their fashionable clothes were talking about the snow. A police captain appeared and stopped Queensberry at the door. "Beg pardon — you're the Marquess of Queensberry, are you not?"

Queensberry raised his snow-wet eyebrows, pleased to be recognized.

"Awfully sorry, sir, the management wishes to have a word with you."

A moment later a flunky in evening clothes arrived, all apologies. "There's been a terrible mistake, sir. We oversold, you see. I'm afraid we shall have to refund your money."

"I bought these tickets the very first day."

"I realize that, sir. It's most regrettable. But I have orders. You're to be given fine seats for any other performance."

Queensberry turned to Tuzzer questioningly, but the fool merely smiled. The theater flunky was too stupid to be threatened. Then suddenly Queensberry darted towards the side door — to discover two bobbies inside, blocking his entrance. One of his own friends must have given him away. Which Judas might it have been? He was afraid he was going to weep.

"Better give up, sir," said Tuzzer Williams. "Put a face on it and take yourself 'ome to bed."

"Bastards," Queensberry moaned, not letting Tuzzer see his face. "Oh, the no-good bastards." He plodded round to the stage door, where two boys were shoveling snow, and handed the doorman the wrapped package of vegetables. "I want this delivered to Mr. Oscar Wilde."

In his lumpy bed that night, Queensberry came as close as he had since childhood to forming a prayer. *Let this play fail,* he begged — *oh, please, if there is any greater power in the universe than our limited intelligence can understand, please oh please make this play a failure.*

The prayer had become a kind of litany by the next morning when he went out through the silent snow-filled streets to buy the *Chronicle. Fail, fail, please make him fail* . . .

He scanned the columns of the theater page with peculiar calm as he stood shivering in the snow. It hardly mattered now what emotion came rushing forth, so long as it was powerful.

Oscar Wilde may be said to have at last, and by a single stroke, put his enemies under his feet. Their name is legion, but the most inveterate of them may be defied to go to St James's Theatre and keep a straight face through the performance of *The Importance of* . . .

After fortifying himself with several drinks at the nearest pub, Queensberry took a cab to Wilde's club. Damn all, he thought. He felt alive again, purposeful, determined.

In the Albemarle, he strode over to the desk imperiously. "Is Mr. Oscar Wilde on the premises?"

"One moment, sir." The guardian looked down the names in a ledger. "Not at the moment, sir, I'm afraid."

"I shall leave my card for him, then," said Queensberry, reaching out his billfold.

"Very good, sir."

With a wry little smile, Queensberry dipped the desk pen into the onyx stand. *For Oscar Wilde,* he wrote, above his own name — and then, unhesitatingly, *Sodomite.* But wait a moment. His attorneys had not as yet produced any evidence worth speaking of. And Wilde would almost certainly sue for libel. Before the word *Sodomite,* Queensberry scrawled in *posing as a.*

"Will you be absolutely certain that Oscar Wilde gets this card? And reads it in your presence?"

"I will, sir. Very good, sir."

Queensberry started towards the door but abruptly halted. *Take back the card,* something told him. *Tear it up.*

He pushed open the outer door of the Albemarle and with a deep sigh strode out into the heaps of piled snow, already turning gray from the city's filth.

PART EIGHT

The Decay of Lying

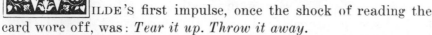

ILDE'S first impulse, once the shock of reading the card wore off, was: *Tear it up. Throw it away.*

He had been out for another evening of celebrating the success of the new play — another curiously empty evening. Then he had come to the Albemarle hoping for some conversation, some intellectual stimulation, some diversion from all the diversion — and found this obscene card from Queensberry.

He could not tear it up. He must stop this lunatic, must keep the fiend from going a step farther. Pride raged up out of him like a dragon breathing fire. Pride — and something more.

"I don't know what to do, Robbie," he was saying, an hour later, in the small saloon bar set up in the lobby of the Avondale Hotel in Piccadilly. "You must advise me what to do."

"Whatever is most prudent."

Wilde could not help being annoyed that Robbie was so full of his own affairs these days, his pursuit of a career in an art gallery. He would have liked Robbie's full attention to remain on *him* and on his difficulties. Also, Robbie was growing ever more sensible, and it was difficult to accept the counsel of sensible people; he shrank from anything common, he liked to say: even common sense. "What *is* the most prudent thing?" Wilde said.

"I don't see how you can prosecute him. That would be madness."

Prosecute? The word had been dancing through his mind, but he had again and again rejected it. Now, hearing it from Robbie's sensible lips, he was shocked. At the same time, in a curious, chilling way, the idea thrilled him. "Prosecute?" But there was no way he could win his case!

"There must be some other way to stop him," said Robbie.

"I? Prosecute the Marquess of Queensberry?" He shook his head slowly. "It would be insanity, Robbie. It would be insanity."

) 2 (

The next afternoon at Tite Street, Arthur announced that Lord Alfred Douglas had arrived. "Show him into my study," said Wilde, drawing on his smoking jacket. He was sulking about a letter Bosie had sent two days earlier, full of insult and vituperation. Nevertheless, the news of this latest gesture of Queensberry's was too delicious for Wilde to keep to himself.

Bosie read the card with growing excitement. "Of course you must prosecute!" he said, appropriating the situation, making it his own special property, his toy. "I promise you," he said, tightening his hands into fists, "it will be the easiest case ever won in an English courtroom."

"I . . . couldn't . . . possibly . . . win," said Wilde, fascinated by the enthusiasm in Bosie's features, for once freshened and alert. He might have just come in from a morning dip in the ocean.

"Think, Oscar! Think of the kindness you will be doing to my poor mother. To all of us! You will be our liberator!" Whatever the thoughts running through Bosie's imagination, they seemed to awe him.

Wilde called for Arthur to fetch his hat and gloves. Faced with Bosie's exhilaration, he felt his own doubts to be less and less relevant to the situation's larger design. "I am going to speak to a solicitor. Charles Humphreys will know exactly what to do." He would, of course, have preferred to go to his dear friend George Lewis — his former dear friend. Lewis had never been the same since the time Wilde had brought Bosie to him for advice on that sordid blackmailing incident at Oxford. Wilde could hardly go to him now — especially over a libel case of this particular kind. No, it was wiser to consult someone who knew less about him.

"Let me come!" Bosie cried, throwing his arms around Wilde's belly.

Wilde gave him a hug and held him tight until Bosie wriggled away. "This is all so dreadful!" Wilde said. "And so exciting! Come if you want to, Bosie."

Bosie wanted to, and very badly.

) 3 (

Beetle-browed and still quite handsome at fifty, despite his bald head, Charles Humphreys was intelligent and witty in a dry, uncompetitive way. "This is absurd," he was saying, over tea and muffins in his chambers in Lincoln's Inn. Once again he read over Queensberry's card. "It makes no sense. Why would anyone write such a thing?"

"Because he is mad," cried Bosie.

"Please, Bosie," said Wilde.

Humphreys's face was smooth except for several large, dramatic lines chiseled about his cheeks, eyes, and forehead. He frowned at Bosie. "Mad, perhaps — but this is not the turn Queensberry's madness usually takes. Not without any provocation. And the man is no fool. I suppose you are aware that he has named Sir George Lewis as his solicitor?"

Wilde stared at him, speechless.

Bosie had been fidgeting on his leather chair; now he leaped up from it. "You have no idea *how* mad he is, Mr. Humphreys. You have heard about my unfortunate brother, of course? Are you aware that it was my father who drove him to —"

"Please, Bosie!" warned Wilde.

The gullies on either side of Humphreys's mouth deepened. "Mr. Wilde, there is — no truth in Queensberry's allegations?"

Wilde's look said that the question was too preposterous to reply to.

"You — are absolutely certain, Mr. Wilde?"

"Mr. Humphreys, I fail to see how you can ask anything so absurd. I am as innocent as — as the day is short."

"I shall apply for a warrant," Humphreys said. "Queensberry will be arrested."

"Oh, excellent!" cried Bosie.

"Being innocent, you shall succeed," Humphreys said. He motioned for the clerk to run out for more muffins. "Now — as to the costs of the trial . . . ."

"Can they wait a bit, Humphreys?" said Wilde, holding forth his cup for more tea. "I have three plays running to packed houses, and yet I cannot seem to get my finances in order. Could I be trusted for a month or two?"

"No need!" said Bosie. "My family will pay the costs." He was standing in a pool of light at the window, smiling and radiant. "It will be cheaper than having my father committed to a lunatic asylum, which is what we had all been planning."

But Wilde was hardly listening. Sir George Lewis — Queensberry's solicitor? It was unthinkable that George had accepted the case out of friendship for Queensberry — he must loathe the man. Had he taken it, then, to somehow strike out at Wilde?

) 4 (

The day of the preliminary hearing was crisp and clear; winter sunshine had pierced the fog. The magistrate's court, on Great Marlborough Street, had none of the dark formality of most of Her Majesty's courtrooms, had even a rather ramshackle look, as if the proceedings there were not meant to be taken too seriously.

As if in compensation, Mr. Robert Milnes Newton was unusually punctilious. Imperiously he granted Queensberry — almost handsome in a new gray suit — permission to sit in a chair outside the rails. When an assistant pointed out that the accused's son was amongst the onlookers, the magistrate made a show of disbelief, as if mayhem had been committed within the precincts of his courtroom, and commanded Bosie to leave at once.

Wilde, as prosecutor, took the stand in the almost empty room.

"Are you a dramatist and author?" Humphreys asked him.

"I believe I am well known in that capacity."

Humphreys frowned at his client. "Only answer the questions, please."

An envelope marked *Exhibit A* was produced. It contained the calling card the Marquess of Queensberry had left at the Albemarle Club. Wilde glanced with distaste at the message written on it. "It is the same."

"Did you read what was on the card?"

Wilde nodded. "I did."

Sir George Lewis's questions were perfunctory, and he seemed to be avoiding Wilde's eyes even as he was staring directly into them.

Leaning on his chin, Mr. Newton deliberated in silence for a moment, and then asked Queensberry if he had anything to say.

"Simply this, Your Worship. I wrote that card to bring matters to a head, since I was not permitted to confront Wilde otherwise. I was trying to save my son from him. And I abide by what I wrote.''

Newton pursed his lips and nodded gravely. ''Then,'' he said, ''you are committed for trial in three weeks' time, on Tuesday, the third of April, in this year of eighteen ninety-five.'' Queensberry was released on bail.

At the Albemarle that evening, Wilde was moodily sipping a brandy and soda with Robbie when he received the news that Sir George Lewis had decided after all not to act for the Marquess of Queensberry in the forthcoming trial. Queensberry, it appeared, had been forced at the last minute to settle on an inexperienced young solicitor named Charles Russell.

Wilde let out a sigh and clinked his glass against Robbie's. ''The gods are smiling on me, after all.''

Robbie nodded, unable to hide his anxiety. ''They always have, haven't they?''

) 5 (

The best possible barrister he could select, Humphreys assured Wilde, would be Sir Edward Clarke. Clarke was the most successful and admired advocate in London at the moment — but unfortunately he was reluctant to take on the case. ''You can persuade him, Mr. Wilde. Of that I feel certain.''

Wilde wondered if Clarke's reluctance was because of his being a protégé of George Lewis's, but he dismissed the thought from his mind. He and Bosie accompanied Humphreys to the Temple, strolling down the cobbled old streets past tight-packed narrow doorways, each surmounted by a haloed lamb carved in stone, on through a cloister to a narrow court made even more solemn by the presence of two gaunt leafless trees.

''I believe it would be advisable for Lord Alfred to wait in the corridor,'' said Humphreys. Wilde lifted his fingers in a vague wave of farewell, feeling a rush of fear — as if he might never see Bosie again.

The offices were cheerful, filled with the scent of furniture polish. Dossiers were arranged about the walls as carefully as books in a well-appointed library, and the furnishings, while utterly conservative, were carefully chosen and tasteful.

Clarke was blessed with grace neither of figure nor of form, and his square heavy face was all lumpy nose and drooping jowls. His gray-streaked hair fanned out from the lump of fat at the back of his neck, proliferating in great tangled snarls about the temples, and culminating in hoary long sideburns like foxtails dangling from his ears. Indeed, he had the look of some rare species of animal, ugly on first view, but assuming nobility when the careful breeding became manifest. Nevertheless, there was no fine breeding in Clarke's background; like his mentor George Lewis he was a self-made man, having drawn himself up from the humblest beginnings.

He was friendly and warm, in a careful way. He spoke of the pleasure he had gotten from Wilde's literary work. At last, after an awkward pause, he came right to the point:

"I can only accept this brief, Mr. Wilde, if you will assure me, on your honor as an English gentleman, that there is not and never has been any foundation for the charges that are made against you."

As if by contrast with his other features, Clarke's eyes — deep and dark, yet piercing — were almost seductive as he studied Wilde with a look of infinite kindness.

Grandly, Wilde threw up his right hand and swore on his honor as an English gentleman that he was innocent of Queensberry's charges. "Is that sufficient, Mr. Clarke?" he said with a disarming smile. Yet for an instant, staring into the bottomless chasms of those eyes, Wilde lost courage, wanted to take it all back, to confess to this good man that he was lying.

"All right, Mr. Wilde," said Clarke, with a troubled smile. "I accept the case."

) 6 (

Frank Harris popped a cucumber sandwich into his mouth and brushed the crumbs from his gleaming black mustache. "We can start with the assumption that you're going to lose the case, Oscar." He had a weary but unquenchably optimistic look.

"Don't be tiresome, Frank," said Wilde, annoyed that Harris had brought his friend Bernard Shaw along to what he well knew was meant to be a serious luncheon. Harris and Shaw seemed to be on more intimate terms with each other than either was with him, which he found vaguely insulting. "Absolutely everything is in my favor, Frank."

He was tired of the Royal. It had begun to seem trite and worn to him, the gilt on the twisting Byzantine columns soot-darkened from tobacco smoke, the caryatids, like the customers, looking weary and unfashionable. He was annoyed, too, that Bosie had not arrived — would probably not come at all. He always felt a quiet, pervasive dread in Bosie's absence — especially now, facing this trial. "Just be my witness, Frank, and everything will go splendidly. I simply want you to vouch, as editor of the *Saturday Review,* that *Dorian Gray* is no more immoral than *The Lives of the Saints* — which is no more than the truth."

Harris looked despairingly at Shaw. "This trial is not going to be a lot of clever chat about books, Oscar! You don't seem to realize what is going to happen to you." He dipped a finger in his glass and stroked brandy into the wings of his mustache, the sweep of which he had copied from Bismarck's, though he insisted it was Bismarck who had copied him. "Queensberry is going to bring up things that will leave art and literature far out of the question. All London is talking about the evidence he's collecting."

Trying to make room in the ashtray to stamp out another cigarette, Wilde frowned. "What evidence could the old brute *possibly* find?" he said thoughtfully. "I have done nothing, Frank, you know that." Harris stared at him as if uncertain whether this was meant to be a joke; only Shaw's presence kept him from exploding into laughter. "Tell me you'll testify about *Dorian,* won't you, Frank? And set my mind at ease?"

Shaw, with his coarse red hair parted in the center over his formidably high forehead, fanned away cigarette smoke, looking from one to the other of them with his sly little eyes. He was, as always, wearing his absurd one-piece suit, worn to prove some theory or other about the effect of wool upon the health. "It should be a simple enough matter, Frank," Shaw said. "*Dorian Gray* couldn't be more moral."

Wilde gave Shaw a smile of gratitude. Shaw was a dazzling writer and talker, witty, well versed, informed on every topic; in other words, insufferable. Wilde liked to say that Shaw was a man without enemies, and none of his friends could stand him. Harris, of course, was the exception.

"I want you to consider the matter carefully, Oscar," Harris said. "You *must* be aware that in matters of art and morality, an English court is the worst tribunal in the civilized world. Look at all the absurd fuss over your *Salomé*."

"Charles Humphreys assures me we shall win."

"Humphreys shall win! Solicitors always win! He will come away with hundreds, perhaps thousands of pounds. Oscar, no English jury is going to convict a father of any action taken to protect his son. Even if he is utterly at fault. Drop the case, Oscar. Go abroad for a while . . ."

Wilde drummed his fingers on the table and looked about, annoyed at the people who were staring at him, equally annoyed at those who were not. "Bosie doesn't want to go abroad."

Harris laughed harshly. "Leave the little snot behind." He poured more Château des Mille Secousses for himself and Wilde, more Vichy water for Shaw. "Take Constance with you. Go to France. And let Douglas and his father fight the whole bloody thing out between themselves. I would say they're well matched."

Wilde found it difficult to speak his mind with Shaw at the table, pompously gazing into his mineral water from under his shaggy red brows. "That isn't a very nice thing to say, Frank," said Wilde. "About Bosie . . ."

"He's using you, can't you see that?" Harris said. "That's all Douglas has ever done, is use people. It's all he *can* do."

"Did you never consider that I might be using Bosie?" Wilde said, with a pained smile at Shaw. London, he decided, was too small for two Irish geniuses; perhaps, indeed, for one.

"Take Constance to France. Then write a letter to the *Times*, Oscar, the kind of letter you alone can write. Tell them that you've decided it was all a mistake. That the Marquess of Queensberry may be a fighter but you are a maker of beautiful things. You are leaving the whole battle, with all its gloves and sponges and pails, to him."

"An excellent idea," said Shaw. "The best way to keep an Irishman out of trouble is to set him to write a letter."

Wilde looked from one to the other of them, beginning to brighten. "A letter to the *Times*?" he said, his imagination already beginning to shape the first paragraph. "After all, that might be an amusing solution."

Shaw chuckled. "We Irish will forgo any pleasure for the pain of putting a few words together on paper, in a more or less logical order."

Wilde leaned an arm on Shaw's shoulder, suddenly liking him enormously. Plain and unaffected as he might pretend to be in his insane woolen suit, Shaw had obviously taken great pains selecting his rust-red cravat, making certain it exactly matched his stringy russet beard. "Do you not find it a tragic thing to be Irish, Shaw? We can't even write good poetry: we are too poetical to be poets! We are a nation of brilliant failures."

"Of failures, at any rate," Shaw said, laughing.

Though neither of them had made any reference to Shaw's unfriendly review of *Earnest* in the *Saturday Review,* it was nevertheless very much part of the conversation. "Yes, we are failures," Wilde said, thinking of what great friends the two of them might have been — if they only had less in common. "All we can do successfully is talk — but Irishmen do that better than anyone since the Greeks."

Shaw looked dubious. "We like to think we have a great talent for creating works of literature," he said, "when in fact our literature has created us."

Wilde sputtered on a mouthful of the Bordeaux. "Shaw! You sound as if you are quoting me."

"I am quoting *myself,*" Shaw said. "I often do. I find it lends spice to my conversation."

Wilde was howling with laughter. "Frank! If even Shaw is becoming 'Oscarized,' what hope is there for the young?" And then, sobering slightly, he said to Shaw: "You were the only theater critic in London I respected — until you were unkind to my play."

"I was never unkind to any of the others."

"But *Earnest* is the best of them!"

Shaw frowned as Wilde lit a new cigarette from the stub of the old one. "Mere verbal dexterity, Oscar. As I said in my review, *Earnest* has no heart."

Wilde sighed, exhaling smoke and guzzling down the last of the wine. "There are no emotions left to write about, Shaw! Shakespeare and Victor Hugo between them used everything up. For the likes of you and me there is nothing left — nothing but extraordinary adjectives. If we could only —"

And then he saw that Bosie was standing in front of the table, arms folded, his face white with fury — as if their hilarity were a personal affront. His new navy blue blazer, with silver buttons, was rumpled and soiled. For an instant Wilde saw him as the others must — a sulking, ungrateful child — and felt embarrassed for Bosie, and for himself. "Do sit down, dear boy."

"I'm sorry to be late," Bosie said, still pouting. "I was contemplating a lily in a vase — and could not tear myself away."

No one smiled but Wilde. "We have been discussing the trial, Bosie."

"Let's have a bottle of Taittinger," said Harris. "Oscar is going to call the whole thing off."

Bosie collapsed into an empty seat, looking stunned.

"Frank is telling me I must write a brilliant letter to the *Times*," said Wilde. "Perhaps he is right."

"It is an ingenious solution," Shaw put in. "Properly worded, a letter to the *Times* could manage to offend absolutely everyone."

As if stung with a sudden headache, Bosie shut his eyes tight. "I see." After a moment he opened them again and gazed sorrowfully at Wilde. "Well? What will you say in this wonderful letter?"

"Something — extravagant, something absurd and beautiful, I suppose."

Bosie gave him a tragic smile, turning his back to the mirror as if afraid of being physically drawn into it. "I hardly think that all the suffering my mother has undergone is material for comedy, Oscar. I won't speak of my own suffering . . ."

"Bosie?" Wilde reached a hand towards him pleadingly. "It could be delicately, carefully phrased. No one would be —"

"Oscar hasn't a chance of winning this case," Harris snapped. "Surely you see that, Lord Alfred."

"He has all the chance in the world. Unless his 'friends' interfere, and turn him into the coward my father insists he is. Do you want the whole of London to treat him as a laughingstock?"

Glowering, Harris reached for his wine but took up Shaw's glass of mineral water instead. After a sip, he put down the glass with a grimace. "It is in the courtroom that he will be made a laughingstock. And worse."

"Hear, hear," said Shaw.

Bosie drew his chair back and rose before them, staring from face to face with contempt. "Your advice, then, Mr. Harris, is to throw in the towel?"

"If you wish to put it in sporting terms, yes. That is my advice."

Bosie's chair went rattling over the marble floor as he started off from the table.

"Bosie!" Wilde rose, staring desperately after the small figure retreating into the rows of potted palms. He picked up the overturned chair; for a moment he seemed to contemplate sitting down in it. "Frank," he said, almost to himself, "that wasn't very friendly." Then he dropped his napkin and hurried out of the restaurant.

) 7 (

Wilde sat on an ivy-framed terrace sipping a sweet cassis concoction thick with fruit, staring down past the pine-dotted hills to where, far below, the rocky shoreline formed fingers of an open hand spreading out into the Mediterranean.

The sun had just set, and the garden leading to the casino, fenced in by close-clipped palms, was streaked with green and indigo shadows. From the midst of them Bosie came bounding over to the terrace, his sunburnt face under a white straw hat looking fresh as an adolescent's. "I've lost again, blast it!" he cried. "I'm going to switch to *trente-et-quarante,* perhaps I'll have more luck." His hands rummaged through the pockets of Wilde's striped coat. "Quick, Oscar! Money-money-money."

The landscape of oleanders and tamarinds seemed to be shimmering under the mossy green humps of the mountain, and villas with tiled roofs bleached by the sun fanned out below like steps in a spiral staircase. "Bosie," Wilde said, halfheartedly pushing him away, "you *must* try to economize." He removed his billfold and began counting out notes.

"I'm on holiday, Oscar! I refuse to let you depress me." He snatched the billfold and took out another, larger note. "I intend to have a wonderful time," he said with a big, boyish smile. "In spite of you!"

Bosie had never been in higher spirits than in the past few days. Wilde took another sip of the drink and put it down, his nostrils quivering. A dreadful cheap perfume diffused itself around the terrace: lemon trees and pomegranates and God only knew what other garish blossoms blowing in the steamy dusk. "Do you know what they call this balcony?" he said. "Suicide Terrace. People come here to — Bosie, *why* did we have to choose Monte Carlo, of all hideous places? I detest gambling. I detest heat. And with so much in London that needs to be done! Why did I listen to you? The trial is *one week away,* dear boy. Do you realize that? It was madness to take a holiday at such a time."

"It would be madness not to." Bosie inhaled deeply of the breeze and twisted his body in a long, indolent yawn. "The trial will take care of itself, Oscar. If you'll only let it! What you need is to think of something else. You'll jinx everything! Come play a round of baccarat. Perhaps you'll change my luck."

"You *know* I cannot abide games of any kind. Bosie, I keep having the most dreadful — premonition. Frank Harris was right, of course. This trial —"

"In a way I wish you *would* do as Harris suggested," said Bosie, taking the seat next to Wilde, stretching his legs out to rest on the balcony's stone wall.

Wilde looked hopeful. "Give the whole thing up?"

"I'm full of dread myself, you know," Bosie said, studying the weave of his straw hat. "Thinking of the terrible debt I should owe you, if you freed me and my family from the domination of that — that demon. It would simply be a different kind of slavery. I would be utterly in *your* thrall. Do as Frank Harris says, if that seems best to you. Write a letter to the *Times.* Apologize. Let my father have the last word."

Wilde turned away. The park behind them was a blur of blossoms, rare blossoms everywhere he looked. Flowers were so disgustingly commonplace in Monte Carlo, while grass was so pathetically rare. Even the strolling women in their elaborate gowns seemed like horticultural specimens. "I have already perjured myself," Wilde said. "I gave my word to Humphreys, and again to Edward Clarke, that your father's charges were unfounded. On my honor as an English gentleman."

"The oath doesn't count. You are an *Irish* gentleman, isn't that what you told me after your interview with Humphreys?"

"Suicide Terrace," said Wilde, looking more troubled than ever.

"How wonderful it would be to not have that trial staring me in the face every morning when I wake."

"Why don't we find a little Italian to stare in your face instead?" Bosie giggled, tilting the hat over his brow. "Yes, do as Frank Harris suggests. Then I will be free! I can start life afresh — as my mother keeps pleading with me to do."

"We could go away, Bosie. Start over."

"We?" Bosie straightened.

"We could live in France, the two of us."

Removing his hat, Bosie regarded it for a moment, then sent it skimming down over the rooftops, down towards the sea. It lodged in the top branches of a pine. "Oscar, old dear," he said with a disarming grin, "if I am purporting to start a clean new life, I will hardly attempt it with the man who corrupted me in the first place."

Wilde moved away, but Bosie reached over to pull him back, facing him with a look of deep gravity, the tawny sunburn making his eyes blaze an unnatural, thrilling blue. "Humphreys? Clarke? Are you going to let yourself stumble over the tired morality of these ordinary men, Oscar? You tower over them! What do their oaths and promises have to do with you?"

"They are far from ordinary men! And in a courtroom —"

"Think of it as a stage. And Humphreys, and Clarke, and all the others, as your audience. Let yourself go back in memory to the first night of *Lady Windermere's Fan*. Remember, Oscar? How happy we were, you and I? You must imagine that the people in the courtroom are that same adoring audience, hanging on your every word. As I shall be. Always. Now, cheer up — and let me have a little more money. Just a *little*."

"I brought no more with me. And we have to pay the hotel."

Bosie glanced about to see if anyone was watching and gave Wilde a quick kiss on the forehead. "Then you shall simply have to wire to London for more!" He started off towards the casino.

"Bosie, please —"

"You can't expect me to stop playing when I'm on a losing streak, now can you!" And Bosie skipped off towards the gaming rooms like a child running off to play.

The cassis was quite warm now, but Wilde sipped at it anyway, mashing slices of orange and lemon against the roof of his mouth to extricate the vile liquid from them. Gloomily he stared down at the harbor, where a single fishing boat with its sail billowing open was being slowly wafted out to the darkening sea.

) 8 (

Back in Tite Street, sunless and gray, a message was waiting from Sir Edward Clarke, charging Wilde to come at once to his chambers in the Temple for a full legal consultation. The message was dated eight days before. Wilde sent a telegram promising to be there the following morning.

Sir Edward was seated at his desk, wearing a stern, fatigued expression. "Mr. Wilde, you should have been here over a week ago," he said testily.

Wilde gave him a warm handshake. "I am so sorry, Sir Edward. I was called away from London — for reasons of unavoidable pleasure." The room was uncomfortably full. Charles Humphreys was there, along with two eager young men whom he introduced as junior counsel; one turned out to be his son. Bosie, too, was very much present, acting most amused by the proceedings. Clarke, obviously irritated by his presence, said nothing.

He led Wilde to a long table neatly covered with papers. "We have all the particulars of Queensberry's plea of justification, Mr. Wilde. They are extremely — but you will see for yourself. I want you to study each document most carefully. And please, Mr. Wilde: this is not a time for levity."

Wilde frowned, slowly circling the table. "Queensberry can't possibly have found anything of interest."

"He has found a number of things of — great interest, Mr. Wilde."

Wilde slid into a chair. The room was stifling. Turning page after page of the beautifully handwritten documents, a slow vague terror coursed through him. He lifted his handkerchief to his nostrils and inhaled the faint scent of lavender. Prominently mentioned in several papers was Alfred Wood. Wood was back from America, it appeared, and had agreed to testify against Wilde. Several other young men in Alfred Taylor's entourage were cited, along with Taylor himself. How in God's name had Queensberry learned all this? One of the youths, Charles Parker, was being given time off from his military service to appear at the trial. His brother was listed as another witness.

The handkerchief was crushed into a tight ball. Wilde read his foolishly exuberant letter to Bosie — once again in a strange hand, this one clerical, pinched, exact. *It is a marvel that those red rose-leaf lips of yours should have been made no less for music of song than for madness of* — The room seemed to be shrinking. The memory of himself, blithely scribbling those words in a Soho café, rose up to mock him. Would he ever be lighthearted again? Without a word, Wilde passed the letter on to Bosie.

"Where would you say our case stands now, Mr. Wilde?" said Sir Edward Clarke.

Wilde ran the handkerchief under his stiff collar. "However do you suppose they manufactured such lies?" he said. "Who can these Parker brothers be? Part of a hoax they've rigged up. Which only proves how desperate they are, Sir Edward, wouldn't you say? When they must resort to such trickery?"

"Is it trickery, Mr. Wilde? All of it?"

Wilde glanced at Bosie, who was hardly bothering to look at the documents; he was eyeing Humphreys's young son. "Every word is a lie," Wilde said.

Clarke began to collect the papers into a leather portfolio. He was scrutinizing Wilde carefully, as if waiting for him to retract. Finally he made an effort at a smile. "In that case, Mr. Wilde, we have nothing to worry about." He snapped the portfolio shut. "Oh, by the way. Queensberry's solicitor has named Edward Carson as barrister for the defense. It seems he was a schoolmate of yours at Trinity College, is that correct?"

"Ned Carson representing Queensberry!" Wilde brightened. Carson and he had carried on a distant but pleasant friendship over the years: Carson would hardly abuse an old Trinity chum in a court of law. "Wonderful news, Sir Edward!"

Clarke nodded, smiling mechanically. "Let's hope it is, Mr. Wilde . . ."

) 9 (

Bosie led the way out through the Temple's warren of doorways, Wilde following in a daze. On Fleet Street, Bosie looked about to see if they were being followed. Wilde walked on ahead of him, and nearly crashed into a passing van. The driver swore at him, but Wilde seemed not to hear.

"It seems your father has left — no stone unturned," Wilde said.

On one half of Ludgate Hill, the traffic was struggling up, on the other, barreling effortlessly down. Bosie waved for a hansom, but Wilde stopped him. He could not bear the thought of being enclosed.

"My father never ceases to amaze me," said Bosie — and the old note of admiration was in his voice. "How did he find out about the Parkers, that's what I want to know. The old snake must have had detectives on my trail every moment for the past year."

"The Parkers," Wilde said miserably. "You were amused by the fact that they were brothers . . ." They walked past old book-shops and buildings dating from the time of Pepys, past Somerset House and Saint Clement Danes and a series of timbered inns. As if under some compulsion to revisit the scene of the crime, Wilde turned into the shadowy courtyard of the Savoy Hotel. Checking their coats in the lobby, he said dreamily: "There is something so perfect about all this. So inevitable. Your father is going to expose — my very soul."

The rear colonnade was cheerless, even funereal. Everyone at the banquettes seemed to be wearing black, as if the entire hotel were in mourning. From the massive windows the Thames, absorb-ing the gray of the afternoon sky, looked like a soiled, badly rum-pled sheet.

"Perhaps Harris *was* right," said Bosie. "Perhaps you should drop the whole thing."

There was no need to order: their favorite waiter — the hand-somest in the Savoy — brought hock and soda unbidden. Wilde smiled up at him absently, then, lighting a cigarette and musing at the match's flame as it inched closer and closer to his fingers, he said: "I don't want to drop it."

"Are you sure?"

He let his fingers burn before he released the match. Then he stared at the charred fingertips curiously. "There is something about the whole thing so perfect. So beautifully crafted — like a superb play. Only — who is doing the crafting? Your father is but a character in the drama. As I am. As you are. No, it is a work fashioned by — a master artist.''

Bosie lay back on the divan, staring up at the intricacies of the coffered ceiling. ''Be quiet, Oscar.''

''You don't feel it? The marvelous inevitability of the whole thing? The hand of the gods at work? Think of all they have granted me: A delightful, amusing life. Money. Success in my work. Two adorable children. Connie.'' Hesitantly, he added: ''You.'' For once Bosie did not contradict. ''The gods have given me so many triumphs, Bosie!'' He downed his drink too quickly, and signaled for a refill. ''Are they going to take it all back?''

) 10 (

''How lovely to see you again, Mrs. Robinson,'' Wilde said, giving the old woman his hand.

She had not so much aged as shrunk, keeping all her elasticity, her sunny smile, her spryness; she seemed a young girl leading a suitor into her parlor.

Close at Wilde's heels was the toy bulldog, who had grown more unmannerly since his last visit. Looking up sideways, the dog emitted low whining sounds at Wilde from deep in his throat. Mrs. Robinson seemed to find these noises as restful as a serenade.

''Your dog is as robust as ever,'' said Wilde.

''Oh, this is Queenie Number Four,'' Mrs. Robinson said, chucking the dog under the muzzle. ''The last Queenie, R.I.P., is enjoying her just reward.''

Wilde returned Queenie Number Four's hostile stare. ''And does this Queenie talk?''

''This Queenie sings,'' she said proudly.

The room was exactly the same, small but cozy, filled with plants and overstuffed furniture, decorated with doilies and tablecloths of handmade lace. Wilde grew restless on the sofa as she served him tea. ''I am about to embark upon a *most* hazardous enterprise, dear lady. I dare not undertake it without your sage advice.''

Nodding, she lifted his hand into her small white one. Studying his face carefully, she seemed to be weighing the hand; then she turned it gently, parted the digits, examined the ridges and cross-hatched lines. She slipped her magnifying glass out from under a cushion.

"Yes, Mr. Wilde, it *is* a most serious affair you have to face."

"Most serious indeed, dear lady."

Her eyes stole across the hand-tinted country landscapes on the wall and stopped at an engraving of Jesus, pointing to his heart wreathed in flames. She stared at it a long while, seeming to receive from it some kind of communication. She smiled reassuringly. "From the serious things, Mr. Wilde, we must not draw back. They are the only things worthwhile. I see a great height to be surmounted — a climb."

"What is at the end of — this climb?"

"Ah, the end of it. Hush, Queenie!" She gave the dog a light tap on his bottom and giggled at Wilde, her blue eyes, under thick white eyebrows, clear and radiant. "Queenie does not realize that *all* his songs are not equally agreeable to human ears."

Once more she reached for Wilde's hand. She closed it over, opened it again gently, pondered a long moment. "At the end of the climb I see — riches. Bliss. All you have ever wished for. Your heart's desire awaits, Mr. Wilde. But first you must get past many obstructions."

"My heart's desire!" Wilde chuckled. "I can transcend any obstruction if it will lead to that!"

"I'm sure you can, Mr. Wilde," she said, releasing his hand. She gazed out through the lace curtains at the clear blue sky. There was something fatalistic, almost tragic in her smile. "I'm sure you can."

) 11 (

Boxes, newspapers, open books were scattered everywhere in the salon, and as Wilde buttoned up his shirt he walked about making an unhappy inspection of what had been, to his mind, at least, the most beautiful room in London. Constance's maid tended to emulate her mistress: once meticulous and energetic, she now seemed to have lost all interest in her tasks.

Constance, in her petticoat and sandals, was mooning about. "Connie, *do* hurry," he said gently. "I have *so much* on my mind, darling — please, please try to get control of yourself."

"Why must *I* go?" she cried. "And with *him?* It's the worst thing to do."

"It is the *best* thing to do," he said, picking up an astrology booklet from the carpet. "People will see us in our box, relaxed, carefree, enjoying the play." He looked about for a place to leave the booklet, finally threw it on the sofa with the rest of the mess. "It is essential they realize how *nonchalantly* we are reacting to the whole silly thing."

"Nonchalantly!"

Absently he picked up a smudged cushion of snow-white silk from the floor. "It is your chance to perform, darling. I always thought you had the makings of an actress." He plumped up the cushion and set it in its correct place on an ivory *fauteuil*. "Think of how magnificently Sarah would handle the situation."

"Sarah Bernhardt?" She knocked the cushion to the floor, then flounced out of the room.

Wilde lay back on the sofa, eyes closed, reciting to himself:

> *"I am weary of days and hours,*
> *Blown buds of barren flowers,*
> *Desires and dreams and powers . . ."*

He peered into her dressing room. Clothes were heaped about everywhere. She was buttoning up the violet-strewn bodice of the dress he had selected for her, a cheery confection of silver-white brocaded silk. "What I cannot understand is why *he* has to come with us," Constance said.

"It's essential, Connie! The whole world must see the three of us together. These vicious rumors must be dispelled outside the courtroom as well as in it." He helped her with the buttons, his fingers as clumsy and nervous as her own. "It's important they realize that, despite all the mud people choose to sling at it, our friendship with Lord Alfred will go on."

"*Our* friendship!" She put her hands behind her neck to fasten the clasp of her pearls; they slid to the floor.

He retrieved them and slipped the pearls back around her smooth, pale throat. "The things they are suggesting are so — so unspeakably vile!" she said. "If I thought there were the slightest bit of truth in them —"

His hands snapped the clasp, then rested on her shoulders. "If you thought there were truth in them — what, Connie?"

"Not even animals engage in practices so vile. I never heard of such — such behavior!"

He turned her around so she was facing him, fury in her eyes. His voice was unsteady : "And your grandfather, Connie? Exposing himself to nursemaids in the Temple Gardens? Was that the kind of behavior you were brought up to think exemplary?"

She stared up as if she would strike him; from the palpitations of her shoulders he knew she was fighting to keep from weeping. "Forgive me, Connie. But we must keep some sense of reality in mind — even about the unspeakable. Please — don't weep. Tears are for homely women, not pretty ones. You're going to be all puffy and red-eyed, darling. Just when I need you most beautiful." He knew that her weeping fed on itself. She would cry until she got a headache, then look at herself in the mirror, and seeing how awful she looked, would begin to weep all over again.

She was glaring at herself in the mirror now, pounding powder into her face with a white puff. "I don't — don't understand you, Oscar. I have never understood you. I never shall." With a towel she wiped away the excess powder.

"You don't *need* to understand me, Connie," he said, trying to keep his tone even. "The important thing is not to understand, but to trust." He reached for her hands, and kissed first one palm, then the other. "Can you trust me, Connie? And love me, perhaps? Is that possible? I need it all the more because — because I do not deserve it."

Skeptically she stared up at him, looking as if she wanted to flee, then suddenly she thrust herself into his arms. Her cheek brushed against his. His heart seemed to wince. *She needs a papa,* he thought, close to tears himself. *That's what they all are looking for.* Pressing his hands around her narrow waist, he whispered, "Darling, darling . . ."

" 'Scuse me, sir," said Arthur at the door, his freckled face aflame with embarrassment at seeing them in each other's arms. "Lord Alfred Douglas has arrived."

She went absolutely stiff, and turned away.

"Thank you, Arthur," said Wilde, staring at Constance imploringly, his face full of pain. "Tell Lord Alfred we shall be right down . . ."

) 12 (

In the interval he left Constance in the box with Bosie and wandered backstage. In George Alexander's dressing room, filled with palm trees and wicker settees, winter was banished: pots of hot coals made the room as balmy as one of the gaming rooms at Homburg, at the height of the season.

Wilde began joking about how much Alexander's performance had improved — but Alexander was not in a joking mood. "Why ever have you come, Oscar!" he said. "With Alfred Douglas! Have you no shame?"

Hurt, Wilde pretended to be interested in a collection of autographed pictures of theatrical celebrities tacked to the wall. "What fascinating people you actors are. The theater is the last refuge of people who are too fascinating." He smirked at Alexander. "Why did we come? To enjoy the best evening of theater London has to offer. In spite of the acting."

"At such a time? With his father on bail after *you* had him arrested? Really, Oscar, it's in the worst possible taste." After a moment's hesitation, Alexander accepted the cigarette Wilde offered, frowning at its tinted paper tip.

"For me to come to my own play? Bad taste?" Wilde lit the cigarettes, and Alexander retreated behind an Oriental screen to finish his costume change. "You might as well say it was bad taste for the *audience* to come, George. Fortunately for both of us, the trial is filling the house!"

Alexander appeared in his white striped jacket, ready for the second act. "Oscar, you and I have never been close friends. But I admire you greatly, and I am very fond of you, as well. May I beg you to drop this case? Withdraw, go abroad. Let the whole nasty thing be forgotten."

"Why does everyone keep insisting that I go abroad?" Wilde said, looking about for an ashtray. "I have just *been* abroad, and had a perfectly dreadful time." Alexander handed him a superb Meissen saucer; with some hesitation Wilde tamped his ashes into it.

"You act as if this were not really happening!" cried Alexander, quickly checking his makeup in the dressing-table mirror. "As if you were a spectator at — at a play! I have heard rumors about the case Queensberry has built up against you."

Wilde drew closer to him, looking around as if to be sure no one could overhear. "But have you heard about Queensberry's *latest* rumor? It is by far the worst of all — and George, it directly concerns *you*."

Alexander collapsed into a chair. ''Concerns *me?*''

''Queensberry is spreading the word far and wide that Lewis Waller's performance in *An Ideal Husband* far surpasses yours in *Earnest*. You can't blame me for prosecuting him after that, can you?'' He laughed and grasped Alexander fondly by the shoulders. ''Dear George. I am touched by your concern about me. But you must have faith, George! That's all there is for us in this impossible world, you know. Faith. It's the only thing that will never, ever fail us.'' At the dressing-room door he smiled again, waving a farewell. ''Everything is going to be magnificent, George. You'll see. Everything is going to be sublime.''

PART NINE

The Trials

RAMED by the somber majesty of white-wigged bar-risters and junior counsel in billowing black robes, Oscar Wilde was impeccable in a tight-fitting pale gray suit with a hint of lilac in the weave, echoed subtly in his lavender spats. The stripes in his trousers were a little wide, thus at once bowing to the fashion and edging slightly ahead of it, and his buttonhole, a modest white carnation with the faintest blush of pink at its heart, formed a counterpoint to the deep rose of his silk moiré tie, clasped with a large, glimmering moonstone.

The courtroom's oak-carved vaults and arches and broken pedi-ments, all wondrous facades that led to nowhere, were reminiscent of a Palladian theater setting. A dome of dull-tinted glass sealed off the sky, but the glittering April sunshine seeped through, cov-ering the spectators with spring light.

After waiting in line for hours for tickets, they were aglow with anticipation, chattering on the rows of hard wood seats as if they were occupying choice places at the Haymarket or the Adelphi. The very gloominess of the courtroom served to heighten their brilliancy, as if for once the set designers had toned down their own contribution in obeisance to the costume designers' skills.

And what costumes they were! Women by far outnumbered men in the galleries, and magnificent gowns were packed tight row after row. Indeed, the dressmakers of London and Paris must have worked day and night to improvise such works of art, each determined that her client should outdo all the others, so that rustling silk filled every corner of the courtroom, and dazzling fabrications of tulle and ostrich feather, ruffle and passementerie spilled out even into the gangways.

The jurymen, by contrast, were undistinguished-looking in their enclosed platform to the right of the bench. But even they contributed to the luster of the scene, like drab supernumeraries selected to set off the star performers' radiance.

And there, clutching his hat in the front of the dock, sat the Marquess of Queensberry, scowling up at everyone and looking, to Wilde, like a misshapen dwarf from a Spanish infanta's entourage.

One by one the sergeants entered and took their places, and then there was a loud cry of "Silence!" and the barristers rose. Justice Collins, in robes of shimmering purple, shuffled to the bench as the usher gave three sharp raps on the dais.

Wilde kept trying to catch Edward Carson's eye, hoping to surprise him into a smile. But Carson sat reading over his documents imperturbably, refusing to notice. At Trinity College, he had been a gangling, homely youth. Time had filled him out, and made his bony frame imposing if not handsome — particularly in his black robes, which might have been designed expressly to dramatize Carson's spare, ascetic features. Even the absurd little horsehair wig became him.

By contrast, Sir Edward Clarke looked clownish and maladroit in his faded, oversize robes. Wilde felt a twinge of despair as the little man rose for his opening speech. In the midst of this glittering congregation, Clarke, with his ordinary square face and undistinguished features, seemed utterly out of key. The ill-fitting wig made the long gray foxtails of his sideburns even more ridiculous.

Still, once he began to speak, Clarke's aura of intelligence and mastery made any impression of clumsiness seem irrelevant. He began by discussing Wilde's relationship with the Queensberry family, and went on to describe the attempt that had been made to blackmail him.

Clarke poked about the exhibits arranged on the barristers' table, picked up a sheet of paper that turned out to be the wrong one, replaced it and reached for another. Clearing his throat, he made his voice light, almost lilting, as he read:

"My own Boy,
   Your sonnet is quite lovely, and it is a marvel that those red rose-leaf lips of yours should have been made no less for music of song than for madness of kisses . . ."

There were loud whispers throughout the courtroom. Clarke handed the letter to the bailiff for the jurymen to inspect. "The words of that letter, gentlemen," he said, "may appear extravagant to those in the habit of writing commercial correspondence —" he paused, pretending to be irritated by the laughter — "or those ordinary letters which the necessities of life force upon one every day. But Mr. Wilde is a poet, and the letter is considered by him as a prose sonnet, and one of which he is in no way ashamed. He claims it is the expression of true poetic feeling, and has no relation whatever to the hateful and repulsive suggestions put to it in the plea to this case . . ."

He called Oscar Wilde to the box.

Ambling up to the bleak brown pulpit, Wilde revised his strategy. In view of Clarke's solemn presentation, his own delivery would have more impact if, instead of the serious demeanor he had planned on, he attempted to sound a comic note.

He lifted his hand, swore to tell the truth, and gave the Bible a light kiss. From the row of herbs lined up on the stand to keep the witnesses' senses fresh, he picked up a sprig of rosemary and inhaled it with a look of mock delight, as if it were some rare bloom. He appeared to be enjoying himself enormously. When he was asked his age, he said in a clear, confident voice that he was thirty-nine.

At that, Edward Carson strode to the box with long, loping steps. Wilde raised his eyebrows slightly, in recognition, but Carson regarded him with chill indifference. "You stated that your age was thirty-nine, Mr. Wilde," he began, without prelude of any kind. "I think you are over forty." He held up to the jury a copy of Wilde's birth certificate. "You were born on the sixteenth of October, eighteen fifty-four?"

Wilde frowned, taken aback. This was not the Ned Carson he knew! "I have no wish to 'pose' as being young," he said. "You have my certificate, that settles the matter."

"But being born in eighteen fifty-four makes you more than forty," said Carson, with a rich Irish brogue that was an affectation: he had never had a trace of a brogue in Ireland. "And Lord Alfred Douglas is, I believe, twenty-four."

Carson clearly had no interest in the case's comic side; if anything, was determined to explore as far as possible its melodramatic overtones. He stalked over to the evidence table and cast

about it, as if randomly, nervousness bringing an intensity to his
movements that held the spectators electrified. Then he held up for
the jury's inspection a slim magazine, which, he announced, contained a piece by Wilde called "Phrases and Philosophies for the
Use of the Young." Opening it, he read:

"'Wickedness is a myth invented by good people to account for
the curious attractiveness of others.' You think that true, Mr.
Wilde?"

Wilde grinned. "I rarely think that anything I write is true."

"'If one tells the truth, one is sure, sooner or later, to be found
out.' Did you write that?"

"That is a pleasing paradox," Wilde said, "but I do not set
very high store by it as an axiom."

"Is it good for the young?"

"Anything is good that stimulates thought, at whatever age."

From high cheekbones the flesh stretched down towards Carson's tight throat. "Whether moral or immoral?" He clenched his
mouth so tightly that no indentation of the upper lip was visible.

"There is no such thing as morality or immorality of thought,"
said Wilde, appearing more interested in his manicure than in the
question.

At that, Carson's thick black eyebrows rose high — to tremendous effect, Wilde saw. The very features that had made Carson
so gawky at college were now his most valuable characteristics.

Carson read again from the magazine. "'Pleasure is the only
thing one should live for.'" He was giving the statement far too
much weight, Wilde decided; it would have had more effect tossed
off casually. How interesting it would be for Carson to have Beerbohm Tree or George Alexander to direct him!

"I think that the realization of oneself is the prime aim of life,"
Wilde said, "and to realize oneself through pleasure is finer than
to do so through pain. I am, on that point, entirely on the side of
the ancients — the Greeks. It is a pagan idea."

By raising one of those wondrous eyebrows, Carson managed to
suggest that this sentiment was a trifle un-English, and more than
a trifle unwholesome. Now he reached for a copy of *The Picture of
Dorian Gray*. He opened to a page marked with a slip of paper.

"'There is no such thing as a moral or an immoral book,'" he

read. " 'Books are well written or badly written.' This expresses
your view?"

"My view on art, yes."

"Then I take it, no matter how immoral a book may be, if it is
well written, it is, in your opinion, a good book?"

Wilde's voice expressed impatience. "If it were badly written,
it would produce a sense of disgust."

"A perverted novel might be a good book?"

"I don't know what you mean by a 'perverted' novel."

Carson looked about the courtroom. "Then I will suggest that
Dorian Gray is open to the interpretation of being such a novel."

"That could only be to brutes and illiterates. The views of phil-
istines on art are unaccountable."

Carson stepped back to the evidence table. His movements,
seemingly broad and rather clumsy, were in fact economical in the
extreme, and he knew how to make the least of his gestures tell.
The way he held up the next exhibit — the letter Clarke had already read — made it seem that the paper was soiled, or emitted
an unpleasant odor. As he glanced at it distastefully, turning the
letter from side to side, his nostrils flared, sending a shudder of
disgust all through the room. He passed the exhibit in front of
Wilde. "Why should a man of your age address a boy nearly twenty
years younger as 'My own Boy'?"

Wilde wished he dared to glance over to the highest part of the
gallery, where Bosie was sitting. "I was fond of him," he said
coolly. "I have always been fond of him."

"Do you — adore him?"

Wilde gave Carson a reproachful look. "I have always liked him."

"Suppose a man who was not an artist had written this letter:
would you say it was a proper letter?"

"A man who was not an artist could not have written that letter."

" 'Your slim gilt soul walks between passion and poetry,' " Carson read, his voice limp with sarcasm. "Is *that* a beautiful phrase?"

"Not as you read it, Mr. Carson. You read it very badly."

At the laughter in the courtroom, Carson's grave, thin, blue-
shadowed face grew graver still. Laughter entered into his courtroom technique very rarely, Wilde surmised, and he obviously dis-

approved of it. All the better. If Carson was going to perform his task with all the added rancor of an old friend, he must learn that Wilde could do the same.

"I do not profess to be an artist," Carson snapped, his voice so low it seemed he was speaking privately to Wilde. "And when I hear *you* give evidence, I am glad I am not."

Sir Edward Clarke rose abruptly. "I do not think my learned friend should talk like that," he said. Then, to Wilde: "Pray do not criticize my learned friend's reading again."

The aura of excitement in the courtroom had grown more intense. Carson waited a long while before his next question; long enough for the gaiety to dissipate, to be replaced by impatience in the spectators, even irritation.

"Mr. Wilde," he said at last, "do you know a young man by the name of Alfred Wood?"

There was no change in Wilde's expression, but he was grasping the brass rail of the witness stand more firmly than before. He told of meeting Wood in the Café Royal and of taking him to dinner the same evening. He had wanted to help Wood, he explained, at the request of Lord Alfred Douglas.

"What about your different social positions?" said Carson.

"I don't care about different social positions."

Carson strolled a few paces, stopped abruptly, then turned in a slow, graceful arc and pointed a long, bony finger at Wilde. "I suggest," he said, hoarse-voiced, "that first you had immoral relations with Alfred Wood, and then you gave him money."

Wilde remained tall, unmoving, expressionless. "Perfectly untrue!" he cried. The mood of the crowd was becoming more difficult to read. The shock pulsing through the courtroom muffled all other reactions.

"Did you consider," Carson said, "that he had come to levy blackmail?"

"I did. And I determined to face it." Wilde dabbed at his forehead with a handkerchief of patterned blue silk, trying to make it seem a graceful act.

"And the way you faced it was — by giving him thirty pounds to go to America?" Carson sounded honestly interested. "Did you not think it a — curious thing — that a man with whom you were on such 'intimate' terms should try to blackmail you?"

Wilde's voice was perceptibly less confident. "I thought it infamous, but Wood convinced me that such had not been his intention . . ."

The bailiff called time: the trial was adjourned for the day. The barristers rose for Justice Collins's departure. Wilde and Sir Edward Clarke left the courtroom together, carrying on a troubled, animated conversation.

) 2 (

Next morning, the Oscar Wilde who climbed to the box was full of subtle changes. He had decided to attempt a simpler attack, to bring less bravura to his testimony. His clothing reflected this change of strategy. His morning suit was finely tailored but as conventional as any banker's, his cravat was of smoke gray, and for once he wore no boutonniere.

Edward Carson, who seemed to have grown a few inches taller overnight, began the questioning by introducing the name of Alfred Taylor. With a sigh, Wilde admitted he knew Taylor, and that he had visited Taylor's home.

"Did his rooms strike you as being peculiar?"

Wilde hesitated. "Only in that he displayed more taste than is usual."

"There was rather elaborate furniture in the rooms, was there not?"

"The rooms were furnished in — good taste." Though many of the same spectators were back, and several were dressed even more splendidly than the day before, Wilde felt that the general effect they were striving for was decidedly more subdued, as if they, too, had thought it wiser to retrench. He approved of the change, regarded it as supportive. Yet he missed yesterday's sense of pomp and grandeur.

"Were the rooms strongly perfumed?"

"Yes, I have known him to burn perfumes." He thought he had better make this seem a fashionable thing to do: "I am in the habit of burning perfumes in my *own* rooms." The spectators would approve, he persuaded himself: those who did not themselves burn incense would surely be inspired to buy some on the way home.

"Did you know that he kept a lady's costume in his rooms?"

Sounding impatient, Wilde said that he did not know it, and

that he had never seen Taylor in such a costume. By his tone he conveyed disapproval of Carson's asking such a question. "Mr. Taylor is a man of great taste and intelligence, and I know he was brought up at a good English school."

Even the courtroom seemed to have changed overnight, he was thinking, to have turned dusty and conventional and dreary.

"Did you get him to arrange dinners at which you could meet young men?"

"No."

"Has he introduced young men to you?"

Wilde tried to make his reply sound casual: "Yes."

"How many young men has he introduced to you?"

It was not the unremitting quality of Carson's questioning that was so fatiguing, but the terrible dryness of it. "About five." What a pity, he thought, that Ned Carson — such a splendid adversary in every other respect — had never possessed a sense of humor.

"Were these young men all about twenty?"

"Twenty or twenty-two. I like the society of young men."

Carson shuffled a few pages. "Among these five did Taylor introduce you to Charles Parker and his brother William?"

"Yes."

"Did you know that one Parker was a gentleman's valet, and the other a groom?"

Wilde was growing increasingly annoyed with Carson's solemnity; worse, he sensed that the spectators were being seduced by it. "I didn't care tuppence what they were. I liked them." He surveyed the courtroom circumspectly to be sure he still had his audience. "I have a passion to civilize the community."

Peals of laughter greeted this, but they were distinctly less robust than before.

Carson seemed more accepting of the courtroom levity today. "What enjoyment was it to you," he said carefully, "to entertain grooms and coachmen?"

He must keep any hint of defensiveness from his reply, Wilde knew — indeed, must act as if he had no position that required defense. "The pleasure to me was being with those who are young, bright, happy, careless, free." He looked away from Carson's penetrating gray eyes — the eyes of a hawk or a falcon. With less assurance, Wilde added: "I do not like the sensible and I do not like the old."

Carson spoke faster. Had Wilde taken Charles Parker to the Savoy Hotel? Wilde said not, but admitted that other young men had visited him at the Savoy. "Did any of these young men have whiskeys and sodas and iced champagnes?"

"I can't say what they had," Wilde answered wearily.

"Do you drink champagne yourself?"

Wilde brightened at the question, even managed to retrieve his smile. "Yes, iced champagne is a favorite drink of mine — strongly against my doctor's orders."

"Never mind your doctor's orders, sir!"

Wilde looked at him wide-eyed. "I never do."

The courtroom shook with laughter. The crowd was Wilde's once again. Carson swerved about to face the gallery, looking as if he might hurl bolts of lightning into their midst. Calming himself, he glanced through his papers with the aspect of a caged, brooding eagle. When the courtroom was silent once again, he returned to the subject of Charles Parker.

"What was there in common between this young man and yourself?" he said, managing to bring something faintly lascivious into his dry voice. "What attraction had he for you?"

"I delight in the society of people younger than myself. I like those who may be called idle and careless. I recognize no social distinctions at all, of any kind; and to me youth, the mere fact of youth, is so wonderful that I would sooner talk to a young man for half an hour than be — well, cross-examined in court."

This time the laughter was mixed with applause. Wilde, moist with perspiration, gazed about the room covering a smile with his handkerchief. He was full of admiration for Carson, was planning, at some time in the near future, to invite him to dinner at Tite Street. How they would laugh about all this — for Carson was so much less stuffy out of the courtroom than in it.

Carson went on to question Wilde about Mason, Alfred Douglas's Oxford "servant." Wilde bristled slightly at the mention of the name. "Did you ever kiss him?" Carson asked.

"Oh, dear, no," Wilde replied, in a mock-serious voice. "He was, unfortunately, extremely ugly. I pitied him for it." There were uncomfortable titters in the room. Wilde blushed, realizing he had miscalculated, had said the wrong thing. He was furious with himself; even more furious with Carson for having made the blunder possible.

"Was that the reason why you did not kiss him?"

Wilde mopped his face with the handkerchief, which was now moist and limp. "Mr. Carson, you are pertinently insolent."

Carson's voice rose menacingly. "Why, sir, did you mention that this boy was extremely ugly?"

"If I were asked why I did not kiss a doormat, I should say because I do not like to kiss doormats," Wilde snapped. "I do not know *why* I mentioned that he was ugly, except that I was stung by the insolent question you put to me, and the way you have insulted me throughout this hearing." He was almost in tears, and had to pause for a moment to collect himself. "You sting me and insult me and — and try to unnerve me — and at times one says things flippantly when one ought to speak more seriously. I admit it."

"Thank you, Mr. Wilde," said Carson, with a cool smile.

Shaken and light-headed, Wilde stumbled from the box, upset that his courtroom debut, so promising at first, was being turned into a fiasco. Sweat was pouring down his body, and he feared that his carefully chosen wardrobe was beginning to look rumpled.

Carson, though, was fresher than at any time heretofore in the trial. Launching into his opening speech for the defense, he looked as if he had just risen from his morning bath.

"From beginning to end, gentlemen," he began, "Lord Queensberry in dealing with Mr. Oscar Wilde has been influenced by one hope alone — that of saving his son." His manner was declamatory and humble, Wilde thought — deceptively so. Thus might Edmund Burke have sounded, addressing Parliament, before starting in on one of his astonishing diatribes. "Lord Queensberry came to know of Mr. Wilde's character, of the scandals in connection with the Savoy Hotel, that the plaintiff had been going about with young men who were not coequal with him in position or in age, that he had been associating with men who, it will be proved beyond doubt, are some of the most immoral characters in London." Yes, he seemed to be modeling himself upon Burke, and Wilde had to admit that the borrowed character was effective.

Carson read the letter from Wilde to Bosie in its entirety, giving it the harsh weight of a villain's speech from Shakespeare. "I am not here to say anything has ever happened between Lord Alfred Douglas and Mr. Oscar Wilde — God forbid," he went on. "But before you condemn Lord Queensberry, I ask you to read Mr. Wilde's letter and to say whether the gorge of *any* father ought not to rise. Lord Queensberry's son was so dominated by Mr. Wilde that he threatened to shoot his own father!"

Sir Edward Clarke drew Wilde aside. Anxiety made Clarke look calm, unruffled. He, too, was a great artist of the courtroom, Wilde could see, although his art was a very different one from Carson's. "We must withdraw from the prosecution," Clarke whispered. "Let me make a statement to the court. We'll consent to the verdict about 'posing.' If the case continues, the Public Prosecutor will arrest you, Wilde. Right here in open court."

Wilde clutched his arm. "Make the statement, Sir Edward." He sat, hands folded in his lap, not daring to look into the audience.

Sir Edward Clarke waddled slowly to the bench, clearing his throat several times en route. He made a short speech in his halting, stammering manner, asserting that the evidence produced might well lead a jury to feel that Lord Queensberry was justified in using the word "posing," and so relieve him of a criminal charge in respect of this statement. Besides which, "without expecting a — *verdict* in this case, we should um, hum, be going through, day after day, hem, yes, um, an investigation of matters of the, um, the most appalling character." He asked Justice Collins to allow his client to withdraw from the prosecution. Edward Carson agreed to accept this.

Seated in the midst of whispering counsel and barristers, Wilde looked stupefied. He caught Edward Carson's eye and thought he saw there, for an instant, a flicker of compassion.

Without leaving the box, the jury consulted for a few moments and returned the verdict that the Marquess of Queensberry was not guilty. The cheering that greeted this was loud and undignified. Queensberry rose and triumphantly lifted his arms to the crowds, his face youthful, a man reborn. When he was formally discharged by the judge, the applause was renewed, this time even louder. The spectators in the gallery lined up to give the smiling marquess their congratulations, as Wilde watched, still too stunned to rise from his seat.

) 3 (

Leaving Tite Street, Robbie walked all the way to the King's Road to pick up the afternoon papers. Reading over the headlines in the hansom to Cadogan Square, he feared that he might become ill.

Hiding out in the Cadogan Hotel seemed another act of folly on Wilde's part. But, of course, the Cadogan in recent months had become Bosie's secret headquarters, the web into which he lured unsavory victims.

"Did you see her, Robbie?" Wilde clutched a drink in his hand and was showing the effects of many more. "How is she?" He glanced fearfully at Bosie, who was lying on the bed with his boots on, munching on a yellow apple.

"Completely shattered." Robbie tossed the newspapers on an easy chair, hoping Wilde was too distracted to look at them. Six green carnations languished in an Oriental vase: Bosie's only effort to impress a personality on the neat, uninteresting room. At the sight of an inscribed photograph of Wilde in a rather vulgar silver frame, Robbie felt a pang of jealousy. "She was hardly able to speak for the tears," he said. "Poor Constance."

"Dear God, what have I done to her! And my boys!"

"She begged me to *force* you to take the boat train, Oscar," Robbie said. "I would if I could." Bosie shifted on the bed, groaning with irritation. Robbie gave him a cold look. "She says you *must* get to France, Oscar, while there's still time."

Of the two luncheon trays on the desk, one was untouched, the other had been picked clean except for a morsel of orange Double Gloucester cheese, which Bosie now popped in his mouth. "*Why* should Oscar leave?" he drawled. "Even if he *were* to be put on trial again, which is hardly likely, he would be certain to win. All he need do is put *me* on the witness stand. As should have been done in the first place." He tossed the half-finished apple out the window, then leaned over to see where it had landed. "See that house across the square, Robbie? With the Norman roof? My family's house! It adds to the sweetness of being wicked, knowing they are nearby."

Wilde was staring at the front pages of the newspapers, dropping them one by one to the floor. "Constance is right, of course. I ought to leave. If I could only make up my mind!" Seeing that the wine bottle was empty, he reached for Bosie's nearly full glass and took a sip.

"Order some brandy, silly," said Bosie. "You can't possibly think things out when you're so nervous."

"Oscar will be arrested if he stays here!" Robbie barked. "Don't you care?"

"Why did Mrs. Robinson lie?" Wilde was saying to himself. "Why did she predict fair things?"

"If you had *forced* Edward Clarke to put me in the box," Bosie said, "none of this would have happened."

"I need to think, Bosie. I must decide what to do."

"Leave England, Oscar," Robbie said. "It is the *only* thing to do."

Wilde had finished the wine in Bosie's glass. "Have them send up another bottle of hock, Bosie, like a good boy?"

Forming his lips into a kiss, Bosie said: "The best cognac — nothing else."

"And you mustn't let me forget to give you the — oh, God! *How* am I going to pay all the costs of that preposterous trial? They will seize everything I own!"

Robbie could not keep silent: "Was your family not going to take care of the court charges, Bosie?"

Bosie, gazing down on the strollers below like a king upon supplicants, turned from the window with surprise. "Now that it has turned into such a scandal? My mother could hardly be expected to lend her name to anything so sordid!"

Wilde had found writing paper in the desk drawer and was scribbling a quick note. "I do this in utter desperation," he murmured, more to himself than them. He was writing to his old friend in Paris, Robert Sherard, asking him to get in touch with Sarah Bernhardt as quickly as possible. Sarah would give him a lump sum for all future royalties on *Salomé* — a few hundred pounds would save the day. Sherard was to forward the money to London by the quickest means possible.

"Post this for me, Robbie?" Wilde said, with a miserable smile. "What would I do without you!"

Robbie put the letter in a pocket and returned to the matter at hand, the one Wilde seemed unable to look at. "If they haven't arrested you as yet, Oscar, it's because they are giving you an opportunity to escape! For no other reason — can't you see that?"

Wilde nodded absently, poking through the newspapers on the floor.

"I know what we'll do, Oscar!" said Bosie, laughing effusively. "We'll dine at Kettner's. We'll show them how little we care for their tedious concepts of propriety. Come with us, Robbie — if you dare!"

Robbie looked as if he might strike him. "Oscar! If you stay you are *doomed*." He was fighting back tears. "You are like a — like a hare hypnotized by the snake about to devour him! Move, Oscar — do *something*, for the love of God!"

"You are perfectly right, Robbie," Wilde murmured. "Perfectly right." He sat at the foot of Bosie's bed, holding his empty glass and staring out the window at the banks of clouds sailing over Cadogan Square like a restless kingdom of dreams. " '*Les nuages qui passent*,' " he whispered. " '*Là-bas . . . là-bas . . . les merveilleux nuages . . .* ' "

He was still sitting that way when the two loud knocks came. Wilde stumbled to the door and opened it to a pair of police officers.

"Mr. Oscar Wilde, I believe?" said the taller of them.

"Yes?" said Wilde, his voice dim.

"We must ask you to accompany us to Scotland Yard. We have a warrant for your arrest."

) 4 (

The cloister was banked with drooping potted lilies, and Robert Sherard sat watching the play of a pair of sleek, gray, blue-eyed cats. The younger sniffed the other's fur excitedly, gave it a few quick licks, then drew away sideways, spitting. Sherard had already been waiting for nearly an hour and, as he kept reminding himself, he was a busy man.

"I am angry with you!" cried Sarah Bernhardt, appearing through a pair of arches at the far end of the cloister. As she charged towards him, her scarlet lips rounded in a pout. "You *never* come to call on me."

He fell to his knees and kissed her hand. "Madame Sarah," he said reverently. She stared down at him like an empress, blazing forth her practiced radiant smile.

Sherard tightened his jaw. "Oscar — the poor devil. Terrible, terrible."

"Ah!" She raised a limp hand to her forehead. "I can hardly bear to read the papers." The tawny red of the tresses piled high above the sacred brow owed much to henna; the pale complexion was heightened with powder; her eyes supported thicknesses of coarse black kohl. "What Oscar must be suffering!" she sobbed, anguish wrinkling her narrow face — which she buried in a white lace handkerchief.

"He needs money, madame. Most desperately."

"Money?" she said, her voice soft. Drying her eyes, she gazed at him thoughtfully, then stepped before a large round mirror with porcelain snakes coiled about the frame. Adjusting the jeweled dragonfly combs in her hair, she said: "How much?"

"He thought you might buy *Salomé* — outright. For ten thousand francs."

"Hmm," she said, lifting one of the cats to her cheek. Was it out of affection for the animal, Sherard wondered, or because the creature's dusky fur so beautifully set off her pallor, at the same time that its eyes were like smaller versions of her own? "In the theater at this moment," she said, "things are abominable. *Abominable!*"

"Oh?" But her plays were doing splendid business.

"I could not possibly purchase that superb, exquisite, heart-wrenching play, much as I long to possess it! Ah! I know what we will do. My beloved Oscar must accept from me a loan. Friend to friend. But I must first see how much money is in the box-office safe. Ten thousand francs, did you say?" She laughed in embarrassment. "I am a fool with money, Monsieur Sherard. An absolute fool. Listen. Today is — Saturday? You will come back Monday at the same time. The money will be waiting for you."

He knelt before her, too moved to speak. Staring down at him imperiously, she closed her tormented eyes a moment and then — as he had often seen her do in *Thaïs* — raised her head ever so slowly as if to communicate with some presence in the heavens only she could see. Without another word, she slipped away into the shadows of the cloister.

When Sherard returned on Monday, the door was opened by a small black page in Moroccan costume. "Madame Sarah? Monsieur, she is not here."

"I can wait."

"No use, monsieur. Madame Sarah will not be back this afternoon."

"She must have left something for me. My name is —"

"There are no messages, monsieur. No messages."

Sherard returned the next day. And the next. "Madame Sarah is gone for the rest of the week," said the page, grinning to show his small white teeth. "There are no messages. No messages at all."

) 5 (

Awaiting trial at Holloway Prison, Wilde was permitted only one visitor each day. He wanted only one.

Holloway, Bosie said, was like a poem, a strange dreadful poem of darkness and despair. He seemed thrilled with the place.

In a row of boxes closed off with wire mesh, the prisoners sat like animals in cages, separated from their visitors by a corridor wide enough for a warder to march up and down in. It was impossible to carry on a lucid conversation: one had to shout over the din of the other prisoners and visitors, who then shouted the louder. It was difficult, some days, to make the effort to speak at all.

One rainy afternoon, when the hall was quieter than usual, Wilde said: "You must go to France, Bosie. It's dangerous for you to stay in London. They'll get you, too."

"I shall never leave."

"The evidence applies to you as well as —"

"The what?"

"The evidence," Wilde repeated, raising his voice. "It is dangerous for you to stay in London."

In his new pale blue suit, Bosie was an angel of light fluttering airily in Holloway's relentless gloom. "I don't care," he said. "I shall stay at your side. They can give us adjoining cells!"

Wilde's heart swelled till it seemed it must crush itself against his ribs. "Go to France, Bosie. You *must*."

"While you are imprisoned in London? Never."

One day, Wilde was persuaded to exchange Bosie's visit for one that he reluctantly had to admit was important. "I have come to volunteer my services, Mr. Wilde,'' Sir Edward Clarke shouted over the commotion of the visiting hall. Wilde was ashamed to look at him: when he did, he saw only friendship in the man's deep eyes. ''I will represent you at this new trial without fee — if you desire me to do so.'' It was difficult to reply for the sobs that racked Wilde's body.

The news Bosie brought with him each day grew worse. Wilde was to be tried with Alfred Taylor, and the evidence against each would no doubt be used to blacken the other. All Wilde's plays had been taken off the boards. His books were no longer on sale in any shop in London. His every source of income had been cut off. Worst of all, the bailiffs had gotten into his house and seized everything he owned.

To pay them would have cost very little; Bosie might easily have gotten the sum from his family. But Wilde was afraid to mention this, afraid it might precipitate a scene between them.

Thus to a vulgar, ravening crowd, his autographed books, his paintings, all his loveliest possessions were sold for virtually nothing at an impromptu auction in Tite Street. Bosie reported every hideous aspect of the sale. Even Cyril's and Vyvyan's toys were one by one auctioned off for a few pennies — a detail Wilde wished he might have been spared.

''All that money going to my father to pay his wretched court fees! It makes me ill,'' said Bosie. Wilde said nothing.

Constance never came to visit; no doubt she did not dare. All the better, Wilde thought. He could not face her. Besides, if she came, he would have to give up Bosie's visit.

Once, as the boy was leaving, Wilde forced a hand through the wire mesh of the cage, cruelly lacerating the skin. The warder rapped his club on the bars until Wilde drew back his bleeding hand.

Then one day shortly before the trial began, Wilde was startled when, at visiting time, Percy Douglas appeared in place of Bosie. His brother was unable to come, Percy explained, but wished Wilde all good luck for the trial.

''Percy, where is he?''

Bosie had left London for Dunkirk, Percy said. Their mother had thought it the wisest course of action. He was taking the afternoon boat to Calais. ''Bosie said you would understand.''

Wilde nodded. ''I understand,'' he said in a choked voice.

) 6 (

The trial began on April 26, and Wilde appeared in the dock beside Alfred Taylor, who was being tried on the same charge: commission of acts of gross indecency.

Justice Charles looked stout and extremely self-satisfied in his purple vestments, and his urbane pastoral manner lent to the courtroom something of the character of a High Church memorial service.

In his opening speech for the prosecution, Charles asked the jury to dismiss from their minds anything they might have heard or read about the two defendants, and to approach the case with absolutely open minds. This request brought smiles to many in the courtroom: as if it would be possible to forget what all London had been chattering about continually for the past month!

Another trial, Wilde was thinking: everything so very much the same, as in a recurring nightmare — but with the nightmare's added horror of being different in small, puzzling particulars. The same courtroom was being used — and yet how unlike last time it was! He thought of some impoverished theatrical group that must use the same poorly painted backdrop for all its productions, comedies and tragedies alike.

As for the spectators, it was as if the court this time had decided to limit entrance to only the shabby and the poor.

For that matter, how different was his own characterization this time! Since he had been permitted in Holloway Prison no such luxury as a haircut, his tresses were long, dirty, stringy, and his face, from the careless ministrations of the prison barber, was torn and bruised. He prayed that his chastened appearance might play on the sympathy of the jury rather than their disdain. And poor noble Alfred Taylor — who had been offered immunity if he would testify against Wilde, but had refused — how far from his natural state of wigs and powder he was, shrouded in a dull black suit. He was like a bird of paradise with all its feathers plucked.

Lest anyone might forget some incriminating detail, Queen's Counsel Charles Gill ran afresh over the catalogue of horrors from the last trial. He lingered over descriptions of the heavily curtained windows and the strange perfumes of Alfred Taylor's rooms in Little College Street.

"Taylor was familiar with a number of young men," Gill droned, in his unctuous, sermonizing way, "who were in the habit of giving their bodies, or selling them, to other men for the purpose of sodomy."

At the word Wilde visibly cringed. But as one youth after another was called into the witness box to testify that they had committed unnatural acts with him, he grew impassive.

Then suddenly in the midst of the crowd Wilde spotted, in one of the front rows, the grinning face of the Marquess of Queensberry, staring right at him. Inadvertently Wilde gasped, and Queensberry bared his teeth like a mad dog.

Alfred Wood took the stand. Why, Wilde asked himself, would Wood want to testify against him?

Wood told of meeting Wilde at the Café Royal through the mediation of Lord Alfred Douglas, and of how Wilde had seduced him. What was still so absorbing was Wood's astonishing physical resemblance to Bosie: indeed, it was like being testified against by Bosie himself. At one point Wood glanced over at him, and Wilde saw in that instant a depth of gloating hatred that he would not have dreamed possible in that beautiful young face. But why? Why?

A masseur from the Savoy Hotel testified that one morning when he had let himself into Wilde's room, he had seen someone in one of the beds whom he first took to be a lady. Then he realized it was a young man. Wilde had told him he was very busy that morning and had no need of a massage.

Expressionless in the dock, Wilde remembered the morning in question, the rays of sunlight streaming in over the disordered room, and Bosie's vile companion lying snoring in the filthy bed as Wilde, barely risen from his own separate bed, had tried to act natural with the nonplussed masseur. Bosie, meanwhile, had been soaking himself in a hot tub, out of view in the bathroom. Wilde closed his eyes.

The chambermaid confirmed this evidence, stating that she, too, had seen a youth in one of the beds. Looking down at the floor, she went on to state that she had been forced to draw the housekeeper's attention to peculiar stains on the bedsheets.

This could not be happening in an English courtroom, Wilde told himself — and surely not to him. It was an evil dream. At any moment he would awake and find himself in a clean, sunny place thick with flowers and fresh lovely things — with his darling boy lying at his side.

Opening his defense, Sir Edward Clarke was more direct than was his custom. "Men who have been charged with the offenses alleged against Mr. Wilde shrink from an investigation," he said. "And in my submission, the fact of him taking the initiative of a public trial is evidence of his innocence."

Clarke too seemed to have changed in the past month: to have become even wiser and far, far older. He looked at the skeptical faces of the jury members with an inner strength of character that gave his every utterance overtones of an almost biblical solemnity. "Men guilty of such offenses suffer from, hum, a species of insanity. What then would you *think* of a man who, hem, um, *knowing* himself to be guilty — *knowing* that evidence would be, ahum, forthcoming from half a dozen different places, insisted on bringing his — his *case* before the world? Insane would hardly be the, hum, hum, word for it, if Mr. Wilde really had been, um, guilty."

Wilde went up from the dock into the witness box, and the crowd's murmuring grew louder. "Order! Order!" cried Justice Charles, with peremptory raps of the gavel. Was this, Wilde wondered, how Jesus had felt when Pontius Pilate led him in rags before the multitude? The only face he recognized was Queensberry's; it seemed the courtroom was filled with Queensberrys, all leering up at him with insane malice.

Mr. Charles Gill rose for the cross-examination.

"During eighteen ninety-three and eighteen ninety-four you were a great deal in the company of Lord Alfred Douglas?" Gill demanded.

"Oh, yes," said Wilde faintly.

"Did he read his poems to you?"

"Yes."

Gill presented his best profile to the court as he searched for a magazine amongst the pieces of evidence, then deliberately turned its pages. He read one of Bosie's poems called "In Praise of Shame." It ended with the line, "I am the Love that dare not speak its name."

"Is it not clear," said Gill, with a sly smile, "that the poem relates to unnatural love?"

"No," Wilde whispered. They had thrown him into the deepest

of wells, and left him to die. But he would not die. He would climb
out, somehow. He would hoist himself up, inch by painful inch.

"What then is 'the love that dare not speak its name'?"

The fact that they were alluding to Bosie seemed to generate
new energy in him. Taking a deep breath, Wilde leaned forward
in the box, tightly clenching the rail. "The love that dare not speak
its name in this century is such a great affection of an elder for a
younger man as there was between David and Jonathan," he said,
his voice somber and low. "Such as Plato made the very basis of
his philosophy. And such as you find in the sonnets of Michelangelo and Shakespeare." Emotion brought a quaver to his voice —
fearful yet strong — that was something new to it. "It is a deep,
spiritual affection as pure as it is perfect. It dictates and pervades
great works of art like those of Shakespeare and Michelangelo —
and that letter of mine you have read, such as it is." He paused a
moment, breathing deep. His voice was louder now: "It is in this
century misunderstood, so much misunderstood that it may be described as — the love that dare not speak its name. And on account of it I am placed where I am now." He was using his voice
like a fine instrument; its resonance surprised and moved him, and
his pleasure brought an even greater richness into his cadences.
"It is beautiful, it is fine, it is the noblest form of affection. There
is nothing unnatural about it. It is intellectual, and it repeatedly
exists between an elder and a younger man, when the elder has
intellect, and the younger has all the joy, hope, and glamour of
life before him. That it should be so, the world does not understand." And now he permitted his voice to go dry, as if he had
exhausted its resources. "The world mocks at it," he said hoarsely,
"and sometimes puts one in the pillory for it."

The courtroom burst into applause, wave upon wave of it. There
were cheers as well, and several men rose in homage. Hisses could
be heard, but they were muffled by the general approbation.

"Order. *Order!*" Judge Charles said he would clear the court if
there were any further such manifestations.

Wilde, moved by the spectators' reactions, seemed to come back
to life. Color flowed into his cheeks, he stood firm and tall. If only
Bosie could be there to see him!

Gill resumed. "I wish to call your attention to the style of your
correspondence with Lord Alfred Douglas."

"I am never ashamed of the style of my writings," Wilde said, with a trace of his earlier arrogance. A rush of approval went through the crowd.

"You are fortunate," Gill said. "Or should I say — shameless?" But Gill had never learned to wield a rapier. "I refer to two passages of your letter in particular. You use the expression 'your slim gilt soul,' and you refer to Lord Alfred's 'red rose-leaf lips.' Do you think an ordinarily constituted being would address such expressions to a younger man?"

Wilde looked about the courtroom, smiling, pleased to find that his audience were far less drab than he had suspected. "I am not, happily I think, an ordinarily constituted being."

Amidst the approving titters, Gill put on a disgusted expression: "I am pleased for once to be able to agree with you." Now it was Gill's turn to be applauded. Obviously pleased, he turned to the testimony of the young men who had accused Wilde of indecent behavior. "Why did you take up with these youths?"

"I am a lover of youth."

Gill sneered. "I suppose you would prefer puppies to dogs? And kittens to cats?"

Wilde smiled faintly, determined to get back the full sympathy of the crowd. "I should enjoy the society of a beardless, briefless barrister quite as much as the most accomplished Queen's Counsel."

Judge Charles rapped for silence in the laughter following.

"Why did you go to Taylor's rooms?" snapped Gill, clearly hostile now.

Wilde felt as sure of himself as if he were tossing off ripostes to a drinking campanion at the Café Royal. "Because I used to meet actors and singers of many kinds there."

"Rather a rough neighborhood, isn't it?"

"That I don't know. I know it is near the Houses of Parliament."

He seemed to be hearing the audience's astonished, delighted laughter at one of his plays. He looked about and feigned surprise.

The sudden upturn of the case had lifted Sir Edward Clarke's spirits; this he manifested by expressing an even deeper gloom than usual. He concluded his stammered, rivetingly interesting peroration by begging the jury members to heed only that testimony which seemed to come from honest, reliable witnesses. "Fix your minds firmly on the, um, *tests* that ought to be applied to evidence before you can condemn a — a fellow man on a charge like this." He looked at them imploringly. "I trust that the result of your deliberations will be to — to gratify those thousands of hopes which are hanging upon your decision, and will, ah, clear from this fearful imputation one of our most — most renowned and accomplished men of letters and, in, uh, clearing him, will clear society from a — from a stain."

Mr. Gill ended his sullen speech to the jury by running down the evidence of the young witnesses once more. "It is your duty, gentlemen," he concluded, "to express your verdict without fear or favor. You owe a duty to society, however sorry you may feel yourselves at the moral downfall of an eminent man, to protect society from such scandals by removing from its heart a sore which cannot fail in time to corrupt and taint it."

The jury deliberated for four hours. When they returned to the box, they announced that they had been unable to arrive at a decision. "The only result we have come to is that we cannot agree." Yet another trial would have to be arranged.

Several in the courtroom applauded. Wilde drew Clarke aside. "You should take a bow, Sir Edward," he whispered, barely able to hide his excitement. "In fact, we both should!"

) 7 (

"The first thing I must do is get to a hairdresser," said Wilde airily, glancing into one of the hotel-room mirrors. "I look like Mrs. Beere playing the Witch of Endor."

"You may find that difficult, Oscar," said Bosie's brother Percy, who was pouring tea for them both. "I think you will find most tradesmen openly hostile."

Wilde stretched luxuriously: to a physique still adjusted to the confines of a prison cell, the pair of cramped, tasteless rooms Percy had taken for him seemed palatial. "Why should my hairdresser be hostile?" he said, burrowing through the suitcase Percy had brought, trying to find something smart to wear. "Why should *anyone* be? I have not been convicted. Nor am I going to be." Softening, he gave Percy a friendly smile. "You saw how they all adored me in the courtroom."

Percy, who was as awkward as Bosie was graceful, poured too much milk in his tea, making it overflow. "Adored you?"

"All but your father!" Wilde sat chuckling on the edge of one of the unsightly club chairs. "Did you notice him, so plump and happy there in the very front row? He is feeding on my ruin!"

Percy produced a flask from an inner pocket and poured a dollop of brandy into Wilde's cup — though most of it landed in the saucer — and then into his own. "He keeps sending horrid, abusive telegrams to my wife. My father is growing madder every day."

"How alike he and Bosie are," Wilde murmured in a small voice. "Never send a letter when a telegram will do . . ."

"He pretends to think of my poor wife as a confidante," Percy said. "Though he hates her and always has! I believe he is somehow jealous that I married. And yet he hates me, too! He hates us all!" Percy lowered his eyes, as if ashamed of this admission. "But I must say something to you, Oscar, and I don't want you to be embarrassed. It's about the money I put up for your bail."

"So *very* generously, Percy," said Wilde, downing the last of the marvelous tea. So this was how it felt to be the one given to, rather than the giver. How devastating! "How can I ever thank you sufficiently for that beautiful act? Men have been made saints for less." He inspected the empty cup in the room's cheery afternoon light, thinking of how lovely it was to be able to order tea when one wished it. How very little it took, after all, to gladden the soul. "But how am I ever to repay you, Percy?"

"It will be perfectly understandable to me if you leave the country. Really, Oscar: it is what I think you should do. I am ready to forfeit the thousand pounds. Gladly. It was my family that led you into these sad straits."

Wilde replaced the teacup on the dresser. "Percy, what a strange idea!" He loosened his tie, heading for the bedroom. "I would not *consider* leaving the country. Even if it had been unnecessary for you to post bail. I am going to be declared innocent at this next trial, Percy. How can you doubt it? And now I am going to have a little nap. Perhaps after that we can have some lunch sent up, a little nourishment might make us —"

There was the sound of a key in the latch and the salon door flew open.

"Oscar Wilde, I believe?" The man looked like a stevedore in Sunday clothing.

Wilde's face went pale. "By what right do you —"

"I am the manager of this hotel. Leave at once."

Wilde turned fearfully to Percy, but Percy was as astonished as himself. Clumsily he got to his feet. "How dare you ask such a — "

"Out! At once!" The man's fists were raised, his muscles bulging under the cheap morning coat. "Is that clear? Do you understand, Mr. Wilde?"

Percy reached for the suitcase and began throwing things in. "There's no sense arguing, Oscar."

Downstairs, a crowd of roughs hovering about the hotel entrance began shouting obscenities when they saw Wilde. "My father is not going to let you go," Percy said sadly. "This is his doing."

"Let us separate, dear generous friend," Wilde said, thinking how unlike Bosie in every way was this befuddled young man. "I shall find lodgings easily enough."

Percy looked as if he might hurl the suitcase at the howling men. "Not so easily as you think, Oscar."

"Percy, you must get it into your head," said Wilde, waving for a cab, "*I have not been convicted!*"

Percy noted that for all his bravado, Wilde — when a hansom drew to a halt before them — averted his face from the driver, as if unable to endure another rejection. Behind them, the hoodlums were waving down two other cabs. As Wilde took off in the direction of Hyde Park, the two cabs followed. Wilde glanced out the window and, with a terrified expression he could not conceal, waved back at Percy.

"God bless you!" Percy shouted.

) 8 (

Percy himself took a cab to Piccadilly. At every newsstand the cab passed, the name Oscar Wilde shrieked out at him from the headlines, like a malediction.

Walking up past the National Gallery, Percy stopped short. In the distance, he saw his father strutting past Saint Martin-in-the-Fields in short quick steps. Percy wanted to turn and run, but decided to stand his ground.

"So! Where is your hero?" Queensberry demanded, his tight features squinching up tighter still.

"I want you to stop sending filthy telegrams to my wife!"

"Do you? Are you afraid she might find out that Wilde is overly fond of *your* red rose-leaf lips?"

"You are insane!"

"Perhaps you've had too much madness of kisses, too — like my other so-called sons."

"Do you realize that you are insane?" Percy screamed.

His father stuck out his tongue, making a rude noise. Percy felt his head spinning as the crowd circled about them. Before he knew what had happened, he was upon his father, or his father was upon him, and blows were raining down from both sides.

"This is my son," screamed the Marquess of Queensberry. A constable was trying to separate them. "This is the one who bailed out Oscar Wilde today. He should not be allowed to walk the streets!"

And then they were tearing at each other again, and the constable could barely pull them apart. He had to whistle for help to haul the two of them, still brawling, into the nearest police station.

) 9 (

The afternoon had lapsed into a raw, windy, rain-spattered night. Wilde, more and more exhausted, had trudged into virtually every hotel in the center of London, had even ventured into the suburbs. None would give him lodging. The two coaches filled with jeering hooligans had pursued him most of the day.

With no feeling left in his legs and feet, near midnight he dragged himself over the sticky wet cobblestones of Oakley Street. His mother's house in the gaslight was shabby and small. He hesitated at the door, fearing to knock. If he should be turned away from here . . .?

The maid was openly disapproving. "Is — is my mother awake, Delia, for God's sake?" Without greeting, she made way for him to enter.

His mother's voice, quavering in song, rang out from a floor above:

> *"Who can tell, or can fancy, the treasures that sleep*
> *Entombed in the wonderful womb of the deep?*

The pearls and the gems, as if valueless, thrown
To lie 'mid the seawrack concealed and unknown . . ."

As he stumbled up the stairs, the old song in her rich, throaty voice brought tears to his eyes.

"Mother —" The room, so much smaller than her home on Park Lane, smelled of beeswax and alcohol and many perfumes. She had still not relinquished a single piece of furniture, and if the last salon had been crowded, this was like a cavern of rolled-up carpets, boxes of newspaper-wrapped china and silverware, porcelain and clocks, tables and cabinets piled atop each other.

"The poet!" she cried. She sat sprawled across her painted gold throne covered with black veils, as if she were in mourning. "The poet!" She staggered across the room to throw herself into his arms.

He forced himself to look for once into his mother's eyes. But she seemed not to see him, to be absorbed with images from within.

"They cannot shame us!" she cried. Her face was blotched red, beneath the veils, and her voice was pitched high with excitement. "What do we care for their morals? Morals are for our servants. We are the Wildes! The Wildes of Merrion Square!"

And as he pondered the ugly oversize pieces on all sides of them, he realized what a great influence on his taste she had been. Where she had wanted everything massive and overbearing, he had devoted his life to seeking out what was airy and light; to being as different from her as he could be. And the more he had tried to be different, the more he had become, somehow, the same . . . "Can I — stay here, Mother? I have no place to go!"

She gripped him by the shoulder and a clawlike hand dabbed at his face. "Foolish child! So long as I live, my home is the home of Oscar Fingal O'Flahertie Wills Wilde! Did they think they could take you from *me?*"

"You have so little space."

"Nonsense," she said, grasping for one of the candlesticks, splashing her black velvet dress with drops of wax.

"It must be painful for you, Mother, moving to houses that get smaller and smaller."

"It is I who get bigger and bigger!" Holding the candle high above her, she led him down the hall, their shadows stretching ahead like goblins dancing over the walls. She flung open the door to a small dust-covered room filled with broken chairs, ancient yellowing newspapers, a stereopticon, handwritten pages in tottering piles. In trying to untie the mattress in the corner, she nearly set it aflame.

"I am so tired, Mother," Wilde said, looking for something to use as a blanket. "So very tired." He collapsed on the mattress and she flung a tattered fur coat over him.

He closed his eyes, pretending to sleep while she went on murmuring to herself, or perhaps to him. For a long while she stood silent in the candlelight, staring down on him. Then once again she raised her voice in song:

> *"The palace of crystal has melted in air,*
> *And the dyes of the rainbow no longer are there;*
> *The grottoes with vapor and clouds are o'ercast,*
> *The sunshine is darkness — the vision has passed!"*

) 10 (

Frank Harris, looking about the house with astonishment, offered the use of a yacht to steal away from England in.

"I am going to be acquitted, Frank! Why does everyone refuse to believe that?"

Of course, much of the time he hardly believed it himself, except when he had imbibed great quantities of hock or brandy, which his mother seemed always to have on hand, though the larder more often than not was bare.

) 11 (

He was seated in the dining room on the ground floor, reading. The works of Matthew Arnold, which had always rather depressed him, now seemed strangely pacifying. The room — the only one not crammed with furniture — looked out on a garden his mother had allowed to run to seed. Something about the very gloominess of the view soothed his racked thoughts.

When the door opened, he did not turn at once, yet he could feel her presence warming the room. "Darling?"

Constance stared at him coldly, shrouded in a dark gray hooded coat, like a figure at a Venetian carnival. "Are you — proud of yourself?"

That was not what she ought to have said. He thought of how he must appear to her. He was wearing a suit his mother had found in one of the closets, a suit left over from his college days, and full of holes. A drunken friend of Delia's had trimmed his hair — crudely as if he had been shearing a hedge. "Proud, Connie? What is left to be proud of?"

If she would throw her arms about him now, he told himself, that one kind natural act would purify him, purify them both, forever. It would have the power to heal — as Jesus had healed. Constance said nothing, did nothing. At last he turned to her and smiled tentatively. "The boys?"

"It is only for their sake that I have come."

"Are they — happy in Ireland? If I could only see them."

Dryly she laughed. "You think of them now? Why didn't you think of them when you were making riot in the Savoy Hotel with —" she bit her lip and turned away.

"You — believe those things?"

"Believe!" The edge of suppressed fury in her voice astonished him. She had never looked so beautiful, so alive. He had always sensed a secret fire burning in Constance. Did it take something so dreadful to fan it to flame? She was fidgeting with two of his mother's little figurines, a Japanese boy and girl grinning at each other from opposite ends of a knickknack shelf. "Are you suggesting the evidence is untrue?" she said.

"And if it *is* true, Connie, can you —"

"You have betrayed me. All these years! Me — and your children. And with — with —" She threw herself onto a broken overstuffed chair, glowering at him. Yes, it was a new Constance he was beholding. "It is a *facade* I have shared my life with. A phantom. I know nothing about the man I married — *nothing!* The imbecile I have been! When I think of it, I want to —"

For all her effort to look stern and unyielding, she appeared so frail that he wished only to embrace her. He fell to his knees, grasped her hands. "Connie —?" She made as if to pull away. "Connie, can you ever care for me again?"

She buried her face in her hands. "You can *ask* such a question?" she said, her voice tremulous. "I — have no tears left." Then, suddenly cold again, she said: "Can you — change? Is it possible?"

"Change?"

"Are you able to *guarantee* that you — that you will alter your way of life?"

He drew away from her and stared into the room's bleak shadows. "You wish — a guarantee?"

"I wish to help the man — I married. A man I once loved very, very dearly. I wish to protect him from — himself."

"And the man you see before you? The man I am right now? In your eyes, does he count for nothing?"

She was regarding him as if he were a stranger. "Do you know what you were to me the day we married, Oscar?" she said, bemused. "You seemed — so much greater than anyone I had ever known, ever dreamed of knowing. My own prince!"

He nodded. "A prince of fairy tales."

"A prince of poets! My very own Keats, my Shelley. That was the worst betrayal. Those secret dreams that I had held all to myself from my earliest days. You betrayed those poor — foolish dreams. I never cared for life. Only poetry. And now — all the poetry is gone." Tears were coming freely, and she made no effort to stem their flow. "The hopes I had for you, Oscar — for us both. Gone. All gone."

Timidly he opened his arms to her. "Some of the greatest poetry germinates in — broken hearts."

She glanced at his open arms, then went to the window and stared out at the disheveled garden. It was full of desiccated willows and rows of lilies and irises gone brown from neglect. "Don't ask me to believe anything," she whispered. "Don't ask me to hope." Her voice rose, thin and fearful. "Lord, dear Lord — listen to this prayer. Never, ever, let me hope — for anything — *anything* — ever again . . ."

) 12 (

In the mornings his mother was cross. "No one appears at my Saturdays since you brought this affliction upon us. And mine was the most dazzling salon in London!"

Wilde smiled despite himself at the memory of those drooping Saturday afternoons when he would be called upon to lift the spirits of the few disreputable guests she had been able to round up.

Her moods kept changing. One morning she went raging through the house shrieking, "Pariah! You have made me a pariah!" Another day she was giddy, laughing at tedious old stories that she repeated over and over to herself.

When dusk came, she would invariably settle down for what she termed "a drop of the spirit," adding that she had well earned a bit of solace in these tormented times.

One evening Wilde was sitting in the *fauteuil* next to her at one end of the dim salon, peering into a cup of hot lemonade heavily laced with Irish whiskey.

She was half asleep on the sagging sofa, with the hot drink in her hand. Suddenly she awoke. "Sit up, Oscar," she said. "The semirecumbent position is bad for the spine — not to mention indecorous."

"Mother? My friends advise me to leave England," he said. The words sounded slurred to him, and he tried to recall how many drinks she had given him. "Well? What is your opinion of that?"

She inhaled the fumes steaming from her cup as if they were a rare perfume. "Escape? A son of 'Speranza' Wilde, descendant of the great Dante himself, run from justice?" She heaved herself up from the sofa. "They are not friends if they advise such a thing!" she boomed forth, and toppled down again into the sofa cushions, raising a cloud of dust.

"Dante ran from Florence!"

"What! For lesser treasons, men have been flogged! Ah, '*Nessun maggiore dolore che — che —*' How does it go?" She stood again, grasping at the door molding for support. "That you have no respect for me is all too evident. Have you none for your ancestors, either?" She seemed to be performing a kind of unsteady gavotte, in and out among the piles of furniture, to music only she could hear.

"I don't think I could bear it if they put me away, Mother. Being detained for even a month was — dreadful. I could not endure any more of it. A long incarceration would — kill me."

"Come, my child," she said, limp. She leaned on him, and hobbled over to her throne, easing herself onto it with a groan. Then she patted her knee for Wilde to sit on — just as when he was a child. Unthinkingly he obeyed, but when his weight proved too much for her, she let him collapse to the floor. He lay there, barely conscious. He tried to speak, but his tongue was too heavy. His head fell forward. She made an effort to raise him by the shoulders, but let go.

"My son, my son," she said, smiling down at him. "They cannot destroy us Irish, no matter how they try. They have tried to dominate us for generations. For centuries. We remain bloodied, but unbowed. In our own weak way, we are too strong for them! In our own wicked way, we are too pure for them! For we have more power than they ever will: the power of the poetry that is in us!" She tried to push herself up out of the seat but gave up the attempt and sank back, her head loose on her neck. "You are Oscar Fingal O'Flahertie Wills Wilde, the son of the beloved Speranza! Let them destroy us! Like phoenixes we shall rise again! No matter *what* they attempt, we shall always — shall always —" A whiskey bottle was tucked in the debris heaped on top of the bookcase; reaching towards it, she fell forward, unconscious, over the crumpled body of her son.

) 13 (

The haggard, unkempt man who stood in the dock on the twenty-second of May bore little resemblance to the Oscar Wilde who had prosecuted the Marquess of Queensberry less than two months before. He was thinner and older, lifeless and bent in his worn black suit.

Sir Edward Clarke began the procedure with enthusiasm, as if he had not had to deal with the sordid details twice before. He petitioned to have Alfred Taylor tried separately, which was agreed on. But the evidence against Taylor was so unequivocal that there was virtually no hope that the jury would find him innocent. And this cast a shadow of complicity over Wilde's trial to follow.

Nevertheless, Clarke cross-examined the familiar witnesses with fresh interest, as if each one of them were new to him.

On the other hand, the new counsel for the prosecution — the Solicitor General himself, Frank Lockwood — seemed to have wearied of the case long before. He was a pale, pockmarked little man with a scraggly beard that climbed about his face like untended ivy, and he was openly distressed by the proceedings.

He questioned Wilde about his relationship with Alfred Taylor and the young men Wilde had met in Taylor's rooms.

"Do you approve of Alfred Taylor's conduct?" Lockwood asked.

"I don't think," Wilde said softly, "that I am called upon to express approval or disapproval of any person's conduct."

Sir Edward Clarke objected to the witness being asked his opinion of other people. The judge, Mr. Justice Wills, a kindly man who seemed to feel pain over all the terrible allegations he was hearing, upheld Clarke's objection.

Lockwood returned to the youths Wilde had met at Taylor's. "Was the conversation of these young men literary?"

Wilde regarded him with some confusion. He was trying not to remember that Lockwood had often been a guest in his home, was trying not to be shattered by Lockwood's worse than contemptuous attitude towards him. "The fact that I had written a play which was a success seemed to them very wonderful. And I was gratified by their admiration." He lowered his head and in a solemn voice said: "I admit that I am enormously fond of praise and admiration."

Not once as the day wore on did he conjure the least bit of humor out of any of the questions put to him. But it was as if, there being no humor, there were no Oscar Wilde, only a specter poised before the court, mouthing words that had lost all meaning.

In his final speech to the jury, Sir Edward Clarke stressed the disreputable character of many of the witnesses. "It is on the evidence of Parker and Wood that you are asked to, um, condemn Mr. Wilde. And Mr. Wilde knew nothing of the character of these men! They were, hem, introduced to him, and it was his — his love of admiration that caused him to be in their, uh, society. These men ought to be the accused, not, hem, the accusers . . ."

Sir Frank Lockwood, in his summary, once again alluded to the letter, which, Wilde felt, everyone in London must by this time know by heart. "It has been attempted to show that this was a prose poem, a sonnet, a 'lovely thing' which, I suppose, we are too low to appreciate." He looked about him with a sardonic grimace that did not sit at all well on his unhealthy white features. "Gentlemen, let us thank God, if it is so, that we do not appreciate things of this sort, save at their proper value — and that is somewhat lower than the beasts!"

Wilde was remembering times Lockwood and he had joked bawdily over dinner. Was this the same Lockwood? Was he the same Oscar Wilde?

"If that letter had been seen by any right-minded man, it would have been looked upon as evidence of guilty passion. And you, men of pride, reason, and honor, are asked to be put off with this story of the prose poem, of the sonnet, of 'the lovely thing' . . ."

Summing up for the jury, Mr. Justice Wills was gentle, firm, and compassionate. "I do not desire to comment more than I can help about Lord Alfred Douglas or the Marquess of Queensberry, but I must say that the whole of this lamentable inquiry has arisen through the defendant's association with Lord Alfred Douglas." One could easily believe, from the gentleness in his voice, that the sorrows of his calling must often reduce this man to tears. "It is true that Lord Alfred's family seem to be a house divided against itself. But even if there was nothing but hatred between father and son, what father would not try to save his own son from the associations suggested by the letter which you have seen from the prisoner to Lord Alfred Douglas?"

The foreman of the jury rose with a question. "Was a warrant ever issued for the apprehension of Lord Alfred Douglas? If we are to consider this letter as evidence of guilt, it applies as much to Lord Alfred Douglas as to the defendant."

"Quite so," said Judge Wills gently. "But we have the guilt of the man in the dock to deal with now."

It was three thirty in the afternoon when the jury retired to make their decision. When they filed back, they had a resigned, tired look.

"Gentlemen," the clerk of the arraigns asked them, "have you agreed upon your verdict?"

"We have," said the foreman of the jury.

"Do you find the prisoner at the bar guilty or not guilty of an act of gross indecency with Charles Parker at the Savoy Hotel?"

"Guilty."

"Do you find him guilty or not guilty of an act of gross indecency with Alfred Wood at Tite Street?"

"Guilty."

"Do you find him guilty or not guilty of an act of gross indecency with a male person unknown in room three sixty-two of the Savoy Hotel?"

"Guilty."

Now Taylor was summoned back to the dock so both the accused could be sentenced at the same time. Judge Wills stared down on them with a look of deep sorrow. ''Oscar Wilde and Alfred Taylor, the crime of which you have been convicted is so bad that one has to put stern restraint upon oneself from describing the sentiments which must rise to the breast of every man of honor who has heard the details of these two terrible trials.

''I shall, under the circumstances, be expected to pass the severest sentence that the law allows. In my judgment it is totally inadequate for such a case as this.'' He was silent for a moment, as if indulging in silent prayer. ''The sentence of the court is that each of you be imprisoned and kept to hard labor for two years.''

Cries of shock went up from the courtroom, muted by an overwhelming roar of approval.

Oscar Wilde teetered backwards, on the verge of collapse.

PART TEN

Out of the Depths

I n a room white as a laboratory, Wilde was told to remove his clothing. His hair was cut by a warder who made no effort to disguise his contempt. He was sent naked into another white room, where three more warders were waiting.

Steam was rising from a tub in the center of the floor. On the water's surface floated clusters of bubbling gray scum.

"This bath has been used!" Wilde protested, his voice hoarse.

"Dear, dear," one of the warders said. He made as if to hurl Wilde into the tub. Closing his eyes, Wilde eased himself into the water.

The uniform with its rough herringbone weave scraped upon his skin: the discomfort seemed more awful to ponder than whatever hard labor they might give him.

"Take a long last look, my beauty," said the warder, holding up a mirror. "There are precious few looking glasses in Her Majesty's prisons."

A bewildering spectacle confronted Wilde in the glass. He tried to look at himself with Bosie's eyes. Could his darling boy ever again accept this shattered relic?

Ecce homo, he thought. And steeled himself for the crucifixion yet to come.

) 2 (

He would never leave Pentonville Prison alive, Wilde felt sure. His cell was exactly the width of the plank bed across one end, and twice that in length. The ceiling was far, far above. In it was a meager window of many small panes, frosted over to keep out

any view of the sky. Even on tiptoe he could not reach up to touch
its bottom frame.

Two years without the sight of Bosie. Could he endure it?

Just as he assured himself that all would somehow be well, he
saw that the cell was shrinking. Trembling, he sank onto the hard
plank bed. Mad? Already? No — he was somehow going to survive, if only to present to Bosie all he had suffered — as a gift.
He was going to survive.

How long he sat, he could not tell. There was nothing to mark
time by, thus time ceased to exist. He ceased to exist. He paced a
bit, sat again. Paced. Sat. The cell grew smaller, the slab of window edged ever farther away.

Minutes: hours. Every trickle of time was equal in length, and
he felt receding in him the ability to conceive of the hours as having perimeters of any sort. His own thoughts had never interested
him, except as they amused or fascinated others. Now there were
to be no others.

And yet he was not alone. Our Lady of Tears had come gliding
into the soundless cell; he knew that she would always be close by.

At some point he lost consciousness — fainted, perhaps, or slept.

The door clanged open. A fat, slow-moving warder placed a cup
and bowl on the table.

"Good — evening," said Wilde. "It — it *is* evening?"

The warder left without even looking at him. The door banged
shut, the locks clicked into place.

The liquid was something like cocoa, something like coffee, with
spots of grease sparkling on the surface, and gave off a putrid
scent. The bread was black and hard: the morsel he chewed tasted
like chalk. He drank down the tepid cocoa, trying not to taste it,
not to gag. Hungry as he was, he could keep nothing down. Into
the battered chamber pot beneath the bed he vomited with a strangled cry.

Then he lay on the plank and prayed to be delivered — into
sleep if God was cruel, into death if he was kind.

Darkness came. The only illumination was the corridor gaslight,
seeping through the cell door's spyhole. Instead of the oblivion he
longed for, the darkness filled with phantoms.

His stomach began to rumble. The cocoa had made him ill. Again and again he had to use the pot beneath the bed. The airless cell reeked with a stench like death.

Prostrate he lay. He prayed for daylight. After layer upon layer of eternity, folding in upon itself, the cell began to fill with chill blue light — and he looked about and prayed that darkness might come soon again.

The door clicked open. " 'Ere, now," said the warder. Wilde stared up at him, feeling feverish. At the smell, the warder drew back. "Kuh-rist!" he cried, running out of the cell, slamming the door behind him. From the hall came the sound of his violent retching. "Oh, the dirty dog," he kept saying. "Oh, the dirty dog."

) 3 (

It began at six, what they called the day. He was given more of the foul liquid, and another crust of bread.

He was led out to a yard where, under a sulky mauve sky, the prisoners tramped a ragged circle. Shuffling and stamping they beat their sullen path, round and round as the sun stole over the bleak suburban hills. Voices kept sounding as Wilde paced, but when he stared into the hard closed faces, every lip would be sealed tight.

Back in his cell, a machine had been set up on the table, a thick column of metal with a projecting lever.

"I want to introduce you to the Crank, prisoner," the warder said. "You two will be excellent friends."

Wilde stared at the machine dully. "What is it?"

"You're to turn that lever all the way round," said the warder.

Wilde pulled it, and the lever made a rasping sound that set his teeth on edge. The figure in the column's small window changed from *1* to *2*.

"Again," said the warder. *3.* "Again." *4.* "You're to keep turning that lever for six hours. By then you should have reached number ten thousand, if you're quick."

Wilde's head began to ache. "What — what is the purpose of it?"

"You must reach number ten thousand. That is your day's work every day."

"But for what purpose?"

"To reach the number ten thousand. That is the purpose."

) 4 (

And then night again. Exhausted as he was, the release of sleep was not forthcoming. He was as one who has awoken to find himself buried alive, left to rot in a locked tomb. He lay awake, or half awake, through hours that were centuries.

Memory would not be silenced. He found himself back in the courtroom again, listening to the droning words of Justice Wills. ". . . the severest sentence that the law allows . . . totally inadequate for such a case as this . . ." As if he were dying, all his life swam steadily before his eyes. Every happy moment seemed to be only a Station of the Cross.

And what was Bosie doing now? Every glowing moment of their friendship came back; no detail was spared him: no strained note of Bosie's voice, no twitch or gesture of his nervous hands.

He paced in the darkness. He sat. He lay on the hard plank. He sat. He gasped the thin foul air hungrily, fearing he might suffocate. He recited the alphabet, determined to exercise his reason, afraid he might lose it forever.

And the night would limp into another endless day. And the day would sag into another endless night.

The week circled around Sunday, and the service in the chapel. Not, certainly, for the quality of the chaplain's dry sermon, which invariably centered on texts of recrimination and guilt, but because in chapel the prisoners were permitted to raise their voices in song. It was the only time of the week the silence might be broken.

He knew he must make no effort to count days. That would lure him into madness. How could the mind fathom the number of hours that made up two years, any more than the stars — when he had been able to look at stars — could, as they stretched forth towards infinity, be given any count?

At some moment, it was impossible afterward to remember precisely when, he began to realize it was all truly happening. He was indeed imprisoned, indeed sealed in this airless, lightless place.

Gradually he reduced all sense of meaning to the stark realities of his cell. The table. The pillow. The chair. Every bit of equipment permitted him must be kept exactly in its place : his cup, his metal plate, his comb, his threadbare towel.

Of the movement of the hours, only the slow shadow creeping across the lime-bleached walls gave any trace. He lived in an imagined monastery where time had no measure, where clocks and moments were feeble concepts as impossible to comprehend — or believe in — as the smiling face of God. He must turn the crank, live his life, day after meaningless day.

Almost crueler than his own despair was the sound of weeping at night from the children's cells in the next block. No child was ever seen : they were kept isolated from the other prisoners. But their sobs in the darkness broke one's heart.

One boy in particular, who sounded no more than seven or eight, wept all the night long. What might the child have done to be thrown into hell ? "Cyril," Wilde whispered, tossing on the plank. "Oh, Cyril, Cyril . . ."

And one thought kept hammering at him : *Where is Bosie now?*

The diarrhea stayed with him for many weeks. He became accustomed to the stench, to the tightness of the cell, to his own misery. He did not go mad.

) 5 (

The cell door swung open and a small white-haired man eased in. He seemed far smaller than in the pulpit. He was looking about him as if he had never seen anything like a cell before.

"Shall I stay, Your Reverence ?" asked the warder.

"That won't be necessary, White. You may leave us." It was a voice practiced in sounding kind. His plump pink face was meant for laughter; instead, he assumed a glowering, forbidding look, peering over his silver spectacles like a funereal Father Christmas.

"I am here to help you, prisoner," he said.

Wilde tried a smile. "I have been wishing we might talk. My name, as I suppose you know, is Oscar Wilde. And yours ?"

Wilde felt the coldness behind the smile as the man stared at him. "My name is Rector Hardwick." When Wilde extended a hand, he made no move to take it. "Prayer is the only thing that can console you in this place, prisoner. I trust you understand that. Prayer and a true spirit of repentance."

"Am I — to have books ?" said Wilde, staring down at his re-

jected hand. He had said no words for so long, it seemed strange
now to speak at all. The tongue, he realized with a tingle of fear,
could forget how language was formed.

Hardwick pursed his lips. "You will be given a Bible."

"I already know the Scriptures by heart. May I have nothing
besides?"

Hardwick looked for a moment as if he were going to sit on the
bed; then glancing down he seemed to find something menacing
about it. "I believe I can find you a copy of *The Pilgrim's Progress.*"

Wilde smiled. "Bunyan is so awfully — dry."

If he had produced his chamber pot for the chaplain to examine,
the man could not have looked more repulsed. "Dry, did you say?"

Perhaps he should fall on his knees; perhaps that was what
Hardwick required. "Can I not have something to lift the spirit
in these long, dreadful hours?" he said, his voice faltering. "Poetry? A bit of Shakespeare?"

Disdain showed through Hardwick's practiced look of compassion. "Only our Redeemer can lift your spirit, prisoner. *The Pilgrim's Progress* will enable you to make contact with Him."

Wilde pulled himself up tall. "Mr. Hardwick, any least sonnet
of Shakespeare's brings me closer to the Divinity than all the de-
votional literature of the world."

"Indeed," said the chaplain, and kicked at the door for the warder to let him out. "And see where it has got you."

) 6 (

He was permitted to receive only two letters a month. One must
be from Charles Humphreys, since only his solicitor might know
if there were any hope for an appeal to Her Majesty, or an early
release.

After much consideration, he decided that the other letter should
be from Robbie Ross. Robbie was in touch with Constance and
with all his friends; Robbie would take care of things for him.
Whereas Bosie —

He was still the only one Wilde truly longed to hear from. But
he was afraid of such a letter. Afraid the boy's selfishness would,
in this place, seem intolerable, afraid of the pompous absurdities

Bosie would write, and even more afraid of what he would not write, could never write.

And then Robbie's letter came, and in it he mentioned that Bosie was in Italy, had moved to a villa in Capri. As he read these lines an adder slid into Wilde's breast and began to feed upon his entrails.

At night his dreams, which had begun to neutralize, grew riotous with images of Bosie swimming in clear green water, Bosie in the grottoes of Tiberius frolicking with sunburnt youths. The cell walls turned colder, clammier. Each night in the garden of his soul Wilde sowed new thorns; each day he reaped them as his numb hand turned the crank.

His recollections of Bosie changed into a much-fingered rosary of betrayal. Obsessively he went over every moment they had ever spent together. The happy times began subtly to change character, to drain of color, as if the drabness of the cell were robbing them of hue.

He would try to push them away, those siren memories, especially the most terrible ones: memories of the rare times when Bosie had pretended to be kind and loving, had proffered him a taste of poisoned joy.

And so the past began to change. Little by little he found himself forgetting the essential things. Often he could not remember what Constance looked like, or the children. Or, if he was able to conjure up the boys' faces, he would be uncertain which was Cyril's, which Vyvyan's.

Then he began to fear that he had not, after all, been removed from home and all things dear and comforting, but that in fact this *was* home, and had somehow always been, and home was the vilest of places that God — who was, it turned out, only Satan in an elaborate mask — had created for the torment of his baffled worshipers. This was home, and the lilac-tinted past had been only a spiteful dream vouchsafed him in order to make the torments to come, by contrast, all the more unbearable.

Every three months he would be notified of the letters that had arrived for him — letters far beyond his ration, letters he was not permitted to read. They would be kept for him until his dismissal. There were letters from old friends and new ones, from enemies, from strangers. But never once did a letter come from Bosie.

One night as he lay sleepless on the plank something slipped rustling into the blackness, something that was itself black. Some-one was with him in the cell. Black dress. Black bonnet. Face white and swollen, weeping.

"Mother! You, here?"

But when he reached out towards her, she was gone.

) 7 (

"You're to follow me," said the warder.

Wilde, terrified, murmured: "What — what have I done?"

He followed through long cold corridors, up a winding damp stairwell, down to a long series of doors. Each opened to a wire-enclosed, cagelike cell. The warder stopped at one of these and motioned him to enter.

Wilde stepped back, trembling. What were they going to do to him, and why? The cage looked out onto a narrow corridor, where two warders were standing at attention, facing each other. An-other cage was directly opposite, with someone barely visible in-side.

"Oscar? Is it — is it you?"

"Constance?"

Was it she — or some trick they had devised to torment him with?

"I can hardly see you, Oscar." Yes, it was Constance's voice. "You seem so — so thin," she said.

"I must have lost thirty pounds." He still thought this might be another dream. "And my little darlings? How are — how are —?"

"The boys are well. In good health. I have put them in school in Switzerland, Oscar. They miss you. Dreadfully."

"Constance, you must tell me the truth. Do I seem myself? I am constantly afraid that I am on the verge of — going mad. Or that I have already gone mad."

"You are — unchanged." She was having difficulty controlling herself. In an unnaturally even voice she went on: "I live in Swit-zerland now myself. Such a — lovely country."

His head was swimming; he held on tight to the bars.

"Oscar — I come with terrible news. Your mother —"

"My mother is dead."

"You — know?"

"I know."

"Without pain. She died in her sleep. But how did you —?"

"Don't you realize? I killed her, Connie."

She began to sob. "Don't say that! She was so — I had to come. I couldn't bear for you to hear it from anyone else, my poor darling. I couldn't let them just — but I can't even see you! Oscar, why is God allowing all this to happen to us?"

Had there been a way for them to touch each other at that moment, all might somehow be saved. But there was no way. "Constance, you must be terribly, terribly careful with the boys," he said. His voice sounded reasonable to him, almost absurdly so — but might that not be a sign of madness in itself? "Cyril, especially. Cyril is so sensitive. You must not spoil them. The way Lady Queensberry spoiled —"

She was drying her eyes. "It is that — *monster* who brought this all about. He did it all. And he goes scot-free." Her hands were pressing against the sides of her cage, as if to keep them from closing in on her. "Are you — are you still in contact with him?"

"Time!" shouted one of the warders standing at attention.

"If Bosie Douglas were here right now," said Wilde, as the door behind him rattled open, "I believe I would — kill him." He stared at the shadowy figure in the facing cell for one last moment, trying to see in her Constance, the Constance of the dead past.

"Oscar — be well."

"Good-bye, my darling," he said, following the warder out into the corridor. "Pray for me. Pray for us all . . ."

) 8 (

Slouching back towards his cell, he felt himself being drawn down into the cold void of horror that all these past months he had been refusing to acknowledge. He felt dizzy, nauseated. The shock of seeing Constance — of having her see him, here — was more than he could bear. Just before they reached the cell block, his legs gave way on the staircase. Down and down he tumbled, striking his head again and again on the metal steps. . . .

Long nails had been driven into his ears, and were slowly rusting there. He opened his eyes. He was in a hard bed under a sheet of coarse, unbleached muslin. The smell of disinfectant made his nostrils quiver. His head was throbbing with a steady, shrieking pain.

"Doctor, what has happened to my ear?" he said to the man in white staring down on him.

"Nothing to worry about."

"I have never . . . in my life . . . felt such pain."

"It is nothing, prisoner. In two days you should be recovered completely. You are to be transferred to Reading, I understand."

"Reading Gaol?" Thank God, Wilde said to himself : change of any kind must be an improvement. "Is Reading — a more lenient place?"

The doctor grinned. "It is considered somewhat stricter."

) 9 (

He sat on the train in his prison uniform, hands cuffed behind his back. A warder sat squeezed in next to him, another on the seat facing. Everyone in the car craned for a look. He heard them whispering. They had no idea who he was, thank God. He was only an object of curiosity to them, not a human being like themselves. The pain in his ear had not lessened; at least it made him forget all else.

As the train drew into Clapham Junction the warder beside him gave Wilde a nudge. "Up."

"But this isn't Reading," Wilde said.

"We change here. We have a half-hour wait." They led him out onto the platform. "Stand straight, prisoner."

The warders took a few steps back, as if they had nothing to do with him. "Here?" Wilde said, looking about frantically, afraid they would leave him there. "Am I to stand in the midst of this crowd? For half an hour?"

"Forty minutes, to be exact," said one of the warders, winking at his colleague. "You should be glad of a little company."

On the windswept platform Wilde stood at attention, all feeling gone from the hands cuffed tight behind his back, as he stared straight ahead, trying not to see. The travelers swarming past would glance at him, recoil slightly, continue walking. Then they would stop, pretending to be studying a book or newspaper as they stole covert glances at him. Some made no effort to conceal their whispers and laughter.

More and more people milled onto the platform. A group of restless children arrived, with their teacher, and pointed at him, openly enthralled. The teacher shushed their questions, but he himself was obviously amused.

A small, fox-faced man stopped in front of him — an older person, rather feminine in appearance, and narrowed his small sharp eyes. "I say," he cried aloud. "Look, everyone. It's the great Oscar Wilde!"

Gasps of excitement undulated through the crowd. "Oscar Wilde!" The name pulsated down to the end of the platform and back. The crowd huddled closer. Wilde's handcuffed wrists jerked involuntarily behind his back. "Oscar Wilde. That man is Oscar Wilde!" His name on their lips was shameful to him, vile, loathsome.

The fox-faced man moved in closer and, clearing his throat elaborately, spat in Wilde's face.

The platform went absolutely silent. Everyone pretended to be gazing in a different direction, but they were all looking at Wilde. The spittle ran slowly down his cheek. Suddenly, someone in the rear began to laugh. One voice after another hesitatingly joined in, and then they were all laughing, the children loudest of all. The two warders made halfhearted attempts to quiet the pandemonium, but bit by bit they gave in, and soon they themselves were as convulsed with laughter as any of the others.

The hands of the great clock in the center of the station reached half-past two. Wilde stared unmoving at those hands until they climbed to two forty-five, and he was led into the Reading train.

) 10 (

The new cell was narrower than the old one; otherwise it was nearly identical. But he was given a new job. Each morning he was marched to a great shed and placed in one of a series of stalls, where he was handed lengths of tarred rope to unravel — rope that had been worn out on Her Majesty's sailing vessels, and could now be torn into oakum.

His fingers by the end of the day would be cut and bleeding, with no ghost of feeling in them. All sensation was leaving his body as all aspiration had left his soul. The terrible thing about prison, he saw, was not that it broke the heart, but that it turned it to stone. Only one thing had the power to move him. Every day at half-past two he would remember Clapham Junction, and he would weep. Those tears were the only sweet thing about his life.

He was able to care about very little. Even his hatred for Bosie, which had become as all-absorbing as his former adoration — indeed, he had come to see that hatred *was* a kind of adoration — had slowly dwindled into apathy. He knew he would never care for anyone, or anything, again.

) 11 (

But then, as he circled the yard each morning, the blurred faces of the other prisoners began to take on features. Some were full of character, even a kind of nobility — so much more so than the noble faces he had bowed to so readily in the past.

He learned to speak as the other prisoners spoke, without moving the lips, so their conversations could not be detected. He learned their names, and began to ask about the lives they had led, what cruel pass had brought them to Reading Gaol.

"It's hard for us," one whispered to him. "But harder for a bloke like you."

"You know me?"

"We know you, Mr. Wilde."

One of the figures marching in the circle every morning seemed particularly interesting, a harshly handsome young man who, the others told Wilde, was soon to be hanged. He was a guardsman — or had been. He had murdered his sweetheart, one man said. No, corrected another, it was his wife. But no one knew how, and no one knew why.

The guardsman, haughty and tall, remained as isolated from the rest as all these months Wilde himself had been. Yet he kept about himself a cool pride and self-collectedness in the face of his destiny that fascinated the others, Wilde most of all.

In the long hours tearing at the shreds of oakum, he found himself brooding upon this guardsman, creating around him a legend. For Wilde this unknown colleague in misery became a kind of alter ego, a dark and tragic saint. At times, in fact, the figure of

Jesus of Nazareth took on, in Wilde's imagination, some of the young soldier's physical characteristics: his detached, faraway look, his military bearing. Memories of the New Testament began to throb with fresh life, especially when he found a copy in Greek in the small prison library he was now allowed to use, and was able to read the overfamiliar passages in their pure, original state. Jesus and the guardsman blurred in Wilde's mind; often when he prayed to the one, his mind's eye would form the handsome visage of the other.

When the morning for the hanging came, Wilde read the accounts of the Passion in the four Gospels. A gun went off. Finished. The man was dead. Tears came, from deeper within him than any he had ever shed for himself. With them came peace.

) 12 (

After that, things seemed to change. A new governor was appointed to the prison, a kind man who eased many of the constraints on the prisoners. Wilde was relieved of his dreary hours making oakum and put to work gardening instead. It was like rising from the grave and being admitted into Paradise. He was allowed to converse again, and he found his voice had become deep and harsh from the months of silence — but that he still had the ability to laugh.

He no longer resented his prison life, but began to accept it as a terrible but rich experience. Even the bitterest of his sufferings — the loss of Cyril and Vyvyan — seemed a necessary lesson: that he could own nothing and no one, that nothing in life could be possessed. Riches and pleasure began to seem to him, indeed, a deeper source of tragedy than poverty and sorrow.

In view of his having been a man of literature, he was given a sheet of foolscap each day on which he was permitted to write for an hour. This sublime consideration he used to pen an examination of conscience, in the form of a letter to Lord Alfred Douglas. Day by day he would spew out the bitterness and sickness that had been festering in him all these bitter months, and many of the months before that. At the end of the day he had to surrender the page to a warder, to be put aside until the day of his release. He was not permitted to correct or revise the pages. It didn't matter. It was not a work of art he was writing, but an act of contrition.

And instead of bemoaning Bosie's inability to care for him, he became grateful for any flicker of love he had ever known, from whatever source.

Any least kindness given one by life was direct evidence of God's grace, he now knew. As he knew that nobody — himself least of all — could claim to be worthy of being loved.

) 13 (

The day of his release approached. He anticipated it calmly, almost reluctantly. With fear he contemplated the life that would be waiting for him. He knew he would be leaving Reading Gaol only to enter another prison. A prison almost certain to be far, far worse.

PART ELEVEN

Each Man Kills
the Thing He Loves

O N the black night waters the boat appeared, a single star in a storm-tossed sky.

"The ferry, Reggie. Wake up!"

The café was on the second floor of the customs shed, and their window commanded a view of the ferry-station bridge and the full sweep of the Channel. Reggie's sleepy, sand-caked eyes made him homelier than ever. Trying to wake himself, he nearly slipped off the chair.

"Please, Reggie!" Robbie grasped his arm. "We must look cheerful and wide-awake and full of high spirits."

Earlier it had seemed a great lark, staying up to greet the Portsmouth night boat, despite Wilde's insisting that they not dare think of doing so. After midnight, though, the world from the windows of the smoke-filled café had taken on a hostile, ghoulish look.

Reggie yawned. "What sad spectacle shall we confront on the gangplank!"

"He will be amusing. Brilliant. Wonderful," Robbie replied, his own doubt all too evident. "As always."

A powerful young longshoreman lumbered past, with a cigarette hanging from his lips. "Why are Frenchmen's bodies so different from ours?" said Reggie admiringly.

Robbie frowned at him.

"Oh, come now, Robbie, there's little enough to look at in this dreary neck of the woods."

The boat's lights shimmered long and golden in the water as it drew closer to the shore. Robbie rubbed his napkin over the windowpanes.

"Less sensitive men than Oscar have been *destroyed* by hard labor," Reggie said. "And by less than two years of it. I am terrified of what we shall see."

"He will be the same. We must believe so. He needs us to believe so."

"Do you know the terrible thing, Robbie? The terrible, shameful thing is — I am afraid someone will see me in his company."

Robbie touched his hand reassuringly. "Whatever happens, we will be patient and loving," he said, collecting their coats. "We will put a delightful face upon it."

They watched through the window as, sounding a long, groaning whistle, the ferry pulled in. The sleepy-eyed, grumpy crowds disembarked, shambling down the gangplank with their valises, parcels, cardboard boxes tied with rope.

"There!" cried Reggie. "Just coming over the bridge."

"That's not Oscar."

"It's him."

Wilde appeared to be lecturing a small group of laughing people, standing taller than any of them. He looked slender and strong. The gauntness made his features bolder, manlier than Robbie had ever seen them, and he had the healthy high coloring of a young athlete. He wore his high bowler hat at a rakish tilt and maneuvered the stairs with grace, helping a woman with her bags.

"But he seems — twenty years younger!" cried Robbie, and went running down the rickety stairs of the café and through the crowds.

" 'Ere, watch what you're about," an elderly man shouted after them. "*Putains anglais,*" snapped a porter.

Robbie stopped, openmouthed, gasping for breath. "Oscar! But how *wonderful* you look!"

"Robbie — my dear, dear boy." For a moment it seemed he was having trouble keeping control of his emotions — but no; he laughed as effusively and airily as ever. "You came to meet me! And dear, dear Reggie. I long to kiss the two of you — only they would surely send me back to Reading Gaol, and you with me!"

Robbie stared at him, tears rising, and impulsively kissed him on the cheek. Wilde laughed, moved. "You darlings — you can't have *got* up at such an hour, you must have *sat* up!"

They passed through customs with surprising speed, and Robbie

noted how few possessions Wilde was carrying in his battered suitcase. Heading for the coach station, they locked arms. "You look
younger than when we first met!" Robbie said in a low, seductive
voice.

"I *am* younger. Nothing is better for the complexion than a
shattering emotional experience." About the past two years, he
told them, he had no regrets, for they had melted his heart. "I am
a new man, a different man. And I am going to write very differently from now on."

"And how was London, Oscar?" said Reggie, feeling a bit like
an intruder.

"Changed. All its gold seems to have turned to lead. Or perhaps
it is simply that I — see differently."

Robbie produced a bottle of champagne that was meant to be
drunk in the hotel. They swigged it down in the coach. "But I
must tell you about my trip from Reading to London," Wilde said,
giggling, as they moved through the dark streets of Dieppe, "accompanied, naturally, by two of Her Majesty's warders. I was
longing for a peep at the *Daily Chronicle*. The only *truly* dreadful
thing about being 'away' is that one is not allowed to read newspapers. 'Let me read the *Chronicle* in the train,' I begged my cap-
tors. 'Absolutely not!' they said, in stern, official tones, 'for the
rules forbid it.' I asked, then, if the rules forbade one to read the
paper upside down. To this they could find no reference in their
book of statutes, so permission was granted. And I must tell you,
darlings, I never enjoyed anything so much! Henceforth I shall
read *all* newspapers upside down. Books as well."

At the decaying old marvel of a hotel, Wilde signed the name
Sebastian Melmoth in the ledger.

"Sebastian what?" said Reggie.

The name was inspired, Wilde explained, by his maternal grandfather's novel, *Melmoth the Wanderer*. And for one who had suffered quite a few of fortune's slings and arrows, Sebastian seemed
rather appropriate. But it would be best if they, too, took pseud-
onyms. Reginald Turner seemed a good name for Robbie. And for
Reggie, how about Robert Ross? Or did the names sound too
studied?

He went on babbling nonsense, exactly like his old self — or
rather, Robbie decided, like someone doing a superb imitation of

his old self, of the consummate Oscar Wilde. He was trying to turn it all into a fairy tale, trying to convert Reading Gaol's gates into portcullises, its turrets into minarets, trying to imagine that the two of them were paladins come to welcome Richard the Lion-Hearted back from captivity. Yes, he was acting, and considering that his personality had always been, by and large, a kind of act, he was in fact giving a performance of a performance, and something of a tour de force! But what, Robbie wondered, must be going on backstage?

"You seem so much — calmer, Oscar," Robbie said, smiling as they sat for a moment in the hotel's darkened salon.

"I have been reborn, Robbie. I feel no bitterness whatsoever. And certainly no shame. Why should I? I have learned gratitude, a new and hard-earned lesson. The only thing I regret is having lived a life unworthy of an artist. And *that* sin I shall soon rectify!"

Will you, dear friend, Robbie wondered to himself. *Can you?*

) 2 (

Reggie had to leave the following evening, but Robbie stayed on for several days. He and Wilde took a trip to the small resort town of Berneval-sur-Mer, which Wilde found enchanting.

"This is where I am going to stay, Robbie! But why don't you stay, too?"

Robbie wanted to stay with him forever, he told Wilde — and in a way it was the truth. It had become quite obvious these past days that Wilde would have liked nothing better than to begin their old romance again. Their love was going into a new phase, he insisted: not so much an Indian summer as an Indian winter.

But though Wilde was the one person in the world Robbie truly loved, and though he was sure that love would never alter, Robbie rebuffed the idea. Wilde had always been a demanding companion; now there was something about his need for unending amusement, continual displays of affection, that seemed voracious, alarming. In the past, being with him had been a strain, but a delicious one. Now, in the midst of all the verbal pyrotechnics, there was an undertow of something new, something frightening, that threatened to drag down Wilde himself and everyone around him.

Robbie was not sorry when the time came for him to return to London.

On his last evening at the Hôtel de la Plage, Wilde invited him to have champagne at the bar overlooking the beach, so that they might watch one last sunset together. He was full of tales about his life in prison, telling them with a feverish excitement that was new to him.

"You're sure you want to stay on here, Oscar — all by yourself?"

"I was given every opportunity, over the past two years, to learn what a delightful companion I am, Robbie! I quite like my own company now. And Berneval is heavenly! Inexpensive. Quiet. Idyllic." Indeed, the beach spread out before them, with its lingering couples under parasols of yellow or Chinese red, might have been painted by Turner or Claude Lorrain. "It is the perfect place to write, Robbie! I shall do fine work here."

Robbie was not convinced.

"Of course, Robbie, two might live in Berneval as cheaply as one . . ."

"I must go upstairs and pack."

"I have not finished telling you about my career as prison gardener!" Wilde said, and started in again about Reading Gaol. Just then the hotel owner's handsome adolescent son ran out with a telegram. Reading it, Wilde went rigid.

"What is it, Oscar?"

Wilde crushed the telegram into a ball. "It is nothing," he said, and resumed his story: "By the time I had to leave, of course, the governor and his wife were so used to seeing me amongst the peony beds, they took it for granted I was the gardener! They begged me to stay on, but of course —"

"You look ill, Oscar. Tell me what that telegram was."

"Bosie is in Paris." He threw the crumpled message to the floor. "He proclaims his undying love, in phrases of purest tinsel."

"Are you — going to see him?"

"Are you mad? Of course I'm not going to see him."

The sun had set, and everyone had left the beach but one small boy, who was pressing the finishing touches into an enormous castle of sand. Robbie got up to go to his room. Inside the café, he paused at the stairway steps and turned for a last sentimental glimpse of the darkening seascape.

Wilde had lit the candle in the frosted glass cup, and in its glow he was pressing the wrinkled telegram flat upon the table, reading its message with anxious, greedy eyes.

) 3 (

For weeks after Robbie left, Wilde was never without companionship. Charles Conder and Ernest Dowson came over from England, as did Will Rothenstein. The actor Lugné-Poe stopped by to discuss the production of *Salomé* he had staged in Paris, and then André Gide arrived. They were all solemn and respectful, like visitors to a ruin.

He welcomed their company. Yet he found himself counting the minutes till their visits would end. When they were gone, he ached to have them back again.

There were letters from Bosie in almost every post. They were warm, effusive, filled with hints of a still smoldering passion. Wilde studied them carefully, unable to react. To think of Bosie seemed to paralyze all feeling in him.

He wrote to Constance in Switzerland, begging her to let him come and visit. He must see the boys. He must see her. Surely they might find a way to start life afresh.

He left the letter at the post office and wandered to the beach café. Sipping a white wine, he watched the dusk draw all the color out of the sea, leaving only a mournful gray darkening at the horizon, bordered by a pulsing line of silver.

) 4 (

Her tea was cold, but she sipped at it anyway, staring out at the neat cobbled streets and, far off, clean gray mountains rising over more mountains. She realized how much she hated it all.

She read the letter again. For all its raw, desperate emotion, she was moved even more by the emotion he had not dared to express. Little as she was able to understand him, that was something she had always understood: his great clumsy store of affection for her and for his sons.

She understood because there was an equal depth of feeling in her — feeling she had always had to curb. One of them must be sensible!

But how tired she was of living a sane, sensible life — especially in this sane, sensible country. She thought of MacGregor, so many years ago. ''It is simple enough, Mrs. Wilde. If you want to love your husband — love him.''

She had determined not to reply to the letter for a day or two, when the emotions it aroused would have settled. Now she tore a sheet of paper from the desk drawer and quickly, nervously began to write:

> My darling,
> Come to Switzerland. At once. The boys miss you so. I miss you even more. I have been cruel, my darling, bad as all the others — worse. I will make it up to you — my poor, dear, impossible, wonderful Oscar. Come — come quickly.

She wanted to rush out to the post office and get it off at once. But she must think about it. Waiting for the water to boil on the small coal stove, she studied the letter over, trying to imagine how he would react.

It was a mistake to say she would make it up to him. If he had indeed changed his ways, he needed to be fortified in his endeavor, and one way to guarantee that was to keep him ever mindful of the depths to which he had allowed himself to fall. She must not for a moment let him think she was blithely accepting it all, lest he be tempted to take it all lightly himself, and fall again. She began a new letter.

> Darling Oscar,
> Come to Switzerland. At once.

But wait. He needed to prove that his intentions were serious. Not so much to her, but to himself. He needed time on his own, free to make decisions, so he could see he had the strength to make the right ones. So he might know he had truly changed his ways.

> Darling Oscar,

she began again. But did that not seem a bit gushy, a bit overblown? Oscar needed to feel he must become worthy of her affection — not, God knew, for her sake, but for his own. She took another sheet of paper from the drawer and wrote:

> Dear Oscar.

) 5 (

When the letter arrived from Switzerland he could hardly open it, he was so fearful and excited. And then he read her cool, prudent words — and threw the page aside.

A letter from Bosie had come, too, full of extravagant pleas of affection. It contained a poem.

> *I bent my eyes upon the summer land,*
> *And all the painted fields were ripe for me,*
> *And every flower nodded to my hand;*
> *But sorrow came and led me back to thee.*
>
> *O Love! O Sorrow! O desired Despair!*
> *I turned my feet towards the boundless sea,*
> *Into the dark I go and heed not where,*
> *So that I come again at last to thee.*

Wilde read it and again read it, wishing he had the courage to toss the frail page to the wind, let it be blown away into the sea. He felt an old conflict, the poet in him cringing at the banality and meretriciousness of Bosie's gift, with all its tired meadows and flowers and fields.

If only Bosie were a great poet, or even a good one. If one's life must be destroyed by somebody, why could he not at least be extraordinary! He ordered a Pernod, despite the early hour. There was no way to get through the day without some drop of solace.

And indeed, how solacing it proved! Once again, life seemed tolerable; indeed, in a bruised way, almost beautiful. He glanced over Constance's letter, smirked bitterly, then called for paper and began to pen a letter to Bosie, exulting over his poem.

From that day on, his replies to the boy — cautious up till then — grew warmer. There was even talk of their meeting again.

But Wilde was afraid. Not only for his own immediate emotional safety. The more practical danger was that any meeting between them might be heard of abroad. The stipend that came regularly from Constance — his only means of support — would be cut off instantly if it became known that he was seeing Bosie.

Worse still, perhaps, was a new threat from Queensberry. The madman insisted that if his son took up with Wilde again, he would rush to France and blow out their brains, Bosie's and Wilde's both.

To behold again that twisted ape face would make him, for once and for all, go mad.

No, he could not stray from Berneval just yet. But he could not bear to stay here, either. The place was only endurable with friends to spirit the hours away. The long dull conversations he held with shopkeepers, barmen, hotel clerks did nothing to dim his loneliness.

He tried to work. He wanted to write a poem about his life in prison, a poem that would at once accuse society and absolve it. It would be about the tragic guardsman who had so moved him in those last months at Reading. It might be a kind of ballad — he was thinking of entitling it *The Ballad of Reading Gaol.* He was able to draft out a stanza or two.

Still, he knew the poem lacked something essential. He was writing from the mind, whereas true poetry could only come from a full heart. Never but when he was brimming over with emotion had he been able to create any work of art.

Would he ever brim over again?

The letters from Switzerland continued to be preachy and cold. Now that he had discharged society's brutal debt, Constance seemed to have decided that it was her turn to punish him. He was going to have to "prove" himself to her. But to be forgiven after one has earned forgiveness — what good is that? How unimaginative she was, measuring out her love when the only thing that could save him now was lavishness of affection, something irrational, something beyond ordinary selfish human love.

The town filled with tourists, and more would soon be coming. Dieppe was even worse. The streets were raucous with cries of hard laughter, with smells of roasting meat, with music from dance halls. The crowds were enjoying their holidays, their liberty. They filled the bars and restaurants, determined to amuse themselves.

Day after day he sat in the crowded beach café, staring out at the writhings of the sea. He had known more peace in Reading Gaol.

And then the tourists were leaving. Boats in the harbor tooted farewell, en route for England. He was alone again.

The morning glass of Pernod became two, sometimes three. They lost their power to enchant the overbright hours. Bit by bit he sank once again into a venomous gloom. Black day followed black day, as if he were reliving his first months in prison, only more horribly, somehow, in this haven of shore and sparkling sea.

He could not get his poem, the ballad of his broken heart, to work. The world was waiting to see if he could still write at all. A masterpiece would restore him in the public's eye. All his future depended on it.

But the very importance of the poem made it impossible to write.

The desire to see Bosie Douglas battened, spread, became overwhelming. It was all he thought of. Why, he wondered, has destruction such a boundless fascination? Why, when we sense our doom impending, do we so yearn to run and meet it?

) 6 (

As the train chugged slowly into the quay at Rouen, sending clouds of steam billowing into the station's glass-topped sheds, Wilde caught sight of the lean figure hovering in the striped shadows along the platform.

His heart sank. Could this be *his* Bosie, this gangling youth with the crabbed, narrow face, squinting at the train windows?

He got out near the station clock, and pretended to be searching through the crowds.

"Oscar — over here."

"Dear boy!" he said mechanically. In his straw hat and rumpled striped blazer, Bosie might be coming from a dull morning at the racetrack. All the poetry in him seemed to have vanished. "How — wonderful to see you, my boy." Was there something accusing, sardonic in his voice? He hoped not — yet he could hardly act as if nothing had happened since their last encounter!

Like strangers they inquired after each other's health, discussed the weather, complained about the French. It was several minutes before Wilde began to see in the young man's taut, sunburnt face the Bosie that all these months he had brooded over so obsessively. They started off on foot towards the heart of town, and discovered they were no longer adjusted to each other's pace.

"Now that I have — lured you here," Bosie said gravely, "I wish almost that I had not."

Wilde eyed him coldly. "Am I such a disappointment?"

"You are — more wonderful than ever," Bosie said, furtively touching his arm, then drawing away. "But seeing you again, I suddenly understand — all I have done. The sorrow I have caused is —'' He was unable to finish.

They were passing through the narrow, curving streets of the town's old quarter, with their sagging beamed medieval houses. ''I believe,'' Wilde said without emotion, ''that these are the very streets Emma Bovary rushed down, hurtling in a closed carriage to her doom.''

''Was she not hurtling to her joy?'' said Bosie.

''And over there, in the square,'' Wilde went on, a trace of hostility warming his voice. ''That is where Joan of Arc was burned at the stake, is it not?''

But Bosie was lost in his own thoughts. ''My soul is full of — mean gardens,'' he said.

''I beg your pardon?''

Bosie stammered that it was a line he was trying to work into a poem.

''A poem,'' said Wilde. Yes, Bosie would have to be seeing something ''poetical'' about all this. He should be angry; instead, he was almost moved. They stopped at a café with waitresses in peasant costume and chairs and tables made of tree limbs, and selected a place outside, screened by linden trees from the blazing sun.

''Have I ever told you of my boyhood, Oscar?''

''Many times.'' Wilde asked for cognac, but when the waitress suggested a fine local Calvados instead, he nodded.

''I was always wicked!'' Bosie went on, frowning. ''I had to be, don't you see? Because I was really such a — such a *good* boy. And if I didn't fight back —''

Wilde nodded. ''With a father like yours . . .''

''My mother damaged me most! It was her kindness that — but as God is my witness, I never wanted to hurt *you*, Oscar.'' Sunlight flickering through the leaves danced over his face, and his eyes were paler, bluer, brighter than in the past. *While you remain young and fresh,* Wilde was remembering, *I grow more and more unsightly, absorbing the ugliness of those sins that leave you more beautiful than before.* ''From the very first, you were like a — god to me, Oscar. That was what was so wonderful. And so terrible. I was totally eclipsed! I could have been — extinguished.''

Touched, Wilde did not dare look at him. The first apple-flavored sip of Calvados filled him with a yearning to be in some quiet country place of apple trees — just the two of them. He must dismiss such thoughts. He must not succumb. "Do I seem as strange to you, Bosie, as you to me?"

Bosie's face darkened. "I thought seeing you would wipe away the memory of these months. It only makes it — more awful."

Wilde closed his eyes. "Not for me." It was as if a great chunk of ice lodged in his heart were melting, and must discharge itself in tears. The brandy's glow both numbed and heightened his senses — or was it merely the aftereffect of the morning's Pernods? "I missed you, Bosie. I am only beginning to realize — how much."

Bosie, looking as vulnerable as when they had first met, smiled up at him miserably. "Don't they say lightning never strikes in the same place twice?" He downed his brandy in a gulp. "They lie, Oscar — they lie." He looked away, his face flushed. "It is only with the greatest effort that I can keep from — throwing myself upon you."

Wilde was blushing, too. "Effort, Bosie, is the enemy of art."

As they rose to leave, Wilde stopped to pat down a recalcitrant lock of Bosie's hair, lightened from many months' exposure to the Mediterranean sun — months, Wilde reminded himself, when he had seen no sun at all. For some perverse reason, this made the boy all the more valuable, all the more beautiful.

They were out in the streets again, and as they turned in and out of squares and time-blackened alleys and sudden patches of greenery and over a bridge with tugboats steaming along the river far below, their hands would furtively brush against each other, their eyes would meet and they would turn away . . . and then they were in a room of the Hôtel de la Poste with the sun seeping in through curtains of thick yellow lace and the memories of all the terrible months seemed only to deepen the pleasures of their lovemaking, only to make the ecstasy sharper and more intense.

) 7 (

The next day Wilde hurried from Berneval-sur-Mer to Dieppe, hoping there would be something for him in the telegraph office. He found what he was praying for. Bosie's telegram said that Rouen, without him, was unendurable.

Hard as his own solitude was to bear, Wilde told himself, the thought of Bosie being lonely was worse. At the Café Suisse, he called for writing paper and a Pernod. Before writing, he stared out a long while at the sea.

> My own Darling Boy,
>   I got your telegram half an hour ago, and just send you a line to say that I feel that my only hope of again doing beautiful work in art is being with you. It was not so in old days, but now it is different. You recreate in me that energy and sense of joyous power on which art depends. I feel that it is only with you that I can do anything at all. Do remake my ruined life for me, and then our friendship and love will have a different meaning to the world . . .

They spoke by telephone and decided that, in spite of everything, they must live together. It was the only hope of happiness for either of them. They would go to the south of Italy — to Naples. Golden days in that sun-blessed city, they assured each other, would heal any wounds still festering in their love-sickened souls.

Their families would be unforgiving. Their friends would disapprove. The English public would be scandalized. What of it? Things no longer had to make sense. The blood was racing through their bodies to a quickened beat. The poetry was rising: what else mattered?

) 8 (

At the first sight of Posilippo, Wilde lost his heart. The golden city, at last!

Bosie found an empty villa overlooking the bay — the very place, they were assured, where Venus first had risen from the foam. The great black pyramid of Vesuvius brooded over the waters, and from its crater a cloud shaped like a question mark melted into the azure sky.

"But are you certain we will be able to pay for it, Bosie?"

"My mother has promised to pay, dearest. Will you ever stop worrying!"

The villa was small and inelegant, and would require refurbishing. But the hills around were dotted with myrtle and pomegranate trees crowded, they promised each other, with full-throated nightingales. And though the place seemed rather quiet as they stared out over the hilltops, they were sure the white feet of the

Muses brushed the dew from the anemones in the morning, and at evening Apollo came to sing to the shepherds in the vale.

To write in, Wilde appropriated one of the large bare rooms; it looked out on a ruined garden. Bosie planned to work in a smaller room with the same view, but in fact, each of them spent more time in the other's writing room than in his own, chatting and gossiping, doing anything to keep from getting down to work.

As the day waned they would sit together on the veranda, sipping tea or chilled Lacrima Christi, and watch the sun over the bay turn to burning copper. "It is like a third-rate picture by Turner, with all his flaws exaggerated," Wilde said. "I love it all the same." Then the sun would sink into Vesuvius, a peaceful ruin at the moment, though always promising to erupt. Without that one romantic threat, Wilde felt, the place might be too intolerably serene.

The *Ballad* began to take shape. Whenever he finished a stanza, Wilde would rush to Bosie's room to read it. A favorable reaction could fill the rest of the day with song; a hostile one tarnished it irreparably. Then there would be nothing to do but console himself with the Pernod he kept hidden in a clothing hamper.

After the first weeks, their life together fell into a placid routine. They read more and more, spoke to each other less and less. Wilde never knew what day it was except when he glanced at a calendar to date a letter: they seemed, indeed, to be living outside time. Neither had ever known such calm before; it was as if both had spent their lives running from anything resembling tranquillity.

Naples, less than an hour away, was a place they swore they must avoid but that grew increasingly attractive. They had determined to save money by eating most of their meals in the villa; but after a series of quiet dinners, with nothing very much to say to each other, they began going out to the city's expensive restaurants, where they might listen to guitars and violins, or to stout, handsome tenors warbling about "Bella Napoli."

Naples, indeed, was like stepping into an opera with all the cast singing out simultaneously, at the top of their lungs. Perhaps inspired by the profligacy of blossoms coloring the surrounding hills, the Neapolitans seemed to think of *themselves* as flowers, and paraded about their city sporting bright-hued costumes set off by gaudy ribbons and scarves. Wilde complained about the tawdriness of the place, yet they began to spend most of their time there — and not just for the food.

It seemed that the exquisite bronzes of Greek and Roman athletes in the museum crept out at nightfall to go lounging about the downtown streets, smoking narrow black cigars and staring one down with black, mocking eyes.

"Naples is a Paradise," Wilde said, smiling at a particularly delightful specimen. "A Paradise teeming with devils."

He had hoped that he would be leading a different kind of life, but now he recognized that there was no changing one's ways: one was doomed to wander round and round the deepening circles of one's personality.

Bosie was finding even Naples too subdued. He made excursions to Capri, claiming that the food there was more interesting. Wilde was never invited to join him on these trips.

Then, what started out as friendly squabbling turned into something more serious. In the beginning, their worst arguments were about money. They talked, for instance, of doing without servants of any kind, a whim that led to many battles. Bosie seemed not to realize that a person like himself was actually *capable* of making a bed or sweeping a floor.

Lady Queensberry, it soon appeared, had no intention of financing Bosie's stay in Naples — once she learned whom he was staying with. She discontinued his allowance. The rent went unpaid. Everything came more and more to depend on Wilde's ability to make money with *The Ballad of Reading Gaol,* which he was finding impossible to finish, even though the publisher Smithers had expressed interest in the project.

"I should be back at the villa, working on my poem," he would say in a Naples café — and call for another Amaretto on ice.

Their fights began to center on the poem itself. Bosie, unable to find anyone willing to publish his sonnets, began to resent the *Ballad.* Why should Wilde be able to get his work in print, he demanded, simply because he could boast a prison record?

"I don't suppose you bothered to see about dinner," he said, returning from Naples one evening to find Wilde hard at work on the poem.

"Of course I did, dear boy," Wilde replied, hurrying into the kitchen. Reappearing with a pot that had been simmering on the coal stove, he lifted the lid to release a cloud of steam scented with herbs. "Gianna gave me her secret recipe for a dish with tomatoes and garlic that is said to drive men mad. It is called spaghetti."

Bosie grimaced. "I am sick of Italian food. I am sick of Italy." He collapsed on the decaying wicker sofa. "I suppose I am expected to listen to your afternoon's efforts."

Wilde set the pot on the dining table. "Perhaps after dinner when you're feeling —"

"Now. I want to listen now."

It was not Bosie in the room with him at all, Wilde told himself. At such times the boy seemed to be taken over by an incubus, and there was no sense arguing. With a sigh he took up the unwieldy manuscript and read the lines he had finished that afternoon:

> *"So with curious eyes and sick surmise*
> *We watched him day by day,*
> *And wondered if each one of us*
> *Would end the self-same way,*
> *For none can tell to what red Hell*
> *His sightless soul may stray."*

Bosie was glowering on the sofa.

"The word that is giving me most trouble is *red*," Wilde said apologetically. "Do you think '*hidden* Hell' might sound less violent? I want an effect of terror, but not violence. If I can only —"

"It sounds trite either way."

"Trite, Bosie?"

"Why don't you accept the fact that you are no longer able to write poetry? You are too old. Or perhaps too broken."

Wilde began taking down dinner plates from the cupboard.

"And why don't you admit," Bosie went on, "that you stole the whole idea of a ballad from *me?*"

Astonished, Wilde laughed. "I did no such thing!"

"Those ballads I wrote when I first knew you — you always admired them inordinately."

The napkins were none too clean, but Wilde slipped the rings onto them all the same. "I have always admired *all* your work, Bosie."

"But you are unable to admit that I am a better poet than you."

"I admit that you write beautifully." Wilde picked up the sheets of his manuscript, careful to keep them in order. He had reworked each stanza so many times, and there were so many stanzas.

"Am I expected to thank you for that great encomium?"

"You will feel better after dinner, dearest boy."

"Don't tell me I will feel better!"

Wilde went into the kitchen for the pasta, and sat for a moment collecting his thoughts. He must remain cheerful at any cost. Humming, he carried the caldron into the dining room, where Bosie was sitting at the table, sulking.

"Have a big, big helping, Bosie," said Wilde, using a fork to lift noodles onto Bosie's plate. "Then you'll —"

"*Don't* tell me what I must and mustn't do," cried Bosie, leaping to his feet.

"I only want you less anxious, Bosie. If —"

Bosie swiped his plate from the table: it crashed on the tiles, the pasta slipping about amidst chunks of broken china. "I am going to spend the night in Capri," Bosie said. "At least there I can breathe." He stormed off to his room.

Wilde stared down at the mess on the floor. He picked up the noodles and the broken plate and carried them into the kitchen. He returned his own plate to the cupboard. He was no longer hungry. He reached for the pages of his manuscript and went into his writing room.

He was sitting in the candlelight, working over a recalcitrant rhyme, when he sensed Bosie standing in the doorway behind him. He waited a moment before he turned.

"Dear boy!" Bosie was dressed in his most seductive sweater, a cream-colored wool with a single narrow stripe of rose. "Bosie, do stay here tonight. I am feeling very — lonely."

"Sorry, old dear," said Bosie, with a hard laugh. "Are you back at that hopeless poem?"

"I must finish it, Bosie. It's our only chance of getting any income." He knew it was useless to plead with Bosie to stay, that begging only made him firmer in his determination to deny. They were both caught in the tangles of the net, for he could no more stop the begging than Bosie could stop the denying. "If you don't stay tonight, then *I* am going to leave," Wilde said. "I will go back to Berneval. Or to Paris. Anywhere. I cannot stay here alone."

"I am leaving Italy, Oscar. I have already written to my mother to announce that I have seen the folly of my ways. You can send my things on to Cadogan Square. Damus may even pay the rent on this accursed place, after all — just to get me out of it."

"You have written to your —"

"Does that shock you? Do you really think I could go on forever living with a self-pitying old man? If you only realized how boring you've become!" Bosie picked up the manuscript and leafed through the pages. " 'It is sweet to dance to violins when Love and Life are fair . . .' I would die with shame if I wrote anything so banal! Everything that was fine in you is dead, Oscar. And I am tired of living with a corpse."

Wilde grasped for the manuscript, but Bosie moved far out of his reach. Wilde smiled at him. "What allowance did your mother promise, Bosie? Thirty pieces of silver?"

"Swine!" Bosie's eyes were gray shields, like a blind man's. "With your filthy lips, you dare to speak of *her?*" He began tearing at the pages of the manuscript.

Wilde was across the room, trying to pull the papers from him. Then they were on the floor, locked together, grunting, shrieking. They might have been making love. At last Bosie got to his feet. He threw the torn pages high over his head.

Wilde lay on the floor as the bits of paper showered down over him. His face was scratched and bleeding. Bosie gave him a hard kick on the shoulder and calmly walked out of the house.

He lay a long while, praying for one single thing, and hating himself for it. *Please, please make him come back.* He began to weep. When at last it was evident that Bosie would not retrace his steps, Wilde went about picking up the scraps of paper from the floor.

The pages that were intact he left carefully to one side. The torn scraps he placed on the desk, one by one, pushing the fragments together into some kind of order.

Some hours later he had several of the mutilated pages in place. Taking a fresh sheet, he began to copy with a steady hand:

> *Yet each man kills the thing he loves,*
> *By each let this be heard . . .*

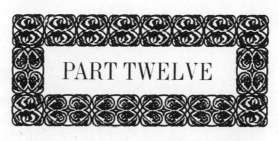

PART TWELVE

The Golden City

ARIS, with her blending of the ancient and the new, had always thrilled him; but now the old parts of the city seemed to have become a museum for gawking tourists, and the new was losing its capacity to shock. He no longer took long detours to avoid the Eiffel Tower: it was beginning to seem an old friend.

What a confounding city she was, though: a whore garbed in precious silks and furs, a virgin mantled in rags of the loveliest blue. It had been a magnificent place to be successful in. For a failure, though, Paris proffered a different kind of splendor. He had been the guest of honor at the banquet; now he was standing outside, staring in, hungry in the cold. But who could say which was the more dazzling view?

He was haunted by memories, each with its tale, its pleasure, its reflection, its pang. His life began to take on, in his own regard at least, the grandeur of an Iliad of forbidden love. Luminaries who had once begged him to grace their salons now pretended in restaurants not to know him. André Gide joined him for an aperitif at the *terrasse* of the Café Francois I, but carefully kept his back to the passing crowd.

Strangers walking on the boulevard Saint-Germain would point him out with amusement or contempt. Everyone knew all about him: no one wished to know him.

He accepted their disdain with a melancholy interest, as if he were watching the unfolding of an opera's last dismal act.

He had little money on the allowance Constance granted him and pretended to have less. Often in conversation he would introduce the topic of his poverty, as if to enjoy the embarrassment it caused. Oscar Wilde foraging for scraps in the streets of Paris: was there not something thrilling about it?

His letters were full of eloquent pleas for help. He began asking for "loans" from old friends and new, pleased when he was given money but pleased in a different way when he was not.

One afternoon as he wandered in the area of the Opéra, trying to think of ways to kill the day, he spied a handsome woman peering into the window of a *parfumerie*, raising the dotted veil from her refined pink face for a better look. Her clothes were English, their severe cut dramatized by a set of superb silver-fox furs that curved about her throat and shoulders. Standing next to her he said: "Miss Melba?"

Startled, she made as if to rush away.

"Don't be frightened — please. I am Oscar Wilde. Surely you remember me?"

Nellie Melba caught her breath, then smiled as superbly as if she were making her entrance in *Roméo et Juliette* at Covent Garden. "Why — of course," she said in her clear, sweet soprano, almost as lovely speaking as singing. She gave him her small hand, sheathed in a long violet glove. "I am very pleased to —"

"I am going to do a terrible thing, Miss Melba. I am going to ask you for money. I am, you see, totally without funds."

Pity melted her strong, well-chiseled features, making them handsomer still, and a dull excitement pulsed through him. Why was he doing this, he asked himself, gazing up at the expanse of sky over the Opéra, filled with small blue stains of clouds. His allowance had arrived only the day before, and his pockets were full.

"How — terrible for you," she said, opening her bag. As she dug out two large notes, she stammered something about how much she had admired *The Ballad of Reading Gaol*.

"I made nothing on it — nothing."

He knew she would be telling of this encounter, in all sympathy, everywhere her fame carried her to — that was the terrible thing, that was the wonderful thing. He pocketed the money and, without another word, turned and took his leave.

) 2 (

It was untrue that he had earned nothing on the *Ballad* — but the small profit he had gained went, like all the money that came to hand, on luxuries. He would spend unthinkingly on a meal, or on a rare book, or on gifts for some sloe-eyed Antinoüs of an evening. For necessities, alas, there was never quite enough.

He needed extensive work done on his teeth, but that must be put aside for now. After the fall he had taken in Pentonville Prison, his ear had continued to bother him. It should be looked at by a competent physician — but that, too, could wait. The frivolities must be taken care of first.

He lodged in a series of cheap artists' hotels in the sunless side streets around the École des Beaux-Arts, paying his rent only when it was absolutely impossible to get out of it. When his arrears went beyond what the proprietor would bear, it would be time for Sebastian Melmoth once again to move on.

He was consumed by infatuations for a series of Latin Quarter street boys, warmer-blooded versions of the lads who had caused him so much trouble at his trials. It always felt like a lifelong passion; it rarely lasted a week. Yet these affairs touched him deeply: it seemed that time, which might antiquate antiquities, would always spare these minor monuments, and he admired them as he had those other misfits, for their struggle to triumph over the merciless exigencies of life. He knew, of course, that they were fated to lose the battle, just as he himself was losing it: that added to their appeal.

"How terrible a thing it is to buy love," he said to Robert Sherard over a cognac in Les Halles. "And yet what purple hours one can snatch from that gray, slowly moving thing we call time."

"How *can* you, Oscar!" said Sherard, righteous as always. He had been delightful young, when they had first met — but he was neither young nor delightful anymore. Sherard seemed determined to see Paris as Hampstead writ large, and Wilde as the repentant sinner begging for society's forgiveness. "Did you learn nothing in Reading Gaol?"

Wilde's hearing was failing; rather than endure the tedium of continually asking people to repeat, he tended to talk more — and louder: "If I had been a patriot, Robert, put in prison for loving his country, I would still love my country, would I not? I was put in prison because I was enchanted by young men. I am *still* enchanted by young men." Then, in a softer voice, he said: "Remember when we were young, Robert? You looked like a Roman emperor on a coin — an emperor of the Decadence."

Clearly it was a subject Sherard did not wish to pursue. "You are drinking far too much brandy, Oscar."

Wilde gave him a withering glance and called to the waiter for another drink. "Of course I am destroying myself!" In this as in so many ways, he told Sherard, he was simply following in the footsteps of his mentor: "I realized in the prison at Reading that Jesus Christ was the true precursor of the Romantic movement — and therefore of my life. How I wish I could have a brandy and soda with him! What strange, harsh-colored tales we might share with one another . . ."

He no longer wrote, no longer wished to. What was the sense of trying to rise a little way from the ground, when his hand had been upon the moon?

"But Oscar," said Robbie Ross, "*The Ballad of Reading Gaol* is a triumph."

"I hope you are wrong, Robbie. It has earned me virtually nothing. What kind of success is that? Besides, there is something vulgar in all success. The truly great men fail. Or seem to fail."

"But your writing is better than it has ever been."

"In that case, dear boy, what better time to stop?"

) 3 (

Paris was not so icy as London in winter, but the cold seemed to penetrate deeper, to chill the very precincts of the soul. Wilde went to bed wearing underclothes, heavy socks, a sweater borrowed from Robert Sherard — and yet he remained cold.

His correspondence with Constance became a mechanical act. He no longer had any power to enchant her, and with that gone there was little left to say. He began to dissociate her from his own sense of doom and to hope she might find some kind of happiness without him.

But no: the news from Switzerland was invariably glum. She missed the boys, who were away at school. Her back was bothering her again. Years before, she had fallen on the stairs at Tite Street, and her spine had given her difficulties ever since. He had no letter for a time, and when she wrote again it was to say that she was paralyzed from the waist down, and would be going to a hospital in Italy for an operation.

When the telegram arrived from her brother, announcing that

Constance had died as a result of the operation, Wilde sat for a long while alone in his dark, narrow room. Dead, he thought. This would have to be part of it. There was no place for you in this hideous world, my darling. Just as there is no place in it for me.

And now his poor, darling boys were in the hands of guardians — guardians who would make sure they never saw their father again.

He felt he did not belong in Paris; there was nowhere left that he did belong. Frank Harris offered him the gift of a winter trip to the Riviera. He humbly accepted: it would give him the opportunity to visit Genoa, where Constance was buried.

All Italy had been covered with rain for days when he arrived, and the skies over the old cemetery were still lowering and black. He walked among the white tombs with his arms full of roses. Most of the graves were topped by strangely realistic statues of the deceased, and searching for Constance's stone he felt he was being watched by hundreds of hostile dead eyes.

He found her stone: CONSTANCE MARY LLOYD. No mention whatsoever of him. Had he expected any?

A bouquet of brown withered blossoms lay twisted on the moist earth. Constance here, and dead? She had not begun to live, had never had a chance to learn what life was.

Constance had been cheated — by life, by God, by him.

And he realized, standing there holding the fragrant roses, that he was angry with her. They had allowed convention to destroy them, she in her way, he in his. And now here she lay, eternally silent and reproachful, in alien ground.

He brushed the dead bouquet aside, then carefully spread the fresh red roses before the tombstone. And then he was stretched out upon the grave, his fingers kneading the black moist clay, and he was crying out, "Connie, Connie," and weeping harsh thick tears that seemed as if they would never stop.

) 4 (

There was beauty enough in the world to arouse his appetites once again, if he wished them to be aroused. He did not. Traveling through the sun-bleached cities along the Mediterranean, he again and again rejected life's siren call.

Sarah Bernhardt was playing *Hamlet* in Nice, a production that had caused as much heated discussion in Paris as the Dreyfus affair. Wilde sent a note, telling her that he would stop backstage before the evening performance.

He wondered if she would refuse to see him. It would not matter. Such incidents were no longer capable of wounding him; he had become all wound.

Nevertheless, he spent most of the afternoon at a café along the promenade des Anglais, fortifying himself with Ricards in the blinding sun and adding very little iced water to the glass.

A maid with an elegant little mustache was waiting for him at the stage door. She led him to the dressing room and rapped on the door. "Monsieur Wilde," she shouted.

It was like entering a familiar garden. Vases of expiring gardenias and mimosa were crowded about the tables and the floor, baskets of ivy hung from the ceiling, great tubs of water held pots of geraniums and herbs. Scattered about were potted palms with electric bulbs concealed beneath their leaves. A harshly plain woman rose from a stool in the middle of the room; grasping his hand, she whisked him inside and slammed and locked the door.

"*Cher ami,*" she whispered, and threw her arms about him.

"My dear Sarah," he said, faltering. "Is it — you?"

He stepped back for a better look. She wore no makeup of any kind, not even a dab of rouge on the lips. Her eyes were small, narrow, piercing; her skin was lifeless and dull. "Look at me closely, Oscar."

"I do not recognize you!"

She seemed not to be a woman at all. Nor a man. Her face had neither character nor personality. Age was in it — certainly the features had been touched by time. Yet it was a face as tentative and unformed as a child's.

"They have stripped away your masks, dear Oscar. It is only fair that you should see *me* the same way."

He genuflected before her — less agilely than in the past: his knee joints cracked. "You are more beautiful than ever before, dear goddess. This is the most thrilling mask of all!"

She laughed ruefully and pulled him to his feet, drawing him into the wings of an eight-sided mirror. "Look at us," she said, holding a candelabra up to their faces. "Clowns, both of us — tragic clowns. Are we not pitiful?"

"Ruins," he said. "Splendid ruins."

"They love raising us high above them — and they love casting us down. They make us more than they are — and less. We are their glory —"

"And their shame," said Wilde, averting his eyes. "My glory is past."

"Ah, *mon cher,* the play is not over!"

There was a hesitant rap at the door. "Seven o'clock, Madame Sarah," said a young boy.

She sighed, and put down the candelabra. "Am I Medea tonight, Frédéric?" she called out.

"Hamlet, madame."

"Hamlet, again!" She stood on tiptoe to give Wilde a kiss on the cheek. "Forgive me, old friend," she whispered. "Time to put on another mask . . ."

) 5 (

"Percy!" cried Lady Queensberry, as her son bounded clumsily up the stairs. "Here at last!"

"He is still —?"

"Still alive," she answered, leading him down the corridor to her bedroom. "Barely." She stopped at a mirror outside the door for a quick adjustment of her silver hair.

"You are *sure* he wants to see me? The last time I saw Papa we were at each other's throats." He shuddered, remembering the dreadful afternoon he had squabbled with his father in Trafalgar Square.

She gave him her old mocking smile, trying to put as much fondness into it as she could. "It was he who insisted that we send for you, silly boy!" She must make an effort to care for Percy more, she thought, sighing. He was kind and good. But his looks were ordinary, his thoughts conventional, his interests shallow. He was a singularly uninteresting young man! She was reaching for the doorknob but stopped and took Percy by the shoulders. "Percy — your father was baptized into the Roman Church late last night."

Percy's mouth fell open. "You must be — My father? A Roman Catholic?"

"Another miracle. Like his wanting to come back here to — You won't vex him, Percy? Promise? He's been wanting so awfully to see you." She threw open the door.

Percy held back, afraid to go in. The room he had so often played in as a child was filled with the aura of death. Bosie, red-eyed, was sitting across from the great canopied bed.

In the harsh winter light streaming in from Cadogan Square, his father looked older than his years, his face drawn and white, emitting a soft blue radiance, his eyes sunk into deep gullies, his nose seeming to have grown larger while the rest of his face had shrunk. Could he still be alive?

"Darling?" Lady Queensberry was saying to the unmoving figure in the bed. "Percy has come. Can you hear me?"

Framed by creamy white sheets the old sunken face made no move. Surely he was dead.

She shook him. "Can you hear me, darling? You were so anxious to see Percy. He is here at last!"

Slowly one of the eyes opened and focused on Percy. Still the body did not move. It was like being watched by a strange white bird. Queensberry released a slow groan.

"What?" said the marchioness, bending closer to his lips. "I believe he wants us to raise him up."

Percy stumbled over to help her, and Bosie brought extra pillows to stuff behind the old man's back. Queensberry stared straight ahead at the window, the black leafless trees. He moaned something, and the marchioness bent close to him again.

"Percy — he has something to say to you."

Percy forced a smile and moved closer to the bed. "It is good to see you again, Papa." His mother hovered at one side of Queensberry, Bosie at the other, their faces twisted with sorrow.

A claw of a hand emerged from the blankets and beckoned. Percy moved closer. The hand beckoned again. Percy moved closer still, till his face was level with his father's. He smiled bashfully at the withered old man.

Queensberry made a sound from deep in his throat. Trembling from the effort, he reached his head far back, and splatted a gob of yellow juice into Percy's face.

) 6 (

On his way back from the Riviera, Wilde stopped in Lyons for a night. He was sipping at a glass of young Châteauneuf-du-Pape and going through an English newspaper when he came upon the obituary notice for the Marquess of Queensberry. He felt no more emotion reading the flowery sentiments than if they had been the final paragraphs of a novel by Ouida.

Back in Paris he picked up the thread of his life again, wandering, dissipating, moving from one cheap hotel to another. Curiously, Constance was with him now in ways she had never been before. On every Paris corner he seemed to confront her and his own young self, exploring the city on their honeymoon. Paris then had seemed the loveliest mystery in the world.

And then he had to ask himself : was the longing that wrenched him at those moments really for Constance — or for the past itself ?

He developed a taste for walking about the city's cemeteries, peering at the tombs of Balzac, Baudelaire, Chopin. The tombs became ever more beautiful, while Paris itself seemed to grow stale. Beloved cities can die for one, he realized, like beloved people. Paris — his Paris — was now lost to him as Connie was, as his mother was. Bit by bit he was destroying every beautiful thing.

One day a *pneumatique* arrived, and he tore it open with a sense of apprehension. It was from Bosie. He had just moved to Paris from London and was living in an apartment on the avenue Kléber. It was silly for them not to see each other, Bosie suggested, after all they had been through together. Wilde was to meet him for an aperitif at Fouquet's.

Bosie in Paris ? Wilde read the message over several times, stunned afresh at each reading. It was hastily scrawled, thoughtless, imperious. No one would insult a friend with such a communication. The only proper response was silence.

Could he stay away from Fouquet's ?

The last thing he expected was to find Bosie in black; but of course, Bosie looked splendid in black.

"Dear boy," he whispered, sliding into a wicker chair with a smile that was both mocking and serious. "Is there any point in saying I am sorry — for your grief ?"

The small, delicate face crumpled up in a quick spasm of laughter, which Bosie covered quickly with a hand. But no, it was not laughter. "I don't expect you to understand," he sobbed. "He adored me. You never knew that. I was the — the apple of my father's eye. And I adored him as well !"

Wilde stared, uncomprehending.

"But *you*," Bosie snapped. "You always hated him. You were violently jealous, that was all."

Wilde reached for Bosie's cigarette case and lit one of the Egyptian cigarettes. "Jealous?" He sat smoking for a time in silence, thinking of how badly he had missed good cigarettes. Now that he had one, he found no pleasure in it at all.

Bosie seemed to be collapsing into another fit of tears — and then Wilde saw that this time he was laughing. "He went over to the Roman Church on his deathbed! Isn't that priceless?" At Bosie's squeals of delight, people from all corners of the *terrasse* turned to stare. "After all those years of ranting and raving against God!"

Sadly, Wilde thought: *How can I ever become a Catholic now!*

They had little to say to each other. Bosie was now twenty-eight. He seemed in a curious way to have aged far more over their years together than Wilde had — perhaps not aged so much as hardened, grown coarser. He still looked younger than his years, and yet there was something very old about him. But Bosie had been born old. His gestures had become clumsy and stiff. He comported himself now with a rustic stance Wilde had never noticed in him before: the stance of the Marquess of Queensberry.

) 7 (

He had never before spent much time in Paris in winter, when the city turned into a poorly taken photograph of itself; he had never known how many variations could be drawn from the single color gray. At one time he might have found the uncompromising *tristesse* delightful. Now it was like too much Chopin.

Through the long evenings, as it grew more difficult to think of ways to pass the time, he pondered on Bosie — Bosie as he once had been — and he would inhale old memories like an opiate. How little love he seemed to feel now for the boy — the aging boy. And yet how happy they might have been, the two of them, if Bosie had not been Bosie, and he had not been —

There were more important things to worry about. Constance had specified in her will that his allowance was to continue at the same rate, but prices were going up, and vices were growing more expensive. His wardrobe kept narrowing as he forfeited suitcase after suitcase to hotel proprietors, and that was a truly serious matter.

"I am back," he said in an accusatory tone to Monsieur Dupoirier, in the dim lobby of the Hôtel Alsace, in the rue des Beaux-Arts.

"Monsieur Wilde," said Dupoirier, trying to twist his kindly face into a scowl. "But I did not expect to see you ever again in this world."

"I decided that I had treated you unfairly last time," said Wilde, dropping his broken valise, held intact by a length of rope, behind the desk. "I have been trying to scrape together the tiny bit of money I owe you, dear old friend. I shall surely have it tomorrow. After all, miserable as your establishment may be, it is the only hotel in all Paris I truly like . . ."

Dupoirier deposited the suitcase outside the desk again. "When no one else will take you in."

"If you say such things, monsieur, I will be forced to suspect you of having bad faith," said Wilde, and used a foot to delicately inch the suitcase back towards the desk.

Dupoirier threw up his arms in a gesture of despair. "But you are impossible, Monsieur Wilde. Impossible!" He sighed deeply. "Nevertheless, I will admit I have missed you. I have missed your stories."

"I have far better stories than before. But I shan't tell you a single one. For you are too unkind." Wilde started for the door but paused in the vestibule. "Any other proprietor would have offered me a Pernod on such a gloomy day. And I think, too, that if I were to decide to live here, you might consider giving me a special rate this time. Having an artist on the premises lends tone to the establishment."

Dupoirier produced a bottle from the bottom drawer of his desk. "I *do* give you a special rate! In any case, you pay no rate at all, since you never put down a sou for rent!" There was a glass on the desk half full of water; Dupoirier poured most of it into a flourishing papyrus plant. To what remained, he added liquid from the bottle. It turned a cloudy jade green.

"Your tragedy, monsieur, is that you have no faith in my future," Wilde said poutingly, accepting the drink. "Without faith, what are we but animals?"

"Oh, but you are a wicked man," said Dupoirier, folding and unfolding his arms on his chest. "You cheat me. You tell lies. When you are drinking you become abusive. When you are sober you are even more abusive! And yet I like you, I cannot deny it.'' He squeezed out from behind the desk and picked up the suitcase, giving it a disapproving look. ''Come. I have a small suite one flight up that I can give you for a special price. And then we will have a little lunch together. And you will tell me a story.''

He led the way up a tight spiral of a staircase that Wilde could hardly manage to climb. He sucked in his belly and pulled himself up by the narrow twisting banister, closely following Dupoirier.

The room smelled of mildew, and the floor, beneath a thin, dirty green rug, was uneven, and creaked distressingly. Soiled torn curtains hid the view of a treeless courtyard. In the way of furniture there was, besides the sagging bed, only a desk covered with burns from cigarettes. ''A 'suite,' monsieur? Both these rooms together would not comprise a decent linen closet! Surely you plan to redo that wallpaper before you ask *any* human being to sleep here — never mind an artist.''

''Take it as it is, Monsieur Wilde. Or do not take it at all.''

Wilde collapsed on the lumpy bed and glowered at the magenta walls, covered with columns of twisting thistles. ''You leave me no choice,'' he said, as Dupoirier stuffed newspapers in the grate to make a fire. ''You have tricked me once again, monsieur. Now about that lunch you promised — could we not have it brought up here?''

) 8 (

When one had no money, Paris became a place of greedy evil-eyed shopkeepers and price tags and hands ever stretching forward for a tip. To soften it for himself, Wilde reread every novel in *La Comédie humaine*. Balzac's Paris was every bit as mendacious, but the passage of sixty years had tinted it in magical colors. How much easier to live in that Paris, or Baudelaire's, or François Villon's, than in his own.

Now, with so few occasions worth dressing for, all his clothing seemed to be wearing away. His suits seemed to know it didn't matter, seemed to find it more appropriate to hang poorly and to bag at the elbows and knees. He kept one shirt for special occasions, which he would send out to the *blanchisserie* on the corner. The few others he owned, he washed by hand.

Since there was no air in his rooms, wet clothing never really dried. Once he left a pair of underdrawers he had washed hanging by the fire, and as he sat reading *La Cousine Bette* he was startled to see smoke filling the room.

He tried to stamp out the fire but could not; and staring at the pathetic tattered bits of blackened cloth, he began to weep, remembering all the lovely things he had owned at Tite Street, and all the lovely times that could never return.

He met with Bosie once in a great while, but there was no pleasure being with him now. Bosie was assuming the airs of an English squire. The more he showed off his new affluence, the more abject Wilde made himself when they were together. They both despised his show of destitution, yet it seemed to bring them both some strange satisfaction.

Just how much money Bosie now possessed, Wilde was afraid to ask. At one time such a question would have seemed perfectly natural between them; now it was only through gossiping with their mutual friend More Adey that Wilde was able to conjecture that Queensberry had left Bosie some fifteen thousand pounds.

He was spending it recklessly, mostly on clothing and parties, to none of which Wilde was invited. He was also, Wilde learned, keeping a sour-dispositioned youth who sold violets to tourists around Saint-Germain-des-Prés.

One afternoon Wilde passed by a little church like one of the homely edifices that dotted the Irish countryside. It had a signboard in English, advertising the day's Masses. Inside, everything was fresh-painted and in execrable taste, from the garish Stations of the Cross to a simpering Saint Anthony of Padua standing before a bank of flickering candles. Yet in the midst of all the majestic churches of Paris, this one had a strange unpretentious warmth about it, a sense of home.

The service was about to begin. The priest was a tall young man, thin as a reed and, in an ascetic sort of way, extremely handsome. His red-cassocked acolytes looked like naughty angels. Wilde slipped into one of the pews near the front, breathing in the perfume of lilies and stale incense.

The young priest seemed to take a voluptuous delight in the Latin phrases he was reading, lingering over the words of the Liturgy, seeming almost to be tasting them, savoring their juices. When the Mass was over, Wilde on an impulse strolled up across the altar to the sacristy door.

The priest looked up, startled, in the process of untying his chasuble. "Monsieur?"

They were alone; the lovely young acolytes had fled to some other part of the sacristy. "I should like to speak with you," said Wilde. "I want to learn about becoming a Catholic." He gave the priest his most disarming smile. "It seems such a — *romantic* thing to do."

) 9 (

Mint pastilles did little to veil the fragrance of absinthe on the breath, but on the afternoons when Wilde went to Saint Joseph's for instruction, Father Dunn seemed not to notice.

He was from Ireland, it had turned out, and the two of them could reminisce for hours about the trials and triumphs of an Irish boyhood. Father Dunn's boyhood, of course, was not very long past.

"I have been in a state approaching despair for months and months," Wilde said one rainy afternoon. The rectory parlor looked out on a side view of the Arc de Triomphe, stained a soft beige by the rain. "Ever since I was released from prison."

Father Dunn's great brown eyes, for all his graveness of demeanor, had a trace of a twinkle in them. "Saint Paul the Apostle lived in despair for twenty years."

"Yes, but — contrary to what people say, Father — I am no saint. Could I not be baptized right away? Could not some special dispensation be made, considering how little I deserve it? It would help me start afresh."

"We must be certain, dear friend — you, more than I — that your desire to join the faithful is not merely a — caprice."

"It is no caprice, Father. But would it not seem more appropriate — considering our difference in age — for you to call *me* Father?"

Father Dunn conveyed as much amusement with a slight crinkling of his smoky eyes as others would with loud guffaws. "How pleased Our Lord must be, Mr. Wilde, to have a man like yourself succumbing to His grace! Even if the Evangelists did not choose to record too many of His sallies, I have always felt Our Savior must be a man of great humor. Perhaps a little like yourself.''

''The pale Galilean?'' said Wilde, with a sigh. ''I am forever being compared with him. I wonder if Jesus tires of it as much as I do.'' He gave Father Dunn a sly smile. ''Every artist's life is an imitation of Christ —''

''There is truth in that, Mr. Wilde.''

''— and hardly any priest's is.''

The young priest tried to suppress his laughter, but it came out all the same — in great spurts that seemed to cause him physical pain. ''You are too quick for me, Mr. Wilde!''

Wilde grasped his thin arm with a look of contriteness. ''Forgive me my little sacrileges, Father.''

''Don't apologize,'' said Father Dunn, smiling warmly. ''I suspect there is more true religious feeling in your irreverences than in the pieties of many of our Catholic hypocrites. Like myself!''

) 10 (

Just when Wilde was wondering where he might borrow funds for a meal pleasant enough to stifle the beetles nibbling at his brain, Monsieur Dupoirier knocked and, barking through the door, demanded *something* down on the rent — or else. Wilde spent the rest of that afternoon in bed. Then, when he knew Dupoirier would be having his aperitif, he slipped past the maid at the desk and went out to the Café des Deux Magots. Sipping a *vin rouge,* he scrawled a message to Bosie, asking if they might have dinner the following evening at the Café de la Paix.

The only suit of clothes he had left was of dusty gray wool that even the moths were weary of. Nor had he a lovely cravat left that might take the curse off it, only a faded green one well past its prime.

Brooding at his ravaged features in the mirror, he tried with a stub of pencil to add some drama to his disenchanted eyes. Talcum toned down the purple in his cheeks, and then a dab of lip rouge about the cheekbones restored some vestige of the flush of youth. With a bit of imagination and the shades half drawn, he saw himself as the Oscar Wilde of a decade before. Would Bosie see him that way, too?

He paused at the bar next to the hotel for a few glasses of Ricard, fortifying them with drops of absinthe, deadly but delightful, and engaging in a silent melancholy conversation with himself. If he were able to view the span of his life from some Olympian height, would he dissolve in tears or rock with laughter? In the composition of some days of love, in a grappling with some hours of pleasure, years and years had rolled away, and the vast perspective of his life had contracted to this wavering, drugged moment. It was so gaudy, so sad. Amongst the glittering costumes in every theater wardrobe, he told himself, was a shroud; in the midst of the most garishly painted sets one could always discover tombstones and crosses, mottled and brown.

He stepped out into the cobblestoned square, tottering a little, and squinted up at the rooftops. Though by cruel daylight he might be forced to loiter in his life's cold ashes, it took only a draft or two of elixir and lo! the drab city was transformed as if by magic into — Paris. Over houses bobbing up and down like sailing vessels at anchor, a goddess seemed to be swimming across the sky in robes of lavender and pink. The sight was so lovely that he had to stop in another *boîte* to try to keep hold of it; but when he came out again, all the shimmering colors were gone.

It had become *l'heure bleue,* and young musicians were strumming serenades in front of the cafés. By the time he reached the omnibus station on the rue des Saints-Pères, people were no longer casting shadows: they had become shadows themselves. The smoke streaming out of the chimney pots was bluer than the sky itself, and over it rose a wizard's moon, ghostly white.

In the foul-smelling omnibus, he felt as expansive as in the old days, and he was sure the evening was going to be gala and sensual, a reprise of their first evenings together. Were new courtiers now ruining themselves in those lovely clubs and cafés? Whoever they were, he prayed that the world might spread as rosily before them, now, as it once had for him.

The restaurant was vast, room after room connected by arched white doorways, and from the artful way in which pier mirrors had been placed on some but not all the walls, each room looked even larger than it was. Glancing through any doorway one saw endless colonnaded hallways stretching forward, filled with tremulous candles, and white-jacketed waiters passing back and forth like specters in a haunted house.

Bosie was waiting at a table in the very center of the room, where the lights and the conversations were brightest. A small orchestra, half hidden by potted palms, played melodies by Offenbach and Johann Strauss. Bosie was handsome as ever in evening dress, but his boyishness was gone. How little we know, Wilde thought, of what we are doing or where we are going; how short a time does a countenance stay fresh and fair.

"I cannot get used to writing 'nineteen hundred,' can you?" said Wilde, drawing up his Louis XV chair.

"I have no difficulty with dates, Oscar. You are getting old." Even his voice was different, Wilde decided: deeper, duller. If they were to meet each other now for the first time, Wilde asked himself, would it be possible for him to be drawn to Bosie in any way?

"The tragic thing is not that I grow old, Bosie, but that I remain young."

"That is a matter of opinion, Oscar." But if they were to meet for the first time now, what would Bosie think of him! Over the fish course — plump mussels saturated in a mustard-flavored sauce — they barely spoke. Wilde longed to enjoy the food, but could not.

"Did you know that I used to believe I was meant to be the first true voice of the twentieth century, Bosie?" He stared at the sharp perspective of candles in one of the mirrors, wondering which of the reflected faces was his own. "Now I see I was only the dying croak of the nineteenth."

"Oscar, for one evening be cheerful? Stay out of the past? Let's try to live *now*. For the moment."

"The moment," Wilde said, more to himself than to Bosie. "Yes, we must experience — the moment." He tilted his empty glass in the candlelight. "Did you see that Walter Pater died? Plucked in the very flower of his middle age?" The waiter poured the last of the Pouilly-Fumé into Wilde's glass. "Poor dear Pater. I am not at all sure Heaven will be up to his standards." The vase in the center of the table held a bouquet of narcissi, camellias, and white lilies splashed with red. "Where, I wonder, is it all going to end between us?" Wilde said suddenly. "What if it never ends at all?"

Bosie exposed his fine teeth in a kind of laugh. "Did it ever really begin? I should pronounce the affair stillborn — smothered by your constant whining."

One waiter removed the fish plates while another served the *Rognons en crème,* and a third poured a new wine, a Château Margaux. "I suppose," Wilde said, "you are referring to the pain I have endured?"

"Back in the past again," Bosie said with a sigh. "I know, Oscar, I know. Your ruin. Your poverty. I caused all of it: it is all because of me."

Why, Wilde wondered, had he ever fallen in love with a youth burdened with so cramped, so arid a range of emotions, a youth without even a personality? Or was it indeed *because* Bosie had so little that he had been doomed to love so much? Was it because Bosie would never be able to respond that he had been so drawn to him — the iceberg upon which his ostentatious galleon must surely crash? "It is not just my world that has crumbled," he said quietly. "All the world has crumbled. I thought I represented the daring, the new. In fact, for all my wickedness I am as stuffy and old-fashioned as an antimacassar or a bustle."

"Now I am supposed to protest about how wrong you are," Bosie said, pretending to yawn, "and assure you about the continuing importance of your gift!"

The kidneys were flavored with a very old cognac; nevertheless, after a bite or two, all Wilde's appetite was gone. "Forgive me for being maudlin, Bosie. It is only that — I cannot work. I cannot do anything." His voice broke. "While you have become — fortune's favorite." He glanced about the room miserably. How many such interiors of cream and gold had he known, how many times had smooth fiddles woven the same thin strains of Strauss. "I understand, dear boy, that you are buying your own stable."

Bosie was on guard. "It is an investment — and a wise one. I don't know, of course, if I can find the money . . . ."

The wine had a fruity taste that kept it from being great: what matter? "So the mad Scarlet Marquis did the right thing by you, after all, dear boy."

"He might have done better. I don't like you calling him that."

"He has made you a young man of substance."

Two of the violinists had detached themselves from the other musicians and were circling the room playing "Partir est mourir un peu." "Even when I had not a shilling to call my own, Oscar, I was a young man of substance."

"And now the tables have turned. You are a man of wealth and promise. While I —"

"They have a way of turning, tables do," said Bosie without interest. The fiddlers paused in front of them but Bosie waved them off.

The scent of the narcissi seemed to fill the room: Wilde could not decide if it was delightful or nauseating. "Would this not be a good time," he said, and cleared his throat — "a good time to set things right between your family and myself?"

Bosie stared at him, puzzled.

"If it hadn't been for you and your family, dear boy, I would certainly never have exposed myself to the folly of that — Bosie, we don't want to go into all that again, do we?"

"Are we back on the famous trials once again?" He signaled for the waiter to remove their plates, his wiped clean, Wilde's barely touched. "What of *my* trials, Oscar? Is it possible, for just a moment, that you might think of somebody besides yourself?"

Your trials, Wilde thought, *have not begun*. He looked after the violinists sadly, unmoved by their plaintive melody, unmoved by anything. *This must be how Bosie always feels!* he thought: Bosie the sentimentalist, always desiring the luxury of an emotion without paying the price. "Obviously," he said, with an influx of excitement bringing back some lilt to his voice, "my character can never be made whole again. Certainly no amount of money on earth could make restitution for one single hour of those two years I languished in Her Majesty's prisons, dying unto myself. I would not dream of suggesting that you could make amends for all that! But am I to go hungry? I cannot see why I should be left penniless when your family — more than comfortably well off now! — owes me a debt of honor."

"A debt of —?"

"You insisted in Charles Humphreys's office that they would pay the court charges. You allowed all my possessions to be sold instead — the money to go to your father! The money you inherited is mine, Bosie. Surely you are aware of that!"

Bosie's face had gone white. "You are saying — I should *pay you off?* And use my father's money to do so? Is that the foul plan you are suggesting?" He looked, Wilde thought, like an evil gardenia, one sniff of which would turn one's heart to ice.

"Hatred blinds you, Bosie. And vanity sews your eyelids to-gether with threads of iron. You come of a race whose marriages are cruel, whose friendships are fatal. A race that lays violent hands either on its own life or the lives of others. You could make some small effort at *atonement*."

"You must be mad!" Bosie cried. "The very idea is — mon-strous. Monstrous! Truly, I cannot believe my ears."

"Don't you realize that our whole situation is monstrous, Bosie? It always has been! Too late to alter that now."

"Do you have any idea how you disgust me?" As heads spun to look at them, Bosie raised his voice. "It sickens me that you could even *conceive* of such a plan." His face shrunken and ugly — the face of the Marquess of Queensberry — he leaped up from his chair. "I will leave you to finish your dinner. We have nothing further to say to each other." He started to walk away, but paused — as always center stage. "Naturally," he shouted for all to hear, "I am expected to pay for your meal." From an ostrich-skin bill-fold he extracted a hundred-franc note, which he laid disdainfully next to Wilde's plate. Without another word, he turned and stamped out of the restaurant.

) 11 (

In the middle of the night Wilde woke, burning hot, parched with thirst, but unable to rise from the bed. He could not move, even to fall to the floor. A narrow silver dagger seemed to be inch-ing through his brain.

Rasping cries, like a faraway child's, echoed through his throb-bing head. He realized that they were emanating from him, that he was screaming in pain.

A key clinked in the lock, the door flew open. "*Mais, Monsieur Wilde*," cried Dupoirier. "*Qu'est-ce que c'est, monsieur?*"

Wilde could not reply. He could only lie back, panting for some-thing liquid to moisten his dry, cracking lips. Somehow Poirier understood. Raising him, he held a cup of cold water to Wilde's mouth. At the first sip of the heavenly chill liquid Wilde lost con-sciousness.

It was daylight. He conjectured from the feel of his beard that he must have been asleep for days.

"The doctor from the Hôtel de Dieu says you must remain in

bed,'' said Dupoirier. ''You are very ill, dear Monsieur Wilde. And you must have the services of a regular doctor.''

There were too many pillows; Wilde knocked one to the floor. ''I cannot afford a nurse, never mind a doctor,'' he said. ''But oh, the agonies within my ear!''

Dupoirier dusted off the pillow and placed it on a chair. ''We will not speak of money,'' he said, and carefully piled extra logs on the fire.

''We *must* speak of money. I have no one, Monsieur Dupoirier. My friends will give me nothing, they have all abandoned me. You are going to have to find some means to keep me alive, because if I die, your bill goes unpaid.''

''Hush, monsieur,'' said Dupoirier, drawing the worn blanket up to his chin. ''Without faith, what are we — remember?'' He shrugged. ''Besides, monsieur has more friends than anyone in Paris. Every day friends come by, inquiring for your health.''

Wilde drew himself up on the pillows. ''What friends?''

''Monsieur Ross comes all the time. And a new one, a Monsieur Turner, from London. Both of them come every single day. They are fine gentlemen.''

''Reggie Turner is in Paris? Does — does anyone else come?''

Again Dupoirier shrugged. ''I am not always at the desk . . .''

Wilde looked about, happy to be alive for another while at least. He even enjoyed the room's ugliness. ''Why am I so very, very tired, Monsieur Dupoirier? What is the matter with me?''

''It is essential that you rest, monsieur.''

Wilde heaved a long sigh. ''It is to my final rest I am going, *cher ami.*''

''Monsieur Wilde is saying stupid things.''

Wilde smiled at the magenta thistles writhing over the wallpaper like blossoms from an evil garden. ''Must I lie here staring at *these* for my final days? Surely you could have the paper torn away . . .''

''We will see, Monsieur Wilde. We will see.''

Wilde pulled the blanket up over his head. ''I warn you: the wallpaper or me. One of us will have to go.''

By the middle of the next week, he was much better. Robbie Ross appeared one noon carrying a basket covered with a white napkin.

"I was having a terrible dream, Robbie," said Wilde, blinking in confusion. "I dreamed I was — supping with the dead."

Robbie cleared the desk for the meal, trying not to disarrange the books. "I'm sure, Oscar, you were the liveliest one at the party."

Wilde roared with laughter, making his back ache. He passed a hand over his cheeks and asked Robbie to help him shave. Appraising himself in the hand mirror, he said: "I have loved only two people in my life — yourself and Constance. Do you realize that, Robbie?"

Robbie held a moist hot towel to his face. "Only two?" he said skeptically. He dipped the towel back in the steaming water and again wrapped it about Wilde's face. This time Wilde opened a little hole in the wrapping for his mouth. "As for Bosie — I was fascinated by Bosie. I ruined myself over Bosie. But I have never really liked him!"

Robbie worked up a rich lather in the mug and swirled it about Wilde's face. "Robbie, do you think Heaven is an amusing place?"

"If you're there, it will be."

"Do you know what we'll do?" Wilde said, watching himself in the mirror as Robbie shaved him. "When the day of judgment comes and we are lying in our tombs of porphyry, with all the trumpets blasting, I will turn to you and say: 'Robbie, dearest — let's pretend we do not hear.' Agreed?" Robbie gave him a kiss on the back of the neck.

Wilde sighed and put down the mirror. "No, it was never love between Bosie and me. We were drawn to each other by hatred, an insane kind of —"

Reggie Turner appeared at the door, carrying a bottle of champagne and a long *baguette* of fresh bread, still warm.

"All my dear ones, coming to say good-bye," cried Wilde. "And you have brought a feast!"

"Coming to say *hello*," Reggie said, giving Robbie a worried look. "Now what exactly is troubling you, 'Hoscar' dear?"

Wilde held him close in a hug. "I neither know nor care. I only hope that it is unknown in all the annals of medicine. To die of some ordinary illness would be too humiliating."

"Don't tire yourself too much, Oscar," said Robbie.

"Robbie is cross with me, Reggie. I am studying to be a Catholic. He, of course, wants to be the *only* one in our entourage."

"It has become so dreadfully common to join the Church," said Robbie, laughing. He finished doling out the chicken, the pickled mushrooms, the apple tart. "Like Aubrey and all the others — even old Queensberry! — Oscar is determined to convert before he —" Stricken, he fell to a chair, burying his face in his hands.

"Robbie," Wilde said, stretching over to touch Robbie's heaving shoulders. "You are far too good of heart to be anything but cynical at a time like this."

Reggie went to investigate a low tapping at the door.

"Father Dunn," cried Wilde. "What a lovely surprise. Robbie, another glass!"

"I am interfering with your lunch. I will come back another —"

"Nonsense. My friends will acquaint you with the world's wicked ways, which will make you a better priest. Or at least a more fashionable one, which in Church circles these days is all that counts."

Reggie opened the champagne, carefully muffling the cork, and with the wine bubbling over he poured generous servings into the four glasses. Wilde insisted they save some to bring down to Monsieur Dupoirier as well — but first he raised his glass to each of them in turn.

"My dear, good friends," he said, gazing lovingly at the meal spread out on his writing table before the worn volumes of *La Comédie humaine*. "Thank you! Thank you for helping me to die the way I lived: beyond my means."

) 12 (

Each time sleep came, it came deeper. And each time, the return was harder than before. He was afloat, sailing out into a night sea, with less and less desire ever to come back.

Steadily he sailed past moss-covered caverns of memory, past the dragon's lair of hope, past desire with its yawning, bleeding jaws.

If they would let in more light . . . but he was too weak to ask.

He was weary of the voyage, but it would not end. Not until he had found that great thing the voyage was created for, that he was created for. Grail, El Dorado, Golden Fleece — he had been seeking it for so long, and where now would he ever find it?

Again they would appear, the important ones. His mother.

Constance. Robbie. So many guises, the face changing, the face of
Cyril or Vyvyan, the face of Alfred Wood or some other cunning
youth he had paid for an hour's feigned passion.

They were all there, for in his way he had loved them all.

But never enough. The more they had delighted him, the crueler
were love's agonies. Or could that be the true joy of love — the
frustration itself?

Bosie was there, of course — in many forms. Child, monster,
saint. The gods had chosen them as instruments to refine each other,
punish each other. That perhaps was all love could ever be.

No. There was more to love than that. More than one could ever
know. More than God himself, perhaps, could ever, ever know . . .

The sea was warm and still, a dark mirror one might walk on —
if one could walk. Someone kept turning the oil lamp up, then
down again. Up and down, over and over. And then he realized
that it was the night speeding into day, the day into night again.
So quickly.

So quickly.

In the layers of deepening dark, he heard from far away the
eager young voice of Father Dunn. Chanting. In Latin. A strange,
sweet song. Prayers of baptism. He was going to be immersed —
in the black mirror. Father Dunn was praying over the sea, to
make it holy.

But how absurd, dear boy! Everything is holy!

He wanted to say something amusing, but there was no strength.
Dear Father Dunn — father, child — don't you realize it was
your love that saved me, not your magic words?

Come, darlings. We acted out our loves like parts in a play. We
were so clever, so cunning, we pretended even to ourselves we believed it all — never knowing that every sigh was real!

Yes, Robbie, our dear charade of passion: it was passion after
all.

Constance.

Mother.

Bosie?

But Bosie's face, like all the others, had been absorbed into another, sweeter face — a face from long, long past. Might it be
Apollo? Or Jesus? A face of purest loveliness, strong, fragile, enduring all sorrow, expressing all joy.

Every face had reminded him of this face — every face he had ever loved. Even though they might be no more divine, any of them, than he himself.

And no less.

Why, hello, dear boy, his heart cried out. He seemed to be sinking faster now into the silence — but in fact the beautiful young man was lifting him to the shore, greeting him, welcoming him, stretching out his strong young arms. Beckoning him forward . . .

There was a chink of light ahead that widened, became a circle leading into other circles, and the young man was pointing to the center, where in the distance warm yellow lights were glimmering, like candles fluttering behind a screen of amber. Domes appeared, and pinnacles, that seemed to be cut out of glowing yellow glass.

He was no longer tired. The boy and he were walking hand in hand. Have you been waiting for me, then? How lovely to be with you at last. Are we really to be together now? Oh, dear friend — the only thing sweeter than *not* getting what you want is — getting it! Does that amuse you, my love?

His laughter seemed to echo in rings of light as the clear-eyed youth led him step by step into the gleaming city, never for an instant dimming his sweet, familiar smile.